Please Don't Call Me Sam!

A Mantha Moore Mystery

Dara Dionne Welms

Please Don't Call Me Sam!

A Mantha Moore Mystery

By Dara Dionne Welms

MANTHA MOORE MYSTERIES

2018

MANTHA MOORE MYSTERIES

Printed in the United States of America

First Printing: 2018

ISBN 978-1-7322625-1-5 (pbk.)

ISBN 978-1-7322625-0-8 (eBook)

Mantha Moore Mysteries
PO Box 198
New York, NY 10018

www.ManthaMooreMysteries.com

Ordering Information:

Special discounts are available on quantity purchases by corporations, associations, educators, and others. For details, contact the publisher at the above listed address.

U.S. trade bookstores and wholesalers: Please contact Mantha Moore Mysteries. Email: info@ManthaMooreMysteries.com.

Dedication

In loving memory of my grandparents, Eunice Beatrice Pittman and John "Pop-Pop" Hadley, who taught me how to tell a story. Your humor, your wisdom, your wit, and your strength are all over these pages, and I celebrate you through this work.

This book is dedicated to my mother, Brenda Gale Williams. Thank you for making reading a nightly ritual in our home and for joining me there in the land of dreams and make-believe. It is because you read with me that I now write for others.

Contents

CHAPTER 1: BETTER NEVER THAN LATE...

I'd seen some ugly nights before, but none like this. A cavalry of clouds converged upon the sky and whisked the moon away like a band of thieves. Stripped of all its stars, the night was especially dark. Through my living room curtains, I spied the fog as it snaked sinuously through the streets, creeping by slowly like an abandoned ship. Every few minutes, lightning would flash up above, and it looked as though the night were undergoing X-ray, each bolt stretching out across the black sky like the white bones of a giant hand. Occasionally, one of those fiery fingers would point at one place in particular, and a tree or a house or whatever it touched would go up in flames. That lightning was vicious! Before you could fully make it out, it was already gone, vanishing just as quickly as it'd appeared. And just seconds behind each dazzling flash came what felt like a volcano exploding underneath us. It thundered, and the whole ground shook as if the Earth had changed her course.

The rain beat its rhythm onto treetops and rooftops as puddles turned into ponds. More than once I was startled by the wind. It pounded on my front door like a pushy salesman, and though I refused to answer, it wouldn't take the hint. That wild wind dragged leaves and fallen tree branches down the empty city streets as water and trash raced along the curbside and into the sewers. It'd been a pretty day, hot and sunny like August, though it was only mid-June. Ms. Jane's girls across the courtyard had been outside jumping rope, singing songs, and playing games almost all afternoon. But as soon as that first cloud

1

rolled over the horizon, it wasn't long before all of Atlanta lay quarantined beneath a canopy of dark, wet night.

Anyone with half a brain would've stayed inside on a night like this, but not me. I had somebody to meet.

"Samantha?" came the voice from behind. It was deep and resonant, like the crooning of a baritone. I swear the wine in my glass rippled when he spoke.

"Yes?" I turned to match a face with the hand I felt on my back. And what a face it was. He stared at me through a pair of deep brown eyes. Long, unruly lashes waved at me with each slow blink. His skin was dark and smooth and shiny. I squeezed the bar to keep from reaching for his bald head. Had he been sunbaked with honey and brown sugar? Or dipped headfirst in chocolate? Whatever the case, I was quickly developing a sweet tooth.

He stood tall, well over six feet. His suit hung from his body like it'd been sewn with him standing in it. Tailored with precision, it fit him and him alone. His left earlobe was adorned with a solitary diamond stud. It reflected light like a disco ball and felt nearly as big. He wore two rings on his right hand, one on his left. Their gold sparkled in the light like glitter. I couldn't quite make out his build beneath his suit jacket, but that was fine by me. I enjoyed imagining what lay beneath that black satin, and my thoughts were definitely X-rated. He smelled of a cologne I couldn't name, probably a mix of his own sweet scents. Had I not checked my reflection in his glistening teeth, I would've forgotten that I was fine, too!

"Samson. Nice to finally meet you." He extended his hand. I wanted to grab that hand right then and there and lead it on a tour across my body, but I shook it instead.

2

"Have you been waiting long?" Mmm. I prayed for him to sing me another word.

"Long enough! You're rather late, Mr. Samson." I leaned away and furrowed my eyebrows in anger. It was a good act, but underneath my red dress, my knees trembled in secret as my toes tap-danced on the footrest that ran along the bottom of the bar. I'm not usually the nervous type, but then again, I rarely find myself in the company of rich and powerful people. Samson exuded an air of confidence, a bold self-assurance that saturated the atmosphere around him like a lavish cologne. Sitting so close, I could hardly breathe.

"Well, it's coming down pretty hard out there," he replied, pointing over his shoulder toward the door. "The wind almost knocked me over." He sat down on the stool beside me, and as his gold wristwatch caught a glint of light and nearly blinded me, suddenly, I felt unworthy to inhabit the same space as a man so refined and well-composed. I took a sip of my wine to steady my nerves and immediately that merlot began to mellow me like a fast-acting medicine, sedating me swiftly like a potent pill. I swirled the wine around in my glass, pinching it by the stem, and studied the tiny tornado that formed and fizzled there like a passing thought. Staring at my drink, I realized I was sipping on my third glass. Samson had kept me waiting for almost an hour and hadn't even so much as offered an apology!

"You afraid of water, Mr. Samson?" It might've been the alcohol speaking, but that wine was reading my thoughts exactly. "I'm sure it wasn't coming down any harder for you than it was for me, and yet I managed to make it here on time." He opened his thick lips to speak, but I beat him to it. "If you aren't serious, Mr. Samson, please let me know now before you waste any more of my very valuable time." I looked him in the eyes and almost got lost. They were deep and dark like black holes, like rips in time and space, gateways to parallel dimensions housed right there in his head. They seemed to be luring me, pulling me in, and again I grabbed the bar to keep from drifting off and away.

"Oh, I'm definitely serious. If I weren't, I wouldn't have come at all." He smiled slyly. "Why don't you let me freshen up your drink?"

"No thank you. It's fresh enough." I rolled my eyes and took another deep sip.

Samson continued to peruse the wine list, thumbing through the specials with his manicured hands. Meanwhile, I scoured the rest of the bar with my gaze, so I wouldn't have to look him in the eyes anymore. For it to be only Thursday, the crowd at Black Jack's was packed in tight as tuna. I might've thought it was Saturday night with the way the wait staff dashed back and forth carrying cocktails and bottles of beer. Rain poured down outside, and a steady libation of drinks were being poured inside as eager alcoholics sipped from bottomless mugs and strangers huddled together like castaways in a cave, waiting for the storm to pass.

Black Jack's was a classy place when it wanted to be, but really, it wasn't much more than a basement. An antique jukebox whispered jazz into the room. There were no windows; soft lights lit the small space. The scent of vanilla crept from incense sticks and disappeared into the air as couples kissed by candlelight and strangers exchanged glances across the dim saloon. The first time I'd made my way down those concrete stairs and wandered into that intimate tavern, I'd thought I'd wandered into a psychic's mystic lair. I half expected to see an old woman in a smoky corner sitting down behind a crystal ball.

This was no ordinary bar. It had long ago been transformed by working people into a world away from work and responsibility, a solace from the rigors and pressures of the grown-up world. Patrons made the pilgrimage there each evening to swap stories and sip away the sorrows of the day. Mostly, it was a place where folks cried their tears into beers and whined into wine, an altar of sorts where anxieties were released and left behind, exorcised by laughter and good company. Yes, any night of the week, Black Jack's was truly a sacred space. Tonight, it was a shelter from the storm.

"Mind if I call you Sam?" His thick, rich voice broke through and shattered my daydream.

"You can call me Mantha, but please don't call me Sam," I said, taking another sip. My mouth kissed the glass, and as my lipstick stained the rim once more, I remember noticing for the first time how perfectly its deep crimson color matched that dry merlot.

"Why not? What's wrong with Sam?" He signaled for the bartender with a slight stroke of his wrist.

"I hate for folks to call me Sam. The day I wake up a man and scratch my crotch is the day you can start calling me Sam. Until then, it's Mantha, Samantha, or nothing at all."

"Scotch...neat," he said to the bartender before turning back to me. "Wow. Are you always this...uh...feisty?" He smiled a boyish smile, flashing those teeth at me.

"Take it or leave it."

5

"I'll take it." He didn't miss a beat.

"Why you wanna call me Sam anyway? You're the one named Samson. How about I call *you* Sam?" He laughed at that. I did not. I was on a roll, and I could tell he found my truculence intriguing. He finished laughing, and then he poured his drink into his mouth and swallowed it whole—two fingers in one smooth gulp.

"Let's get down to business," he said after slamming his glass against the rosewood bar. He stared at me and licked his lips slowly. His tongue, too, was thick. It was like a beast. Finally free from the prison of those pearl-white teeth, it slithered out of his mouth and molested his lips.

"Yes, let's," I said. I turned my whole body to face him and stared deep into his eyes—or really his forehead. I couldn't handle those eyes anymore. "Three hundred dollars an hour, two thousand for the whole night."

He didn't wince or flinch at all. His right hand reached into the breast pocket of his jacket and pulled out a snakeskin wallet. All the while, his dark eyes stared into mine. A sudden smirk overtook his face as he looked down to unfold his wallet. *What was that about?* I wondered. *That smirk.* It was like he'd read my mind and suddenly held the answers to all my questions, like he'd unlocked the code to all my secrets. Maybe I had run into a psychic here at Black Jack's after all.

He pulled a stack of neat hundred-dollar bills from a compartment in his wallet. He counted the money, laying each bill Benjamin-side up on the bar. Never had money looked so good to me. It was all green and crisp. I might've believed he'd ironed each one of those bills flat, but I knew better. Samson was not the type of man who ironed. He'd sooner have his money dry-cleaned.

"Eighteen, nineteen, two thousand." He didn't stop there. "One, two, three, four, five, six, seven, eight, nine, a thousand." He assembled the money into two piles: one of two thousand, the other half as much.

"You're gonna make me ask you, huh?" I said, staring at the money. I never could save money, so I'd never seen that much of it all at once. I was reluctant to take my eyes off it, fearing it might up and disappear like a desert mirage.

"Ask me what?" I'm sure he was smiling at me, but I wasn't looking at him. I had my eyes fixed on that green. I'd been looking over my shoulder for weeks trying to steer clear of Mr. Tennison—that's my landlord. I was two weeks behind on the rent, and I feared if he saw me on the street, he might just whoop my behind—or at least he might try! I was afraid to answer my phone for all the bill collectors. They'd started calling me by my first name— that's when you know they mean business. I was down to my last. Couldn't even pass by a vending machine without the candy bars laughing at me. No chile, he might've been smiling, but I wasn't paying him any mind at all. I had my eyes on that money, and as far as I could see, Samson was no longer the most beautiful thing in the room.

"What's the extra grand for?" I looked him in the eye.

"That's a little bonus for if you do it right...the way I like it." He extended his hand to my face and brushed my skin softly with the backs of his fingers.

"Well, then, that extra grand is money in my pocket, Mr. Samson." I grabbed his hand, the one that caressed my

7

cheek, and inhaled his index finger in a long, slow suck. I closed my eyes and worked my tongue around. His finger was salty to the taste. I opened my eyes to witness his frenzy. A bead of sweat gathered on his brow, a symbol of the elevating heat between us. With my teeth, I pulled off a ring and held it hostage beneath my tongue. He didn't feel a thing, and how could he? The blood had left his head; it had abandoned his entire upper half. He was floating too close to Heaven to notice my devilish deeds. "You'll like it, Mr. Samson," I said, drawing back with a smile. "I promise you, you'll like it."

|•|•|•|•|•|•|•|•|•|•|•|•|•|•|•|•|•|•|•|•|•|•|•

The rainfall had downgraded to a light spray, but I could tell the storm was far from over. Thunder rumbled like a hungry stomach, and lightning cracked the sky into pieces, as if the night were made of glass. You could barely see past your eyelashes for all the fog. From way up on the fourteenth-floor terrace of the Bell Sheraton Hotel, I watched it roll through the streets like an old ghost, the dense brume devouring everything in sight. I was making a couple clouds of my own, puffing on a Newport Light. In between drags, I sipped on Jack Daniels and ginger ale. I felt good standing there in my red dress being bathed in moonlight, showered in rain. And I could feel myself falling deeply in love.

No, not with Samson. I was in love with penthouse Suite 1401! It was a palace compared to my place on Bouldercrest Lane. I was living in Apartment B-19, a one-bedroom, second story walk-up in the Connelly Homes Housing Projects. Up until moving there a few years ago, I'd been renting rooms when and where I could from all kinds of lowlifes and crooks: unscrupulous slumlords renting glorified outhouses, sometimes just a toilet and a cot. The only sort of service those misers cared about was the service of eviction notices to outspoken tenants, to anyone who dared to demand more for their money than destitution and squalor.

Apartment B-19 at Connelly Homes was my first solo apartment, and with all the love I'd poured into it, it was much more of a home than many of the other residents could claim. I had a couch, a loveseat, and a chair in my living room. I had food in my refrigerator, a TV to watch, and even a few pieces of art hanging up along the walls. Sure, my bathroom faucet had a perpetual leak, and from time to time I had roaches for roommates. But despite every shortcoming, every mundane fault, I delighted in the peace of having that one small portion of the universe to call my own. And I took great comfort in knowing that only my key could turn that lock. I was the queen of that castle, the master of that domain. And at night, when I laid my head to pillow and thought back over my life, I was overcome every time with thankfulness and gratefulness for the safety and security those walls provided. Still, I would've traded those walls easily for penthouse Suite 1401.

I finished my cigarette and flicked it over the balcony. The orange butt sailed through the night like a comet before disappearing into the fog down below. I stepped back through the sheer white curtains and into the lounge where I set my empty glass down on the minibar.

My red stilettos sank deeply into the plush carpet; it almost
swallowed my feet. The cathedral ceilings rose at least
thirty feet high, and a crystal chandelier dangled regally
over the centermost point of the room. Colorful cascades
of light fell down in all directions as shadows hid like
cowards under tables and behind chairs.

Fresh-cut flowers of all types dressed each table,
and abstract paintings filled with bold, vibrant colors clung
to every wall. A tall set of double doors on the far wall
opposite me led into what I suspected was the bedroom.
Aside from the front door we had entered and the bedroom,
there was only one other doorway. Samson emerged from
it shaking the water from his hands, and I gathered that it
was the bathroom.

"Sorry I took so long. Wanted to wash my face."
More likely, he was probably in there *watching* his face,
but I kept that comment to myself. He touched a hand to
the circular dimmer on the wall beside him and turned it
slowly. The chandelier had been like the sun, lighting and
warming the world below. But with one gentle touch from
Samson, the chandelier began to fade like a long summer
dusk. Shadows rose from the dark corners of the room to
dance along the walls. And candles that had been burning
in the background began to cast their glow center stage.

Samson crept toward me, undoing his tie, and I took
a shaky step back. I don't scare easily, but something
about his countenance frightened me. That sly smile was
back, and there was a sizzling look in his deep, dark eyes
that was almost inscrutable. It was primal, but seductive,
dangerous, yet somehow romantic. Standing there in the
path of his gaze, I couldn't tell if I was about to be kissed
or killed—or one of each! He threw his necktie to the floor

and unfastened the top three buttons of his shirt. Minus his suit jacket, he was all the more beautiful. His chest and arms were hard and perfectly sculpted, like he'd been chiseled from a block of mahogany. I took another step back.

"You scared?" he said with a smirk, stepping toward me slowly. "You were talkin' a big game back at the bar. Now it's showtime." He licked his lips. "Checkout's at noon, so you got all night to earn that extra grand."

He undressed me with his eyes—and then his hands. My dress fell off my shoulders and stacked upon itself around my ankles. No sooner had I stepped down out of my heels than he swept me off my feet and up into his arms. He held me close and carried me through those tall double doors, where he placed me on the king-size bed and laid his weight on top of mine. He kissed my neck and shoulders. Then my mouth. His kisses were wet and sweet like fresh fruit—must have been passion fruit, if you catch my meaning!

He was an experienced lover, I could tell. He didn't yank at my bra until it relented, nor did he just pull at my panties until they ripped. I'd had many a bra and panty set ruined by overzealous lovers. No, Samson was skilled, honey. And smooth. He massaged his fingers into my back, and the bra came off just like that! He rolled my panties carefully over my hips and down my legs, caressing my skin with his fingertips. Then he dove between my thighs like a world-class swimmer, licking me like a lollipop or some other tasty treat. He pressed his lips against my labia and sucked on me like a peach, the juices dripping down his hands like nectar, sticky and sweet. And when I had been thoroughly pleased, he brushed his lips against my inner thighs and left a trail of wet kisses leading all the way down my legs to the soles of my feet, where he sucked on each of my toes like a babe at the breast. His thick, long tongue made a meal of my body, and I writhed in delight, anxious to be devoured.

Now I'm usually the seductress, but before I even knew what was happening, I had been seduced. I found myself intoxicated by his sweet scent, and I felt powerless against his charms. I lay there naked beneath his sloppy kisses, vulnerable to his tender touch. I unbuttoned another of his shirt buttons—and then another and another until finally I felt the full contact of his skin on top of mine. I pulled his shirt back over his arms, our bare chests pressing together like magnets. Lying there, heart to heart, breast to breast, I felt him throbbing against my thigh, and honey, I knew definitively that in a jungle somewhere far away, an elephant was missing its trunk!

I began working on his pants. And as I unhooked his belt buckle, I felt his heart beating wildly against me like a drum. Our bodies moved together in perfect rhythm, dancing to that primal beat. With each breath, each rise and fall of his chest, with each sensual kiss, each careful caress, that heartbeat grew stronger. It pounded faster. And faster. And faster still. I'd just unfastened his zipper when it stopped. The drumming. The nectar-sweet kisses. The teasing touches. Those warm breaths against my neck. The war cry that echoed between us as our bodies danced together. Everything stopped. His brown eyes stared into mine, and as I stared back up at him, it was like seeing a stranger for the first time. Like I barely knew him. The deep gaze that had been reading me all evening was suddenly shallow and glossy, as if a gate had been closed behind his pupils. He was dead.

CHAPTER 2: A TALE OF TWO KISSES!

For a moment, I lay there frozen, just like the dead man who straddled me from above. And as I stared up into his perfect face and beheld those cold, empty eyes, I shuddered at the irony of my bald-headed Samson now so weak, so powerless, and blind, just like his biblical namesake from so many millennia before. Had I been his Delilah? Was his death my doing? Had I held him in the wrong way? Did I squeeze him too tightly? I'd always been a proponent of safe sex, and yet that night it seemed my lips had been lethal. My kisses had somehow killed. I was armed and dangerous, wielding passion like a dagger, a secret weapon lurking deep down within that, until that moment, I hadn't even known was there.

I was still in shock as Samson's lifeless body held me down like a paperweight and anchored me to the bed. But as soon as the reality set in that I was lying with a corpse, chile, I shot up out of those sheets so fast you would've thought there was a crocodile in the covers! I searched the bed for my panties and found them, but my bra seemed to have disappeared. I swear I nearly turned that whole room over looking for that bra. You ever been in a situation where you couldn't find your keys and had to be some place quick? Well, multiply that feeling by ten! Twenty, honey!

She works hard for the money! Single,
professional woman seeking a man of means
for companionship and more...a lot more.
Only serious individuals need inquire. #667

That's what I'd said in the ad I placed in *The Atlanta Sun* last month. Cost me twenty-five cents a word, and it ran for three weeks before I'd gotten so much as a hello. Samson responded earlier that morning and left me a message saying he wanted to meet. I replied and gave him directions to Black Jack's. And I took that opportunity to tell him that I was a businesswoman, and not to forget his wallet. After that, I really didn't expect him to come, and I was just getting ready to get up and leave when he showed up at the bar. I realize now that Samson's tardiness had been an omen, a sign that I should've taken my behind home! I should've just paid the check and split; I should have tipped my hat and gone. But instead, I summoned the bartender again, watched him refill my glass for a third time, and waited for the storm to send Samson drifting my way, to carry him ashore like foam on the evening tide.

I gave up on the bra and ran out of the bedroom into the lounge. My dress and shoes were right where I'd left them. I stepped into them both and slipped them on simultaneously. Then I snatched my purse from the glass coffee table, and while I was at it, I ran back over to the bar and grabbed the empty cognac glass that I'd sipped from earlier and dropped it in my bag too. My bra was a lost cause, but I figured I'd better do *something* to limit the evidence of my presence. Then I raced for the door and was halfway into the hallway when I remembered. I had two thousand dollars in my purse. *Only* two thousand. For all the trouble he'd put me through, Samson owed me that extra grand, so I told myself.

I turned back into the suite and ran into the bedroom. As much as I hated to touch him, I patted Samson's pants. No wallet. It might've been my imagination, but in that little stretch of time, it seemed like his skin had already stiffened to the touch. My mahogany man was becoming a mahogany statue. I ran back into the lounge and rummaged through his satin jacket. No wallet. By this time, I was sweating like a race horse and moving nearly as fast. I couldn't imagine where that money could be. Then it hit me, of course. The bathroom. Samson had spent a good while in there, long enough for me to have a drink and a cigarette.

I pushed open the bathroom door and flicked on the switch. The lights around the vanity momentarily blinded me; they were bright as a stadium. The first thing my eyes fixed on once they adjusted was that snakeskin wallet. It sat perched like a lizard on the edge of the porcelain sink. I bolted in and grabbed it. Then I counted out ten hundred-dollar bills and started to put the rest back. *What kind of man carries over three thousand dollars in cash on him?* I wondered. Whatever his reason, I decided to go ahead and take the whole wallet. Not to sound insensitive, but he didn't exactly have much use for it anymore, I figured.

I stuffed the dead man's wallet into my purse and left the suite—this time for good. And you should've seen me. You talkin' 'bout scared? All the way down the fourteen flights of stairs, I was crouching low, ducking behind corners. I swear you would've thought I was auditioning to be a ninja! And walking through that lobby? Honey, I was tip-toein' like a ballerina!

|•|•|•|•|•|•|•|•|•|•|•|•|•|•|•|•|•|•|•|•|•|•|•

Francine. That's what they were calling her. Every station I turned to was broadcasting the same story: more on Hurricane Francine. I was glad Samson and I had taken separate cars, but to be honest, I would've rather been behind the wheel of his truck than in my old Chevy Nova. The streets had begun to look more like rivers, water racing around like whirlpools. Tree branches, road signs, and utility poles that had been snatched down by wind now blocked the roads like dams. I found myself detoured at least twice, and trying to drive around all those obstacles, I felt like I was trapped inside a video game!

Visibility on the road in front of me was down to almost zero and not just because of the rain. Chile, my wipers were about as dull as a game of golf, and my defroster was working in reverse. Seemed like the more it blew, the foggier the glass. To top things off, ole Milsey—that's what I named my car—was acting like she'd rather die than drive. According to the radio, the storm was still working its way through the Caribbean Sea, lurking just off the coast of Cuba, ready to strike. It hadn't yet hit land and was still nearly a thousand miles away, but it seemed to me like the storm was racing right alongside me, following me through the darkness. And after a lifetime of running, I was sick of being chased.

"Hey!" he shouted. "Hey! I'm talkin' ta you. You speak English or what? You slow, girl? You stupid or somethin'?" He grabbed my wrist and spun me around. "Hey!"

"Hay is for horses," I finally replied. "If you don't know my name, that's a sign that you ain't got no business talkin' to me." I broke free of his clutch and kept on stepping. He gave chase and snatched my arm again.

"Where you think you goin'?"

"Let go of my arm!" He squeezed me tighter. I couldn't take it. "Turn me loose!" I hollered. He pulled me close and silenced my scream by sticking his tongue in my mouth. I tried to fight, but suddenly he held both of my wrists. My eyes bulged out of my head like they wanted to jump out of my face, like they couldn't bear to witness what was happening. I smelled his breath. I tasted his tongue. I felt his whiskers against my cheeks. They scratched and pricked like the hard bristles of a cheap brush. As our faces touched, I was smeared in a mix of sweat and oily excretions. He reeked of Old Smuggler whiskey and Old Spice cologne. I tried to scream again, but no sound came out; he was holding my mouth hostage with his foul kiss. I heard people in the distance. They saw, but did not care. I began to cry, tears watering my face like Niagara. I was scared, but not helpless. I had one weapon. One defense. Channeling all my strength, I bit down hard. He released me, hollering. Howling. He fell to the ground, clutching his face. I spit his blood and saliva from my mouth and gagged violently. I felt like I might vomit, but each painful heave was dry. I backed away, shaking. I clutched my bruised wrist, and I was angry. I lunged forward and kicked him in the stomach, stabbing him with my silver stiletto. Then I turned and ran. I ran like I was on fire, looking back every few steps to make sure he wasn't chasing me. I kept running, and all the while, I'm thinking of how much I hate working Commerce Boulevard and how tired I am of running through life looking back over my shoulder.

In a flash of white, electricity filled the sky and jarred me from daydreaming. I swerved out of my lane for a moment, but thankfully, mine was the only car on the road. Lightning flashed again, and with it, the heavens began to rumble, a chorus of drums beating wildly in the rippling wind. Why didn't my killer kiss work when that drunk had attacked me on the street last month? Or the month before that, when I had to fight my way out of another lunatic's car and ripped my favorite blouse on his door handle in the process? Where was my kiss of death then?

In my line of work, the risks were often greater than the rewards, and there was the potential for danger lurking beyond every tinted window, around every dark corner, and in every approaching silhouette. That's why I'd placed that ad in the *Sun*. I know it was unconventional and maybe even a little strange to advertise a service like mine in such an unusual forum, but after my recent run of bad luck, dealing with one dangerous jerk after another, I was desperate to avoid the hazards of the streets. But this new path I traveled seemed to be paved in the same chaos and regret as the old one; this new road led me to the same place as the last. The seemingly safe alternative I'd chosen over strolling down Commerce Boulevard proved ultimately to be no less dangerous. After all, a man was dead now, half naked and sprawled out across a hotel bed.

The fog crossed in front of me as I drove, hovering over the road like a fallen cloud. Rain spilled from the sky, drowning plants and saturating the streets. Thunder resounded through the city and sent a chill all down through my body, no doubt a warning that trouble was headed my way. I held the wheel tightly, and as I laid into the gas, I prayed for the strength to weather both storms.

CHAPTER 3: SHHH! MOM'S THE WORD.

I was a sack full of skin and nerves by the time I turned onto Bouldercrest Lane. I could barely hold the wheel steady for all my jitters—which is dangerous, honey, when you ain't got no power steering! It was late, and all I wanted to think about was getting home. I kept looking in my rearview mirror. Samson's death was still my little secret, but for some reason, I felt like a hurricane wasn't the only thing coming.

I turned into the Connelly Homes lot and parked way in the back in my regular space. And just as I turned off my headlights and pulled the keys from the ignition, I couldn't believe it. The rain stopped. A sudden silence befell the night as the bustling city settled into stillness, every soul awaiting its fate, dreading the hurricane's impending wrath. I reached over and pushed in my cigarette lighter. Then I dug into my purse in search of a smoke. The lighter released itself with a click, and I put my last cigarette to my lips. I closed my eyes, relaxed my shoulders, and let my head sink deep into the leather headrest. This should have been a peaceful moment and I should've felt soothed, but I just couldn't escape the image of Samson's lifeless body lying on that hotel bed. Samson's face was plastered indelibly on the backs of my eyelids; even with my eyes shut, I saw him still—literally still.

Clutching my purse beneath my arm and my cigarette between my lips, I got out of the car. Even with the keys out of the ignition, Milsey's engine knocked and ticked softly. Around two corners, underneath a concrete overpass, up a shaky metal staircase, and I was home. Finally. I grabbed my keys again and went to unfasten the first of my three locks, but upon a mere touch, the door drifted open. Beyond its slow swing, my TV and stereo lay on their sides, and the tall brass lamp that had once stood regally in the corner of the living room now lay prostrate, straddling the sofa. Knickknacks, papers, and pictures that had adorned the shelves of my bookcase were now strewn all across the floor. I stood there breathless and confused. I mean, sure, I had a couple of little things, but nothing much worth stealing. Hell, a thief robbing *me* would have to just be practicin'!

My coffee table was now just a metal frame, and shards of glass from it littered the entryway. I heard them imploding beneath the soles of my feet, felt them grinding into the carpet as I inched further inside. I stepped to the left toward the hallway. I could see that the bathroom door was closed and the bedroom door at the end of the short hall was slightly ajar. "Hello? Who's there?!" Hearing my own shaky voice, I realized something. If every horror movie I had ever seen was true to form, then I was likely to either be tackled by a thug or eaten alive by a monster. I suddenly realized that if, by chance, I was not alone, I wasn't at all prepared for an encounter with the culprit. And so, I reached down and picked up a long, icicle-shaped shard of glass.

Weapon in hand, I clutched the hallway wall as I inched slowly toward the closed bathroom door. Once in front of it, I grabbed the knob with a tight grip, took a deep breath, and flung it open. The force of my swing caused the door to hit the wall with a bang. Aside from my startled reflection in the bathroom mirror, everything else looked fine. I proceeded the rest of the way down the hall toward my bedroom. A light was on inside. I snuck up to the door and pushed it open slowly as the hinges creaked and whined beneath the pressure of my touch. The sheets on the bed were pulled back, exposing the worn mattress underneath. Clothes spilled out of the closet and piled onto the floor. The dresser drawers were open, and undies of all kinds and colors burst from within. I stood there, beholding a room in total disarray. I smiled and exhaled a sigh of relief to see that it was just as I had left it!

I stepped back out of the bedroom and past the living room to the kitchen. Nothing and no one there either, although the throw rug I'd so stylishly placed cattycorner in the center of the floor had been stained with the soil from my overturned baby ficus. I'd placed the plant up on the windowsill earlier that day to get some light. It had hastily been given a new home atop the linoleum. I'm no detective, but while bending over to pick up my plant, I did notice part of an extra-large boot print stamped into one of the mounds of dirt. Just knowing that a stranger had been walking through my home sent a shudder running through my body. And I decided I'd better leave. I was tired, I was scared, but more than anything, I was offended. That's right, offended! None of my costume jewelry had been touched. Not one piece was missing. If my faux diamonds, brass bangles, and artificial earrings weren't foolin' the lowlife who'd ransacked my apartment, I shuddered to think who *else* they weren't foolin'!

I stepped out of the apartment, pulled the door closed, and rested my forehead against it. The wine had run its full course through my body, and Mr. Jack Daniels was waving his farewell. I wanted nothing more than to rest my weary head. The warm wind raced through the housing development and tossed my hair about. And just like that wind, I also found myself running with nowhere on Earth to go.

I certainly couldn't call the police. Even if I hadn't met Samson that night and borne witness to his death, I definitely didn't need any cops poking through my things and nosing around my home—especially since my own backyard was far from clean. And if Mr. Tennison, my landlord, saw the current state of my place, chile, I'd be out faster than ribs at a picnic in Mississippi!

"Who is it?"

"It's me, Mantha. I know it's late."

The door seemed to open itself. She stood there, tall and still. Her robe, silky and blue, rinsed over her figure and gathered at her feet. The light behind her spilled out onto the concrete walk where I stood. Somewhere between knocking and waiting, I had swallowed my tongue. Held there, hostage in her shadow, my knees quaked beneath me. Words gathered in my throat, too chicken to step out and be heard. "Yes, baby?" she asked. Her voice fell down around me like soft rain. Underneath it, my heart slowed from speeding. And for the first time since I'd left the hotel, I was no longer afraid.

"I need your help." I stepped inside, glancing back over my shoulder as the door closed gently behind me.

"I'd take ya' coat, but you ain't got na'am."

"I know—"

"And look at you...you soakin' wet."

"I know, Ms. Jane." I stole a way into the conversation. "You don't know what I've been through tonight—"

"And I don't wanna know either!" interjected Ms. Jane again. "Not right now, anyways. Let's get you outta' those wet clothes. I'll put some tea on the boil."

|•|•|•|•|•|•|•|•|•|•|•|•|•|•|•|•|•|•|•|•|•|•|•

The clock on the wall read ten something. Its time was partially obscured by the steam that crept slowly up its glass face. Like a virulent disease, the steam from my bath had also claimed the mirror above the sink and frosted the tiny window just above the toilet. I lay there in silence, watching the damp haze consume the room while the condensation dripped down the shower walls like tears. I, too, was crying a bit, a hundred or more questions racing through my mind. Even more persistent, though, were the usual thoughts that I could never seem to shake.

"Samantha Moore?"

"Yes, ma'am. Right here," she answered. I hadn't yet learned to speak for myself.

"You can come on back." I grabbed my book bag and my fluttering chest and followed the nurse and my mama through a doorway and down a short hall. My heartbeat was fast, powerful enough to break a stethoscope. "Have a seat." She motioned to me. I did as I was told and hoisted myself onto the table. It seemed especially high, and I felt especially heavy. "You can have a seat over there, Mrs. Phillips." Mama sat down on the stool in the far corner, poised like a boxer between bloody bouts. And she glared at me as if I were her opponent, some mysterious adversary who'd come with the intention of challenging her title. She sat there, never blinking, intensely focused. I was on the other side of the room near the door, yet that didn't seem far enough away. "I just have a couple questions." The nurse turned her eyes to me, clipboard in hand.

"Yes, ma'am," I mumbled timidly.

"Age?"

"Thirteen…and a half." Her pen wrote vigorously. I could hear the ballpoint scratching wildly against the stiff wooden board.

"Father?"

"Pardon?"

"Who is the daddy of this child, dear? This is not a game." The nurse took a stern stance to match her tone. Mama rose a little higher on her seat.

"I won't say."

The nurse turned her back to me with a fury and collected her papers. As mean as she was, I wanted to beg her not to leave. Before exiting, she leaned in and whispered, "It's a shame what you're doin' to your poor mother, little girl." Then she turned to Mama. "Doctor'll be in shortly, Mrs. Phillips. God bless you." Mama nodded as the door drifted to a close. Then she braced the windowsill for support and rose from the corner stool. It seemed like she would never stop standing; she felt ten feet tall to me.

Her eyes still fixed to mine, she walked slowly toward me. I burst into tears and stared down at my dangling feet. She placed one hand on the top of my thigh

25

and lifted my chin with the other. Our eyes met through our tears.

"You did right. You hear me?" she reassured. "You hear me?" I nodded. "Can't nobody ever know. You did right. Can't nobody ever know."

Those were his words, too. He would steal a way into my room in the middle of the night and mount me, gently holding a hand over my mouth. He was never vicious, never violent, and that was precisely his crime. If only he'd been violent and vicious in manner, I wouldn't have mistaken his lustful touch for loving affection. If only he had been hostile, I wouldn't have confused our careful secrets for the bonds of intimacy. If only he had been aggressive, cruel, and sadistic in his ways, I wouldn't have looked for him in the night to darken my doorway, and I wouldn't have cried at his goodbyes. If he hadn't kissed me so softly, so sensuously, maybe my emotions wouldn't have been jumpstarted so prematurely. Maybe I wouldn't have spent so many years afterwards sifting and sorting through men of all types and kinds, searching for that same touch, that furtive feeling that only occurs in darkness and in secret, after midnight and before dawn. Each time, when it was over, his whiskers would graze my ear, and he would whisper softly, "Can't nobody ever know."

But then my belly began to swell, and what my lips kept quiet, my body began to tell. The nausea and weakness I'd begun to feel could not be hidden nor denied. And thus, only months after our secret was born, so was our baby. Ten pretty fingers, ten pretty toes, and a pair of hazy gray eyes, all wrapped in bronze skin smooth as silk—except for a small chocolate circle on her left shoulder. A tiny birthmark just as uniquely beautiful as its wearer.

If I had held her any tighter, I would have hurt her. I didn't want to let her go, but the choice was not mine. I held her long enough to name her, and then Mama gave her to a lady I was told was a social worker. "Trinity." The name fit so well. Trinity, the child of me and my mother's husband. The proof that one plus one can sometimes equal three. I prayed that in her new home, with her new family, she would never know the scandal of her conception. Mama signed her name and mine along a dotted line, and with that, she willed away all that was and would ever be truly mine. I sobbed in Mama's arms, still a baby myself. And our foreheads touched, perhaps in symbolic agreement that we were forever slated to share the same painful memory, just as we'd shared the same dreadful man.

"You alright in there, honey?" I jerked suddenly. A bit of water spilled from the tub and onto the floor. "You stay in there too long, and you gon' be lookin' like one of them California Raisins."

"I'm alright, Ms. Jane. Be out in a minute." My stormy night that had begun at Black Jack's Tavern was just one out of a series of bad days, disappointments, and unsolicited twists of fate for me, just another cog in the ever-spiraling wheel of my existence. My life ain't never been ordinary, honey, but even with all the challenges and bizarre ventures and misadventures of my past, and all my strange luck thrown in besides, I just couldn't understand this night's events. What would cause a seemingly healthy, virile man like Samson to just up and die like that? And my apartment? Who would tear up my place and not take a thing? What were they looking for? Or who? Things just didn't add up. For one, there were too many unknowns in my equation.

My curls had already been threatened by the afternoon's rains. I figured I'd rather have them flattened by *my* hands than those of Francine. And so, with a deep breath, I slid down into the suds and submerged my whole head—hair and all—beneath what used to be steaming hot water; it had cooled a bit. I closed my eyes and listened to the distant whirls of the water as it splished and splashed back and forth against the walls of the tiny tub. I prayed to emerge from the water like a dreamer. Finally released from the grasp of sleep and slumber, I hungered to be free, to live and seek every good thing my mind had dared to conjure. I longed to arise from the water into a realization that the whole evening had never taken place. I yearned to be baptized, washed clean, and renewed, to emerge from the shallow pool like an innocent babe. I sat up in the tub and opened my eyes to behold the same dimly lit bathroom. I looked down to see the same breasts and arms and legs, the same ole soggy me.

"So much for second chances," I said aloud before lifting myself from the tepid waters.

CHAPTER 4: FIGHTING CHANCE!

"Jesus, Jesus, how I trust Him… How I've proved Him o'er and o'er." Ms. Jane's voice soared down the hall. "Jesus, Jesus, precious Jesus… Oh, for grace to trust Him more…" While the words were beautiful, her voice was anything but. Sound spilled recklessly over her lips and out into the air like pollution. Now, I'm no musician, but I'm pretty sure Ms. Jane was in the key of Z! I laughed to myself as I stepped from the bathroom, the carpet soft and warm beneath my toes.

Ms. Jane had given me one of her nightshirts to wear. It was so long the entire Lord's Prayer was written down its front in big cursive letters. I felt like a little girl playing dress-up in her mother's closet. A long string of pearls and some oversized pumps would've completed the silly set. I didn't care, though. I was dry.

I followed Ms. Jane's voice down the long hallway toward the living room. Ms. Jane's place was just about identical to mine, but it had an extra bedroom that the girls all shared. Their door was open halfway, so I stopped and peeped inside. The four of them slept head to toe on a shabby wooden bunk bed: two on top and two on the bottom. They lay motionless under the faint glow of a tiny nightlight beneath the wardrobe. I'd never known Ms. Jane's girls to be so silent and still. I mean, that room was so quiet you could hear a cotton ball bounce!

The four little girls *I* knew were grown, sassy, and stereo loud! For the last few years that I'd been a tenant at Connelly Homes, it seemed not a day had gone by that Kyla, Kierra, Kia, and Kimmie weren't outside raising some sort of hell. They'd start off nice enough with their

29

hula-hoops and roller skates. And often they'd partake in a friendly game of dodgeball, tag, or kickball with the other boys and girls in the development. But as soon as those jump ropes came out, so did the beast in each of them!

Jumping rope was a rite of passage, a ghetto gauntlet, honey. Only the bravest of souls dared to defy those spinning circles, stepping forward out of the shadows and into the contest like knights in armor ready to joust. And all along the sidelines stood girls from all over the neighborhood, teasing and taunting the gladiator in the ropes like a tribunal of challengers and champs. And so, the tournament began!

"Bluebells, cockleshells, eevy ivy over! I like coffee. I like tea. I like the boys, and the boys like me!" I'd hear them singing as they jumped in and out of the double-dutch ropes with speed and precision. And when they got going real good and had worked up a shine, sweat lathering on their faces like soap, I heard the sidelines shouting, "'A' begins the alphabet, so be on time, 'cause the school bus leaves at a quarter to nine!" Those girls jumped and jumped and jumped, pushing through the pain of exhaustion like world-class athletes training for a decathlon. And as the competition stiffened and the intensity mounted, the boys halted their nearby games and gathered around the girls to watch this clash of preteen titans.

"Postman, postman, do your duty, 'cause here comes Kierra, she's America's beauty! She can jump, jump, jump! And she can twist, twist, twist...but I bet she can't do this!" And then they stopped the ropes and spun them 'Irish', backwards in the opposite direction. The ropes looked alive there and even took on the shape of a

DNA double helix as they twirled and intertwined. And the jumper got bold and started doing tricks right there inside those whirling wires. That girl would hop on one foot and touch the ground. She'd twist and turn and shake around and never miss a beat as the ropes slapped the cement and orbited only inches above her afro puffs. "Click-clack, click-clack," the ropes themselves would sing as hands clapped all around the swarming circle. One false step, and those ropes would sting your ankles worse than an ocean full of jellyfish, a hive full of bees, and a hundred hot combs!

      Those songs and sounds were the score to my childhood growing up in Mississippi, and just hearing them again caused the warmth of nostalgia to envelop me like a gentle hug. I'd spy Ms. Jane's girls and all the other children through my bedroom blinds, and for a second, I'd bask admiringly in the sounds of youth, remembering and relishing the simplicity of pre-adolescence. Then, all of a sudden, "Clapsies!" someone would yell, the most dangerous word on the playground, signifying the possibility of foul play somewhere: the intentional tampering and hampering of the ropes. And the call of clapsies was almost always succeeded by someone pointing and shouting, "She double-handed!" This was the ultimate insult, calling into question the rhythmic aptitude of one of the girls governing the ropes. And honey, after the contest had been contested, an inquisition began. And that nice game they had been playing would turn into an all-out shouting match, where angry accusations of cheating and treachery, fuming allegations of trickery and treason, would be tossed about. Next thing you know, Ms. Jane's girls would be hurling both insults and punches, scratching and

31

biting like dogs. I mean, they would fight anybody, no matter how big, how small, or how many! Now, in that tiny bedroom, there they lay in darkness, silenced by sleep and—for once—peaceful.

I kept on moving down the hall and stepped into the living room as the eleven o'clock news sang its start and rolled its beginning credits across Ms. Jane's TV. "Got to know what's goin' on in the worl', chile. People's crazy anymore!" Ms. Jane declared as she emerged from the kitchen, ducking underneath the doorway and wiping her hands with the tattered apron she wore over her robe. By most standards, Ms. Jane was almost a giant, standing at least six foot eight if she was an inch. She hobbled over to the TV set and turned the sound down a bit before sitting in her rocking recliner. She nestled deep into its plush upholstery and wiggled her hips a bit—I assume to align her backside with the contours it had created through the many years of crocheting, hair-braiding, and channel surfing. Her favorite program of all, practically an obsession, was the news. And she tuned in eagerly to every broadcast, morning, noon, and night.

To many tenants living there in Connelly Homes, Ms. Jane herself was the news. She knew everyone in the whole complex, which consisted of six buildings with twenty-four units each. And if that weren't impressive enough, her tentacles stretched even beyond the gates of our development and spanned the entire city. After over half a century living in Atlanta, Ms. Jane was an institution, a fixture in all the communities. And she was tapped into the pulse of every living soul. Though she rarely left the house herself anymore, she seemed to know even the most intimate of details about every man, woman, boy, or girl:

from innocent tidbits such as birthdays and anniversaries to juicy morsels like who owed who money, whose husband was cheating with whose wife, and the gamut of unlikely, but nonetheless torrid, love affairs—or lust affairs, whichever.

What she didn't know, she could find out in a flash. She had a secret constituency consisting of all types: suspicious old ladies plagued by fear who surveyed the neighborhoods like guard dogs, blabbermouth youngsters who'd sell their soul and yours for a sweet treat or any drink with a straw in it, watchful winos who wandered the streets like nomads witnessing every secret transaction and clandestine encounter. Ms. Jane had an army of her own, a waiting militia whose very identity was itself a secret known only to its commander-in-chief. She was a living, breathing pool of knowledge, a well of truth, a fountain of secrets—a pay fountain, that is.

That's right. Ms. Jane had information for *sale*, jack! Sometimes, she would charge cash. On other occasions, she'd require a buyer to join the ranks of her growing group of minions, to become one of her secret troops—or snoops, as it were. Most times, finding it difficult to place a dollar amount on her brand of classified intelligence, she traded favors, services, and other acts of goodwill. It was a tight operation, really, and every little bit of support Ms. Jane could scrounge together to help provide for those four nightmares that lay dreaming in the back room was warmly welcomed and happily obliged.

"So…what's your trouble, chile?" She turned her glance to me.

"Ughh!" I sighed, plopping down on the squeaky sofa. "Ms. Jane, I don't wanna burden you with all my sad

33

---

stories, but I just don't know what's goin' on. I met a friend tonight…"

"A friend?" Ms. Jane interrupted curiously.

"A stranger," I corrected myself. "I met a stranger tonight…at a bar…from a personal ad…"

"Talk about looking for trouble." Ms. Jane shook her head with a chuckle.

"I had him meet me at Black Jack's. He was late—"

"Yeah, yeah, yeah. What did he *look* like, honey?" Ms. Jane smiled, leaning her head back into her chair and closing her eyes as if preparing the slate of her mind to imagine Samson's likeness.

"Bald head. Tall, dark. Handsome and strong. Perfect, really."

Ms. Jane opened her eyes. "Now, ain't *no* man perfect, honey, 'cept for Jesus of Nazareth! And he wouldn't have answered no personal ad and met you in no bar!" She chuckled again, her shoulders bouncing up and down with each giggle. "Mantha, I done known you quite a while, and somethin' tells me you wadn't out lookin' for no love connection. What gives?"

"You know how I been so tired of dealin' for dollars with these same ole creeps."

"Yeah, you said you was through workin' them streets."

"Yes, exactly, which is why I placed that ad instead. I thought it would be safer, you know, if I could sorta' do some screening."

"Well? Was it?"

"He's dead, Ms. Jane."

"Who? Mr. Perfect?"

"Yes, he's dead."

34

Ms. Jane leaned forward in her chair. "You mean to tell me you witnessed a murder tonight?" A sudden look of horror arrested her countenance. "You didn't kill him, did you? Did he hurt you?!"

"No, no, Ms. Jane. Nothing like that. He just died." Restless, I rose from the couch and paced the floor. "We were in the hotel room, and he was on top of me, and we were kissing, and then he just died."

"So you *did* kill him!" Ms. Jane laughed.

"This is funny to you?"

Ms. Jane turned her attention back to the news. "Here go the lottery numbers." She leaned into the television and squinted despite her bifocals.

"Ms. Jane! You gon' ignore me for that stupid lottery!" I shouted as loud as I could whisper. I definitely didn't want to wake the girls.

"Shhh!" Ms. Jane waved a hand at me as she studied the numbers on the screen intently. "Look at that. Missed it by that much." She snapped her fingers with a thunderous click. "Girl, I was almost a millionaire!" Ms. Jane leaned back in her chair and laughed again before turning back to me. "You see that?"

"Yes, I saw," I said. I may have even rolled my eyes a little. I was trying to talk seriously, and Ms. Jane didn't seem the least bit interested. Perhaps I had chosen the wrong confidante to confide in.

"No, no, no. Did you *really* see?" Ms. Jane repeated with a wink.

"See what?" I asked.

"All those lil' balls bouncin' 'round that tank. Yep, they start those balls to bouncin', then the machine sucks one up, and the pretty lady reads it off. That's how they

35

pick the numbers for the lottery. Until that ball pops up outta' that tube, nobody knows what the number will be. Now, in those few moments while those balls are stirrin' in that tank and poppin' up one by one, a person's everything can be changed. A man who's been broke all his life can suddenly pick himself up and dust off every speck of poverty and disparity. And a woman like me, strugglin' to provide for her grandchi'ren can change both her life and the lives of generations that ain't even been thought about yet. You understand what I'm sayin'?"

"I understand, but what does this have to do with anything right now?"

"Sit." Ms. Jane pointed to the couch and I sat back down on the end next to her chair. "Every time you step out to do what you doin', meetin' these sleazy men and rompin' around in seedy motels and shady backseats and dark alleyways and what have you, you stirrin' up that tank. Just like me, you takin' a chance. Now, when I take *my* chance and guess wrong, it only cost me a dollar. All it takes is for one crazy fool to reach his hands 'round your neck out there in them streets, and girl, *yo'* number is up! Don't you see that your whole life is at stake? And your life is worth a hell of a lot more than my dollar."

"Ms. Jane, I don't need no—"

"No, no, I ain't through yet. Now, if I win—if they call my numbers just as I played 'em, I get to have a whole new beginning. I get a fresh start for me and my babies, and for you too, 'cause you know you like a daughter to me. Just think of how different all our lives would be if I won! Now, ain't *no* winner to the game *you* playin, chile. Not a one. So whose lottery sounds mo' stupid, yours or mine?"

I folded my arms and stared into the TV. If I had a dollar for every time I'd heard a similar lecture, I wouldn't need a lottery to begin with—neither kind. Ms. Jane looked to me for a response, some reaction that illustrated that I'd heard what she'd said and had been moved in some way. I denied her the satisfaction. I sat still, eyes ahead, focused on a commercial for cough syrup, pretending to be ignorant and impervious to her words of wisdom.

I was fourteen years old when I left Mississippi, and I'd been running ever since, navigating solo through life's coarse waters without a compass or guide. At an age where most kids were just discovering themselves in so many ways, learning to embrace life with curiosity and to taste and savor each day with excitement, I had already had my fill. I'd borne the scarlet stigma of pregnancy, every friend, foe, and stranger pointing their fingers at me and making their judgments. I'd been living out a life sentence of small-town contempt, suffering under a barrage of snide remarks whispered behind my back and even the occasional insult said right to my face. Outside my house, my name rested comfortably on everyone's lips. Inside my house, lips were sealed.

Mama's husband had gone, leaving Mama and I both with a mouthful of regrets—regrets so thick in our throats they seemed impenetrable to words. We moved through the empty house like the inner workings of a clock: mechanical, methodical, calculated. She'd enter the room where I'd be sitting, maybe studying my textbooks, and I would schedule my exit. Or, on occasion, I'd sit beside her on the couch in front of the television, and she'd excuse herself to the bathroom or kitchen. When she returned—if she returned—she would seat herself on the chair or

37

loveseat, the furthest spot away from me. He left, and it was as if he'd packed away all the laughter, all the music, all the joy in his leather suitcase. He left and carried away with him the very piece of our hearts that allowed us to love. It was as if he'd stolen the sun from us and left us to dwell in darkness, in coldness, a never-ending solstice of winter and ice.

I couldn't bear the cold season any longer. And so, I packed my bags too. I ran, fleeing something my child mind couldn't altogether articulate, in search of a feeling I was too immature to define. All I knew, all I understood, was that I had to go. I ran, and when I tired I walked. Using my smile as currency, I hitchhiked here and there, but mostly I rode my legs and feet, a teenage girl, cursed with curves and beauty, traveling without a plan, a wayfaring wanderer, drifting through the countryside with no clear agenda.

I should have felt victorious and in control. I should have felt empowered and in charge. Instead, I felt like I was locked out of the world, yet somehow still caged. There, in all that open air, free to roam to my heart's content, I found myself more bound than I'd ever been. And though my belly was full with freedom and independence, I was hungrier than I'd ever known. My hunger, it seemed, could not be quenched, and my pockets echoed their emptiness. I wanted to tell Ms. Jane that when she'd pulled that dollar bill out of her brassiere and used it to purchase her lottery ticket, she'd made a choice. She'd volunteered herself to be the victim of chance. She'd willfully decided to submit to fate, to win or to lose. I had not chosen this. I'd never chosen to be the object of my stepfather's desire. I'd never decided to feel unloved and

unwanted in my mother's home. I'd never elected to be
mocked and ridiculed by a town full of snobs and gossips.
I'd never even fully chosen to make myself vendible, a
product to be bought and sold. I'd simply chosen to
survive, to live and to breathe another day.

"Um…for the record, Ms. Jane, those days are over.
I don't do alleyways and backseats anymore. I got too
much class for that."

"Honey, you got too much class for all of that
nonsense, if you ask me."

"Too much class…not enough cash," I retorted
before burying myself in the sofa. It squeaked and
squished as it surrendered to my weight. I didn't mean to
go to sleep. I just wanted to rest my eyes, but somewhere
within that brief blink, I drifted off and away. Lying on
that sofa was like lying on a giant feather. I floated to sleep
feeling weightless, burdenless, temporarily unhinged from
the gravity of the night's events.

CHAPTER 5: RAIN OF TERROR!

Drip......drip......drip......drip. I had no wristwatch, so at first, I was appreciative of that sound. It helped me to keep track of my seconds spent in solitude. Drip......drip......drip. Every moment assigned a sound and alliterated by that slow leak from above. Drip...... drip......drip. That leaky ceiling overhead was a like a metronome, its tempo steady and concise, like when a drummer counts off the rhythm so that the band can begin. Drip......drip......drip......drip. But the band never played. Sometimes, I'd practice holding my breath and slowing my breathing to see if I could synch my heartbeat to that drip......drip......drip. But like so many ventures in my life, I could never get it quite right. Those drops were too precise, way too perfect, like they'd been calibrated by a Swiss timepiece, drips and drops right on schedule like ticks and tocks.

Drip......drip......drip......drip. In the beginning, I was thankful for those relentless drips drowning out the sounds of mice foraging for food in dark corners and the scuttle of cockroaches scavenging in unclean crevices. There, amid the persistence of those calculated drips, I was able to ignore the constant footsteps in the distance, the pacing of my captors just outside my cage. Under the sound of those droning drops, some nights I was lulled to sleep right away. But most nights, I just lay there awake, thinking, rethinking, overthinking. One night, while sleep eluded me, I remember pondering the phrase "sleep like a baby," so often used to describe a peaceful night's rest. I thought about how inaccurate that idiom was, because there were far too many nights that I'd slept like a baby, and I knew firsthand what that really entailed: sleep a few hours…roll over…wake up…cry…rinse and repeat.

Nights like those, when sleep only flirted with me, when slumber would tease, when rest would ring my doorbell and run before my body could answer, I prayed for that ceiling to come crashing down, to collapse in on me, to open up and release the floodwaters. I prayed to be drowned once and for all. I practiced the act of dying and imagined how I would look once the waters subsided and my lifeless body had been excavated from the floor of that soggy cell: cold, saturated, and blue. Drip……drip…… drip. Some nights, that incessant leak wasn't overhead at all. It was my own tears hitting the pillow *under* my head that threatened to submerge me forever like a tidal wave, a tsunami of sorrow and regret.

"I suppose you know why you're here?" he asked, pulling a folding metal chair from against the cinderblock wall.

"And upon what notion do you base that supposition?" I replied.

"What?" he asked as he positioned his chair directly across from me and sat down. The confusion in his eyes was real. He was about five feet tall and looked to be about the same distance around, his big protruding belly resting on the table like a Christmas ham. His beady eyes stared at me over a pair of bent wire spectacles. A piece of discolored masking tape held the temple in place on one side, but not enough to keep the flimsy glasses from sitting lopsidedly on the bridge of his pointy nose. The bristly hairs in his ears and nose were visible even from my vantage point clear across the table, and those errant hairs,

41

those rogue whiskers, seemed to be the only healthy patches he had. His hairline had receded to the point where a thin coat of fuzz circled only the sides of his head. Meanwhile, the crown of his egg-shaped cranium was so bald and barren, it was a wonder I couldn't see straight through to his thoughts.

"I was dragged down here without so much as a word; no one's told me anything," I complained.

"Notion? Supposition, huh?" He laughed. "You can use all the big words you want, lil' lady," he said in a slow drawl. "They ain't gon' get you out of the trouble you're in. So why don't we stick to the small words…okay? Like whore. Thief. Liar. Surely you understand those words, right, Miss…uh? What you say your name was again?" he asked with a smile.

"You're the detective, you figure it out." The handcuffs were tight behind my chair, and my thighs were numb from sitting there so long—at least four hours by my estimation. There were no windows in the room, and the clock on the wall was stuck with both hands at twelve. It could've been midnight or noon—or neither. "You can't keep me here like this. Even whores have rights, fat ass." I mirrored his smug smile. "Now are you going to charge me with something, or am I free to go?" I asked calmly. Suddenly, the big little man pulled a thick manila folder from somewhere beneath the table and slammed it on the tabletop equidistant between him and me. The folder was overfilled and bursting with papers.

"Your licentiousness has finally caught up with you, lil' lady." Then he whispered, "How's that for a big word?" He laughed wildly, and his big belly shook like a pile of gelatin. "You know what this is?" he asked, pointing at the fat folder. The smug smile that had once graced his face was suddenly gone.

"Hmm…lemme guess…your lunch receipts? Oh, I know. These must be your cholesterol reports back in from the lab." I laughed. His eyes narrowed in on me as if he were looking down the barrel of a rifle.

"Make your jokes, dear. Make all the jokes you want. Just remember. I can always lose this weight. You can't unsuck those cocks, you shameless whore. You think if you just sit up straight and use a few big words, that'll undo the harm you've done? You think we're so stupid we'll believe this to be a simple case of mistaken identity and send you on your way?" With each turn of phrase his volume rose. "You think that just 'cause you can win a game of Scrabble with that fancy vocabulary of yours, that exonerates you from the crimes you've committed?"

"What crimes?!" I yelled back with a stamp of my foot. I was trying to unnerve the big little man, but he didn't even blink. Instead, he curved his lips again into a sly smile, the yellow teeth in his mouth flashing like caution lights on the interstate.

"I thought you'd never ask." He opened the manila folder and spread its contents across the large table, angling the pages toward me so I could read the typeface. "Your reign of terror ends today, Samantha Anna Marie Moore." And just like that, all sound ceased, and the world stopped spinning, like there'd been a rip in the space-time continuum. An invisible vacuum sucked all the oxygen from the room, rendering me breathless. And time stood still as if the clock up on the wall had been right all along! I had been using aliases for years, and occasionally, I'd gone by my first name only, but here, this man somehow

43

knew the full name I thought I'd left back in Mississippi. And there in front of me, beneath the dim lights of that interrogation room, were the blueprints of my secret life, all my crimes and indiscretions there in black and white. I had to force the pigment to return to my face.

"Reign of terror?" I repeated. "Isn't that what they call it when you drop in on the all-you-can-eat buffet?" I threw my head back in contemptuous laughter. "Listen, you heart attack in pants, I don't know what you think you have on me, but you're both mistaken and misguided."

"That's where you're wrong, Sam."

"Please don't call me Sam."

"I'm trying to be nice to you. But fine. Have it your way, Miss Moore." He leaned back and clasped his hands behind his head, revealing the sweat stains beneath his armpits. "Ya' see…we know all about your little racket. You see a gentleman…maybe in a bar…or on the street…usually some schmuck in a suit headed home from work to be with his family…or in town on business… You intercept him…offer him a smile…some polite conversation where you impress him with a bit of intellect and sexy talk…flashing your smile and displaying your cleavage like a peacock fanning her feathers…bending over to show off that pretty tail… The dumb fuck doesn't stand a chance…doesn't even know what hit him… Ya' get him alone…ya' do him….and then you roll him. Isn't that right? Now this poor unsuspecting schmuck pays you for a roll in the hay, and it's only after you've gone that he realizes you've stolen his wallet or his watch...his ring…even his car keys. Sound familiar to ya'?"

"First of all, shit-for-brains, it's the male peacock that fans his feathers, not the female. I bet you wouldn't

44

know a fact unless it was deep-fried and covered in cheese." I laughed. "I mean, really. Is there anything else in that pea brain of yours other than speculation and conjecture…and the Burger King value menu fully memorized?" I pursed my lips together like a clamshell and stared into his beady eyes.

"You want facts?" He said flippantly, laughing. "Here's a fact. You're a con artist! You know all these men are probably married…or have some standing in the community and would never report to the police that they'd gotten tangled up with common gutter trash like you. And so you prey upon their vulnerability and walk away scot-free like the she-devil you are…and it's on to the next victim. Am I right?" He flashed that dingy smile at me, and I knew his question was rhetorical. "I bet you even pat yourself on the back each night for a hard day's work. You're so pathologically screwed up you don't even see any wrong in what you've done. Right?! How's that for fact?"

"You're a joke. You know that? I mean, you ought to seriously consider taking this act on the road. Maybe a sideshow in the circus. I can see the headline now. World's shortest, fattest man…" I announced, "will amaze you with tall, spindly tales pulled right out of his ass!" I let out a boisterous laugh in mimic of a circus announcer and heard my voice echo through the cinderblock room.

"Enjoy it while you can, Miss Moore. The last laugh is always mine." And I did just that. I erupted in another wild cachinnation and heard my booming voice reverberate again through the room. On the inside, though, I was fighting off the urge to cry. The papers and pictures on the table stared up at me, and if they'd had legs and

45

arms to move, they would have surely stood up and pointed in my direction. Those crimes on the table were mine, and I knew it. Yes, I laughed outwardly, but inside, I feared that the fat detective would eat me alive. And judging by his appearance, I believed his appetite might've been voracious enough to do it. "You see," he continued, "you were picked out of that lineup today, my dear."

"That's bull. You said it yourself, fatso. Even if I *were* guilty of these alleged crimes—which I'm not—no man would risk his family and reputation to pursue these allegations."

"You're absolutely right. No man would. But how about a woman?" He brought his arms down and rested his elbows on the table. "It wasn't one of your johns behind the glass, my dear. We have a female independent eyewitness who saw the whole thing…a third party who has no vested interest in this case other than her interest in justice being served. She is willing to testify to having seen you lure an unsuspecting victim into the alley beneath her window last night. She then witnessed the two of you performing lewd and lascivious acts of a sexual nature, at which time she dialed the authorities. We've got the 9-1-1 recording where she describes you to a tee right down to the jacket you're still wearing and the shoes on your pretty little feet. She then witnessed the exchange of money from his hand to yours, and watched you pull his wallet from his rear right pants pocket while he hugged you goodbye. So, thanks to the testimony of this eyewitness, a trusted woman in the community with no ulterior motives and no horse in this race, we're now prepared to file charges against the *both* of you: you for solicitation and theft and him for disorderly conduct. Now listen closely, sweetie. This is where it gets interesting."

The short detective leaned in, and the garlic on his breath assaulted me like a nightstick to the face. "The johns you rolled all tell the same story." He laughed. "They never say outright that they were with a prostitute, of course. They're not idiots. But they did each come down to the station to report being robbed after their respective encounters with you. Nineteen incident reports here. See that?" He pushed one of the pages closer to me. "And this one? And this one? And this one?" He slid the papers forcibly across the table. "All of them describing the same perpetrator. A female. Your age. Your height. Your weight. Your build. Your hair color. Luring them into your web of deceit with that big fancy vocabulary of yours, that innocent smile, and all that youthful charm. With today's independent eyewitness detailing your M.O. and fingering you in that lineup, we thought it prudent to bring these nineteen gentlemen back in today to give *them* an opportunity to identify you as well. So, right after the lady plucked you out like a bad apple, I'm sure it wouldn't surprise you to know that you were subsequently IDed by all nineteen of your victims. Probably not the first time you got fingered by a bunch of men," he added with a guttural laugh from deep within, "but I'm sure this time it hurts."

The detective finished his hearty laugh and then leaned back again in his chair, interlocking his chunky fingers together on top of his bald head. "That, of course, was enough to obtain a warrant for search and seizure of your apartment and any property contained therein…hence us keeping you here all these many hours." He yawned. "And naturally, it was during that search that we found the john's wallet tucked under your mattress." He paused to watch me squirm. "So, like I said, Miss Moore, I always get the last laugh," he added with a chuckle, rising from the table. Then he placed his palms flat on the papers and leaned in until he was only inches from my face, his rotund belly sweeping the tabletop. "See, dear? You're not the only one in this room who knows how to grab somebody by the balls." Then the big little man drew back, turned, and exited the room, slamming the metal door behind him, my freedom close in tow.

Thanks to Ms. Jane and her network of secrets and favors, I was able to obtain a real attorney and not just some apathetic public defender. Nearly all of the counts against me were thrown out due to a preponderance of only circumstantial evidence and a lack of physical proof. But I couldn't escape the testimony of that eyewitness and the wallet they'd recovered. And so I was found guilty on the charges related to that last case and sentenced to eighteen months in a women's correctional facility in northern Georgia with eligibility for release in a year with good behavior.

Good behavior. What had so-called good behavior ever gotten me? When my stepfather swore me to secrecy about our illicit acts and I willfully obeyed him, wasn't that good behavior? Or no? When I'd done all my chores and maintained good grades in school, wasn't that good behavior? Mama only rewarded me with silence and loathing, so I wasn't sure. The line between good and bad had been blurry all my life, ever since I was a little girl in pigtails and rainbow tights. In my experience, a pretty face and a gentle nature—especially when combined—are only magnets for trouble. And good behavior is no match for trouble when it sets its sights on you. The only cure for trouble is more trouble, and sometimes, you have to fight fire with fire. Somehow, I managed to make parole, but staying out of trouble thereafter felt about as possible as riding a unicorn to the moon.

That's why I couldn't call the police like a normal person in my situation. I couldn't have simply alerted the authorities to Samson's death and let the wheels of justice turn in my favor. There was no favor for a convict like me, no justice, no mercy, no benefit of grace. Not even the truth could set me free. And as I pushed Samson's corpse off of me and the adrenaline coursed through my veins like electricity, I was reminded of the electric chair that surely awaited me if I were to be connected in any way to that rich man's death. All I could think about as I paced that hotel room was the concrete cell I'd paced for three hundred sixty-five long nights and the beady-eyed detective who'd put me there. I couldn't go back. I would rather die than go back, and in no uncertain terms, I knew I *would* die if ever I saw those prison walls again.

It's true that death is an inevitability that none among us can escape, but I wasn't ready to die just yet. So I fled that hotel room rather than stay and face the law. But as I drove through the rains that night, I still felt death looming around every corner, setting traps for me at every turn. And after seeing my apartment in shambles, I felt like death had already written my name in its great book and was busy making arrangements for my arrival: sending this storm my way to lure me far from shore, like a ship without an anchor, stuck adrift at the mercy of the wind. And it was only a matter of time before I would be lost forever to the ocean, pulled down under, dragged deep into the chasm of that quiet unknown.

Drip......drip......drip......drip. I sprang up like hot toast. There was darkness all around and silence everywhere except for the pitter patter of rain drops on the window sill. Drip......drip......drip. For a moment, I thought I was still in confinement, still trapped in that tiny concrete cell, just me and the mice. But the softness of Ms. Jane's couch wrapping itself all around me felt like a reassuring hug. Those soft cushions held me and told me that I was free and safe and that everything would be okay in the morning. As I nestled in for another round of sleeping, I chose to believe those sweet little lies.

CHAPTER 6: THE GOOD FIGHT!

"Mantha! Mantha!" It seemed no sooner had I fallen asleep that I felt Ms. Jane's big hand nudging my shoulder and rousing me again into consciousness. But I could tell from the light that peeked from under the heavy drapes that some hours had passed and morning was on the rise.

"What?! What's goin' on?!" I sat up and stretched my neck slowly from side to side. "What time is it?" The gentle giant hobbled over to the TV.

"I think they talkin' 'bout yo' bald-headed man on the news!" Ms. Jane exclaimed, pointing at the screen where a whitehaired reporter with stern eyes and a deep voice was squinting to read from an off-camera teleprompter. A bulletin flashed red just over his head, the words "Breaking News" displayed in large font.

"A police investigation is underway this morning," he explained, "following the gruesome discovery of a dead body at the popular Bell Sheraton Hotel and Resort in downtown Atlanta. No names have been released as of yet; however, inside sources tell us this may be a case of foul play. Stay tuned for more to come on this developing story," he concluded.

"They didn't show no picture of him," Ms. Jane added, turning down the volume on the old TV. "But ain't that the hotel where you was at last night?"

"Y-yes," I stuttered.

"Well, nobody saw you, did they?"

"No, I don't think so. He and I came in separately and obviously I left alone...but how can I be sure?"

51

"Well, you can't really. So long as you ain't leave no evidence behind, I guess you'll be okay."

"Well, other than the few thousand fingerprints I left all over the place…no, I didn't leave no evidence behind," I said sarcastically, burying my face between my palms.

"Mm, mm, mm. Girl, you in a worl' of trouble. I tole you that yo' way of livin' would catch up with you one day." Ms. Jane placed a hand on her hip and nodded her head in agreement, as if someone else had just spoken her words. With all her wisdom, I felt like Ms. Jane was foolish to think that I was oblivious to the consequences of my lifestyle, that I was unaware of the dangers of my surreptitious acquaintances. The choices and mistakes I'd made over the years haunted me constantly and threatened my sanity with each passing moment. But more persistently, I found myself haunted and threatened by Visa, MasterCard, and Mr. Tennison! The name of the game was money, honey, and I had to come up with it the best way, or rather the only way, I knew how. I sat back on the couch and crossed my arms over my bosom. Holding myself tightly, I remembered something terrible. I had left my bra in that hotel room, too! I sobbed silently to myself, feeling—in more ways than one—exposed.

"Ain't no use in cryin', chile. What chu gon' do?"

"What can I do?" I searched Ms. Jane's face for an answer. She sat down in her big chair, eyebrows furrowed in thought. After a few moments, she stirred and turned her face to me.

"Well, honey…if you didn't do it, then I s'pose you need to figure out what killed dat bald-headed man of yours. I mean, folks don't just up and die, chile…not young folks, anyways. What you know 'bout him?"

"Well, nothing, Ms. Jane. I told you I just met him; he was a stranger. A nobody."

"Well, girl, the night he died, you were with him at a public bar. Then y'all checked into a fancy hotel downtown. Seem to me like you better find out all you can about that *no*body before *some*body remembers you…and tells *every*body!" Ms. Jane turned back towards the television and pushed down on the wooden lever on the side of her recliner. And without a moment's hesitation, she was asleep. Her breaths began to whisper through the quiet room, her chest rising and falling in perfect, gentle rhythm.

I lay back on the couch, praying for the same peace to come and overtake me too. But no. Sleep never showed up to relieve me, and so my mind was working overtime. I pondered Ms. Jane's words over and over. She was right. I knew nothing at all of Samson—other than the obvious, of course, like that he was observably refined, certainly bred from sophisticated stock. Cufflinks and wingtips weren't exactly staples in the wardrobes of most men I knew—or most men period. No, Samson was far from common. Even his manner was unusual to me. He was curiously self-assured, oddly confident, all of which lent to the air of mystery that shrouded him. And the fact that a man could be mysterious to *me* of all people, I had to admit, was pleasantly surprising. I mean, you'd be hard-pressed to find someone with more experience with the opposite sex than me, chile. But in the short while that I'd spent with him, Samson had defied my expectations and challenged every notion I'd had about my own expertise.

53

I agreed with Ms. Jane that I had better find out more. But how? I didn't even know his last name or where he lived. And then, of course, I remembered: I had Samson's wallet! I darted up from the couch and found my purse hanging amidst the scarves and jackets on Ms. Jane's coat rack. I reached inside, sifting through papers and loose change, lipsticks and eyeliners. I had pulled out a pack of gum, a pair of stockings, a bottle of mouthwash, and my own change purse before I finally found what I was looking for. I sat back down on the couch and held it for a moment. It was heavy in my hands, and I suspected that his snakeskin masterpiece probably cost more than everything in my closet combined. I undid the gold clasp and spread the wallet open, all its tender secrets revealed in the dull morning light.

I went straight for the driver's license. Samson Brodice. 428 Aldine Road. Lithonia, GA. Just a few towns over. It was a twenty- or thirty-minute drive, depending on traffic and the weather, of course. I could still feel the hurricane approaching as the rain came down outside. The steady taps against the window sounded like fingertips clawing, scratching against the glass, Francine frantic to make her way inside.

"Hey, what chu doin' here?" said a tiny voice. I turned to find a set of big black eyes peeping at me from around the hall corner. Her hair stood on top of her head in a huge, unruly puff. She crossed the room and wrapped herself in Ms. Jane's chocolate arm. The sleeping giant remained undisturbed.

"I'm just visiting, sweetie. You hungry? Want me to fix you some cereal and then you can watch TV?" Kimmie was the youngest of Ms. Jane's granddaughters and, quite frankly, just about the only one I could stand. I motioned for the little one to come to me and I tried to smooth down her mane, but with each pass of my fingers, her tangled tendrils bounced back in rebellion.

"Cheerios," she whispered through a gummy smile.

"How old are you now, honey?" I asked, still trying to shape her massive tufts by sweeping them backward behind her dainty ears.

"This many." She held up four little fingers and lowered her head shyly. I stood and led her into the kitchen, her miniature hand in mine, where I found Cheerios and milk, eggs benedict to the four-year-old palate.

"Eat up, honey," I said before disappearing out of the kitchen and into the bathroom to get dressed. When I snuck out of the apartment that morning, Kimmie was sitting in front of the TV, eyes glued to cartoons. Ms. Jane and Kimmie's big sisters were still sleeping, lulled by the rainstorm and spiraling ever deeper into that dream-filled abyss.

|•|•|•|•|•|•|•|•|•|•|•|•|•|•|•|•|•|•|•|•|

A quick stop back at my apartment for a change of clothes, and I was on my way. This time, I wore blue jeans and a gray hooded sweatshirt. I stuffed my feet into a pair of tall rain boots and slipped an umbrella into my purse. I crammed a few things into a duffel bag too and threw it in the trunk. The time was 8am as I turned onto the highway, but the morning looked more like dusk. The sun was totally obscured by hundreds of charcoal-colored clouds.

They seemed to be moving faster than usual, as if the wind were chasing them across the sky. And down below, the wind was no less aggressive, bullying me around like a schoolyard thug. Those angry gales barreled between buildings and toppled trees, and at one point, Milsey and I were nearly lifted off the road. Traffic lights swung side to side like a therapist's pendulum, but the stubborn storm refused to relax. And even though their bright lights flashed green through the thickening fog, colorblind Francine was seeing red.

According to KZOP, one of the few stations my raggedy radio could pick up, Francine had ravaged the Caribbean during the night and crossed over into the Atlantic. The death toll in Cuba alone was well over thirty and climbing. She had been upgraded to a Category Three storm with winds approaching a hundred miles an hour. The weatherman seemed to be unsure if or when the storm would reach the mainland, Florida's southernmost tip, but talks of evacuations were already underway. Apparently, there was still a chance that Francine could make her way further east toward warmer waters and miss the U.S. altogether, but there was no way of knowing just yet.

Chile, you know these weather people don't know jack! Last week, they'd said that by now we'd be on day three of a heat wave. Then, somewhere over the weekend, they snuck in this here hurricane as if they'd never told us to head down to the shore today with our beach towels and chairs. Good thing I listen to the news every day, 'cause if I was to go to the beach now on last week's advice, chile, I'd be swept out to sea! I was sick of all those weather folks and their flimsy calculations. Besides, I had a few predictions of my own.

Atlanta was no coastal community. As a matter of fact, my fair city was over two hundred miles from the Atlantic. The mere fact that I could see and feel the effects of the storm this far inland so vividly and so clearly, gave me a sense of Francine's magnitude and momentum, her size and scale. I could tell deep in my gut that the storm had no intention of turning away. And the fine hairs that stood up on the back of my neck told me that she wasn't backing down. Francine had already killed, and now she was out for blood. I switched the radio off to drive in silence. I'd had enough of the rain talk and was more interested in my own forecast. What was to become of *me*? As I raced to the dead man's house, not even my best guess or wildest estimation could help me to imagine what might lie in store.

When I finally crossed over into Lithonia, I pulled over to the shoulder to fetch a map out of the glove compartment. Yes, I know it might've been faster to look up the address on my cellphone, but if you really must know, I hadn't paid that bill either! I unfolded the map and traced the lines with my fingertips until I found Aldine Road. Butterflies rose in my belly when I realized just how close I was. I pulled back onto the highway and followed the directions I had memorized. In just a few moments, I was turning onto Samson's street, and it was like wandering down memory lane. The view reminded me of back home in Mississippi: big country houses with long gravel driveways surrounded by endless land and trees. I hesitated to call it a neighborhood, since the next neighbor had to be at least a hundred feet up the road from the last. There were no streetlights or lampposts, no curbs or sidewalks, just long stretches of trampled grass on either side of the asphalt, where I imagined the school children marched to and from class.

"Ya' name Samantha, ain't it?" She ran up alongside me and matched my stride. I had heard her coming, so I wasn't surprised.

"Yeah, so?" I kept walking.

"Stop, lemme talk to you for a minute." She smiled.

"I don't know you." I wasn't lying.

"Oh, you don't know me?"

"Nope." I sped up. I could hear the snickers in the distance behind me.

"Oh, okay. Well you know Marcus, right?"

"Marcus who?" I asked coyly. I buried my hands deep into my pockets, so she wouldn't see them trembling.

"Damn, iss like dat? You do it to so many boys, you don't even remember they names, huh?" She grabbed me by the elbow, pulling me into the street.

"Oooooh!!" the crowd shouted in unison as they trailed behind. They leapt with excitement, boys and girls alike, eager with anticipation.

"Git off of me!" I warned, wildly shaking myself loose from her sturdy grip. "I don't know you, and I don't know no Marcus neither!" I shouted, stepping back onto the footpath and out of the road. A tall, bird-chested boy in a dirty T-shirt emerged from the crowd and yanked my book bag from off my shoulders. The crowd laughed at the act.

"I know you did it to my boyfriend behind the gym, so don't lie!" the big girl accused. Her fists were balled up at her sides, and I saw hatred in her eyes.

"I don't know what chu talkin' 'bout," I retorted with a snap of my neck, "but anybody who would go with somebody like *you* ain't good enough for somebody like me!"

"Ooooooh!" the crowd roared all at once before bursting into laughter. The big girl's eyes grew twice as wide, and her chest swelled with air as though she were a balloon about to burst. Again, I stuffed my hands deep into my pockets. The crowd surrounded us, blocking my path on all sides. "Git her, Cleo!" someone yelled. "Oh, I know you ain't gon' let her talk to you like dat!" shouted another. And with that, she made her move, charging me like a linebacker.

I stood there, frozen in her path, petrified with fear. But just as she stepped within arm's reach, I pulled my hands from my pockets and hurled my fists in her direction. The first one connected with her chin, and the crowd hollered. She stumbled beneath the sting of my blow, and as soon as I saw her falter, I swung my fists again in wild fury, beating her face and neck like a drum. She fell to the ground, and I pounced, a wild animal caged within the swarming crowd. I turned her onto her back and pummeled her without mercy until someone yanked me away. The crowd disbursed in no time, disappointed at the victor. They helped the big girl up, and she cursed me as she limped away amongst her friends, a parade of cowards and spectators. When I finally unclenched my fists, the two stones that I had pulled from my pockets fell to the earth, bloodstained and wet with sweat.

I've been fighting dirty all my life. It's been me against the world for as long as I can remember. The only child of a poor working mother, I was left alone most evenings and early mornings while Mama cleaned office buildings. Each week, she was paid just enough to sustain us until the next week, and by the time I hit the seventh grade, I was already working a job of my own, bagging groceries to help out. I never saw a penny of my paycheck, but Mama never let me go hungry, so I suppose survival was my pay. Growing up, the only thing withheld from me more than money was time. But I understood. I mean, how could she give that which she did not have?

I could identify with how Mama must've felt when she met that man and married him so quickly. He had money and seemed stable, a successful salesman and inventor. He was a dreamer hell-bent on being wealthy one day, striking it rich with one of his big ideas. When he came into the picture with all his hope and all the talk of the future and its endless possibilities, he offered Mama's simple life new meaning. He gave her a new reason to endure, to fight, to strive, a new will to live other than the nagging obligation of having my big mouth to feed. I completely understood his appeal. I understood, because the relief Mama felt when she met my stepfather was the same relief I, too, would feel when I met Marcus Dixon a few years later.

A smooth-talking, tall, skinny boy with curly hair and caramel skin, he was two years my senior—although in the same grade. He played basketball for Piedmont Junior High School. I was a cheerleader for Marymount and met him one fall afternoon when our two teams played. The second I saw him, I was interested. And I suppose the feeling was mutual with the way he smiled at me from the free-throw line, flashing his braces and flaunting his jump shot. Between that silver smile and those acrobatic alleyoops, it's hard to say what caught my eye first. I was immediately impressed and made sure to throw a little extra sass into my cheers that day, already utilizing those feminine wiles that puberty had just brought me only a couple years before.

It began innocently enough. He would come all the way over to Marymount and meet me after school. Even though the autumn frost had chilled the air, we'd stop each day for lemon ices on the way home. I could get anything I wanted, actually, a hot dog, a soda, chips. He always seemed to have the money, which, I'll admit, was attractive, alluring even. I would let him carry my book bag and hold my hand. And after a few weeks, I even allowed him to kiss me in front of my doorstep, and we'd stand outside hugging for hours beneath the afternoon sky.

He was sweet and charming. But in all our courting, the slow strolls to and from school, the crumpled love notes that passed between hands, the flirtatious phone calls behind my mother's back, he never mentioned a girlfriend. Never once did he speak of the tall, husky girl who wore his initials in her earrings, the faithful girl who stood waiting for him by his locker when classes let out. The girl so love-struck, she dared to seek out and fight a stranger for his affection. Cleopatra Jones, a cruel name for an ugly girl. Crueler still, though, was the boy who held her heart within his hands and bounced it around like the basketball he'd mastered.

Yes, he had been sweet and charming. I now know those to be the first two ingredients in the making of a liar. I mean, there I was, thinking that Marcus walked me home the long way because he wanted to spend more time with me, when, more likely, it was because he didn't want to be seen holding hands with me on the main roads. And I later learned that Cleo was the daughter of a local dentist and suddenly understood where Marcus got all that money from for snacks and afterschool treats.

I tell you, standing there on the roadside that day, watching the crowd disappear back over the horizon and wiping the dust from my book bag and clothes, I wished I could dust off those saccharin kisses that he'd given me. I wished I could wipe away the feel of his fingertips across my body. Yes, I did it. I surprised him the day before and did it to him there in the shadows behind the Piedmont Gymnasium. I had made up my mind that morning that I would give myself to him that day. Marcus had been nice to me and had given me time and attention. In return, I was ready to give him all I had: me. I hadn't yet learned to place any worth or importance in myself, and so, in my mind, the exchange was fair.

The secret between Mama's husband and I had already come out, and he had already moved out. Mama could barely look at me, and when she did, I saw nothing but loathing and disgust reflected in her eyes. I was only in junior high school and already a motherless child and a childless mother. I'd been snubbed and shunned by everybody at school, teachers and kids alike, and I found myself friendless too. Deprived of all affection, I dove into Marcus's arms, and I appreciated him for harboring me there, for being a refuge from Mama's rage and a distraction from all the hurt. I appreciated him because, where others saw nothing, he saw something. He saw me. He heard me. He understood me. And during those stolen moments we spent together, I was alive, no longer just a whispered rumor, no longer invisible like a forgotten ghost. I was real. I was here, live and in the flesh.

Our lovemaking, though rushed and hushed, was fun and exciting. He said he'd done it before, but his clumsy kisses and awkward gropes proved otherwise. He ejaculated on my thigh in under six minutes and blushed with embarrassment, but I kissed his rosy cheek, and we laughed before doing it again. Our playful experimentation was gratifying at the time, but looking back, I should've known better. Following the experience with my stepfather, I could've written the book on heartbreak. And yet, I was still too stupid to read it. Like a fool, I chose to love again, just as bold as I was blind.

After I'd given all I had to Mama's husband and Cleo's boyfriend, I felt ashamed and embarrassed, stupid and naïve, unloved and unwanted. And now, almost fifteen years later, as I pulled my old car up in front of a dead man's house, I was sad to realize that neither my feelings nor my reality had yet changed in all these years. I was just a grown-up little girl, still walking the streets alone, fending for myself and defending myself, still poor, easily enticed by the lure of fast money, still sweeping up the pieces of a shattered heart and forever fighting dirty. Just me. Against the world.

CHAPTER 7: DICE!

"This can't be right," I said aloud as Milsey's engine idled in front of number 428. I leaned over the passenger seat to squint at the numbers on the tattered mailbox. 4-2-8, they read clearly in irrefutable confirmation. The gravel driveway was balding in some areas, exposing the dirt and grass underneath. And at the end of the driveway stood a one-story house, built from wood and painted white. The home looked more like gray, though, years of dust, dirt, wind, and rain slowly tinting its lackluster finish. The shades were drawn all along the perimeter, so from the roadside, I couldn't tell much. I turned in slowly and parked on the lip of the driveway, just barely off the street.

I pulled the keys from the ignition, and like always, the engine ticked loudly, like a big rusty clock. I was hoping to be discreet, but ole Milsey seemed insistent upon announcing my arrival. I stepped out onto the gravel and into the rain. The driveway sank beneath my feet, and mud rose to coat my pink boots in a murky brown sauce. While looking down at my feet, I noticed a set of faint tire tracks leading up and around to the side of the house. At the end of the tracks, a brown station wagon was parked. The rear windshield was cracked but still intact and covered in plastic to keep the rain at bay, I supposed. I followed the tracks uphill but left the trail to stand directly in front of the house.

A couple of old rusty oil drums decorated the front of the home where bushes should have been. And a matrix of pipes was exposed through a crack in the cement foundation. I stepped toward the porch. The steps were just wooden slats that stretched from one rickety post to another, but where there should have been six steps, there were only four. I took the stairs two at a time to keep from falling through to the dark, wet depths below. A bunch of children's toys littered the porch, among them a battered rocking horse, a water pistol shaped like a .45, and a plastic yellow tub filled with miniature cars and trucks—most of them rusted over, not unlike the wagon in the driveway.

I was just eying the lopsided screen door that was hinged only at its base when, without warning or provocation, the inside door swung open from within. I hadn't yet rehearsed what I would say, since I had almost assessed the house as being abandoned and hadn't yet planned to knock.

"Can I help you?" asked the woman of about my same age, height, and stature. She held a little brown baby on her hip, and I gathered immediately from his long lashes and deep-set eyes that he was Samson's son. He spied me curiously, and I confirmed his paternity from that trenchant gaze. The woman's hair was jet black, not at all flattering against her pale, peaky skin. She wiped it from her eyes before asking again, "Can I help you?"

"Uh...yes. I'm looking for Samson Bro-diss?" I stuttered. I couldn't think of anything else.

"Pssh." She rolled her eyes. "Honey, you and me both! And he better hope *you* find him before *I* do!" The baby began to cry under the sound of his mother's harsh tone. "Hush dat noise!" she scolded before turning her attention back to me. She looked me up and down from head to toe, as if she'd just seen me for the first time. "And who are you?"

65

Who was I? A good question. I hadn't yet thought through what lie I would tell. I certainly couldn't tell the truth. No woman wants to hear that her man is unfaithful, and she damn sure don't wanna hear it from the heifer that's sleeping with him!

"My name is Alice. Alice Johnston. I'm with Dugan Financial. It's regarding the money that Mr. Brodice and I spoke about? You must be Mrs. Brodice?" I extended a hand even though the screen door was closed between us.

"It's Bro-dice," she corrected. "As in roll the dice?" She opened the screen door slightly, just enough to shake my hand.

"Oh, indeed. My apologies, Mrs. Bro-*dice*." I placed special emphasis on the second syllable. "So sorry for the gross mispronunciation," I said with a smile in my most polished voice.

"If you and my husband spoke over the phone, then how come you don't already know how it's pronounced?" She was sharp!

"Well, I suppose he never corrected me." I laughed nervously. "And, then again, maybe he did. I must admit I handle so many clients and cases, I sometimes forget." I shrugged my shoulders and smiled anxiously. The dead man's wife probed my face for some sign of sincerity, scarcely trusting my explanation. "And while I'm apologizing, let me ask you to please excuse my appearance this morning. This is just an informal visit, and with it raining the way it is"—I pointed over my shoulder— "I decided to leave my suit on the hanger!" I smiled. Her silence made my stomach tense.

"Sure, well, come in," she said hesitantly, pushing open the flimsy door to make way for my entrance. "Leave your boots on the porch."

The interior of the home was pretty much as I expected. Dusty shades and dark curtains, no two alike, covered each window, creating a dim light throughout the house. A few vases and knickknacks were placed here and there, but all in all, the living room was nearly barren, just a brown and orange floral sofa and two mismatching chairs. A wooden coffee table stood—or rather leaned—in front of the couch on just three good legs. The tan wall-to-wall carpet barely masked the rickety wooden floorboards underneath; I could feel the unevenness with each shaky step. And the creaking of that floor was loud enough to make me wonder if the house weren't alive, screaming to be condemned and put out of its misery.

I'd removed my boots at the widow's request, presumably to keep from dirtying the floor, but now, as my socks swept up dirt, grit, and grime, I wondered if perhaps I'd been invited in to clean it! The dining room wasn't much better than the living room. It consisted of one long, rectangular fold-up table surrounded by metal folding chairs such as might be seen in a school auditorium. Even though we were indoors now, the rain seemed strangely audible. That's when I noticed that in one corner of the living room, a large black cooking pot sat on the floor collecting the water that seeped through the decaying roof. The pot was already half-full, each raindrop landing in a splash and sending a wild ripple to the cast-iron edge. Suddenly, I realized that the random vases and flowerpots placed all about the room were not for mere decoration.

Their purpose was not fashion, but function, each one nearly filled to its brim with Francine's tears.

"Have a seat," she said. I chose a chair and sat down, and she sat down on the couch across from me, the miniature Samson perched on her knee. He wore a set of powder-blue pajamas, and so did his mother. And they were about the only two things in the entire space that matched.

"Can I get you something to drink? Coffee maybe?" she asked.

"No, no, nothing for me, thanks." I folded my hands in my lap to keep from fidgeting.

"So talk to me about this money," she said, wasting no time.

"Money?" I repeated, as if I hadn't understood the first time.

"Yes, you said you were here to discuss money matters with my husband?" she reminded me.

"Well, uh, yes," I stammered. "It's all a bit complicated, but to simplify things as best I can, essentially, your husband, along with several others, has been named as joint heir and beneficiary to a significant sum of money." I had known quite a few lawyers and insurance types, and I surprised myself at how much of their lingo I'd picked up over the years. "To put it plainly, Mrs. Brodice, someone died and left your husband an inheritance."

"How much?" She rose in her chair. Even though I sat there telling one lie after another, I admit I found it rather appalling and quite telling that Mrs. Brodice's first question was "How much?" and not "Who died?"

"Well, the deceased's assets are still being evaluated, so the official, final amount hasn't yet been confirmed. And even so, at Dugan Financial, we take our fiduciary duties quite seriously, and discretion is of paramount importance. Surely you understand. I really must speak with your husband directly. When are you expecting Mr. Brodice's return?" It was a terrible question to ask, considering what I knew. The minute I said the words, my stomach sank. But they had already been spoken and could not be taken back.

"Well, never," she answered, "considering the fact that he don't live here." A look of confusion must have taken over my face, because, without me having to ask, she began to explain. "He may have given you this address, but he ain't lived here in almost six months. We're separated."

"Oh, I see," I said with concern. "Sorry to hear that, Mrs. Brodice."

"I don't know why. I'm not! And you can call me Jackie," she said, wiping crumbs from the baby's mouth with her thumb. "It is what it is. He would rather chase after a pair of dice than get a steady job with benefits and keep food on the table, so it's better this way."

"Pair of dice?" I repeated.

"My husband has a gambling habit, honey. A bad one! And it's gettin' worse by the day! That's why if you got any money matters to discuss, I'm the one you need to be speakin' to."

"What's going on?" I leaned in closer. "If you don't mind me asking, of course."

"I don't mind, but to be honest," she said with a sigh, "I don't know what's goin' on with him. He just…changed."

"Well, gambling can be a serious addiction, a sickness, really. I imagine things must have been very difficult for you." I nodded my head in sympathy.

"Honey, you have no idea. I'm telling you…unless you've been through it yourself, you have no earthly idea."

The steaming oven. It was Mama's husband's own invention: a portable electric stove whose only practical use was steaming vegetables. He bought a patent and paid to have a hundred units built immediately. Each contraption weighed a whopping sixty-five pounds, and that was *before* you poured in the water. And energy? Chile, that thing consumed more power than a plutonium rocket bound for outer space!

It was an awful idea, really, and an even worse investment. But Mama believed in him, and she had plenty of cause. Within the span of just a year, we had moved to a new neighborhood into a larger home and Mama was driving to work instead of riding the bus. As far as she could see, he was taking good care of us. And so, when he came up from the basement that night, wiping the oil from his hands, wearing that grin, and declaring that he'd invented a device that people would stand in line to buy, Mama believed.

Next thing you know, the postman started bringing us final notices in the mail and the collections calls started waking us up in the morning before our alarm clocks. She confronted him about it, and he told her to trust him, that this was a new investment that was bound to pay off soon. She believed him. When they cut off the lights the first

70

time and she had to pawn her jewelry to have them
restored, when the faucet ran cold and she stood in front of
the stove boiling pots full of water so she and I could bathe,
even when the dealership took back her car and she found
herself dusting off that laminated bus pass, still she
believed. Right until the very end, when she came home to
that notice of eviction posted on our front door for all the
neighbors to see, she was humiliated, but she looked into
his eyes, and he promised to take care of it. He begged her
to believe, and she did.

Meanwhile, he was racing through the savings with
Olympic speed, and the checks began to bounce like they
were printed on rubber. Money was disappearing faster
than they could make it and the stack of unpaid notices on
the kitchen table proved that the money definitely wasn't
going toward the bills. And so Mama started searching
through his things for some evidence of what was
happening to him, some clue as to what was happening to
their hard-earned savings. In his jacket pockets, she began
to find the stubs to the high-stakes poker tournaments
aboard those fancy riverboat casinos. She started to come
across the racetrack tickets and the football score sheets
where he'd circled his picks. Once she started looking, she
started finding. She even came across a box of lottery
tickets and scratch-offs stuffed under his side of the bed,
packed tight and over-flowing, tiny paper symbols of his
growing desperation. He wanted to recover the money he'd
lost from his bad investment, and he wanted to get it back
by any means, taking greater risks despite even the most
unlikely of odds.

I believe, somewhere inside herself, Mama must
have known that he was out of control, but when he held

her in his arms and looked into her eyes and told her everything would be okay, she needed something to believe in. Really, they were both gamblers. They were both sick. He was *her* addiction, her compulsion, her obsession. The chips were down, the ante had been raised, and yet Mama refused to fold. Led by love, she went all in. And in short order, we were all put out. I'll never forget the day we were escorted off the premises by the sheriff. And afterwards, the Red Cross put us up in a motel for three weeks until, finally, circumstances forced us back into public housing. I never blamed Mama though. I harbored the same deep need to believe in something, in someone. So how could I judge her? I understood then, and still I understand.

"Yes, I understand, Jackie," I said, leaning forward with concern. "Trust me. I know the pain of gambling addiction more than I care to admit."

"You have kids?" And there it was. Probably my least favorite question to be asked. I swallowed hard before lying.

"No, ma'am, I don't."

"Nine hours of labor," she began. "You hear me? Nine...hours...of labor. Now, I don't even wanna do nothin' that feels *good* for nine hours!" she declared indignantly. "And that was just the beginning. Then came all those months of cryin' and screaming and hollering— and girl that was just me! I ain't even talkin' 'bout the baby yet!" she laughed, pointing at the miniature man on her lap. "One day when you have your very own kid, you'll see," she nodded her head. I cringed. "Yo' baby will cry and scream and holler and poop and pee and spit up...but it's yours. It's yo' baby and you love it. In your children, you see something…something…I don't even know how to say it. I'm not sure it can be said. Tryin' to describe it is like tryna' tell somebody wit' no tongue what chocolate taste like…like tryna' explain to somebody who ain't nevah been outdoors, what the breeze feels like when it blows against your skin. Human words just won't do. There ain't enough of 'em! Some things in life just got to be felt…experienced firsthand. All I can say is…there's a joy that takes over you. And all the pain you go through in having children and all the aggravation that follows, somehow it's all worthwhile when you see that baby smile for the first time…"

She stood the baby up on her lap and bounced him gently. "When you hold him heart to heart and look into those eyes"—she brought the baby in for a hug— "when you touch that baby skin and smell that baby smell…" The baby cooed as if he understood what she was saying. "Afta' while, girl, even the cryin' sound like music to ya'. Make me wish I had ten more just like him." She looked into the baby's eyes again as they rubbed noses. "Plus, they fun to make!" She winked at me.

"I loved Samson, I did…and I still do…but girl, one morning, I woke up, and the cupboards were bare, the diapers were out, and the baby's formula was down to just a few sprinkles left in the can. I woke up that morning, and honey, I woke up! There's nothin' like hearing the sound of your own baby crying, and you can't feed him or change him or comfort him. So, in the end, I had to make a choice. And I chose us." She cuddled the baby again. "I borrowed against my pension and bought this old house and that old wagon parked out front. They ain't much, but they enough! They mine, and I ain't ashamed." She scoured the room

73

with her gaze, and to my surprise, one lone tear spilled from her eye and traced her cheek. "I ain't ashamed of nothin', 'cause every old thing you see in here I worked hard for it, it's mine, I own it outright, and can't nobody take it away from me!"

She rubbed the baby's temples with her fingertips and rocked him gently, all the while staring into space. I could tell she was replaying the last few months of her life over in her head. And suddenly, she seemed regal and majestic sitting there, even despite her meager surroundings. Telling her story to me seemed to have encouraged her, all but transformed her. It was as though she realized for the first time just how far she'd come, just how strong she'd been. Though her words were originally intended to educate me on Samson, they had graduated to greater purpose. They had inspired her own soul and spoke of a power within that, until now, she hadn't realized was there.

Jackie may have been my same size and stature, but looking into the face of a woman who had taken her circumstances by the reins and created her own fate, I felt so small, so puny, so weak. I'd been playing with the cards that life had dealt to me, while Jackie had overturned the table and gotten up!

"So, is that when you left Samson? I guess when you bought this house?"

"Yep! Shole was! But you know how it is, girl. I wasn't here three weeks before he came a-knockin' and I let his sorry behind in. Still lovesick, still dumb and thinkin' I could still make the relationship work so long as I was careful not to lose myself in him again. So stupid!" she scoffed. "If you can't trust yo' man enough to let go

74

and lose yourself in love, then what's the point?! That's why they call it *falling* in love! Cause you s'posed to slip in it, and fall down in it, and roll around in it! You s'posed to get lost in it, to get tied up and tangled, to lose control. Any other way just ain't right." She smiled as she scooted back further on the couch. The baby nestled in for another hug, and she kissed his forehead gently, smoothing his fine hairs with her fingertips.

"I let Samson stay with us again 'cause I wanted us to be a family for the baby's sake. That's all I ever wanted. But girl, I got tired of takin' care of two babies when I only gave birth to one! Okay? So I put his ass out! Excuse my language," she said, covering the baby's ears. "I put his behind out. I hated to do it, but I know it was the right move. He was runnin' with some real shady folks. A few weeks ago even, two big men in dark suits came to the door looking for him, and I knew from the look in their eyes that if they found him, they'd kill him—or us! So I'm glad I showed him the door once and for all. But Samson know he s'posed to come by here at least once a week to spend time with his son. That was the deal. We ain't seen him since last month!"

"Wow. I'm certainly sorry to hear—"

"Like I said, it is what it is," she interrupted. "If he can't make time for us, we shole don't have no time for him!" she declared with a swivel of her neck. "And now you understand why you and I need to discuss this money. I ain't sittin' up here tellin' you all my business for nothin'! Whatever cash Samson got comin' to him, surely, as his wife, I can do something to put that money away somewhere so some good can come of it. Believe me, honey, if Samson gets hold of it, it's as good as gone."

75

"I see. Well, uh, I certainly understand your predicament, Mrs. Brodice—I mean Jackie. And trust me, I'd like to help. But please understand that I have to speak with Samson in person. Do you know where I might find him? His real address? His last known employer maybe? Uh…any places he might frequent regularly? Watering holes? Gambling spots? Any information you might have would be greatly appreciated."

"Sista, why should I help you? For what? You not helpin' me, and you damn sure ain't helpin' Samson! I mean, do you really think you helpin' a gambler by givin' him more money to gamble with?"

I took a breath. I wanted to say the right thing. After all, without Jackie's help I had nothing. "Jackie, we're talking about a substantial sum of money here, and I'm not unsympathetic towards your position. I want to see good things come of this money…good things for you….and this cutie-pie." I reached over and tickled the baby's bare toes. He kicked his legs wildly and laughed, the drool escaping his chubby cheeks. I turned back to Jackie. "We're going to work together on this, okay? But you've got to trust me. Show me where I can find Mr. Brodice so we can get this ball rolling and get you paid." I had come for information on Samson, and I was determined to get just that. The widow thought for a moment and then let out a long sigh.

"Well," she said, sighing again, "I can write out a list for you. Some names…addresses..."

"That would be great, Jackie. A great start. Do you also have a photo of Mr. Brodice that I can have? Just so I'll know him when I see him?" As it was, I couldn't shake

Samson's image from my thoughts, but of course, I had to play the part.

"Yeah, sure," she said, rising from the couch. "It ain't no use to me anymore."

"Oh, and—just as a formality for all the claimants—I also have to ask…does Mr. Brodice have any health issues or pre-existing medical conditions that you're aware of? Major…minor…anything at all. High blood pressure? High cholesterol? Is he a smoker?" I was praying for the widow to tell me about heart troubles or an all-cheeseburger diet or a longstanding history of stroke in Samson's family. If that were the case, I could've ended my investigation right then and blamed his untimely death on poor choices or bad genes.

"That depends. Does stupid count as a pre-existing medical condition?" she asked. I almost laughed out loud, but then her faced donned a serious look, and I realized she wasn't joking.

"Uh…I don't believe so…no," I replied.

"Then, nope. Healthy as an ox! Never even had so much as a cavity." *Dammit!* I thought to myself.

Jackie turned to leave the room but stopped abruptly. "Listen, Alice. I realize you're going out of your way to help us. All those other cases and clients you have, and look at you, making house calls—and in the middle of a rainstorm, no less. I want you to know I really do appreciate what you're doing for us." She kissed the baby's forehead again. "I just hope you don't get in no trouble."

"Trouble?" I swear my heart stopped. What did she know? "T-trouble for what?" I stammered.

77

Dara Dionne Welms

"You know…trouble with your company for all this attention you giving to us poor folks." She laughed before heading toward the back. Her words lingered in the air.

"In trouble with my company?" I repeated aloud. The company I kept had already gotten me into more trouble than she could imagine, and it was that same trouble that had led me to her doorstep in the first place.

CHAPTER 8: LIFE'S A BUTCH!

I had come that morning to get answers, but meeting Samson's wife had only left me with more questions. As I backed out of the driveway, Jackie waved goodbye from the porch—still a stranger and holding that all-too-familiar child. Knowing Samson as I had known him, seeing him as I had seen him, with his wingtip shoes, his tailored suit with the satin lapels, I was confused and troubled. How could he afford to wear the clothes he wore and drive the truck he drove while his wife and child sought refuge in a home hardly fit for living? And the dozens of crisp hundred-dollar bills that now lined the bottom of my purse? The gold ring I'd pilfered from his manicured finger? Where could he have gotten that kind of money? A big windfall perhaps? Was this inscrutable man living a double life as both prince and pauper? Driving through the gloom, I contemplated these mysteries intently as the widow's shack became just a tiny speck in my rearview mirror.

Straight ahead, though, the storm climbed over the horizon in my direction, spilling rain all over the roadway before me. Driving in a straight line was next to impossible, due in part to the slick conditions, yes, but also 'cause my tires were about as bald as a baby's behind! Milsey's hood took a vigorous beating, and water ricocheted off of it and up onto the windshield. I used my bare palms to wipe a porthole into the glass in front of me. Yes, chile, the fog was so bad even my window needed a window! Francine's blustery breaths whipped unyieldingly through the tall, wild grass that divided each property. Those breaths had even split trees into pieces, their sodden branches littering the roadside, their soggy leaves covering the asphalt in a slippery green skin. That wind seemed to be taunting me, calling me, howling my name. And I answered by stepping on the gas. A trail of dark exhaust burst forth from Milsey's tailpipe as I created an angry wind of my own.

I can still hear that name floating on the wind: "Thaddeus..." She called it so meekly. "Oh, Thaddeus..." she sang his name so sweetly, yet we dared not be fooled. I remember how all us kids would run and take cover, none wanting to be stopped and interrogated by Miss Miller for her young son's whereabouts. "Thaddeus..." she beckoned as we took our places in the bushes and up trees, none wanting to be the snitch and pay the price. For if anyone dared to so much as point the way, we knew a black eye from Thaddeus the next morning would be as inevitable as morning itself. Miss Miller was actually the only one I knew to call him Thaddeus. The rest of the neighborhood knew him as Butch, a name much more befitting a brute of his magnitude.

Butch wasn't just your typical neighborhood bully. No, sir, he was more like a bully mutant, like he'd been genetically engineered to terrorize. Just about a whole foot taller than all the other kids his age, he also had muscles where the rest of us were still covered in baby fat. He ran the fastest and the furthest. He jumped the highest and climbed the tallest trees. At the tender age of twelve, he was an impeccable athlete, precocious and advanced. And he used all that talent to torment the rest of us, to steal our quarters, eat our goodies, and chase us home. He was like an animal, in both prowess and temperament, a lion, the king of our jungle. And we were his insignificant subjects, playthings fit only for his amusement.

"Thaddeus…" Such a sweet summons it was, but Butch was much too clever a fish to take the bait. For in Miss Miller's thick, brown, leathery hands, she almost always carried a thick brown leather belt. It was too small in the waist to be hers. No, honey, this belt was used especially for whooping. And you could look at Miss Miller and tell she knew just how to use it. Her arms were big enough to be a pair of legs, and her legs…? Chile, from afar, you might've thought she was *Mister* Miller coming at you—if there was a Mister Miller to speak of.

Most days, Butch managed to steer clear, but on occasion, Miss Miller would happen to sneak up on him. On those days, we saw clearly the origin of his cruelty. She would ambush him, belt in hand, and beat him like a dusty rug. We never knew her reason, but she whirled that belt like a propeller, and each strike would paint him black and blue. Sometimes, the lashes would cut, and as he limped home behind her, his blood would stain the sidewalk—a gruesome roadmap leading all the way to their doorstep. It was a tiny, two-story house about a quarter-mile up the street from where Mama and I stayed.

Some evenings, somebody would shout, "Butch gettin' a beatin'!" and us kids would race our bikes up the block to see the show. If you stood across the street from Butch's house, you could hear Miss Miller yelling and cursing. And the boy's wild screams were tangible; you could feel them running up your back. If the Millers were on the first floor, you could see clearly in the curtains the shadowy silhouette of him running around the room trying to escape her. And if they were upstairs in one of the bedrooms, the bright light behind them would play the whole scene simultaneously on the lawn down below—their shadows twenty feet tall, reenacting the event, a twilight massacre for the neighborhood to behold.

As much as we feared Butch, and even loathed him, none of us laughed. Not a one of us smiled. Watching Miss Miller whale on him like that, we feared for him. We wept for him. We prayed for him. And one day, we rejoiced for him, because as soon as he got old enough to go the distance, Butch made his move. He disappeared far out of reach of his mother's summonses, long out of range of that brown leather belt. And in his wake, he left behind only two things: the name Thaddeus that his mother so loved to call and a crumpled letter that was delivered in the mail a few weeks after he vanished. It read simply,

I'm gone for good
and it feel good to be gone.
~Butch

I know about the note, because Miss Miller sat in my dining room—her favorite seat in *anybody's* house—and read it aloud to my mama. They worked together a few days a week cleaning office spaces and had become friends somewhere along the way. I eavesdropped from the kitchen and rolled my eyes as Miss Miller sobbed and Mama consoled. I wasn't a bully like Butch, but still, somehow, I identified with him, and I suppose it's no great mystery why. The story of Butch Miller appealed to any misfit kid who had stared up at the stars and longed for a new life somewhere far away. It seduced and beguiled any outcast who had closed his eyes and prayed to disappear.

Butch had become a legend to the rest of us, and his story was studied like scripture, told and retold on playgrounds and in schoolyards, whispered in the back rows of math classes and in lunch table huddles. We passed Butch's story around like candy, and like candy, we couldn't get enough of it. It was a new testament, offering fresh hope for new beginnings to those of us who needed just that. That's why a few years later, when I had finally had all I could take and decided to run away myself, I recalled the story of Butch Miller and felt empowered. I drew strength from his bravery as I packed my little bag. I remembered the pain he had endured at the hands of *his* miserable mother, and I channeled that energy, harnessed that power, to escape mine. And now, as I knocked on his apartment door that dismal morning, I prayed that ole Butch would lead the way and be my hero once again.

"Hoes makin' house calls now?" he said with a chuckle as he opened the door. He held the knob with one hand and a bowl of cereal with the other.

"Call me a hoe again, and you gon' need a doctor that makes house calls," I retorted as I pushed past him. He laughed heartily and raised his arms in surrender.

Butch lived on the far side of town in a section of Atlanta prone to crime and unrest—so much so that news vans full of eager reporters lay in wait, parked on side streets and alleyways like tourists on safari, praying for glimpses of lions and prey. Police officers in plain clothes circled the blocks in unmarked vehicles, scouring the streets, looking for trouble—even if that meant creating it. Black helicopters whirled low in the sky just above the rusty steeples of dilapidated churches and the crumbling rooftops of battered tenements. And telescopic lenses peeked and poked from third-story curtains surveying the land below, poised to capture all manner of dereliction and delinquency both day and night.

Southeast Atlanta was no paradise to begin with, but it had recently become an all-out warzone. Only two short weeks before, three police officers had been killed and a half dozen more injured in a shootout following a bank robbery. The bandits were still at large and undoubtedly being harbored somewhere nearby. Although most folks were hardworking, law-abiding, productive citizens, the entire southeast—Atlanta's largest and most populated ward—was under intense heightened surveillance. A full-fledged manhunt had been launched, and every resident was a suspect, irrespective of their guilt or innocence. Every man and woman had already been framed for these crimes by media, dubbed coconspirators by police, found guilty in the court of public opinion, and were now sentenced to a tortured version of house arrest: every soul stripped of their liberties, lumped together, and scrutinized like ants trapped in an ant farm, like fish gasping in a shallow bowl, men and women herded and locked down like zoo animals after closing time.

Earlier, as I drove through the city under siege on my way to Butch's place, my paranoia made me wonder if every distant siren and hovering chopper was coming for me and if every barking dog was part of a pack of thirsty bloodhounds that had picked up my scent and was hot on my trail. For once, I was thankful for Francine. It was only ten after ten in the morning, and her overcast was dark as dusk, allowing me to cross stealthily over enemy lines, undetected beneath the pretense of night.

"Hungry?" Butch asked, taking a bite of cereal.

84

"I couldn't eat even if I wanted to," I said as I meandered through his modest abode.

The décor inside Butch's apartment was meager, to say the least. There was just the one room in which we stood and a small bathroom off to the side. A stove, refrigerator, and countertop ran along the back wall to make up what I suppose was the kitchen. The kitchen and bathroom were the only distinguishable spaces architecturally, but the room was adorned with one lone piece of furniture off to the side: a rickety black futon that served as both couch and cot. The walls in the place were mostly bare, with the exception of the occasional crack in the cinderblock façade.

I had been to Butch's place many times, but since my last visit, a transformation had occurred. Stacks of big square record sleeves stood as tall as me all throughout the space. They had been arranged in long aisles, and while walking between them, I felt like I was shopping in a dimly lit thrift store or standing amongst troves of trinkets at a flea market. For every stack of sleeves, there was an equally tall pile of naked vinyl records, each one separated from the next by a thin sheet of parchment paper. And flush against the walls of the apartment were stacks of milk crates that had been turned on their sides and packed tight with everything from Dizzy to Duke, Oscar Peterson to Charlie Parker.

I pulled one record sleeve from its makeshift shelf and observed Thelonious Monk hunched at a piano, his eyes filled with wonderment as if even he was surprised by the magic escaping his fingertips. On another cover, Louie Armstrong's cheeks were inflated like two big balloons and sealed with a tight pucker, a passionate kiss through which he romanced a glistening gold trumpet. And while he wooed her, his fingers tickled her in secret places, causing her to moan and squeal and emote sounds that had never before been heard by human ears. His big shiny eyes bulged out like a cartoon animation, yet there was real love reflected in them, tangible, palpable evidence of a sizzling courtship between man and music.

Suddenly, I heard a scream and was startled momentarily until I realized it was coming from a vintage record player in the corner. A wild saxophone screeched out a few sad notes over a piano that seemed to be laughing, dancing, taunting, teasing. The sax soared to great heights and then let out another shriek as if it had suddenly been hit. Then it fell deep down to the bottom of the scale, where it sulked and brooded amongst the low notes plucked from an upright bass. A stiff snare struggled to beat a rhythm into the sax, but the horn wouldn't give in. And so the tune continued, the quartet cutting in and out of one another, sometimes fluttering like butterflies, alternating paths in playful syncopation. And sometimes, it was a dangerous game of chase, the volatile drum exploding in each measure, stalking that inexorable sax to cage it in rhythm, to lock it in time. It was a sweet and sour blend, a lively amalgam of joy and sorrow, pleasure and pain, a strange and disjointed melody, enchanting, haunting, untamed and alive, beautiful, ugly, harmonic, dissonant, breaking all the rules of form, no structure, no shape—just moods and memories, wrapped up in tears, sprinkled with laughter, and painted blue. I knew the song. It was my song, the soundtrack of my turbulent life.

"Let me borrow this one," I said, reaching for Billie Holiday and the gardenias pinned among her shimmering curls.

"Hell no." Butch snatched the sleeve from me quickly, yet carefully, displaying all the gentleness of a father saving his wandering toddler from the danger of the street. The love he had for those records was made abundantly clear in the way he nestled Billie in the crook of his arm and held her close to his chest.

Imagining Butch listening to jazz in solitude, being moved by chord progressions and key changes, was like imagining ice cream flowing from a volcano. The two notions just didn't blend. I was happy to call Butch my friend. After all, he was funny, charismatic, and dependable. But there was an undeveloped space in him, a primitive place lying just beneath the surface where he was still a boy pulling the wings off of dragonflies and chasing the girls with snakes. I'd known Butch when he was a wild child and a terror, and I'd come to know and accept the grown-up Butch too, the wild man, the troglodytic barbarian whom I had seen bash in the heads of men for no good reason and with no real remorse.

As I watched him holding Billie there in the lock of his muscled shoulders, for a moment, I was afraid. Seeing him express such concern over those records probably should have ingratiated him to me, but instead, it made me think of a sociopath, the kind that kills women and children under the cover of night and then hurries home to feed the cat. I stood there, as perplexed as I was petrified, staring at the phenomenon standing before me, the paradox wrapped in flesh. How could someone so cold show such care?

Such sensitivity? How could someone pick and choose when to be human and when to be beast?

"You know how much these things is worth?!" Butch scolded as he slid the record carefully back into its crate.

"Where all these records come from anyway? And that player? I ain't never known you to even listen to music, let alone collect it."

"A lot of things you don't know 'bout me. Have a seat," he said, pointing at no place in particular. Then he sat himself on the floor against a wall. His long, muscular legs stretched out in front of him. His cereal bowl sat in his lap, just barely covering the hole in his striped boxers. Butch was handsome, but his baby face was almost completely obscured by a thick and unruly beard. The bristly hairs climbed up his cheeks and all down his neck, giving him the appearance of a wolf man beneath a full moon. He wore a gray T-shirt and gray tube socks—at least, I hope they were gray. They could've just been dingy. I sat down on the wobbly futon across from the boyish beast. "You came all the way over here to ask me 'bout my musical tastes?" he asked with a smirk.

"I wish that was all I had to ask," I said while pulling Jackie's list from my purse. As I had requested, the widow had scribbled out the names of people and places for me to check out. "I need your help. I'm lookin' for somebody...well...not exactly." I took a deep breath and stumbled through the story of Samson and Jackie Brodice and my ransacked apartment and the news report that Ms. Jane and I had seen that morning about the discovery of the body. I omitted the part about the money in Samson's wallet and Samson's affluent appearance and brand-new car. I knew Butch fairly well, and the more I knew of him, the less I trusted him where money was concerned. As I sat there editing the truth for Butch, I felt like a little girl again, sitting before him on my bicycle, hair in pigtails, surrendering my quarters while hiding the dollar bills in my shoe. "So, long story short, I need you to come with me. You probably already know a bunch of these places, don't you?" I asked as I handed the list to Butch along with the photo of Samson that the widow had given me. "I would feel safer if I had some company…some protection… somebody with me I could trust."

"They probably ain't gon' raise too much fuss over this prettyboy," Butch said with a laugh. "I wouldn't worry 'bout it if I was you." He took another bite of his Cocoa Puffs.

"I can't take that chance, Butch. You know how these police is. Hell, just look outside! They don't care if they find the right one or uncover the real reasons. Long as they got somebody to blame for the crime, they'll be satisfied. I got plenty reasons to be scared. They fillin' up jails like airlines fill up seats on a plane…like hotels book rooms…or concert halls sell tickets. We ain't nothin' but coals fit for the fire. They don't take the time to distinguish one coal from the next. Long as they black, they'll burn." I struggled to hold in the tears. I didn't want to show weakness in front of a man like Butch. Some animals smell weakness like a pheromone on the wind. And suddenly their instincts overpower their training, and they can't help but go in for the kill.

"And it don't help matters if you ain't a hundred percent on the up and up to begin with," I continued. "You can lose yo' job today and steal a three-dollar steak from

89

the grocery store to feed yo' starvin' kids…and in they minds, you just as sick as one of them fools that robbed that bank. They don't make no distinctions. They don't factor in your circumstances as context for your crimes. They just stand us all together in a single-file line and pull the trigger—one razor-sharp bullet piercing us all in the same place at the same time."

I needed a cigarette. I don't know where the urge came from so unexpectedly and why it came on with such intensity, but suddenly I needed a cigarette, and I would have chosen it over water or air. "I need your help, Butch. Come with me. Help me clear my name," I pleaded. "You know more than anybody how far I've come and what all I left behind. I got too much to lose now."

"I ain't no bodyguard," Butch barked without emotion before tilting the cereal bowl to sip on the milk.

"I can pay you."

"When do we leave?" Butch smiled, and it was like an oyster yielding its pearl, like the ocean offering up treasure with the incoming tide.

For many hours after that, Butch and I studied the list and crafted our plan. At first, we struggled to decipher Jackie's crude penmanship, but before long, we were fluent in Jackie's chicken scratch and had ingested every word as if we had crafted each letter ourselves. We were like two war-torn generals, pacing the floors of a secret room, devising the perfect plan of attack. We brainstormed and debated—even argued—working tirelessly to calculate our next step together, to extract some sense from all the confusion that shrouded this curious case. And just like a top-secret unit of Special Forces, we planned to make our move after nightfall, to infiltrate Samson's world when it was up and running and in full swing.

One of the places on the list was a nightclub called The Wild Goose, and Butch suggested we hit this spot first, since he'd been there before and knew the way. As Butch laid out his strategy, my mind departed momentarily, and I had the sudden epiphany that I was a fool! I mean, there I was, seeking out people I'd never met and actively planning to visit places I'd never before been, all in search of clues about a strange and mysterious dead man that may or may not even help me. Butch droned on more and more about the swanky nightclub, and I—the fool—knowingly, purposefully, willfully agreed to jump headfirst into this journey, heedlessly embarking upon a fool's errand, a kamikaze pilot flying directly into harm's way, Icarus headed for the sun.

CHAPTER 9: FIRST SUMMER...AND THEN THE FALL...

When that final bell rang, and school let out for the last time, chile, it was like Thanksgiving, Christmas, and a hundred birthdays all mixed in together. We flung our book bags off one last time, and with them, we rid our minds of all the book reports, all the tedious science experiments, and all the impossible math problems. We shook ourselves loose like pups fresh out of the tub, every lesson learned already long forgotten by the time our heels hit the curbside.

To parents, the summer was a time of freedom. It was an opportunity to relinquish control, to rid themselves of the nagging responsibility of minding their kids twenty-four long hours a day. And so, parents began to act more like landlords during summer, evicting their kids each morning and leaving them to fend for themselves for the day. The dangers of today weren't yet making headlines back then, and parents could put their kids out and lock the doors behind them with peace of mind. And with that turn of the lock, they were free.

To us kids, the summer was also a time of freedom, but freedom of a different sort. Parents got to let go, and us kids got to grab hold, to take charge. Summer was a time of personal empowerment, each kid in full control over how to spend the long day ahead. And with the sun on our faces and the warm wind at our backs, we marched to the sweet symphony of the cicadas, exiles exploring, hopeful refugees forging new ground, unrestricted and free to roam as far as our imaginations could take us. And the day was like an empty canvas waiting to be filled with all kinds of colorful experiences, an artist's blank slate waiting for inspiration and poised to capture any excitement we dared to envision.

Some days, we were pirates who had drifted ashore in search of treasure, and as such, we scoured the neighborhood for gems and artifacts with no stone left unturned. Some days, we were astronauts probing a new planet in the name of science, excavating the creek for toads, salamanders, and any other extraterrestrial lifeforms hiding deep amongst the moss-covered rocks. And often times, we spent our days entertaining fantasies far more mundane, like when we'd pretend to be grown-ups working construction, building huts and treehouses from discarded scrap metal and slats of wood. Our structures were far too flimsy to be safely inhabited, but that didn't matter anyway, because as soon as they were erected, they were promptly forgotten. We moved on to other pastimes, like lying in homemade hammocks and conjuring shapes from the clouds that passed overhead.

By August, though, we were tapped out of ideas, especially as the summer's harshest heat threatened to roast us alive. On this one particular day in mid-August, the sun was so hot above us that I began to imagine God as just some great big inquisitive kid burning ants below with a magnifying glass. I was sitting on the steps with Chewy, this really quiet kid from way down the hill in the 487 apartment complex. We were melting in the sun like a couple of ice cubes, when, all of a sudden, Chewy says, "You know what we should do? We should go up to the park and play some baseball. It's nice and shady up there and we might catch us a breeze."

I decided that Chewy's idea was a good one, and we snuck inside his house to pilfer a couple of baseball gloves from his room and a couple of popsicles from the freezer. Then we headed on up the hill to the park. As we walked, we were joined by other kids from the neighborhood. Finally free from the prison of our porches, we all marched up the hill together. There was Carl from 572, Brandon and BJ from 600, and Marisol from 621. An even bigger tomboy than I, she had the best bat ever, a real heavyweight standard issue like they use in the major leagues!

We're all walking and talking and laughing along when suddenly…sirens. Lights. A squad car slams up the curb and blocks our path. Another one blocks the street. Traffic builds. Horns blow. "On the ground!" they yell, guns drawn. As I lie on the sizzling ground, being handcuffed with a knee in my back, I watch the ants attack my half-eaten popsicle. The popsicle reminded me of an animal carcass, left for dead in a pool of its own cherry-colored blood. And the ants were like scavengers that had picked up the scent of death on the wind and come running. As the cuffs tightened around my wrists and my bare knees scraped the ground, I felt the blood trickling down my legs, and I became cold inside and numb all over, yet another popsicle bleeding under siege. After being handcuffed, we were lifted from the ground and thrown screaming and kicking into paddy wagons while neighbors and spectators watched.

I was eight years old when this happened. Eight. But let me back up a minute. All us kids loved summer, yes, but my love affair with summer was something special. The other nine months of the year were quite different. Growing up, I probably had the most overprotective mother ever, and freedom was a concept I couldn't even fathom, let alone experience. I couldn't stay outside late and play like the other kids, because I had to come in when the streetlights came on. And it was kind of hard to play "Follow the Leader" with my friends when I was only allowed to ride my bike for a span of ten sidewalk squares, which, by the way, had been carefully chalked out—in red. I had to ask permission to cross the street until long after it was necessary. No, I wasn't a bad child, and yes, my grades were good. But still, every day, like clockwork, I had to withdraw from all the fun and games and go inside. I'd stomp angrily up the steps of my porch, with the warm afternoon sun on my back, listening to the rhythms of bouncing balls and jump ropes slapping against the broken cement. I'd stand at the top of the steps wondering, *What is Mama so scared of?*

The world I acknowledged as an eight-year-old consisted of kickball, tag, and blowing bubbles. It carefully excluded most boys, which I had decided were the carriers of the highly infectious, extremely contagious cootie virus. My world began at my porch and extended only as far as I could see. Mama, however, was conscious of a far more dangerous, vicious world. On that hot August afternoon, our two worlds collided, and I was catapulted into the ominous place Mama had tried so desperately to shield me from: a land where a group of young African-American and Latino boys and girls couldn't walk to the park to play a friendly game of baseball without being mistaken for a gang of bat-toting hoodlums. It was then that I was first introduced to the complex and pervasive notion of "perception" and made its lifelong acquaintance. It was then that I finally understood what Mama had been so scared of, and instantly, I was afraid of it, too.

A blaring siren raced down Butch's street, just beneath the window, and I rose from dreaming. For a moment, I didn't know where I was. There was darkness all around, and I couldn't tell where the dream ended and reality began. Was I still eight years old? Where was Mama now? As I sat there composing myself in the darkness, the sounds of the city poured through the window, and the screeching tires and sirens that sped by revealed quite clearly why my mind had dared to venture so far back into my childhood to unearth such a distant memory.

As I placed my bare feet on the floor to make my way to the bathroom, I contemplated the irony of Mama being so protective of me back then, the way she kept me in isolation, quarantined from the dangers of the outside world, only to open the front door herself a few years later and invite in a predator. For a moment, as I washed my face, I imagined the guilt, the confusion, the betrayal she must have felt when she exposed us both to the wolf who would in due time separate us from one another to devour us each. And as I turned the knob in Butch's shower, instead of pure water, the feelings and memories of my past poured out of the metal spigot overhead and covered me in a sadness that could not be washed away.

Standing there, soapy and naked, I recalled how I had been held so tightly by Mama's rules and mandates. I was like a newborn baby, snug and warm, swaddled and secure in the boundaries Mama had set. But after the wolf had come and gone, there were no more rules, no more curfews or household regulations to abide by, no more

96

careful restrictions set for my good. I was no longer her baby, and she just couldn't will herself to care anymore. And so I went from feeling swaddled and safe to being let go—dropped. I found myself in a dangerous nosedive, plummeting, free-falling, arms flailing with nothing and no one to latch on to, and no cushion in sight for my inevitable demise.

CHAPTER 10: WILD GOOSE CHASE!

Butch and I were headed to the car by 8pm. He wore a slim-fitting, camel-colored, single-breasted suit and a pair of chocolate leather boots that may have been calf skin they looked so soft. The boy beast had shed his flocculent beard to expose a face that had scarcely changed since we were kids. His countenance was perfectly symmetrical and clean-shaven, giving him a look of innocence and purity—even beauty. But a sleek fedora cocked slightly to one side covered his perfectly round head and cast a deep shadow over his left brow, giving him an air of mystery and sex.

His left wrist showcased a shiny gold watch covered in rows of tiny white diamonds. Butch had never worked a regular full-time job in his life, so I knew a watch that extravagant couldn't possibly have been obtained through honest means. And I tried not to imagine where or from whom it had been stolen. Besides, who was I to judge? I had never exceled and elevated through the ranks on a job or climbed the corporate ladder anywhere myself, and I winced at the thought of how many wives and children had gone without so that my services could be afforded. As I admired the fine fabric of his camel suit, I couldn't help but admit that Butch and I were cut from the same cloth.

I had packed a taupe-colored gown in my duffel. It had always been a head-turner for me, the way it looked nude against my skin. And I wore a cute pair of strappy sandals on my freshly painted feet. The rhinestones on my five-inch heels glinted under the moonlight and made me feel chic and refined—if only for a moment. A pair of drop earrings and a few bracelets completed the elegant look. The clear glass in my jewelry pretended to be diamonds, and I, too, pretended to be something I was not. Butch had decided my name for the night was to be Clara Wells, and I had just relocated to Atlanta from West Texas. I belonged to Atlanta's upper echelon, the newest member of the Black aristocracy. And Butch was my cousin Winston, also a recent transplant to the Atlanta area. Our faux family had made its money in textiles, and Winston and I were stepping out tonight to enjoy the spoils of our labor.

As we crossed the parking lot together, I added extra sophistication to my stride and elongated my neck as if balancing books atop my head. That night, Butch and I dissipated like dust in the wind, and Clara and Winston emerged from the darkness to take our places. And chile, if there was an elite fashion magazine holding auditions somewhere nearby, Clara and Winston would have been elected by the masses to grace the cover. They were secure and successful and happy, everything Butch and I had longed to be but could never quite seem to achieve. But when they arrived at Milsey's dented doors and beheld the chipped paint in her vapid exterior, the fantasy imploded. Butch and I were pretending to live out our dreams, but Milsey told the secret of our reality. Despite our dignified appearances, we were just two counterfeits, imposters in nice shoes.

"How the hell you expect us to blend in when we pull up in this hooptie?" Butch's gruff voice spilled from Winston's beautiful face and startled me momentarily.

"Well, unless you got a Rolls Royce parked up yo' behind, shut up and get yo' tail in the car!" I replied as I opened the driver's side door. "You gotta get in on this

99

side, though, and scoot over, 'cause the handle on that door is busted." Butch's right eye, the one unobscured by shadow, narrowed in on my face, and honey, if looks could kill, my funeral would've been on Wednesday at eleven!

"Wait here," the man-child commanded before turning and disappearing across the lot. I did as I was told, until the seconds turned to minutes and the minutes reached almost half an hour. At one point, a helicopter passed by overheard, and I crouched down beside Milsey as the chopper's searchlight scanned the parking lot. Somehow, she and I managed to remain concealed in darkness, but my jittery nerves were becoming harder and harder to hide. The thought of being caught with Samson's wallet on my person and being tossed back in jail terrified me deeply, especially considering that having possession of somebody else's wallet was the nail that had sealed my coffin and sent me to jail the last time. And so I pulled the dead man's wallet from my purse and locked it away in Milsey's glovebox among the random loose papers, bills, receipts, and fast food napkins that were already there. And, while I was at it, I removed my own wallet too. I had no idea what the night would bring, and I figured I could probably benefit from a bit of anonymity while I went undercover. Taking those wallets out of my purse was like lifting a two-ton weight from my mind. Instantly, I felt a tiny bit better, and that little bit of relief was just enough to keep me sane as I waited for the belated Butch. I was just arriving at the conclusion that I had been abandoned, when an engine revved suddenly from behind, and a pair of headlights blinded me as I turned around. The headlights went out, and as my vision returned, I made out Butch's image standing up through the sunroof of a midnight-blue Ferrari FF.

"Where the hell you get this car?!" I shouted. I heard my voice echo through the endless parking lot and felt uneasy and vulnerable all over again.

"Don't worry 'bout that. Let me swap the plates with yours, and we'll be on our way," Butch said as he emerged from the driver's seat, his face stretched from ear to ear by a gargantuan grin.

"Butch, I'm not playin'. I don't need to get in no mo' trouble than I'm already in. Where you get this car from? This is too much!"

"I got it from a luxury dealership over on Main. Don't worry, plenty cars over there. They ain't gon' miss just one," Butch said as he fumbled to remove Milsey's rear license plate with the Swiss army knife he'd pulled from his breast pocket.

"Butch, you sound like a damn fool!"

"Now, we both know I ain't no fool," he said as Milsey's plate finally gave way and came off in his big hands. "We'll return it before sunrise. Trust me." He stood and turned to walk over to the sports car. "Besides…they had a sign over there that said, 'Everything must go.' Hell, I was just followin' orders!" He laughed as he turned his back to me to kneel before the mighty Ferrari.

"I'll be back." I turned and walked away. There was no use arguing with Butch, I knew. And I also knew that I couldn't drive old Milsey into an upscale joint like The Wild Goose without being laughed at and turned away. But what could I do? Surely, there was a better alternative available to me than grand theft auto, right? I searched my subconscious for that voice of reason most folks claim to hear when faced with a predicament. Nothing. There I stood on the precipice of a major dilemma, deadlocked and confused, and as usual, my desperate introspection and deep contemplation was met with nothing but silence. I needed direction. I needed clarity. Quickly! And so, I dropped fifty cents into a nearby payphone and dialed seven numbers I knew well.

"Good evening," the voice answered, and that peaceful tone in my ear was like a healing tonic running its course through my body, calming all my nerves along the way.

"Ms. Jane, it's me. Mantha. I'm sorry to call so late. I hope I didn't wake the girls."

"Oh, that's alright, baby. You know I give those chi'ren a strong brew at night, and they sleep straight through to morning. Dead to the world." Ms. Jane chuckled. "I'm just glad to hear yo' voice. You ain't in jail, is you?"

"No, no, Ms. Jane. You heard anything more on the news? I ain't even had a chance to watch TV all day, and I can't bring myself to buy the paper," I said, fighting back the tears that threatened to escape my eyes and ruin my make-up.

"Yeah, chile. They ain't release no names yet, but they say they workin' on a lead. I shole hope it don't lead 'em to *you*! Where you at?" There was worry in Ms. Jane's voice, and I admit it felt good to know someone somewhere felt concern for me.

"Well, right now I'm wit' my friend Butch. You know Butch."

"Hmmf!" Ms. Jane scoffed. "I know that boy is trouble! That's what I know!" she proclaimed.

"Yeah, I know, Ms. Jane. But I found Samson's address—the dead man—and went to his house and met his wife and kid, and I told her I was an insurance agent, and she told me where I had to go to find Samson, 'cause you know she don't know he dead yet," I blurted all at once. "And anyway, so now I know where to go to find out more about Samson, but I need Butch's help with this part. And you're the one who told me I need to find out more about Samson, Ms. Jane."

"Yeah, yeah. I guess I did say that," Ms. Jane admitted. "Well, what y'all fixin' to do?"

"Please deposit twenty-five cents for the next three minutes," warned the automated voice. "If twenty-five cents is not deposited within fifteen seconds, your call will be disconnected." I reached into my clutch and dropped another quarter in the slot.

"Sorry, Ms. Jane…uh…yeah…we 'bout to go to a nightclub over near Madison City where Samson liked to go. Butch just stole a car so we can pass as rich folks over there."

"Lawd hammercy!" Ms. Jane exclaimed before sighing into the receiver. "Honey, I've told you this many times, and I'm tellin' you again. Maybe this time you'll hear me." Ms. Jane paused, perhaps to make sure she had my attention, but more likely for dramatic effect. "If you'll lie, you'll steal. And if you'll steal, you'll kill! You hear me? Now, you done already lied to this po' widow talkin' 'bout you an insurance agent and ain't even told the po' thang that her husband is dead. Now here you are stealin' cars? You know what's next!"

"I know, Ms. Jane," I conceded as I looked around the empty lot. The asphalt was damp, and there were puddles everywhere from where the water had collected over the course of the day's rains. I looked down at my red toenails and reconsidered the shoes I'd selected.

"You gettin' in deeper and deeper in this mess, and you know that Butch ain't no good. Hmmf!" she sneered again. "That innocent look on his stupid face don't do nothin' but remind me that even the devil used to be an angel…mm-hmm. I wouldn't trust him if I was you, chile! Shole wouldn't."

"I hear you, Ms. Jane, I do. But listen. I'm calling 'cause I need a favor from you."

"Sure, baby. What is it?"

"I need you to see what you can find out about a man by the name of Nathan Dobbs. He goes by the name Doughboy. Samson's wife gave me his name, and unless you can help me find something on him, he's a dead end. I'll call in the morning to see what you turned up."

"Okay, honey. I'll see what I can do. I'll shake the tree and see what falls out, but I need you to do me a favor too."

"Sure, Ms. Jane. Anything."

"Be careful!" she demanded sternly.

"I'll try, Ms. Jane. I'll try. Just…just say a prayer for me tonight, will you?"

"Ha haaaaaa!" Ms. Jane laughed. I held the receiver away from my ear and looked at it. I was angry. I mean, what could possibly be funny right now?

"Please deposit twenty-five cents for the next three minutes," warned the automated voice again. "If twenty-five cents is not deposited within fifteen seconds…" I searched my clutch for another quarter. After no more than a moment, I dropped my last coin in and held the receiver to my ear again.

"Hello? Hello? You still there?" I heard Ms. Jane ask.

"I'm here. Almost hung up on you for laughing like that, but I'm here."

"Aww...don't be sore baby. It's just that prayer don't work that way. You can't sit down to a plate of pork chops, fatback, potatoes, and gravy and think that if you just ask God to bless it, you won't end up in the ICU sooner or later." Ms. Jane chuckled again. "Chile, God don't unclog arteries. And He shole don't ride shotgun after you steal a car so you can pull up to a nightclub in style. Now, don't get me wrong. He been known to perform a miracle or two under extenuating circumstances, but you ain't exactly Moses leading the Israelites out of bondage, and yo' problems ain't the size of the Red Sea. I mean, I know I tole you before that God helps those who help themselves, but you musta' misunderstood. That don't mean you can help yo'self to somebody else's car just 'cause you think you need it! Now, if you really and truly want the good Lord to watch over you, make sure He don't look down and catch you lyin', cheatin', and stealin' when He do! Make up yo' mind to do right, chile, and from here on out, choose wisely!"

"Please deposit twenty-five cents..."

I held the receiver to my heart and mulled over Ms. Jane's words. I was out of quarters, out of ideas, and running out of time. I said goodbye, hung up the phone, and headed back toward the car. *Choose wisely*, the words echoed across my mind. *Choose wisely*.

The car had already been borrowed and my license plates were already on it so what difference did it make if we returned it now or later, as long as it was back in the lot by morning? And it's not like we have any other options, I rationalized to myself. And my argument sounded perfectly cogent at the time. As I approached the Ferrari, Winston revved the engine. I opened the passenger door, but it was Clara Wells who stepped in and sat down. Lightning flashed in the distance, and we sped out of the parking lot into the soggy night, two hardheaded, impetuous kids who'd forgotten to grow up, each of us still playing dress-up and make-believe, forever hiding…and seeking.

CHAPTER 11: JAZZ MEN IN BLOOM!

The Wild Goose rose from the darkness just up ahead. At least four stories high, the posh nightclub looked more like a palace. Spotlights on the plush green lawn pointed upward and illuminated the monstrous structure from below, showcasing the Goose in all its architectural splendor. Seeing it standing there so tall and regal amidst the surrounding farmlands and fields was like watching a king haggling for bread amongst peasants and commoners; His Highness was out of place and simply didn't belong.

The Ferrari crept toward the Goose like a panther on the prowl, crouching and crawling low on all fours. And its powerful engine purred like a cat as we inched up the long circular driveway toward the valets in red coats and white gloves. I rolled my window down as we approached and heard the excited chatter of friendly voices and the click-clacking of high heels and dress shoes: proud patrons making the long walk toward the entrance. The muted sound of big band jazz seeped from behind the nightclub's doors and out into the starlit night. As our tires rolled to a stop and the valet opened my passenger door, I felt like the Ferrari was some kind of miraculous time machine. Stepping out of it and hearing the buzz of the partygoers and the sounds of jazz on the wind, I felt like we were stepping out of a Studebaker in early twentieth-century Harlem, lining up to enter the Savoy.

Beautiful people, variegated in all shades of brown and dressed in gowns and suits of all kinds and colors, paraded up the long path before disappearing into those tall double doors. Winston and I were proud to take our places among them as we turned the keys over to the valet. The

night air was warm and eerily still as Francine loomed in
the distance. She was still hundreds of miles offshore, but
just as we stepped inside the building, thunder grumbled
overhead with such an intensity, I thought one of those
silver stars might just shake loose from the heavens and
come crashing down to Earth.

     Just inside the front entrance, we were patted down
gently for weapons by two large men in gray suits.
Standing there being frisked, I was glad I had convinced
Butch to leave his Swiss army knife in the car or else our
little adventure might have been over before it began. We
were then asked to sign a guestbook, and Winston paid our
admission from money I had given him. The maître d'
pointed the way, and we followed the crowd, the music,
and the tantalizing aroma of warm cakes and exotic
cuisines toward a narrow opening in a red velvet curtain up
ahead.

     While walking, we passed beneath several
translucent veils that hung from somewhere high above.
They were thin and lightweight and seemed almost alive as
they danced on the wind of the frequently opening door.
The veils were undoubtedly sewn from silk and were
multicolored with flecks of gold and glints of silver. There
was red wine and burnt sienna, canary yellow and deep-sea
blue, emerald green and royal purple, endless colors, the
next one bolder and richer than the last. And at the end of
the delicate rainbow, we finally passed between those red
velvet curtains. They were held open by two handsome
waiters in tuxedos holding serving trays filled with
champagne flutes. Winston and I each took away a glass as
the nightclub's glorious interior took away my breath.

The décor was modernist and fresh, but classic with strong hints of Moroccan influence. The coffered ceilings rose the entire height of the structure, just like the ceilings of an old church or cathedral, and they were held up by huge pillars wrapped in colorful tile mosaic: golds and burgundies and shades of green. The walls were tiled as well, but only partially. At about ten feet from the ground, the tile ended, and brilliant white paint climbed the wall the rest of the way. That white paint must have been mixed with glitter, because slivers of gold twinkled from the walls, reflecting light from the dozens of crystal chandeliers overhead. The sparkling paint gave the illusion of flash photography in the distance and made me feel famous and important standing there, like a movie starlet making a grand entrance at her own premiere.

Champagne in hand, Winston and I descended the small staircase that led onto what felt like an endless dancefloor. On the other side, against the far wall opposite the entrance, an enormous brass orchestra, comprised of at least twenty men all in black slacks and white jackets, swung their horns to Count Basie's "One O'clock Jump." The bandleader waved his baton with vigor and delight, glancing back every couple of measures to behold the frenzy of the dancing crowd. And what a crowd it was! They were a work of art, really, a live installation depicting the unbridled freedom of vernacular dance. The band would call out in song, and the dancefloor would respond with an effortless display of style and grace. Beautiful men and women shook their behinds and shimmied their shoulders to the captivating rhythms pounded from the percussionist's drum. The bassist finessed that bassline and walked his fingers all up and down the groove while the people shouted and clapped their hands in soulful syncopation. And when the horns came in all together, there was a wave of gladness that washed over the dancefloor, like when a preacher turns a phrase just right on Sunday morning and sends the church into a fit of praise.

Everywhere I looked, my eyes beheld elegant tableaus, poetic vignettes of beautiful brown bodies poised and posed in joyful expressions. I'd blink, and in the millisecond it took for me to reopen my eyes, the scene would be changed: heads angled differently, bodies repositioned and stretched in new directions, arms raised high, and feet stomping rhythms into the marble down below.

For a moment, again I was transported back in time, way back, long before my birth. I found myself wandering through gardens of nostalgia, drifting through labyrinths of déjà vu, entranced, engrossed, enchanted. Like a cobra hypnotized and seduced by the snake charmer's melody, I was locked in a beautiful delirium, lost in a rhapsody that only music could incite, a fantasia that only jazz can inspire.

Winston nudged me and pulled me back from the brink of aural bliss. He stepped off to the left and motioned for me to follow. I yanked myself from the music's grasp and somehow managed to navigate through the sea of dancing couples to follow Winston over to the dining area. Traveling from the busy marble dancefloor to the plush dark carpet of the dining area was like emerging from restless waters and stepping onto an oasis of dry land. The restaurant held about fifty round tables immaculately set with luxurious tablecloths, glistening flatware, towering centerpieces, and cloth napkins sculpted into delightful shapes. Each table was large enough to accommodate up to ten chairs. Winston found a table near the back with two empty seats, and we sat ourselves between two couples: a boisterous two on our left who were arguing quite vigorously in hushed tones and a spiritless pair on the right who appeared to be suffering from a mix of boredom and apathy—matrimony at its worst.

I took a sip from my glass, and as the champagne bubbles tickled my upper lip, seducing my senses with their sweet effervescence, I realized that it had been over thirty-six hours since my last real meal. A waitress standing nearby must have heard my stomach growl because, only seconds later, she approached the table and placed two menus before us. We perused the menus for a moment, and I elected to order the Fish Tagine, a spicy Moroccan stew with tomato, cilantro, potatoes, carrots, and peppers, served with couscous. Winston ordered a steak extra rare with mashed potatoes, steamed veggies, and a fried egg.

As he touted his order off to the pretty young waitress whose nametag read "Eve", I scanned the room. The band began playing a short and mysterious overture that artfully unfolded into the familiar jazz classic "All of Me." And the surrounding tables lit up with joy as the song introduced itself and stirred up fond recollections all around. Couples took to the dancefloor while fingers snapped and hands clapped. Glasses clinked in the near distance, and there was the constant murmur of conversation in the air, indistinct voices with happy tones, forks scraping against dinner plates, and the occasional burst of joyous laughter.

Sitting there amidst all the activity, suddenly I felt small and out of place. Even despite my makeup and my fancy getup, I felt like an outsider sitting there among those people, like I was standing in a herd of zebras and covered in spots. Those people were unashamed to laugh. They had reason to smile. They had already found their diamonds, and I was still looking for the rough. They were the real and true embodiment of all I was pretending to be. They were happy.

In the presence of such happiness, such confidence, such affluence, I felt like a brown rose petal in one of those fancy floral arrangements, like a soup stain on one of those linen tablecloths—an obvious flaw in the midst of perfection. The waitress named Eve, who wore a black satin cocktail dress embroidered in silk lace, took our menus and left the table. And with her went every last bit of self-confidence I had accrued. It hurt deep down to know that even while sitting there in my most expensive dress, I had been bested by a waitress in uniform!

And all at once, I felt vulnerable and embarrassed of the faux diamond earrings that hung from my earlobes and kissed my neck. I looked down at my hands and winced at the cheap polish I'd brushed over my spurned cuticles. Anxiety rose within, and I began to imagine the voices around me to be whispers behind my back, my name being spoken over lips and across tables. My heart raced from beat to beat as my mind jumped to conclusions. I was convinced that I'd been made, fingered, pointed out by everyone in the club as a charlatan in chiffon.

Winston must have seen the upset in my eyes and the sweat building on my brow, because he leaned in and whispered, "Try to keep it together." I suppose that was as close as he could come to offering encouragement. After all, Winston was a fabrication. I wondered how it was that

Butch seemed so cool and relaxed. How could he be so at home playing a character like Winston in a room full of real Winstons? He and I had come from the same humble beginnings, and yet here I was, about to unravel at the seams like the hemline of my cheap gown, and Butch seemed as comfortable as a pair of old pajamas.

"I wanna…go home," I yelled between gasps. We had been running for what felt like forever, but I knew that if I stopped to catch my breath, I myself would be caught.

"What?!" Butch called back over his shoulder.

"I said…I wanna go home!" I yelled again, wiping the hair from my face and a tear from my eye. Bullets rang out overhead and ricocheted off of the dumpsters that lined the alley on either side. I ducked as Butch grabbed my hand and pulled me hard to the left down an intersecting alleyway. This new corridor was narrower than the last, and although it hadn't rained in weeks, there were mysterious puddles all around. And from those puddles emanated the unmistakable stench of urine mixed with the rancid aroma of leachate, trash liquefied under the summer's relentless heat. I resisted the urge to vomit as Butch and I leapt over litter and garbage. The feral screeches of stray cats permeated the air and crawled up my back. Or maybe they weren't cats at all, but rats full as ticks from feasting on yesterday's discards and last week's trash.

Butch was a much better runner than me, but I surprised myself at my ability to keep up despite the cumbersome knapsack I carried beneath my arm. Suddenly, there was a loud pop. And then another and another, bullets shot recklessly into the night. Butch let go of my hand and ran ahead. "Wait!" I called at his back, but the athlete had already disappeared into the shadows ahead.

The footsteps of my pursuers echoed from wall to wall throughout the narrow passage and made it sound as though I were being chased from all sides. My heart was ready to burst from my chest, and I was contemplating giving up when suddenly I heard, "Psst!" I slowed to listen, crouching low beside a rusty barrel overflowing with cans and bottles. "Psst!" I heard again. I looked up and saw Butch standing in the shadows of a second story fire escape. The ladder was near me but at least a foot out of reach.

"I can't!" I whispered at Butch's silhouette. "I can't reach it!"

"You have to!" Butch insisted. I pulled the knapsack's leather strap over my head and slung the big bag across my body like a pocketbook. And as the sound of footsteps grew nearer, I leapt almost out of my shoes toward the hanging metal ladder. My fingertips grabbed the bottom rung, and I hoisted myself up with all my might. Butch reached down to help me the rest of the way, and as I joined him there in the shadows of that second story balcony, the gunmen on our tails ran by below: three fools afoot, chasing our ghosts and shooting at the benign shadows that stirred in darkness.

Butch took my hand again, and we climbed the fire escape from floor to floor, Butch peeping in windows at every landing. Somewhere around the fifth floor, Butch stopped and used his elbow to break the glass of a large window. "Wait here," he said as he climbed inside. I did as I was told. The lights were off inside, but I stood there trying to make shapes out of the darkness—anything to keep my mind off of my fear of heights as I stood out there on that shaky metal ledge.

After some minutes, Butch flipped a switch on inside and came back to the window to retrieve me. "Gimme the bag," he demanded, holding his arms out to receive the knapsack that I'd hoisted onto my back. I removed the bag and handed it to him, careful not to cut myself on the jagged shards of glass jutting from the busted window. Butch took the bag, set it down, and then reached for me. I stepped inside and nearly collapsed in his arms, exhausted from our marathon through the streets and the long climb that had brought me to that fifth-floor apartment. "Breathe. We safe now," Butch reassured.

I stepped back from Butch's embrace and observed my surroundings for the first time. We were in a bedroom. The bed was neatly made, and a pair of his and hers bathrobes lay across the foot. Amongst the lotions, perfumes, and deodorants on the dresser, there was an eight-by-ten picture of a handsome couple in their mid to late thirties. The husband was pushing his wife on a tire swing while a golden retriever panted in the foreground. All three of their mouths were agape with joy and laughter. "Come on," Butch commanded from the doorway.

I followed Butch out of the bedroom and down a short hall to a small living room. The living room was furnished quite nicely with a tan leather sofa and two matching recliners. A coffee table straddled the middle of the room, and there were neat piles of magazines, books, newspapers, and other periodicals on top of it.

"We should get out of here before they come home," I said as I stared at the dozen or so pictures that adorned the living room walls. In one photo, the couple

115

wore sunglasses at the beach. And in another photo, they were bundled tightly, holding ski poles in each hand. And there they were again; this time, she seemed to be accepting some type of award as he kissed her cheek with loving admiration. The wooden plaque was also mounted on the wall just beside its photo, and the inscription read, "Kimberly Carick - Teacher of the Year."

"We'll be alright. They pro'ly still at work or out to dinner somewhere," Butch said, turning on the TV before disappearing into the small dining area that was adjacent to the living room. That small space contained a marble-topped table surrounded by four leather-backed chairs and a tall hutch filled with china and wine glasses, no doubt heirlooms passed down through generations, symbolizing thousands of meals shared and stories told. The small dining room was adjoined to a kitchen that seemed oversized in comparison to the rest of the apartment. "When was the last time you ate?" Butch called from the kitchen.

"Couple days," I answered from the living room. As the TV warmed up, Vanna White revealed the letters of a giant puzzle while an old lady named "Diane" spun the wheel of fortune. And for a moment, I felt like an invited guest in the happy couple's home. Standing there amidst their photos, awards, knickknacks, and books, I imagined them coming home each day to sit together on that soft couch and call out letters to Pat Sajak. And after dinner, they'd settle into those recliners to eat cake or smoke a pipe, the golden-haired hound at their feet. I was a girl of just fourteen, a recent escapee from a bitter and broken home. And deep down inside, I longed for that kind of normalcy, so much so that it physically pained me to stand there a moment more.

I passed through the dining room, stepped into the large kitchen, and sat down. Half of the kitchen table was filled with plastic containers full of leftovers Butch had pulled from the fridge. Butch had dumped out the contents of the knapsack, and the other half of the table was covered in piles of money, mountains of crumpled dollar bills. Some of them were wet and sticking together, some were even torn. Traces of lipstick and glitter on the folds told the story of their origin, dollars stolen from a strip club's till.

Butch counted the loot while I tasted the teacher's meatloaf. After one bite, I deduced quickly that she would never win any awards in the culinary arts, but my empty stomach was thankful even if my taste buds weren't. As I sat across from Butch, I watched him mouth the numbers as he counted the money, and I thought back to how many times I'd seen him count in the very same way after he'd stolen from the neighborhood kids, myself included. I had just been reunited with Butch the night before after hitchhiking from western Mississippi. For months, I had held on to Butch's note. Butch's mother had shared the letter with my mother, and when she'd left our house that night I'd rescued it from the trash to study it myself. In my lowest moments living there in Mama's house, I went back to that letter again and again for comfort, for inspiration and encouragement. Even more intriguing to me than the message was the postmark: Tuscaloosa, Alabama.

I fantasized about Tuscaloosa. In my child mind, I romanticized and revered that city as a place where oddballs and misfits, rebels and loners, could go to escape

their troubles and find community. Tuscaloosa was my
Atlantis, a magical city where freedom and happiness were
more than just distant ideals but realities, both tangible and
attainable. Even its name had an alluring and rhythmic
meter, a melodic cadence that I loved to repeat.
Tuscaloosa. Over and over, I dreamt of breaking free from
the pain of my life and making it to that distant land, that
haven, that sanctum. In school, I'd read all about the Black
Warrior River that runs through it, and I'd imagined living
off the land and fishing in its namesake lake. And so, when
I left Mama's house, I wandered the countryside and took
comfort in knowing that somewhere out there existed a
special place that wanted me just as much as I wanted it—
according to my wishes and prayers.

When I finally made it, when I finally crossed over
those city limits and stepped into the land of my dreams, I
was deeply underwhelmed. I was devastated to discover
that the city I'd puffed up to be so grand in my fantasies
was a mere figment of my imagination. With no money in
my pocket, I found myself loitering amongst the dregs of
society: burnt out youths bored with life before it had even
begun, winos and weirdos looking for a fix to make them
numb to the pain of the world. In those sad circles, I asked
about Butch and described the man-child to all who would
listen. And in just a few days' time, I found Butch, and we
were reacquainted. He offered to let me stay with him a
while and to help me find work right away. Butch and I
had never been friends growing up, and I had no earthly
reason to trust him, but when surrounded by strangers in a
strange land, a familiar face can often feel like a friendly
one. And so Butch, my former foe, took me under his wing
and dispatched me to Lucky Lady Gentlemen's Club that

day to inquire about a job as a dancer. It was an upscale burlesque house in one of the city's busiest districts.

As a fresh-faced fourteen-year-old with a perky bosom and curves in all the right places, the management took an immediate interest in me and whisked me downstairs to the owner's office. He was somewhere between handsome and ugly, but neither label fit. His features were both soft and hard depending on which angle you observed him from and how the fluorescent lights above him cast their rays upon his chiseled face. His hair was sleek and shiny and contained one lone streak of white down the side, making him appear distinguished and debonair. He was brown-eyed and olive-skinned, with an exotic, yet untraceable accent. His nameplate simply read "Mr. C," a title equally as cryptic as his ethnic origins.

I sat there in the basement office, being interviewed by this enigma in pinstripes, and my mere presence there seemed to have set the club abuzz and to have captured the attention of nearly all the employees. Just about the entire security staff waited outside the office door, sniffing like dogs in heat, hoping to catch a glimpse of my taut behind in tight jeans. And the seasoned dancers were no less curious; they gathered there in the hallway to size up the competition and assess the threat. As I sat there lying to Mr. C about my age and being double-jointed, one lone shot rang out from upstairs in the club. The shot was followed by screams, and I heard the scrambling of the security staff outside Mr. C's door rushing back up to the parlor upstairs. Another gunshot rang out, and I nearly jumped out of my skin.

"Wait here, young lady, until we secure the situation," the mysterious Mr. C advised before rushing out of the office to follow the guards toward the chaos upstairs. I sat there alone in the mystery man's office, listening to the thuds overhead of patrons running for cover and the thunderous footsteps of folks pouring out of the club. And the hairs on my neck stood as I heard the screams of dancers stampeding through the halls in their high heels. I sat there as I was told, waiting for the proprietor to return, and the minutes felt like dynasties passing by.

All of a sudden, I heard a faint tapping at one of the basement windows. I turned to find Butch's smiling face motioning for me to come near. The basement windows were up above my head, and I had to climb up the front of a bookcase to unlatch the pane.

"Butch!" I exclaimed.

"Shhh!" He held a finger to his lip.

"What you doin' here?" I whispered, confused. A look of even greater confusion overtook Butch's face.

"What chu mean? I told you I would help you find a job."

"Yeah…and?"

"Well…this is the job!" Butch held up a green army knapsack and lifted the flap to reveal the green bills stuffed inside. And slowly my naivety began to fade like a cheap perfume. I realized that I was just a pawn to Butch, just a means to a deceitful end, a sacrificial lamb sent for the slaughter. I was downstairs having what I thought was a real job interview, and meanwhile, Butch was upstairs tying up the clerks in the champagne room and stuffing bills into his bag.

"Come on before they get back!" Butch urged, holding the window open for me. I stepped up higher on the bookshelf, and a large ceramic vase came crashing down. Butch's eyes met mine, and we both shared the same look of horror. "Let's go! Let's go!!" Butch yelled, and I spilled out of the window onto the ground outside. As I looked back over my shoulder, I saw Mr. C and his henchman burst into the office to discover my empty chair and the broken bits all over the floor. Butch and I ran for our lives, jumping bushes, dodging bullets, and cutting through the matrix of alleyways that led us to the Carick's apartment to eat cold meatloaf and mashed potatoes.

"One thousand nine hundred and ninety-four dollars!" Butch shouted with a smile. "Good money for a few minutes work."

"Are you crazy?!" I asked in all sincerity. "We almost got killed!"

"No, we didn't," Butch said, reaching for a drumstick on my side of the table. "Those assholes couldn't aim for shit. I bet they piss all over the floor every time they go to the toilet!" Butch laughed and slapped the table. "We got almost two thousand dollars here!"

"That money ain't ours, Butch!" I protested.

"Neither is that corn on the cob, but ain't those yo' teeth marks?" Butch laughed. "Ain't nobody gon' give you nothing in this life. You want something, you gotta take it! Or you starve."

As I chewed on that meatloaf for far longer than meatloaf should have to be chewed, I mulled over Butch's words. I'd been hitchhiking and wandering for months and couldn't even remember the last time I'd eaten. And after less than twenty-four hours in Butch's presence, I had food in my belly and money in my pocket. How could I argue?

"I gotta use the bathroom," I said, excusing myself from the table.

Dara Dionne Welms

"Don't get lost," Butch said. He smiled with his mouth, but there was a threat in his eyes.

I walked through the dining room, through the living room, down the hall, past the bedroom with the broken window, to the back of the apartment, where I found the bathroom. I flipped on the light switch and stared at myself in the mirror. I wondered how I would ever be able to face that girl again, knowing my crimes. And before I knew it, I was crying—sobbing uncontrollably. I turned on the water to drown out the sounds of my despair. Then after a few moments, I composed myself, turned the water off, and flushed the toilet. I wiped my eyes and adjusted my clothes in preparation for rejoining Butch, but still I heard sobbing, a sobbing that could not be contained. But it wasn't me. I pulled back the shower curtain and found Mr. and Mrs. Carick lying there in the tub, bound and gagged. Their golden retriever lay between them, its neck snapped back and slit open, flesh popping out like a freshly opened can of biscuits.

"Mantha!" I jumped. "What the hell is wrong wit' chu?" Butch whispered. And suddenly, I remembered where I was and why I was there. Butch had turned me into a common criminal years ago, and as I sat there fidgeting in the belly of The Wild Goose, I resented him for how many times *my* goose had almost been cooked on account of him and his antics. I hated him for leading me down a path of destruction and into a life of crime, for making me an unwilling, unknowing accomplice to his craziness.

I hated Butch, and I hated myself too, for being so weak, so needy, so helpless, so incapable of doing anything on my own. I mean, the only reason Butch sat beside me that night was because I had all but begged him to come. I was the one who'd come knocking on his door that morning, just like I had come looking for him so many years ago on the streets of Tuscaloosa. And with that realization, suddenly, smack dab in the middle of loathing Butch, part of me was busy loving him. I was equal parts hateful and grateful. Butch was wicked and no doubt insane, but he was on my side, on my team, always ready to use his evil powers for my good—whether I liked it or not.

"Fish tagine served with jasmine infused couscous," Eve announced, approaching the table with a large serving tray. Steam radiated from the bowls and plates as she placed our meals before us.

"Steak…bloody…with garlic mashed potatoes, steamed vegetables, and a fried goose egg."

"Thank you," Winston and I said together. I dug my spoon into the stew and cooled it with my lips. The broth was immensely fragrant. I inhaled the savory aromas of saffron, curry, and jasmine, and those sweet-smelling, ambrosial scents began mending my soul almost instantly. With one bite, I was rejuvenated, revitalized, replenished. I felt the nourishment coursing through my veins like an IV drip, and for a brief moment, everything in the whole world was fair and all right. For a second, Samson, the widow, and even Francine were all distant memories from a former life, just rumors on an ephemeral wind.

CHAPTER 12: FAIR GAME!

"Somewhere there's music…how faint the tune. Somewhere there's heaven…how high the moon. There is no moon above when love is far away too…till it comes true…that you love me as I love you…" The stage was nearly black, the band blending together in darkness, just vague contours hidden amongst the shadows. One lone beam framed the soloist in a light so bright it felt as though she were the last living woman inhabiting a deserted Earth. Her eyes were closed tightly as her bright red lips wrapped themselves around each lyric. A perfectly placed mole decorated the space between her nose and upper lip, and her graceful neck was long and elegant enough to make even a giraffe look twice. Three gentlemen stood behind her off to the side, contributing the occasional ooh and aah while that lead singer offered up melodies into the atmosphere so sweet, I imagine the angels above must have been moved to put down their harps and listen.

"The darkest night would shine if you would come to me soon…until you will, how still my heart…how high the moon…" Her hair was the color of wine and was stacked high into a bouffant, making her look ten feet tall standing there. Her bright green dress was covered in dazzling sequins that glinted in the light and moved when she did. Ample cleavage peeked from behind a sweetheart neckline, and that sparkling green dress clung to her curves like a second layer of skin, like gills on a fish, all the way down to her knees, where it blossomed out like a flower the rest of the way to the floor. I felt honored watching that

124

lady in green, like I'd been invited to a private concert by a real-life mermaid on loan from the Atlantic.

"How high the moon...does it touch the stars? How high the moon...does it reach up to Mars? Though the words may be wrong to this song, we're asking how high, high, high, high, high is the moon..." The entire room was mesmerized by that siren's song, transfixed on her every word, the way she crooned that ballad so artfully, so masterfully, weaving the story together like a basket, bending the notes with her throat until they were black and blue. And just when we thought she was through, she swung her voice around in a wild scat that grabbed each of us like a lasso and ushered us one by one into a state of ecstasy.

Eve had cleared our plates and placed two slices of strawberry cheesecake before Winston and me. And right there at the table, she drizzled each piece slowly with thick, warm fudge. I took a bite, and the sweet decadence that danced between my cheeks made me pause involuntarily to savor the experience. The rich flavors married on my tongue and evolved over and over again in my mouth, essences unfolding like a caterpillar in its cocoon, a metamorphosis of taste that would forever transform my palate. No more corner store cakes or fifty cent pies for me, chile! My taste buds had been elevated to new heights, and with each mouthful, I gleefully relished that newfound altitude.

The food, the music, the ambience, the people, everything about the Wild Goose ministered to my senses that night, but as Eve poured me my second cup of Moroccan coffee and the aromas of clove and nutmeg beckoned from the mug, I was reminded of the widow

Jackie and little Samson Jr., who sat in squalor under a decaying roof that contained more holes than a cheese grater. I imagined them peeking together through the dingy curtains of their sad shack, watching for the headlights of a father who would never return. And immediately I was refocused on the business at hand, the plans that Butch and I had laid.

"Uh…Eve," I whispered, and the pretty waitress bent down to hear me over the din. "Does this man look familiar to you?" I pulled Samson's picture from my clutch and handed it to her.

"Oh, yes," Eve replied, holding the photo in one hand and the coffee carafe in the other. "I've seen him many, many times. He's hard to miss." Eve winked and handed the photo back.

"Yes, well, he's a friend of mine, and he told me that the Wild Goose is the place to be if you've got an itch that needs scratching." I smiled at the waitress.

"An itch?" She smiled back.

"Yes, an itch," I repeated as I pulled one of those crisp hundred-dollar bills from my bag. "You see, I've got all this money burning a hole in my purse, and my friend from the photo told me that there's a lounge somewhere in this place that has a poker table?"

"Mmm…I see." Eve leaned in closer. "Well, your friend has a big mouth," she said coyly, "because the Golden Egg is a private room. Invitation only. Costs a hundred dollars just to get in there and another grand to sit down at the table."

"A thousand-dollar minimum buy in?" I repeated in disbelief. "That's all?" I smirked. The pretty waitress returned my smile and stood.

126

"Come with me." Eve motioned, and Winston and I rose from our seats, bidding farewell to our tablemates. As we snaked through the many tables in the dimly lit restaurant in pursuit of the pretty waitress in black lace, I wondered if *this* Eve would lead us to perdition like her namesake from the scriptures. Would I regret this journey in the morning? Would I even be alive in the morning? In jail? I tried not to let my fears get the best of me as Eve, Winston, and I boarded a small elevator at the back of the restaurant.

The elevator was right beside the kitchen, and as we waited for those heavy doors to close, the clatter of cooks searing and chopping and flambéing almost masked the music in the air. So close to that kitchen, the epicenter of all those fragrant and exotic dishes, the smells were greatly intensified. I felt like I was being choked standing there, assaulted by the very scents that had been enticing me all evening—like I'd been flirting with a handsome stranger from across a dark room all night only to discover later, up close and in good light, that he had been ugly all along. As the elevator doors closed gently between the three of us and the outside world, I took that odor as a warning, a noxious reminder to proceed with caution.

Eve reached for the buttons on the wall and pressed the number two and four simultaneously. The whole panel lit up brightly and began to flash, but instead of feeling the elevator move up or down, I felt a centrifugal force, the elevator turning slowly clockwise. Then there was a loud click followed by a quiet hum as we felt the elevator sliding sideways along a track. "Wow," I said aloud. "That's...uh...different."

"Yea, it's weird, I know." Eve laughed. "This is the only one of its kind. The only elevator in the world that doesn't just elevate! It spins and moves from east wing to west wing and back. Cool, right?"

"Very," I said nervously. The only form of transportation I hated more than an elevator was a train. And here I stood locked inside a fusion of both: a small steel box on rails, a nightmare within a nightmare.

"Very expensive too," Eve added. "They say this little elevator cost more than any other feature in the building."

"I bet," I replied. The look in my eyes and the tone of my voice conveyed interest, but truthfully, I didn't really care. I hated that elevator, and the only thing keeping me from counting every second of my confinement was the paltry exchange of idle chitchat between the waitress and me.

"Yep. And speaking of bets..." Eve cleared her throat, "May I remind you that entry to the betting tables will run you a hundred dollars?" She held out a manicured hand.

"Yes, sure...of course." I gave Eve the hundred-dollar bill that I still had folded in my fingers, hoping she wouldn't notice the dampness from my sweaty palms.

"Each!" Eve said, looking at Winston. The man-child pulled his wallet out and handed the waitress another crisp hundred. She folded both bills and stuffed them beneath her bra strap. "As you know, this party is invitation only, and now"—Eve patted her bosom, where the money lay hidden— "you're both invited!" The elevator came to a sudden stop, and the heavy doors began to part slowly. "Lady and gentleman," Eve announced, "I give you..." she added in a whisper, "the Golden Egg."

Eve's dramatic introduction was actually quite apropos, because just beyond those elevator doors was a room so bountifully extravagant it could have made King Tut's tomb look like a country swap meet on the side of the road. Everything that could be gold...was gold! The vases filled with English roses? All gold. The oversized planters burgeoning with exotic shrubberies, flourishing ferns, huge Madagascar dragon trees, and towering Kentia palms? Gold. The tabletops, stools, and fixtures? The wallpaper, the carpeting, the curtains? Gold, gold, and more gold! The room itself was large and round—oval-shaped actually, like an egg. And suddenly, it was clear how and from whence the secret room's title had been derived.

Winston and I stepped forward, and the elevator doors closed behind us, Eve's smiling face disappearing behind the gold mirror finish. To our left, a man with a golden complexion, wearing a shiny gold suit, played soft sounds on a gold grand piano. Aside from the ambient piano music, the golden slot machines that circled the room along the walls played songs of their own, flashing and blinking, chiming and ringing like a chorus of Christmas bells. Patrons stared into the slot machines like zombies on stools, but everywhere else there was much excitement. The room was abuzz with buoyant banter as clusters of people stood around counter-height tables laughing and playing games. A lively tournament of dominoes was taking place at one table nearby, and other tables throughout the room hosted everything from keno to Uno! Bid whist, Pitty Pat, pinochle, gin rummy, tonk, hearts, spades, you name it! One table even had a roulette wheel built into it. And standing around that table was a much more focused bunch, their heads following that wheel around like patients under hypnosis, like awestricken cavemen staring into the magnificent sun. The room was filled with joy and a wonderful lightheartedness, beautiful women winking coquettishly and handsome men flashing their teeth. Waiters armed with champagne bottles stood by, poised and ready to refill glasses as the guests sipped and chatted, telling truths and lies.

In the center of the room, amidst all the activity, there was a tall, round table with a green felt top—it was probably velvet, actually. In the middle of the table was a large opening, and inside the opening stood a dealer expertly shuffling a deck of cards. He wore a visor on his head and a smile on his face. And as he stood there, I wondered curiously how that tall man got in and out of that donut-shaped table. Six tall stools surrounded the dealer's cage, and four of them were already occupied by three attractive men smoking cigars and a handsome older woman puffing on a slim cigarette. Half-filled cognac glasses sat in front of each of them as the tobacco smoke swirled slowly in the light above their heads. The men looked to be about my age, but the streaks of white and silver in the woman's short curls exposed her as being in her mid to late sixties. The men wore dark suits, and the woman wore a red satin gown. Her jewelry glinted even under the dull lights, and everything about her demeanor, manner, and austere appearance boasted of tremendous wealth.

"Two seats still open at the table, folks. Ten lightning rounds of Texas Hold 'Em startin' in five!" the tall dealer announced. Then he reached somewhere under the table and brought up a bottle of McDowell's, an aged brandy, and began refilling glasses. I was impressed to see that he was both dealer and bartender at that high-roller table. But it wasn't his ability to multi-task that impressed me, it was his hustle. I had run a couple of scams in my lifetime, and I had even been the victim of a few, but this one was especially clever. Imagine a dealer listening to the woes of the players, stroking egos, offering advice, swapping stories, and telling jokes, all the while pouring liquor down their unsuspecting gullets and collecting their chips for the house. It was a blatant conflict of interest, yet wonderfully inconspicuous, like when a mechanic pokes a slow leak into the tire he just replaced to get you back in for another repair, or when the doc prescribes you a sedative, so he can treat you later for depression. It was a brilliant con. An ingenious racket! The perfect plan, foolproof and eighty-proof, impenetrable enough to be bulletproof.

"You need to get a seat at that table, Mantha," Butch whispered with a nudge. "Give me that picture."

"It's been years since I played poker. I don't think I remember how," I said as I pulled Samson's photo from my bag.

"Perfect! As far as they concerned, you the best kinda' player." Butch laughed. "Don't worry 'bout playing cards... You just play the table. Work that old lady and those three suits over there. See what you can find out about ya' boyfriend. I'll work the room." He snatched Samson's photo from me, and before I could protest any further, he patted me on the shoulder and stepped away. I suppose he was right, though. Butch had a manner and a presence about himself that was far better suited for blending in and performing that kind of quiet reconnaissance. He was like a special ops solider, naturally gifted with the ability to camouflage his agenda and skilled at operating calmly and efficiently deep undercover behind enemy lines. And so I focused my talents and efforts on converting Clara Wells, the confident, successful southern belle, from fiction to fact.

"Last call! Two more seats at the table everybody. Game startin' in just a few," the dealer cried as I sashayed decidedly toward the velvet circle. I placed my clutch on the table, but before I could pull out my stool, a hand touched my back gently.

"Allow me," said one of the three suits. I was concentrating so hard on being Clara, I hadn't even seen him stand.

"Why, thank you," I said with a smile as I stepped up onto the seat.

"My pleasure," he said, and as if on cue, a twinkle flashed brightly in his dark eyes. The man returned to his side of the table and sat between his two buddies. They were all three equally handsome and covered in the same shade of bark-colored skin. The woman in red took another sip of her brandy, and I remember thinking how perfectly her amber complexion matched that sweet liqueur.

"What's your name, beautiful?" asked the man in the middle. A thin mustache straddled his upper lip.

"I'm Clara. Clara Wells," I responded in my sweetest voice. "And you are?"

"I'm Reginald Burris. You can call me Reggie. And uh…" he continued, "this here is Ellis Hill"—he pointed at the man on his left— "and Jeremiah Wilkes," he motioned to the man on his right. "Jerry for short."

"How do you do?" both men said in unison as they tipped their hats in my direction.

"Pleased to meet you, Reggie, Ellis, Jerry." I nodded at each as I spoke his name. "So refreshing to find such well-mannered gentlemen this day and age."

"Ha!" blurted the woman in red, slamming her glass on the velvet table. "Are you kiddin' me?" she asked with a chuckle. Her voice was gruff and gravelly, and its timbre was only slightly higher than the men at the table. "You think any one of these fools helped me onto my stool when I sat down?" She pointed at Reggie and his friends. "I had to damn near tie a grappling hook and hoist myself up here like a rock climber on Mount Kilimanjaro!"

"That's not true!" Reggie disputed with a laugh.

"Are you calling me a liar, Mr. Burris? If it weren't for Jimmy here refilling my glass every ten seconds"—she pointed to the card-dealing bartender— "I might've believed I was invisible. Then this pretty young thing comes gliding over to the table, and suddenly you three have more hospitality than a five-star hotel!"

"It's not like that, Mrs. Barrister," Jerry pleaded.

"Not at all," added Ellis.

"I would've offered to help you too, Mrs. Barrister," Reggie interjected, "but you looked like you had things well under control."

"Under control? I'll tell you what's under control. My bladder!" She turned to me and leaned in close. "I've had to pee for a half-hour now…but with no help from these three dopes…I was afraid I'd have to rappel down this chair like Batman in order to make it to the can!"

"No, no, no!" the men protested with a laugh.

"I'm sorry, Mrs. Barrister." Reggie and the other men stood. "Let us help you down."

"Hmmf! That's more like it," she said as the three men took her by the hand and helped her to the floor. "You come with me, honey." She motioned to me. "That way I can badmouth these boys properly!"

"Aww, Mrs. Barrister, don't be like that," Ellis said, sighing.

"We said we were sorry now," Jerry added with a smile.

"Mm-hmm." Mrs. Barrister rolled her eyes. "Not as sorry as my poor kidneys!" The woman in red hooked her arm in mine. "Come now, girl."

There was a tall doorway a few paces from the poker table, and as we made our way toward it, I saw Butch looking at us in my periphery and felt safe knowing I was still on the mercenary's radar.

The bathroom was just as fancy as I imagined it would be. Just inside the entrance, a female cellist sat playing long meter sonatas on a golden cello. And an attendant stood in front of the huge mirror, offering soaps, perfumes, and other amenities. The sinks were lavish, with ornamental fixtures, and there was a posh clawfoot couch along one wall. A huge painting of ocean waves crashing against a deserted shore dressed the wall above the couch. The painting seemed to be calling me, and I felt myself being pulled toward it instinctively, like a bear to honey, a moth to a flame. The colors were so vivid you could almost hear the seagulls overhead and taste the saltwater on your lips. I reached out to touch those blue waters, and an intense tranquility, a powerful serenity emanated from that seascape and enveloped me like heat coming from the sun.

"Careful dear!" Mrs. Barrister warned. "That painting is new, and the oil may still be a tad wet." I drew my hand away from the inspiring portrait and stepped back. "Come. I'll race ya'," Mrs. Barrister said with a wink as she headed into one of the stalls. I smiled and entered a stall a few doors over. It felt good to have a moment of privacy, to be plain old me for a minute. "So where are you from, dear?" Mrs. Barrister shouted over the stalls. I rolled my eyes and sighed to see that my moment of solitude was already ancient history.

"West Texas originally. I just moved to Georgia earlier this year," I shouted back as we both relieved ourselves. I was thankful then for the cellist and her sad music drowning out the sounds of our biology. "And you?"

"Oh, I've lived in Georgia all my life, darling. That's why I can't stand peaches." She laughed as the toilet flushed. "What brought you to our fine state, if I may be so bold as to inquire?" I hurried and finished my business as well so as to avoid the embarrassment of being too long on the pot.

"Well...many reasons..." I replied as we both exited the stalls. "So many wonderful connections to be made in Atlanta and the surrounding areas. Look at how many captains of industry have dug their roots here. So many budding businesses, emerging markets, and there's a culture of entrepreneurship here that I like. Great things happening all around. I mean, just look at this place." I motioned to the décor of that elaborate ladies room. "Obviously, there's money to be made here...and adventures to be had. You ask why Georgia. I ask…why not?" I winked at Mrs. Barrister as the attendant squeezed a dab of liquid soap into my hand.

"You've done your homework, my dear," Mrs. Barrister acknowledged as she washed her hands in the marble sink. "Most young girls who pass through here have the IQ of an amoeba." She shook her head while shaking the water from her hands. The attendant handed her a warm towel from what looked like an oven in the wall. "I see them strutting through here. Talk about a circus! Faces painted up like clowns…tits popping out of their gowns like helium balloons…parading around here in heels so high they may as well be on stilts!" The attendant handed me a towel to dry my hands as well. "I think they come here just to shop for a husband or a…whatchamacallit? A baby's daddy! You know what I mean." I laughed at her candor as the attendant squirted a glob of scented lotion on my hands. "I'm glad you find that funny, my dear, 'cause, to be honest, I had you pegged as one of the same." My smile fell faster than a drunk on skates.

"I beg your pardon?" I asked.

"Oh, don't be angry, love," said the lady in red as she applied more lipstick to her thinning lips. "I was obviously wrong. And I must say"—she traced her lips slowly with the red pencil— "that in and of itself intrigues me, as I'm so rarely wrong." She pressed her lips together and blew a kiss at the mirror. "Those other young women out there are no better than the common prostitute as far as I'm concerned," she added, fluffing her curls with her fingertips. "Throwing themselves at men for the promise of money, security, a little prestige. So crass. So tactless.

136

And lewd, I might add!" Mrs. Barrister shook her head in disgust before turning to me. "It's quite obvious to me now that you're much more dignified, my dear, and your agenda here is far more laudable. And you have a keen eye for good art to boot!" Mrs. Barrister motioned toward the painting on the wall. "You're nothing at all like those whores. Come now." She offered her elbow with a smile. "Our poker game awaits!"

And just like that, I was wounded. Slain! A mere thirty seconds ago, I felt good. I actually felt comfortable. I felt like I belonged. Standing there in disguise, passing for rich, pretending to be someone new, someone improved, someone better, someone else, I actually felt accepted for the first time since I'd stepped foot in that nightclub. And then boom! She dropped those syllables like hand grenades, and with all the ease and precision of a career marksman, she aimed her words at me, zoomed in, and picked me off like a sniper. I felt my soul plummeting to the ground like wild game, and tears threatened to seep from my eyes like a fresh gash, bloody and wet.

You're nothing at all like those whores. I was no stranger to that word: back home in Mississippi, when the other girls in class would cut their eyes at me and my protruding belly, when Mama would lock herself away in her room to keep from seeing my face, when Cleo and her friends had ambushed me along the roadside on my way home from school, later, in Tuscaloosa, when Mr. C's goons had chased me through the streets, even just a few weeks prior, here in Atlanta, when that derelict had grabbed my arm on Commerce Boulevard and forced his kiss on me. The instances were plentiful.

I'd been called a whore more often than my own name, but never had I felt as powerless as I did standing there with Mrs. Barrister. I couldn't react or respond, nor could I run away without outing myself and exposing the mission. When dressed as a lion and infiltrating the pride, I suppose the slaughter of gazelles should come as no surprise. Mrs. Barrister's hateful, snobbish words, spoken in my presence so casually, had made my poor soul a casualty. But my wounded feelings were merely collateral damage, the cost of doing business, of operating covertly, the price of passing successfully undercover. And so I swallowed my hurt quickly like a shot of bourbon and put my mask back on: a tortured smile mustered up from somewhere deep within.

As Mrs. Barrister and I exited the ladies room together arm in arm, the pretty painting on the wall that had once offered me so much peace, the same painting that had been calling me and drawing me and pulling me in like a gravity, was now a toxin to me, taunting me, teasing me, killing me slowly with its insincere assurances, all those empty promises. That ocean view could never be mine. Those tranquil waves would never caress my skin. I'd never feel that warm golden sand beneath my toes. The only commonality between me and that pretty bathroom painting was the certain fact that both of us had been hung out to dry…and were stuck in shitty places…with our backs up against a wall.

CHAPTER 13: EGG OVER EASY!

"There they are!" the bartender exclaimed as Mrs. Barrister and I rejoined the table. "Thought you two had lost your way." He smiled, drying shot glasses with a gold hand towel.

"Ha!" Mrs. Barrister chortled. "Trust me, Jimmy, at my age, I know my way to and from every restroom in a ten-block radius!" The gentlemen laughed. "Did you boys miss me?" she asked as Reggie, Ellis, and Jerry rose to help her back up onto her stool.

"Of course," Reggie replied. "Wasn't the same without you," he added, apparently the spokesman for the bunch. Then the three men turned to help me back up as well. "I hope Mrs. Barrister didn't defame us too badly in there?" Reggie asked. The gleam in his eye was flirtatious yet coy. The gleam in his wedding band, however, was bold and brash.

"I assure you Mrs. Barrister went very easy on you gentlemen and kept the slander to a minimum." I smiled as he and Ellis each took one of my hands and Jerry pulled out my seat. "You can call off your attorneys." The men laughed, as I knew they would. From the minute I laid eyes on those three I knew them like the proverbial back of my hand. A year ago—hell, a day ago—I would have set my sights on them and had their money, their jewelry, and their hearts before closing time.

My life in the streets had given me an advantage, a special education in analyzing men and situations, a kind of clairvoyance with regard to the opposite sex. Over the years, I had developed and cultivated a built-in barometer, a keen insight that allowed me to swiftly yet thoroughly

139

interpret the mood of a man, to guess his likes and dislikes, to assess his strengths and weaknesses, anticipate his every move, and steer him in the direction of my choosing. I could read a man like a library book, honey, from cover to cover in just a few seconds, and then use his own story against him. His appearance, his conduct, his behavior, every action, reaction, and inaction was a clue I fashioned into a weapon to be used in my conniving. Then, when I was done checking him out, I would return that man to the library, to the same shelf where I'd plucked him from, but not before ripping out his spine and leaving him slumped there, flaccid and limp.

"Wait a minute!" Mrs. Barrister extended her arm out like a crossing guard halting oncoming traffic. "Aren't you forgetting something, my dear?"

"Uh…am I?" I asked quizzically.

"Your chips!" she exclaimed, pointing at the empty area in front of my chair. "You haven't any chips to play with, darling."

"Ugh," I sighed. "Where's my head?"

"Window's over there." Reggie pointed to the other side of the room, where a line of people stood in front of a plate-glass window. A set of red velvet ropes kept the line in order as the teller behind the glass called up patrons one by one to exchange cash for chips and chips for cash. As I made my way across the room to the back of the line, I observed the workers behind the glass moving all about, opening and closing drawers, counting and recounting chips and bills like busy bees in a translucent hive. Two security guards in dark gray suits stood tall and still on either side of the window, like English guards defending the gates of Buckingham Palace. I suppose their purpose

there was to stave off the possibility of threats or
handwritten extortions being passed through to the tellers,
like in all the great bank robbery films. Still, I found their
presence to be a bit redundant, since every patron had
already been checked for weapons and vetted at the door on
the way in to the Goose. I surmised that the payload caged
behind that glass must have been quite large to warrant the
added layer of security.

"How's it goin'?" Butch snuck up from behind me
and startled me from my thoughts. He spoke in a whisper,
and like a trained ventriloquist, his lips scarcely moved.
"Turn back around so no one sees us talking," he directed
in a hush. I turned around just as the line inched forward. I
took a step toward the window. "There you go," Butch
whispered. "Now what chu find out over at the table?"

"Oh…uh…" The line crept forward again, and I
took another step. "Not much. Haven't had a chance yet."

"What about the old lady in the bathroom. You ask
her 'bout ya' boyfriend?"

"Stop callin' him my boyfriend!" I shouted in a
whisper. "And no. I was too busy trying to maintain my
cover. She kept askin' questions." The line moved
forward again. "What about you? Find anything?"

"Yep. Plenty! Your boyfriend is pretty popular
around here. Shhh!" Butch warned in my ear. The line
moved up again, and I found myself next in line to step to
the window. The burly bouncers stood only a few feet
away, scanning over the crowd, looking at no one in
particular. I opened my clutch and counted out ten
hundred-dollar bills from the money Samson had
bequeathed to me. I felt like kissing them goodbye, since I

knew they would soon be relinquished in the poker game I was getting ready to lose.

"Next guest!" The teller beckoned. She was an older woman with long dark hair swept back into a loose bun. A pair of cat eye reading glasses sat perched on the edge of her nose. Her uniform consisted of a shiny gold vest and a white short-sleeved blouse. And she wore latex gloves on both hands—I imagine so as to avoid the microscopic germs crawling all over that money. Even as she smacked quite vigorously on a piece of chewing gum, she offered me a warm smile through the cold, hard glass. I smiled back, and as I stepped forward to greet her, without warning, I felt an arm wrap around my throat, yanking me backward. I tried to yell, but nothing came out. The arm around my neck squeezed my windpipe like a boa constrictor, silencing my would-be screams. The security guards drew their guns in tandem and pointed them in my direction.

"Put it down!" one yelled.

"Put down the knife!" shouted the other. I heard the hysteria and screams in the room around me, but my eyes only saw the teller behind the glass. A look of sheer horror arrested her, and as she clutched the crucifix that dangled from her neck, I felt her prayers reaching for me. I felt her soul interceding on my behalf, appealing to the saints and deities of her faith for my safety and protection. Her fervor sent me into a panic; I knew something terrible was happening. I began kicking wildly, but my resistance was useless against my attacker. I was powerless, lame, impotent, captive to an unknown assailant. I was grateful that I'd brought Butch with me. Whoever was holding me hostage would soon regret it! And then I heard it.

"Guns down, or she's dead! I'll slit her goddamned throat, I swear!" It was Butch's voice. There were more screams all around, and the ambient piano music that had been serenading us all night was instantly gone, leaving an eerie void in its place, a stark and blatant silence. The standoff continued, the guards inching closer and Butch inching back, dragging me with him. "Stay right there!" Butch yelled. "Take another step, fat boy, and her blood is on your hands!" he threatened one of the guards.

Both guards ignored Butch's intimidations and continued to step forward. My life flashed before my eyes, and I saw failure after failure. I closed my eyes to keep from seeing anymore. And then I felt the tears cascading down the slopes of my cheeks, eyeliner and mascara painting lines into my face as I stared down the barrel of two guns and felt the tip of Butch's knife at the base of my neck.

"Stop it!" I heard a familiar voice shout from across the room. "Stop it! Do what he says!" Mrs. Barrister commanded from the poker table. The men lowered their weapons slowly under her authority.

"Put 'em on the ground!" Butch yelled, and the reluctant men looked over to Mrs. Barrister. "Now!!" Butch demanded.

"Curtis and Ralph!" Mrs. Barrister called. "Do as he says!" she shouted adamantly. The two guards placed their weapons on the ground.

"Now kick your guns over to me, Curtis and Ralph!" Butch mocked Mrs. Barrister's gruff tones as he spoke the guards' names. The big guards did as they were told and gently kicked their guns toward Butch. "Back up!" he commanded. "Back up against the glass!" The two men stepped back as instructed until their backs were against the teller's booth. "Now listen, bitch. I want you to reach down there slowly and pick up both those guns," he directed. "You hear what I said, bitch?!"

Butch shook me wildly, and I felt the sharp knife poke me deep. I didn't even realize he was talking to me! Butch and I had always called each other names in jest, but never had he called me a bitch like this, and never had he physically harmed me. He was like a domesticated tiger who had suddenly turned against his caretaker, against the one who loved him most. The boy-beast had grown up in an instant and was now just beast, one hundred percent animal, holding that knife to my throat.

I bent down slowly to retrieve the guns, and Butch crouched with me, the knife held to my neck all the way. "Easy does it," he coached as I grabbed both guns. Then we rose together. Maintaining a firm grasp on my neck, he deposited one gun into his waistband and then slid the long knife back inside the jacket pocket from where it had been pulled. There was a hole in the bottom of the pocket that allowed the blade to slide in easily like a makeshift holster. Then he held the second gun to my temple.

"Listen up, everybody!" Butch called out. "Put your hands in the air. Higher!!" The crowd complied. "I'm armed, and you bet your ass I'm dangerous! If anybody wants to be a hero today and to try me, I suggest you think long and hard right now about everybody in your life that you love. Think of your mothers and your fathers. Picture your daughters and sons...your husbands...your wives. Don't make them plan your funeral. Don't make your mothers lay out their black dresses. Don't make your children grow up too soon. 'Cause if you fuck with me, I will kill you, and that's exactly what will happen. Everybody got that?!"

I saw the look of terror reflected in everyone's eyes as he turned me clockwise around the room so everyone could behold the two of us, the maniac and his horrified hostage. Even the two guards, Curtis and Ralph, were cowering under Butch's threats.

"Sir, if I may," called that familiar voice again. "My name is Theresa Barrister, and this is my establishment. I own the Wild Goose, and I assure you that if you'll promise not to harm anyone, you will have the full support and cooperation of my entire staff. Please, let the young lady go, Sir. She has nothing to do with this," Mrs. Barrister pleaded. I had wondered why everyone there seemed to know her name and why they showed her such great respect. And I'd wondered how she could have possibly known that the pretty painting in the bathroom was new and perchance still wet. I had hoped to have those questions answered under more affable circumstances, but Butch's violence had fast-forwarded my courtship with the lady in red and revealed those facts prematurely.

"Everybody take your cues from the boss lady here. I expect nothing less than your full support and cooperation," Butch warned the room. "Boss lady," he said, addressing Mrs. Barrister, "what's this guy's name?" He pointed the gun at the pianist. The piano player's eyes bugged out in fright, making him look like a boardwalk caricature drawn in haste.

"His name is Cecil," Mrs. Barrister replied.

"Cecil, go over there and call for the elevator. And when it comes, you hold it open. Try anything funny, and

I'll kill you and five more people in here just like you. Got dat?"

Cecil nodded his head rapidly in a wild yes and scurried like a beetle over to the elevator.

"Boss lady," Butch called, addressing Mrs. Barrister again, "what's this lady's name?" He pointed at the teller behind the glass, who stood there squeezing her crucifix like a good luck charm.

"That's Rosemary," Mrs. Barrister replied.

"Rosemary, I need two empty cash deposit bags." The frazzled teller seemed confused and panicked as she whispered prayers and gripped her necklace tighter. "Rosemary, look at me." The teller stopped and looked at Butch and the gun that was now pointed in her direction. "Get it together, or they'll be no need for prayers 'cause you'll be talkin' to your maker face to face! Now hurry up!!" he screamed. The terrified teller found what she was looking for and shoved the empty sacks through the slot under the glass. "Curtis and Ralph! Each of you take a bag!" Butch commanded, and the two big men rushed over to the window to retrieve the large sacks.

"Now listen up!" the madman shouted, addressing the room again. "Curtis and Ralph here are gonna take up a collection on my behalf. I want everybody to dump your wallets, your rings, your necklaces, your earrings, your cellphones, your keys…everything you got…dump it in the bags as these two nice gentleman make their rounds. If you have loose change, I want it. If you ain't got nothing but a ball of lint and a stick of gum, I want it! I designate this area right here"—he pointed to a random corner of the room with the nose of his revolver— "as the body area. If I catch anybody holdin' out on me, I will kill you and stack

146

the corpses over there. Got dat?! And the first two I kill will be you two fat asses!" Butch barked at the bouncers. "Make sure I get *every*thing!" And with that final threat, Curtis and Ralph were dispatched around the room on a quest to fill those deep sacks. Just then, there was a high-pitched ding, and the elevator doors began to part slowly.

"I got the elevator, mister!" Cecil called from the entrance.

"Good job. Now hold that elevator like your life depends on it. You know why?" Cecil shook his head from side to side. "Because it does!" Cecil swallowed that threat deep, and his Adam's apple looked like an elevator in its own right, the lump descending slowly down his boney neck.

The room was filled with weeping and the clinking of valuables being thrown into the bags and stacking within.

"Rosemary!" Butch called to the window. "I need you and your girls back there to fill up as many of those bags as possible with money from the till." Rosemary nodded her head vehemently, and the ladies behind the glass sprang into action. "And I want all hundreds, you hear me?" Butch yelled. "If I find any dollar bills, fives, tens, and twenties, I'm coming back there and stacking your bodies where?" The ladies behind the glass all pointed together to the body area previously designated by the madman. "That's right. Glad to see you ladies are paying attention. Rosemary, you make sure they get it right, or else I'll have to take that nice necklace with me too." Rosemary gasped at the thought of parting with her precious crucifix and began directing the others with newfound resolve and determination.

147

"Boss lady," he called to Mrs. Barrister again, "what's this guy's name?" He pointed at one of the waiters against the wall, near the abandoned piano. The waiter was holding a bottle of champagne, and as he stared down the barrel of Butch's gun, his hands trembled like a diver suffering from hypothermia.

"His name is…his name is Charles," Mrs. Barrister called back. Her attention was divided between the madman Butch and the guard Ralph. The big bouncer was over at the poker table now, collecting valuables from her and the three suits.

"Hey, Chuck," Butch called to the waiter nonchalantly. "Get me a couple of those serving carts, the kind you penguins wheel around with the tablecloth on it?"

"Yes, sir. Right away!" the waiter acknowledged as he perused the room for serving carts.

"Curtis and Ralph! How we doin' wit' those bags? The clock is tickin'!"

"Just about done, sir!" shouted Ralph.

"Same here!" echoed Curtis.

"Rosemary, how many bags you got together so far?"

"Tres bolsas, señor!" Rosemary replied through the opening in the glass.

"What?" Butch shouted back.

"Lo siento… I'm sorry, sir. Three bags. Three bags so far! We're working on number four." The poor teller was so traumatized she'd inadvertently slipped into her native tongue.

"Nice!" Butch replied. "Bring all four out here soon as you're done!" The teller nodded as her partners frantically filled the last bag.

148

"Here are the carts you asked for, sir," Charles announced, wheeling the two over.

"Make sure they're empty underneath," Butch instructed.

"Yes, sir. They are," Charles confirmed. Right then, Curtis and Ralph approached, each holding full sacks of loot plundered from the affluent crowd.

"Okay, you two tie those sacks and sit them under one of these carts," Butch directed. While the big men did as they were told, Rosemary and another teller emerged from a hidden door in the gold wall. I didn't even know it was there until it opened. They each dragged out two heavy sacks. "Nice job, ladies!" Butch congratulated. "Curtis and Ralph, tie these bags up too and haul 'em over." He motioned toward the carts. The brawny men lugged the bags over to the carts and loaded them accordingly. "Then load the carts on the elevator over there."

The men went to work, and Butch addressed the room again. "Alright folks. I thank you for your benevolent hospitality. Truly, I appreciate these charitable donations." He laughed. "But I'm afraid I must be going now. And if anybody here is thinkin' about callin' the cops after I leave, just remember...I got your wallets, and I know where you live. And trust me...you don't want me knockin' on your door." As Curtis and Ralph loaded the elevator, Butch backed up slowly toward them, the gun still planted firmly in my forehead.

"Let her go!" Mrs. Barrister pleaded again. "We've given you everything you've asked for, now let the young lady go! It's my club; take me instead. I'm the better hostage!" As Mrs. Barrister bargained with Butch, I

149

wondered if she'd be so quick to trade in her life for mine if she knew who I really was. If she had known from the start that I was nothing more than a "common prostitute" and just another opportunist "whore", would she have ever even instructed her guards to drop their weapons in the first place? *Not likely*, I supposed. She would've probably had them open fire and kill us both. Then she and the rest of these rich folks could have returned to their games while the custodial staff heaved our lifeless bodies into the trash. Just another cleanup on aisle five.

"Yeah, right." Butch sucked his teeth. "You think they just gon' let me walk out this building with you? The owner? You and I both know *she's* the better hostage." Butch poked me again with the barrel of his gun. "But nice try."

"Carts are on the elevator, sir," Ralph reported as Butch and I backed into the steel box.

"Everybody, arms back up! Arms in the air!!" Butch commanded. "Now count to five hundred. Everybody!"

"One, two, three, four, five…" the crowd began to chant.

"Louder!" Butch yelled. "Louder!"

"Eight, nine, ten, eleven…" the crowd shouted together.

"You boys join me on the elevator. I'm gonna need you to wheel these carts to the curb," Butch insisted. The two goons boarded the elevator with Butch and me, and as the doors closed slowly and we left the golden room behind, we could still hear the counting faintly as the elevator made its trek back to the restaurant. "Now you listen up good, Clara Wells," Butch began, "I'm gonna put

150

this gun away, but if you try anything…and I do mean *anything*…I will spray your guts all over that dancefloor. You hear me?!" I nodded my head yes. "Now wipe your face. All that eyeliner runnin', you look like a zebra."

Butch put the second gun in his waistband and handed me the handkerchief from his breast pocket. I wiped off my ruined makeup and soaked up a few new tears. I couldn't believe that just a few minutes ago, I had been boasting to myself about how well I knew men, how I could read a man like an open book. And all the while, the man I'd known the longest and trusted most was willing to fillet me like a fish even despite my love and loyalty. Butch's knife had been held to my throat, but in my *back* was where I had been stabbed! Part of me wished he would have just pulled the trigger when he'd had that gun pressed to my temple. At least being riddled with bullets would have been quick. But, no. The pain Butch chose to inflict on me that night was slower than a glacier and equally as cold.

Just as I finished wiping my face, the elevator stopped abruptly with a jolt. Then, with a loud click, it began to spin counterclockwise. "Showtime, folks," Butch cautioned. "Let's make it look good."

The elevator doors parted, and I was immediately assaulted by the powerful scents emanating from the busy kitchen. The two guards exited first, each pushing a cart. Butch and I brought up the rear. The restaurant was still abuzz with lively conversation. Waiters and waitresses crossed every which way, delivering platters and pitchers and slices of pie. No one seemed to lend much attention to us, and so our little caravan continued undetected. We crossed over onto the dancefloor, and as the men shimmied and spun all over and the women sweated out their perms, we tried our best to keep to the edge of the party and out of the way of the dancers.

When we approached the small staircase near the front of the club, I worried what problem those steps would present for the carts. Butch had already proven himself tonight to be crazier than I'd ever imagined, and I shuddered to think how he might react if we couldn't get those carts out. But then Curtis and Ralph, at home on their native turf, turned, and I noticed the ramps on either side of the staircase. We ascended the ramps without a problem and bid farewell to the same smiling waiters who had first greeted us hours ago. Once again, we passed through those red velvet curtains and beneath the colorfully clinquant veils that hung from the rafters. And as we approached the security checkpoint at the front doors of the nightclub, Curtis and Ralph nodded to the guards on duty, and we exited without hitch or hindrance.

As we made the long walk to the valets standing at the circular driveway, I heard a familiar sound, the powerful purr of the mighty Ferrari. It was waiting right in front of the entrance, its tinted windows making it look all the more like a panther lurking there, stalking the Goose like a nocturnal predator. The trunk popped open, and I wondered how on earth the valets knew we were coming? And how did they know to open the trunk? Curtis and Ralph loaded the sacks into the back of the car obediently while Butch opened the passenger door for me.

"Hop in!" she called out, and my heart stopped so abruptly I thought it might beat backwards! What the hell was going on? Butch slid the front seat forward, and I climbed into the back. Then Butch sat down on the

152

passenger side and, as the trunk slammed shut, he called out to Curtis and Ralph one last time.

"You boys be good now!" And with that, he slammed the passenger door, and the FF peeled off down the driveway. We turned the corner, and the tires screeched again as the Ferrari fishtailed around the curve, flexing its powerful muscles all over the slick road. As the tears welled up in my eyes, Eve and Butch slapped hands and released a shout of triumph through the sunroof that sounded like two old wolves baying at a new moon.

CHAPTER 14: PROS...AND CONS...

"Are you shittin' me right now? What the hell is goin' on?!" I had been taken through the entire range of human emotion that night. I'd been nervous, anxious, happy, sad, afraid, surprised, and now, as the rage rose inside of me like mercury in a desert thermometer, I was pissed!

"Relax," Butch replied from the front seat, and his nonchalance made me overwrought with fury.

"Relax?!" I screamed back, and the Ferrari swerved momentarily with a startled Eve at the helm. "You just held a knife to my throat and a gun to my head, and now you tellin' me to relax?!"

"It's okay, honey," Eve consoled from the driver's seat. I heard her voice, but all I saw were her pouty lips moving in the rearview mirror. "You're safe now."

"Heifer, the question is are *you* safe? I ought to choke the..."

"Calm down!" Butch interjected. "Eve cool. She on our side."

"I wanna know why she's drivin' this car!" I yelled at Butch before turning back to the mouth in the mirror. "Why the hell are you drivin' this car, Eve?" The pretty waitress donned a frown for the first time all evening. "What the hell is goin' on?!" I seethed.

"Don't worry. We'll cut chu in!" Butch assured me, as if his scant remarks had answered my question.

"Cut me in?!" I repeated. "You just tried to cut me *up*! Or have you already forgotten?! Now I wanna know what the hell is goin' on here!" I demanded. And the man-

child finally appeased me by explaining the whole sordid
story from the beginning.

Apparently, Butch had already known Eve and had
already been a guest at the Goose. He and the waitress had
already discussed at great length the wealth that walked in
and out of those doors every weekend, and they'd spoken
about Mrs. Barrister, the club's owner, and all the inner-
workings of the staff and procedure. Whatever questions
Butch had about the Goose, Eve was able to find out
covertly and report back. And armed with that inside
intelligence, Butch began to devise and design the perfect
heist. But even with all his evil genius, all his cunning and
conniving, Butch couldn't quite figure out how best to seize
the ironclad facility—especially its secret golden room
filled with treasure. And then, that morning, like a rare and
beautiful finch flying right into the birdwatcher's palm,
unsolicited and uninvited, I came knocking on Butch's door
with the widow's list.

To Butch—ever the opportunist—it seemed kismet,
like fates aligning, like destiny being written. Me showing
up there that day and mentioning the very nightclub he'd
been casing for months felt to him like the universe
beckoning, calling him to action. And so, as I bared my
soul to him about Samson and my quest to clear my name,
Butch was busy plotting to use me as cloak and cover for
his own agenda. And that afternoon, as I napped on
Butch's futon, he and Eve whispered over the phone and
placed the finishing touches on the devious plan that would
lead us all to this moment.

As Butch recounted all the events that precipitated
the heist, I replayed each second in my mind
simultaneously and was mortified at the elaborate ruse I'd

155

been sucked into unknowingly. I mean, every detail seemed to have been planned out carefully in advance. The cover Butch had assigned me, Miss Clara Wells? Butch had learned from Eve that disguising me as a professional woman would appeal to Mrs. Barrister's snobbish nature and ingratiate me to her quickly. Even the way he'd protested at the sight of ole Milsey when he'd seen her parked there in the lot earlier that night? He'd been planning to steal that Ferrari all along to serve as the perfect getaway car. And I thought about how those two empty seats just so happened to be available at Eve's table despite the jam-packed restaurant, and understood that—unbeknownst to me—they'd already been reserved. Everything I thought to be mere happenstance, pure serendipity, and sheer coincidence had been premeditated and orchestrated, already concocted well beforehand by the criminal prodigy.

And honey, I was fuming mad! But not so much at Butch and his sidekick anymore. I was mad at myself and had turned the blame on yours truly for allowing myself to fall victim to Butch's trickery yet again. I'd been used as a prop, a pawn, a patsy! And it wasn't the first time I had aided and abetted that maniac; I should have known better. When we'd first walked into the Golden Egg and observed such obnoxious wealth, even *I* had contemplated stealing a vase or two when no one was looking.

If my novice mind had dared to venture down that path, I should have known instinctively that Butch's master mind was busy masterminding, plotting, and planning a dangerous ploy of a similar nature. But I believed that Butch was there acting solely as my agent, an ambassador of my will. Surely, he would be on his best behavior.

Surely, he would yield to my needs and place my plight over his own, right? And I thought that even if he *were* hatching some sort of scheme, we were both unarmed and trapped in a secured room that had only one exit, an iron elevator that moved at a snail's pace. I believed not even Butch was crazy enough to try anything under those circumstances, and so I dismissed my trepidations. As usual, I was as wrong as granny's mustache.

"See, that's why I couldn't tell you, 'cause I knew you wouldn't go along wit' it," Butch continued. "Look how square you acted when I borrowed this car!"

"Butch, I had a right to know. I can't believe you played me like this…again!"

"You could barely keep your cover as it was! If I woulda' let you in on everything, them folks woulda' seen right through you!" he pleaded. "I needed you to be legitimately scared. I needed you to be convincing!"

"But what about me, Butch?! What about my needs? I was there for a purpose," I cried, trying to be vague so as to keep Eve in the dark about my deathly secrets, "and we left without me finding out anything! And now I'm in even *more* trouble than when we started, 'cause you got me *robbin'* the damn place!"

"See, that's the best part," Butch said, smirking. "You ain't in no trouble, 'cause you ain't you!"

"What?!"

"You Clara Wells from West Texas," Butch said with a wink, "and as far as anybody knows, Clara Wells was the *victim* of a crime tonight…not the perpetrator!" That gargantuan grin was back, stretching wide across Butch's baby face. "And as for ya' boyfriend…I told you I got plenty info on him. I made sure I did that first. Don't worry. I'll tell you what I found out when we get where we goin'." Butch turned back around.

"See? Everybody wins!" exclaimed Eve from behind the wheel. "I know a guy who'll give me cash for all that jewelry and shit..."

"And we all get to split the money and everything three ways!" Butch added, slapping the dashboard with excitement.

"Don't forget about Curtis and Ralph," Eve corrected.

"Oh yeah, no doubt. We'll give them their cut off the top and divide the rest." And with that, Butch and Eve studied the road ahead while their imaginations went to work, already busy spending the treasure that lay entombed in the trunk of the car.

"Car?"

"Pardon me?" I replied, not understanding the question.

"Do you drive? And do you have access to a reliable vehicle?" she clarified. Her first-floor office faced Peachtree Street, one of Atlanta's main arteries. And as we conversed, I heard the occasional horn from drivers in the near distance and saw frequent pedestrians walking by her window on the sidewalk just outside.

"Yes, and yes," I answered with a smile. "I drive, and I have reliable transportation." The office was bright and beautiful, washed thoroughly in the midday sunshine that poured gratuitously through the many windows. The walls were laden with framed certificates, degrees, and awards, all of which boasted of her success and advanced education.

"Great! And are you willing to travel for work? I assume you have a passport?" she asked, checking off the boxes on her wooden clipboard. Her desk was meticulously organized but filled nonetheless with piles of papers and manila folders. Her beveled glass nameplate read "Meredith Petrucci – Chief Executive Officer," and several rubber stamps sat alongside that fancy nameplate. I imagined that those piles of papers were important documents that awaited her sign-off and consent.

"Yes, I am, and yes, I do," I replied, still smiling. "Ready to travel anywhere. Send me, I'll go!" My foot tapped nervously against the shag carpeting, and I had to pinch the underside of my thigh to keep my leg from shaking.

"Wonderful! Have you ever been convicted of a crime or served time in jail?" She looked at me over her horn-rimmed glasses.

"Absolutely not!" I replied, as if her question were an accusation. Just like the papers on her desk I, too, was hoping to receive her stamp of approval.

"Great! And it says here you have previous sales experience?"

"Yes, I do." I nodded.

"Here at Petrucci Paints"—she removed her glasses and let them dangle from the chain around her neck— "we pride ourselves on achieving customer satisfaction through knowledgeable, courteous, and experienced sales professionals." Her posture shifted as she crossed her legs under the oak desk.

"Yes, I've been in sales nearly all my adult life." It wasn't a lie. I'd been trading and selling for years, but I left out the fact that I myself had been the commodity.

159

"Impressive." She placed her glasses back on the bridge of her nose and lifted my resume close. "You don't seem to list very many former employers," she stated curiously.

"I've been…self-employed for most of my tenure in sales," I explained. "I've managed to become quite successful as an independent contractor," I added to bolster my explanation.

"I see." She examined my application again. "And it says here you studied Business Management at Spellman College? Graduated magna cum laude?"

"Yes, that's right." Okay, now that was a lie, I admit, but I had no choice. Putting my real story on that application would've been like wearing my inmate jumpsuit to the interview, like walking into her office wearing stripes and lugging a ball and chain behind me. This was my sixth interview since my release, and without a college degree—or high school diploma for that matter— I'd been applying for every opening I saw that met my qualifications: box lifter, tree climber, dog walker. I was willing to do anything and everything to turn my life around, but I wasn't even fit for a paper route with the glaring admission of having been a recent ward of the state listed under my name. So, I simply removed that tidbit and resorted to my most cultivated skill: lying.

"So, then, you're familiar with monitoring inventory levels, tracking sales and data trends, markups, discounts, P&Ls, forecasts, projections, supply and demand, and so on? We're really looking for someone who can dive right in." Data trends? P&Ls? Supply and demand? She might as well have been speaking the language of the dolphins. My understanding of sales terms, business jargon, legal mumbo jumbo, and the like had been gleaned from the many men I'd met over the years. On its face, my knowledge in these areas may have seemed solid and sound, but really, it was nothing more than a magician's trick, smoke and mirrors, a bluff. As I sat there nodding yes, the truth was I had no idea what she was talking about. But I figured maybe I'd get at least one paycheck out of this gig before I was fired.

"Well, look no further," I professed with a smile. "I'm your woman!"

"Great!" She fumbled in her desk drawer for a moment and pulled out several papers. "This sounds like a perfect fit. We'll just need you to complete these few simple forms." She slid the papers across the desk to me. "Standard procedure. Nothing out of the ordinary. We just need your consent for a criminal background check, credit check, reference check, and a hair follicle drug test. All our new employees must undergo the vetting process in order to gain access to sensitive data such as our financials and metrics. I'll give you a moment to complete these, and I just need to run and get you a W-4 to complete as well for tax purposes." She rose from the table with a smile. "I'll be just a moment, okay?"

"Sure. Thank you!" I replied as she left the room. I took a moment to thumb through all the documents and read all the legal disclaimers in fine print. Mrs. Petrucci was looking for someone that my past wouldn't allow me to be. She needed an educated, confident sales professional with years of experience and expertise—a real pro. And I lacked all those qualifications. She wanted someone who was willing to travel for work. I was willing, yes, but the conditions of my parole forbade it. She was looking for

161

someone to jump right in, to meet the demands of her growing business, someone who could hit the ground running. And after I climbed out of her office window, that's exactly what I did. My feet hit the pavement, and I took off running down Peachtree Street, vanishing into the bustling crowd, my tears glistening in the afternoon sun.

Ms. Jane had worked out an arrangement with Mr. Tennison for my rent the entire year I was away. And now I owed her *and* him. Ever since I'd been out of jail, I had been leaning on what was left of my credit and trying to build a life by honest means. I met with my parole officer each month, but I was just a name and number to him, a signature on a dotted line, and a paper cup filled with urine. Nothing else about me mattered as far as he was concerned. The state wanted me to stay out of trouble but didn't care to show me how. How could I rise above the stigma of having a criminal record? How could I avoid the biases and prejudices of potential employers? And who would pay my rent while I figured all that out? With no help, no resources, no benefits or cash assistance, I was left to my usual devices, and I turned back to my wicked ways. And it seemed like my problems only begat more problems, misfortune metastasizing like a cancer all throughout my life.

"Butch, I gotta know something," I said, breaking the silence from the backseat.

"What's that?" He turned to me.

"How you get that knife?"

"Huh?" His eyebrows furrowed in confusion.

"That knife in your pocket! The one you held to my neck. I watched the security guards at the front door pat you down. Was they in on it too?" The boy beast laughed as he pulled the knife out again from his inside pocket.

"Nah, they weren't in on it."

"Then how you get that knife?"

"Why you think I ordered that tough ass steak?" the genius replied. "Eve brought it out with the meal, and I pocketed it when we got up from the table. You know I like my meat well done." He turned and stared back at the road ahead, still brandishing the serrated blade. Eve smiled in the rearview mirror, and I rolled my eyes and snarled at her full lips and perfect teeth. But suddenly, her pretty smile disappeared.

"Shit," Eve whispered.

"What is it?" Butch asked from the passenger seat. And before Eve could open her mouth, the flashing lights behind us answered Butch's question. I turned and saw three police cars approaching fast from behind. They must have been stalking us in the darkness, and now they gave chase. Like a pack of ravenous lionesses in the grasslands of the Serengeti, they were pouncing, leaping forward out of the shadows, and moving in for the kill.

CHAPTER 15: A RUN FOR THE MONEY!

"Fuck! What do I do?" Eve shouted from the driver's seat. And suddenly, the sirens began to wail from behind, piercing the night, rippling through the quiet like demon screams, a poltergeist in sound. "What do I do?!" Eve yelled again, both hands gripping the steering wheel like a lifebuoy.

"Put this motherfucka' in overdrive!" Butch commanded. And with that, Eve squeezed that wheel and laid all her weight into the pedal calling forth every bit of that 651-horsepower V-12 fuel injection engine. In just seconds, the speedometer was at 90 and climbing. The squad cars were still hot on our trail as we raced through the darkness, and at this speed, the gentle mist that had filled the air now began to look more like torrential rains hitting the windshield. Eve flipped on the wipers as the speedometer rose to 105.

I looked back again through the rear window, and where there had originally been just three police cars in pursuit, I now counted five—and then six! With our trunk overflowing with the wallets and valuables of bigwigs, dignitaries, and other VIPs, it was no wonder we had the entire Madison City Police Department locking in on us like a pit bull's jaws. Not to mention, there was the ongoing emergency of a one Miss Clara Wells, whose life was still in jeopardy according to all eyewitness accounts. That beautiful young professional was still a hostage of the deranged, knife-wielding, gun-toting madman as far as anyone knew. It dawned on me then that those cops would never stop until they'd lodged a bullet between Butch's eyes and rescued me, the poor damsel in distress, from his evil clutches. And of course, once they freed me, they would soon discover that Clara Wells was a farce and place the *real* me back in jail just as sure as a bean is green! I turned back around to the front and hurried to fasten my seatbelt as I fought off the urge to hyperventilate. I spied the speedometer approaching 130, and it felt like we were taxiing down a runway, preparing for takeoff.

"Faster!" Butch demanded.

"I'm trying!" Eve yelled back. And then she reached over to the dashboard and pressed a button. The button turned red as it engaged, and suddenly the Ferrari's deep purr took on a stereo surround-sound effect, as if there were subwoofers built into the chassis and a microphone under the hood. The flashing lights were still behind us, but as the FF stretched its legs across the road and the speedometer hit 201, it felt like the wheels left the ground, and we took flight. In a matter of moments, the cops that tailed us were just infinitesimal dots in the rearview mirror, and the shrill sirens that once screeched like banshees in the night were now muted by the throaty growl of that powerful engine. It was like I'd been strapped to a rocket, launched like a missile, shot out of a cannon at supersonic speed, Mach 1 and climbing. And as the scenery passed by in blurry indistinct blobs, the road ahead looked as though it were alive, animated, and coming at us, instead of us moving toward it. I was grateful to have eluded the police, but I feared my face would soon melt if we continued at that pace. And as we sped through the countryside, water splattering against the windshield, our tires barely touching that slick black terrain, I knew without doubt that we were three fools tempting death: crash dummies in waiting.

"Slow down," I managed to yell, "before you kill us, girl!" Eve pressed the button again and took her foot off the gas. The magic spell lifted, and the car began to coast. The needle on the speedometer made its slow descent, and I half expected to hear a pilot's voice over intercom announcing our approach. My buttocks were clenched so tight I thought I might hatch a diamond right there in the backseat. And as the speedometer plummeted to a cool 130, I gasped and realized I hadn't been breathing.

"Turn off here," Butch instructed from the passenger seat, and a frazzled Eve applied the brake gently and turned down an intersecting road. This new road looked the same as the last. We passed more trees, more meadows, more fields brimming with tall grass, vast swaths of countryside, herds of cows, and infinite rows of corn. "Turn in here," Butch advised, and Eve slowed and turned into a long, dirt driveway. "Headlights off," Butch added, and Eve reached beyond the steering wheel to manipulate the controls. The headlights went off as we inched up the long dirt path shrouded in blackness. "Alright, now stop," and Eve brought the automobile-turned-rocket to a halt. "We gotta ditch the car," Butch advised as he opened the passenger door and stepped out.

"What?" I protested. "This car just saved our behinds!"

"Get out!" Butch insisted as he pulled the seat forward to allow my exit. As I stepped out of the car, my heels sank into the ground, and I felt the mud rise between my toes. And just then, the night took on a breathtaking lambency as lightning flashed overhead. That brilliant sheet spanned the entire sky, turning night into day for an instant, like God snapping pictures from above, compiling evidence to be used against me later when I stood before the pearly gates.

Eve exited from the driver's side door, and her once lissome, graceful gait was now clumsy and irregular. She stumbled a few steps and vomited into the tall cornfield that abutted the muddy driveway. The mere sound of someone retching in my presence had always made me want to heave right along with them, and so I wrestled against my own inclination to puke. Eve stumbled back toward the car and staggered around the front to join Butch and me on the passenger side. Even by moonlight, I could see that her complexion was now pale and pallid, and as she shoved her lengthy bangs back into a slipshod ponytail, I saw that her forehead was sweatin' up bullets.

The three of us stood there for a moment, quiet as three deaf dogs. And as we each caught our breath, the dense humidity that enveloped us like an atmosphere gave way to a light and gentle drizzle. The rain was cool against my skin, and I knew that refreshing shower was just what the doctor ordered for the ailing Eve. She unfastened a button on her satin dress and took deep breaths of the country air. Meanwhile, Butch opened the passenger door again and reached across the front seats to pop the trunk.

"Come on," Butch whispered, and we followed him to the rear, where all of our plunder stared up at us from inside the car. Butch fiddled inside the trunk for a minute and then slid two bags forward and sat them upright. "Okay…you two each take a bag and untie it. Then go through it and turn off all those cellphones in case we bein' tracked somehow." Eve and I started in on the bags, and Butch stepped back around toward the front of the car, but he didn't stop there. He began ascending the long driveway, walking further toward the massive farmhouse that stood at its end. The night was pitch black, so I couldn't make out much, but between the rain and the steady glow of moonlight in the distance, the silhouette of that old dark house looked ominous and threatening, like a vampire's castle perched on a cliff in the mountains of Transylvania.

"Where you goin?" I whispered loudly.

"Just shut off the phones!" Butch commanded in reply. "I'll be back." Then he turned and walked away, trudging through the gravel and mud. Just then, thunder rolled, and a light breeze began to whisper through the towering cornstalks, pushing the tall plants into a soft sway. I heard wind chimes jingling from somewhere nearby and the rustling of leaves. And it might've been my imagination, but deep in the background of that soundscape, I heard the lingering howl of sirens echoing across the pastures and fields. Lightning flashed again and illuminated the old farmhouse for an instant, and I wondered if the monster named Butch would be any match for the Dracula that might be waiting for him inside.

As Eve and I dug through the bags, I contemplated hitting her upside the head and speeding off in the car to the nearest police station. I would simply tell them the truth and take my chances. If I returned all the money, that would prove my innocence, right? But then I thought about rolling up to the precinct in a stolen car with a trunk full of stolen money and knew that my lazy, apathetic parole officer would have me back in lockup before the ink dried on my statement. I had tangled with the police enough in my lifetime to know that the beginning and middle of the story were inconsequential. It was the bottom line that

168

mattered; all they cared about was the end result. I knew I wouldn't be able to talk or explain my way out of this mess, so I followed Butch's instructions and powered down the cellphones in accordance with the madman's will.

"Can I ask you something?" Eve whispered, stretching one arm deep inside her bag.

"What?" I replied as I fiddled with a phone.

"What's your name?"

I paused and looked at Eve, and it was in that moment I realized that she and I were perfect strangers. I contemplated giving her a fake name, but as I stared into the eyes of my fellow coconspirator, I figured offering an alias would have been inane.

"Samantha," I replied.

"Nice to officially meet you, Sam." She smiled and extended a manicured hand.

"Please don't call me Sam," I replied as I sorted through watches, jewelry, and cash in search of another phone to deactivate.

"Oh, my bad, Samantha." Her hand was still waiting. "My name is actually Evelyn, but I hate that name."

"Why?" I asked as I finally broke down and shook the pretty girl's hand. The color had finally returned to her face.

"I don't know. It's so ordinary. I think Eve is much more fun!"

"Right now, I'd kill for ordinary. Nothing fun about the mess we're in." I sighed.

"Definitely. I think I may start goin' by Evelyn after all this is over." She laughed nervously. "You think we'll be alright? I never imagined goin' to jail. Butch said

169

this would be simple and all I had to do was get you guys inside the Egg and drive the getaway car. He assured me no cops."

"Butch told you what you wanted to hear, girl. If there's one thing I've learned tonight, it's that Butch has revolutionized deceit! That man has turned deception into an art form." I fetched another phone from the bag. "Looking into somebody's eyes and lying right to their damn face is a technique he's innovated so well, he ought to apply for a patent with the U.S. government!" Eve threw her head back in laughter.

"Well, first he needs to grow a brain if he's gonna trademark intellectual property," Eve added, and for two seconds, I actually liked the hussy.

"How'd you get mixed up with him anyway?" I asked, digging through my bag.

"Well," Eve began, "one night, some prick was giving me a real hard time. From the minute he walked in the restaurant, nothing was good enough. He sent back his appetizer…said the pasta salad was too mushy…then it was too al dente. I brought his steak out three times. First it was too rare. Then it was overcooked. Then I brought it out a third time, and he tells me it's perfect…but now he wants fish!" Eve placed a hand on her hip and shifted her weight to one side. "He even sent back the hors d'oeuvres, and shit, they were complimentary!" The anger was just as palpable on Eve's face as her nose, mouth, and eyes; I could tell she was still vexed by the mere memory.

"So," she said with a sigh as she dug back into her bag for the next phone, "he was just really, really mean to me…a real jerk. Butch was sitting at the next table over. I didn't even see him there until he walks over to the guy and

170

whispers something in his ear. And girl, all of a sudden, the guy transforms." Eve smiled as she recalled. "I mean night and day! Suddenly, everything's delicious, and everything's fabulous, and he's complimenting me like I cooked the shit!" Eve laughed. "And after he and his ugly wife leave, I go back to clear the table, and I see that he left me a hundred-dollar tip!"

Eve paused for effect. "So naturally, I go over to Butch and I say, 'Excuse me, sir, but I just gotta know what you said to that guy to get him to be so nice to me.' And Butch goes, 'I told him he betta' act like that food is to die for or I promised him, it would be!' I laughed so hard. And from there, we started talkin' about all the snobs that come through that place, and I started venting about the management and the pay and the hours, and next thing I knew...we were talkin' about what it would take to knock the place over. It was just a joke...or at least it was supposed to be. I never thought he was serious, you know? And when I finally realized that he wasn't playin', it was too late to back out."

"So he threatened you into going along with the plan?" I asked as I deactivated my last phone.

"No, not so much threatened. More like...strongly advised." I understood exactly what Eve was saying by picking up on what she was trying so hard *not* to say. Butch had a way of convincing you to do something in such a manner that you'd think it was your own idea. Or he'd make it sound like a suggestion and not a demand. And he wouldn't outright threaten you, but somehow, you knew you'd better do exactly what he said. Getting reunited with a master manipulator like Butch was the very

171

event to which I credited at least ninety percent of my demise. The other ten percent was me, I'll admit.

Before getting tangled up with Butch back in Tuscaloosa, I'd been a fighter! My heart had been turned into a doormat and trampled beyond repair by Mama and her husband. And yet I'd survived. I'd survived the gut-wrenching agony of being forced to give up my baby. I'd survived Marcus, my junior high school sweetheart who'd played me like a piano, dating me and professing his love, all the while betrothed to another. Even the snares of poverty and homelessness that entangled me from time to time were no match for my spirit down within. Like a fierce rat, I was still alive and breathing on the trap, ready and willing to chew off my own tail if necessary. That's right, I was a fighter, dammit! But Butch's hold on me was just too strong, much too powerful. It seemed inescapable, like a terminal disease, unavoidable as the plague.

Eve continued to rummage through her bag, and watching her there was like gazing back in time and seeing my own self: young, naïve, impetuous and impulsive. I swear it was like looking in a mirror. And just like a real reflection, Eve was repeating after me, doing everything I did, copying my every action: chasing after a lunatic, submitting to his every maniacal whim like a marionette on a string. I feared for that doe-eyed girl and prayed that she would have better luck escaping Butch's tentacles than I'd had, that she'd somehow be able to break the spell that Butch had cast over her life and finally cut the strings. And maybe once she'd succeeded in finding her freedom and broke herself loose, she'd come back like a slave abolitionist and release me from bondage too.

"Y'all done yet?" Butch walked up alongside the car, and Eve and I both jumped ten feet.

"Where you come from, boy?" I asked with a smile as I grabbed my palpitating heart. Underneath my grin, I was wondering how long he'd been lurking there and if he'd heard our conversation.

"You scared me!" Eve added.

"Y'all done, yes or no?" Butch repeated.

"Yeah, I'm done," I said, retying my bag.

"This my last one," said Eve as she placed her final phone back into its sack.

"Good, let's go," Butch commanded as he slammed the trunk shut.

"Go where?" Eve asked.

"The farmer who owns this property invited us in," Butch explained, pointing toward the house.

"And why would he do that? He don't even know us, and it's almost midnight!" I challenged while squinting to read my watch in the moonlight.

"Did you...hurt him?" Eve asked timidly, a suspicious glare in her eye.

"No, I ain't hurt nobody!" Butch contested as if he were truly offended by the outlandish accusation. "I offered him some money. I took one look at this piece-of-shit farm, and I knew his ass could use it!" And with that said, Butch ushered Eve and I up the slippery driveway toward the big, eerie house. The rain fell down in a soft spray, and every few seconds, lightning zigzagged across the sky like an electric eel. My calves became sore as my heels dug into the mud, and the walk to the house seemed like an eternity as I plowed on through the pain.

The house had been dark, but now the first floor was all lit up. And as the bright lights poured out of those large, ranch-style windows, I saw the home's structure for the first time. It was more like a mansion, actually. It was two stories high, and its face was filled with several large windows, each one mounted between a pair of rickety wooden shutters. A plantation-style porch, complete with four large pillars, wrapped around the whole first floor. And the second floor had a large outdoor porch of its own, a big balcony that spanned the entire perimeter of the home's façade. Wooden rocking chairs and rusty swinging benches decorated both porches, and they squeaked softly as the wind rocked them gently to and fro.

As we approached, I caught whiff of the unmistakable smell of manure, and it was then that I noticed the tall barns that sandwiched the house on both sides. A towering silo on one barn and a huge windmill on the other made both edifices seem monumental as they rose to meet the stars. We stepped up onto the enormous porch, and I heard the neighs and whinnies of horses and the deep-bellowed moos of cattle resonating across the property. Butch held the screen door open, and as Eve and I reluctantly entered the mysterious mansion, I trembled at the thought of what horrors might lie within.

CHAPTER 16: TICKLED...TO DEATH...

"Come in," his lips said, but his eyes screamed in terror, like they'd seen a ghost, an apparition from his past floating through the doorway. As I stepped beyond the threshold and into the warmth of the living room, he remained behind the door as if it were a shield, a barrier of protection between us. Immediately I heard the blare of the huge TV that was mounted above the fireplace. A giant in navy blue shorts dribbled a ball across the screen as the camera zoomed in on a stern-faced coach dressed in suit and tie. I, too, was pensive as I stood there in that strange house.

"Take ya' coat?" he yelled over the TV as he finally closed the door. His booming voice was nearly overpowered by the roar of the stadium and the sportscasters who narrated the game with playful banter.

I slipped my coat from my shoulders and handed it to the man. He was tall, maybe six foot two, and in his early thirties. He wore a thin, brown sweater, camel-colored slacks, and leather sandals that showcased his pretty toes. His eyes were almond-shaped and not quite hazel, more of a medium brown. They lay encased on his face behind a chic pair of rectangular, tortoise-print glasses. His skin was the same complexion as mine but had a red hue underneath that made him look sun-kissed and exotic. And even while performing the simple task of hanging my coat on the wrought iron rack, the muscles in his back and shoulders clenched and tightened like a bodybuilder posing before a panel of judges. His hair was long and curly, yet neatly styled atop his head. And as he turned back to face me, I noticed the one lone curl that dangled over his brow just above his glasses, and wondered if perhaps I'd stumbled into the secret lair of a real-life Superman. Instead of Clark Kent, the superhero recluse was posing as a man named Keron and hiding out in the suburbs of Charleston, South Carolina. Just behind him, I noticed several other coats, scarves, and hats resting on the hooks of that coatrack and wondered to whom they belonged.

"You live with somebody?" I asked sheepishly.

"Uh…yeah. I do," Keron replied, and I heard the nervousness in his tenor. "Why don't we take a seat over t'ere." He motioned toward the huge leather sectional sofa that wrapped around the small living room. And for the first time since we'd been talking, I detected a tiny trace of some kind of accent, a slight rhythmic inflection, definitely Caribbean, some place warm and colorful like Jamaica or Antigua perhaps. Maybe Grenada or Saint Lucia? As I stepped toward the couch, I inhaled a bevy of savory spices and scents, and those brilliant aromas drifting from the kitchen confirmed his island heritage with indubitable certainty. "I was just sittin' 'ere watchin' de game…lemme turn dis t'ing down," he said as he lowered the volume on the massive TV with a tiny remote control.

I pretended to look up at the game, but really, I was zeroing in on the photos that lined the mantle below the television. I saw the smiling faces of children at various stages of their development. They all looked familiar, and yet I knew them not.

"Aah…you're so beautiful." Keron leaned in to steal my attention away from the mantle. "You know dat?" He grinned. I rolled my eyes. If only I'd received that kind of validation back when it counted, maybe I wouldn't have sought it so desperately in the eyes and arms of others.

Maybe my life would have turned out differently. Maybe I would have had a chance.

"I look like you," I replied.

"Indeed, you do." He nodded as he reached a hand to my face and pushed the curls away from my eyes. "Indeed, you do. And 'ow is mum?"

"She's fine, I guess. She's back at the hotel," I lied. I'd left Mississippi over a month ago and hadn't spoken to Mama since. And since she and I had scarcely communicated even before my departure, I didn't miss her presence in my life at all. I doubted that she'd posted any signs for me or filed any reports. She probably saw my disappearance as a wish granted, a prayer answered, her luck finally turning around. "I don't remember you," I said as I winced under the strange man's touch.

"I know. You were just a wee chile when I…when I left," he stuttered. "A gyul of maybe two or t'ree years old. You was such a fat little t'ing!" He smiled and laughed with fond recollection. "You 'memba I used to bounce you on me knee for hours. Look meh still got strong calves from all dat liftin' up and down!" He squeezed his leg below the knee. "And you used to run in de room and wek meh soon as de sun rise up and you shout, 'Tickle meh! Tickle meh!' And I tickle you 'til ya' tummy turn red, and you use to laugh so 'ard 'til you pee ya' diaper and da snot roll all down ya' nose!" He laughed. "Aah, gyul…you may not 'memba me, but I never ever forget you!" He smiled, and although I wasn't ready to receive it, I felt his warmth, and it seemed sincere.

"Why did you leave?" I asked. It was my million-dollar question. It was the reason for my journey. I'd left Mama's house with no finite plans, just roaming the world

177

leisurely, dawdling through my existence, lollygagging
toward a purpose. But there was one thing I knew for sure,
even at the tender age of fourteen. I couldn't even begin to
move forward toward the future until I went back to deal
with my past. I'd been without a father for my entire life;
even my earliest memories excluded him. And so, when
I'd seen his handwritten letters and cards and those
unopened packages all addressed to me, my curiosity had
begun to bud and bloom. They had been tucked away in
Mama's armoire, accumulating for years, and ironically
enough, it was Mama's husband who had first shown them
to me, undoubtedly as a ploy to earn my trust and devotion.

"Eh...das a long story, dat one. You doh 'ave de
time for me to tell dat tale, but suffice it to say, me and
your mum wasn't gettin' along and fightin' all de time. De
trut' is," he confessed, "we were bot' way too young when
we brought you into dis worl'...and we got married in a
'urry because de worl' expected it and your mum's family
demanded it. Her and me was nevuh 'appy toget'er, and
afta while, t'ings become 'arder and 'arder between us.
Ya' mum was a good woman, but eh...our timing and
compatibility was all wrong. Understand?"

"Why didn't you take me with you?"

"Oh, chile, de way you clung to your mum and
carry on so, you nevuh would 'ave come back 'ome wit'
me." He laughed.

"Back home?"

"You ever 'ear of Trinidad and Tobago?" I nodded.
"I was born on de sista' isle of Tobago way out in de bush,"
he began. "And afta' me and ya' mum split, I went back
'ome to regroup and clear me 'ead. No place for a little
babe like you gyul. Back 'ome, we used to fish in de ocean

and dig for crabs err' day just so to eat. And for fun, we used to build cages for hours from vine and sticks and lure de kiskadees inside. We catch dem and play wit' dem and turn dem loose to watch dem fly. We climbed trees and shake de branches and eat sweet mango and sour plum and suck on chenet 'til our stomachs 'urt so bad." He laughed. "And we swam wit de dolphins and sharks and stingrays. We didn't 'ave no TV or video game like 'ere in dis country." He pointed at the big screen on the wall. "We made pets from goats and snakes...and shoot, gyul ...you used to run from de 'ousecat... No way in de worl' you wan' live 'round all dat wildlife!" He laughed again and placed his arm around my shoulder.

"How come you never came to see me? Not one visit my whole life."

"Yeah, I sorry fuh dat. Even afta I come back to de states, I never lost touch wit' your mum, because I always wanted to know you were okay, but your mum didn't want me to be in and out ya' life. She tole me she say, 'Keron!'" He wagged his finger as he imitated Mama, "'Eit'er stay in her life or stay out! You come, or you go! No in between!' So, I respect her wishes. I sent you birt'day cards and Christmas gifts and random letters 'ere and t'ere. I dunno if she give dem to ya' or no, but I try me best. To be honest, I'm surprised your mum bring you all de way up 'ere to see me...alt'ough I'm not surprised she choose to stay in de 'otel. I guess she still never forgive meh."

I hadn't had a home-cooked meal in weeks, and as I sat there on the plush couch, inhaling the celestial aromas of dinner in the making, my stomach called out loudly in a desperate whine.

"Ya' 'ungry? I 'ope ya' stay fuh lunch," he offered.
I knew that he'd heard my empty stomach growling, and I
blushed with embarrassment. But just as my stomach had
outed me, his eyes were busy exposing him. Ten minutes
ago, he'd had no idea I was in town and no idea I would be
stopping over. I'd called him from a payphone on the
corner and invited myself there that evening. I could tell
from the look on his face that his offer for me to stay and
eat was merely a polite gesture, and as his brows furrowed
and his jaws clenched tightly, I knew he was praying that
I'd decline.

"Yes, I'll stay," I agreed in defiance, and he
swallowed his misgivings in a deep gulp. "But it's almost
six o'clock. Time for dinner, not lunch," I corrected.

"No, no," the man named Keron said with a smile.
"It's suppa', but on Sundee, we 'ave what we call Sundee
lunch."

"What's that?" I asked.

"Ahh, gyul, ya' in fuh a treat!" His arm was still
wrapped around me, and he squeezed my shoulder tightly.
"Imagine a feast of stewed chicken, provision and
dumplin', black-eyed peas, callaloo, white rice and pelau,"
he said, his eyes lighting up as he rattled off the menu,
"macaroni pie, potato salad, coo-coo, plantain, and soft-
shelled crab." I had no idea what half those dishes were,
but the saliva rose beneath my tongue, and my mouth
watered nonetheless. "And t'ere is mauby and swee' drink
and, for dessert, chocolate biscuits and chip chip!"

"We?"

"Huh?" He cocked his head curiously.

"You said *we* have Sunday lunch. Who is we?"

180

"Ahh…just me wife…and kids." He paused to gauge my reaction.

"You're married?" I asked, fidgeting with my hands.

"Ten years dis June."

"And so I have siblings?"

"Yes, I 'ave one son and t'ree daughters…including you." He poked my chest playfully as he boasted with pride. Then he did something I hadn't counted on. He squeezed my shoulder again, leaned in, and kissed my forehead. As his lips lingered on my skin and his strong arm hugged me tightly, I felt like an old appliance. After years of dormancy, I had suddenly been plugged in, and now I was no longer dysfunctional. All the lost years of love and affection came pouring into me like an electric current, filling vacancies inside me that hadn't been inhabited in a million forevers. I felt like I'd tapped into an endless power supply, an infinite storehouse of care and concern, like I'd hit the jackpot and won myself a father. "Would you like to meet me wife now?"

"Yes…Daddy," I replied. He kissed me again, and we rose from the couch together, hand in hand. He led me out of the living room, past the staircase, and through the dining room, where a big round table was stylishly set. As we moved through the little house, I couldn't help but imagine myself as a permanent fixture there: descending those steps each morning for school, doing my homework at that dining room table before Daddy made me push my books aside for dinner. I imagined movie nights in front of that giant TV and falling asleep in my daddy's arms on that big leather sofa. We continued to follow our noses through the house, summoned by the fragrance of that home-cooked meal, and as I spied the huge backyard through a window on the way, I was so glad that I'd made the desperate journey north to find my father and to seek out the alternate life that had been waiting for me all along.

Within moments, we arrived at the kitchen, where a woman stood in front of the stove with her back to us. The kitchen was large but narrow, and both sides of the space were lined with lengthy counters and tall oak cabinets. The lively sounds of soca music poured from a little radio that sat on the windowsill just above the stove, and Keron's wife danced and sang along to those island anthems as she stirred her pots to the rhythm.

"Babe, we 'ave a visitor," Keron announced. She looked back over her shoulder and saw me there, and I could see the look of wonder all across her face.

She turned her body to face me, and I was in immediate awe of her magnificence. Her complexion was the color of a fresh pot of coffee, dark and rich. Her skin was smooth and shiny, like patent leather, and when she smiled at me, her teeth looked milky white there between her full red lips. A small gap between her two front teeth added a warmth to her smile that made me want to hug the beautiful stranger. She wore a long and colorful homemade dress that was loose and flowing, as though she were draped and wrapped in light, yet luxurious fabrics: reds and yellows, oranges and blues. The ceiling fan that spun above our heads blew its gentle breeze against her gorgeous garb and made her look magnanimous there, like a pheasant in flight.

"Well, aren't you a pretty one?" she extoled, spoon in hand. Her smile was so bright it could've had a wattage. "And 'oo might you be, me dear?" I looked to Keron to make the introductions; suddenly I wasn't sure just who I was.

"Sam, I wan' you to meet me wife, Dinelle." He motioned toward the model-in-residence. "Dinelle, dis 'ere is Sam…me daughter." The smile fell from her face like it had been shot down by friendly fire. And in its place, a look of shock and betrayal overtook her. She waved the wooden spoon like a flyswatter as she digested Keron's words.

"Daughter?" the beautiful woman repeated, drops of sauce flying from the spoon in all directions. "Daughter?!" she exclaimed again in disbelief. "Ya' never temme 'bout no daughter? How ole dis gyul?" She looked at me like I was a dead mouse, disgust and repulsion now gracing her face where all the beauty had been.

"Dis gyul…is fourteen!" I retorted, sticking out my tongue as punctuation.

"Ooh! And her got a big fresh mout' too!" Somehow, her hands managed to find her hips under all those layers of fabric. "Where de 'ell she come from all of a sudden?" She pointed the spoon at me. "And wuh her doin' 'ere in me 'ouse?" she demanded of Keron.

"Calm ya'self, woman!" Keron shouted back. "I tole ya' meh got a daughter from me fuss wife! I tole ya 'bout her err' time meh send a card in de post!"

"Him say he sendin' a letta' in de post to Sam," Dinelle explained to me, pointing the spoon at Keron now. "Him no say Sam is a gyul. And him nevuh say you his chile!" Dinelle insisted.

"Well, now ya' know! Set anot'a place at de table!" Keron shouted back.

"Ya' wan' dis gyul break bread at me table?! Right 'long side me chi'ren?!" Dinelle gasped at the thought. "First ya' horn 'round and cheat on meh wit' dat gyul Vanessa…and now dis chile come outta nowhere…eyes like you!" She pointed the spoon at Keron like a sword.

"Not in front of de chile!" Keron cried, trying to silence his wife and keep his indiscretions discreet.

"Oh? You doh wan' dis gyul to hear de trut'? You wan' make style and show off for dis gyul and pretend like you so good?" Then she turned to me. "Lemme tell ya' 'bout *Caren*! And *Wendy*! And *Simone*!" she yelled. "Him say Lisa jus' a friend from wuk, den meh wek up in de night and him keys dem gone. Meh pack up de babies and drive 'round 'til meh catch him comin' out de gyul 'ouse at t'ree in de mornin'…and her standin' in de doorway nekkid as de day she born!"

"Dinelle!" Keron warned again.

"Him cyaan be trusted!" she continued. "A liar straight down to de bone! When his mout' closed he keepin' secrets…and when it open…him doh temme not'ing but lies!"

"Dinelle!" Keron shouted.

"How many more bastard chi'ren you got out t'ere in de worl', huh?" Dinelle demanded. "Ten? Twenty?!"

"She de only one!" Keron confirmed.

"Aah, Lawd'a'mercy!" Dinelle exclaimed. "Meh so vex make meh feel to cry!" Then she slumped over the countertop, buried her face in her arm, and wept into her colorful dress as if it were a giant handkerchief.

"Eh, quit dem tears now!" Keron shouted as his wife sobbed softly. "Ya' embarrass meh in front of me chile. Now set anot'a place at de table, and doh give meh

184

no back chat now, ya' 'ear!" And with that, Dinelle lifted her head slightly and aimed one eye at Keron. That scowling glare pierced so deeply, I was afraid that not even my Superman could withstand such a razor-sharp gaze.

"You wan' meh make plate?!" She slammed the wooden spoon down on the granite countertop and dashed over to the opposite counter, where several covered platters were neatly arranged.

"Wha' you doin', woman?!" Keron called out as Dinelle ripped off the lids and tossed the contents wildly onto the linoleum floor.

"You wan' meh make plate?!" She dumped another platter out into a heap on the floor.

"You gwyne mad?! Stop!! Wha' ya' doin?" Keron shouted at his hysterical wife.

"He ya go!!" She dumped another container and another and another until the countertop was bare. Then she raced over to the stove, where several pots were simmering.

"Doh you dare!" Keron warned as Dinelle lifted one large pot high above her head.

"Ya wan' summore? He ya go!!" she yelled as the scalding hot contents splatted on the floor and the pot bounced and rolled in our direction. Then she emptied another pot and another and another until the stovetop was bare save for the flames that still flickered from where the pots had been resting.

"Calm ya'self! Before I call de people on ya'! Ready to be fit for a straightjacket!" Keron shouted as his wife snatched a pair of red oven mitts down off the wall beside the stove, put them on, and pulled the oven door open like a drawbridge. "No! Doh do it!" Keron pleaded.

But Dinelle's rage was in no mood for negotiations. She reached in the oven and yanked out the huge roaster that lay within.

"You wan' her to eat? You wan' dis gyul be part of de family?!" She tossed the roaster up in the air, and everything in it rained down onto the floor like soggy confetti. "He ya go!! She can eat off de floor like de family dog!" Then she collapsed in front of the stove and wept, the piping hot feast littering the ground between us like an uncrossable moat.

"Get up now! Ya' actin' like a damn fool!" Keron shouted again. And Dinelle jumped to her feet once more, snatched the little radio from the windowsill, and hurled it at his head. Fortunately for Keron, she'd forgotten to unplug it, and before it could reach his handsome face, the cord became taut, and the radio fell to the floor, where it smashed into bits. The music stopped at once, and Dinelle collapsed again to the floor. Keron and I stood there in the doorway, petrified like a pair of window mannequins.

"Umm," he leaned in and whispered, "maybe I just make you a sandwich to go, eh?" We backed out of the kitchen slowly and walked back toward the living room as the sounds of Dinelle's mournful cries soared through the small house like the bird she resembled. As we walked, Keron placed his strong arm on my shoulder again. "Doh pay her no mind," he said. "She be okay in a few minutes...or days...couple years at de most." He laughed nervously and scratched his head.

I wanted to laugh it all off too, but while still in earshot of Dinelle's doleful bellows, I just couldn't find the humor. Never had anyone expressed their disdain for me so outright. My own mother had been the queen of

186

passive-aggressiveness, expertly exhibiting a non-violent resistance toward me that was pervasive and difficult to pinpoint. She could make me feel like trash just by the manner in which she said hello. And, conversely, she could make me crumble to pieces like stale bread simply by not saying hello at all. Even the unspoken words between us were loaded with antipathy, pregnant with friction and animosity.

Meanwhile, my new stepmom had shown a whole new brand of hatred, a whole new level of contempt. The bitterness she'd displayed for me that day could have made a lemon seem sweet. I didn't have to speculate on how she felt, because she'd left nothing to the imagination. She loathed the very sight of me, and even though I'd already left the kitchen, the lingering thought of me made her writhe in pain, sick with despair. My existence preceded their relationship, but, to Dinelle, I was still nothing more than a reminder of her husband's infidelities, secrets, and lies. Unable to ignore those haunting memories, she chose to ignore *me* instead, to erase me like words from a page, to scribble my existence from the face of the earth. And so, for me, this was no laughing matter. The only thing hysterical that day was Dinelle's inconsolable cry.

"Ahh, yes!" Keron exclaimed as we ambled back into the little living room. "Let's 'ave a seat and enjoy de rest of de game, okay?" But before our behinds could hit the couch, they came running.

"Daddy, wus wrong wit' Mommy?" asked the tallest of the little girls.

"She cryin' like crazy!" added the boy as he leapt into the room.

"I'm hungry," offered the youngest girl, obviously indifferent to her mother's suffering. All three of them seemed to notice me at the same time.

"Who she?" asked the youngest girl as she grabbed my hand without qualm or hesitation. Almost instantly, there was a connection between us, her palm fitting perfectly within mine like two pieces of a jigsaw puzzle.

"Kids, dis 'ere is Daddy's friend Sam." He pointed at me. "She stopped by to say 'ello to me and your mum, but now she gwyne back 'ome. Say 'ello," he instructed.

"Hi," they all said together in a monotone unison. *Daddy's friend Sam*, I repeated in my mind. I suppose that in light of his wife's reaction to my presence, he didn't want to risk having a repeat performance by his children. And so, in less than a half-hour's time, I had been promoted, demoted, and now relegated to mere friend. For a moment, I'd had a father, a new mother, a brother, and two sisters, but the sands quickly drained from the hourglass, the spell wore off, and my life turned back into a pumpkin.

Keron, my daddy twice removed, pulled a few bills from his wallet, thirty-seven dollars to be exact, and handed them to me. "I'll grab ya' coat." He hurried over to the rack. The three kids stared at me, and I stared back at them. We were in a kind of eerie standoff, like two territorial yet skittish groups of alley cats, each one waiting for the other to make a move.

"She look familiar," said the little boy.

"Ain't we seen you somewhere before?" asked the tallest of the girls. Meanwhile, the youngest continued to squeeze my hand as she swung from it like a vine. I wanted to inform them all that what they perceived to be a familiar connection was actually a *familial* connection, but before I could part my lips, Superman draped my coat over my shoulders like one of his own capes and nudged me toward the door. But I refused to budge. I planted my feet firmly there like the roots of a thousand-year-old tree. Somehow, I knew I'd never see any of them again, and at the very least, I just had to know one thing.

"Wus y'all names?" I asked the bunch.

"Come now, Sam. You should get going before it gets dark." Keron tugged at my shoulder again.

"Wus y'all names?" I asked again, refusing to be moved.

"I'm Amber!" shouted the little one, who climbed my leg like a koala. "I'm five and a half years old, and I'm in kinneygarden!" she added with excitement.

"I'm Shawn!" shouted the boy. "I'm seven!" He smiled with a wave.

"Gettin' late, Sam. Your mum will be worried sick!" Keron nearly shouted.

"I'm Samantha," said the oldest girl. "I'm eight."

"Samantha?" I repeated.

"Yeah. Just like your name except with an A-N-T-H-A on the end. Samantha!" She smiled like a spelling bee contestant. Suddenly, I felt a cool breeze against my back and looked over my shoulder to find the front door wide open.

"Say goodbye, kids," Keron commanded.

"Bye." They waved all at once. And in that moment, as I trudged toward the door, I died. I died and became the ghost that Keron had seen when I'd first arrived. That little girl had spelled out the letters of her name and pronounced me dead. And what an unremarkable death it was. Like the blowing out of a match. So quick and unceremonious. My corpse was still warm to the touch, and yet I'd already been replaced. The world never paused to grieve. There was no moment of silence. Life just carried on without me; the Earth continued to spin. There was no inconsolable mother throwing herself at my casket. No father to curse and plead with God. No child to carry on my values and beliefs. I died without a legacy, minus any mourning. No reminiscence, no solemn retrospection, no warm recollections. There was shamefully little memory of me left in the world.

I'd been wondering how my father could bear my absence, how he could live so long without his once-treasured little girl, and now it was all clear. He'd simply given my name to his next child, thereby overwriting my existence like a computer file, exchanging the obsolete for the new and improved. Despite all the hugs and kisses bestowed upon me that day, he hadn't missed me at all. The cards and letters over the years had only been empty gestures, just like his reluctant invitation for Sunday lunch. And I knew they were empty gestures, because they were empty! Never once had he sent any money. Never had he even tried to contribute to my well-being. Just the occasional Christmas gift plucked from the bargain bin of the dollar store. Love on clearance, discounted as defective.

Mama and I had been living hand to mouth for most of my life, and I had been bagging groceries after school for months. Every week, we struggled to keep the lights on and the cold out. And meanwhile, my father and his new family had been tucked away in suburbia in that quaint little house with big screen TVs and a satellite dish, feasting every week while I was busy starving. And if that weren't bad enough, my trip to Charleston had also revealed to me that my papa wasn't just a rolling stone. He was a falling rock, squashing the hearts of women everywhere. And now I was just one more casualty, the latest entry on his list of forlorn loves. I felt naïve for placing so much hope in a dream. I felt foolish for allowing myself to receive those counterfeit kisses, all those hollow hugs. And I felt stupid for opening my ears and heart to those romantic words, spoken in pity and falsely altruistic, Keron proudly thinking he was doing me a favor, performing some great service, by whispering lies.

"Bye, Sam," Keron mumbled as I walked by. Each heavy footfall felt like yet another stride in my own funeral march.

"Please." I paused to look him in the eye one last time. "Don't call me Sam."

As I left that house and the door slammed against my back, I stepped into the afterlife, the hereafter, the great beyond. And nearly a decade and a half later, as Butch, Eve, and I stepped inside that ghostly manor, I was unchanged, still a zombie, wandering mindlessly, haunting the living, and drifting eternally from one hell to the next.

CHAPTER 17: WHO?

As we stood in the doorway with the light rain behind us, there was a sudden blast of thunder. And with it, almost concurrently, lightning ripped through the darkness, puncturing the night like a jagged-edged sword. Butch, Eve, and I were each jolted out of our skins for a moment, and Eve cupped her mouth to keep from screaming. The moon was so bright it looked almost sunny floating there. But as soon as those dense clouds scurried by and began to swathe that big white rock in blackness, the fulgent moon disappeared altogether, swallowed whole by a starless night. The hurricane had been fairly calm the last few hours, sprinkling only light rains here and there, but now, Francine seemed to be emerging from a siesta and rearing her head again. I hurried to shut the door on her grisly face.

The ceilings of that grand foyer had to be at least thirty feet high, and orbiting smack dab in the middle was a dimly lit chandelier. Just about all of its bulbs were blown except for a handful. Every time lightning flashed outside, those last few remaining orbs would flicker wildly like a candle at the end of its wick, like flames in the wind sputtering on the brink of extinction. And the whole house would turn pitch-black for an instant as electricity surged across the heavens and down through the home's antiquated wiring. A slight draft blew through the empty room and sent a chill running up my spine. That quiet breeze, together with the intermittent moments of darkness, made me feel as though the old house were on life support, breathing shallowly and blinking at us tearfully, dying right before our very eyes.

Just beyond the front entrance, two spiraling staircases, one on the left and one on the right, rose up and around to meet in the center of the second floor, perfectly symmetrical. Aside from the chandelier that dangled lifelessly there like a noose and corpse, several small metal sconces mounted all throughout the room offered their own little bit of brilliance to the glow of that stately space.

At first glance, the old mansion seemed to be fairly well cared for and preserved, but as soon as I took my first step inside, the chips in the wooden staircase begged to differ, as did the brown mold in the crown moldings, and the cracks in the striped wallpaper. I could tell that at one time, that grand space had been elegant and alluring, probably the venue for dozens of cotillions, cocktail parties, and other country gatherings. But over the years, the dignified home had fallen gradually into disrepair, a victim of age and the changing times.

All of a sudden, I was overcome with the eerie notion that we were being watched. That's when I noticed that even though the three of us stood there alone, there were eyes all around: a dozen or so oversized oil paintings and sepia-colored photographs displayed all throughout, portrait after portrait of grim, unsmiling faces. They seemed to spy us with indifference, unimpressed with our presence there.

"This way," Butch directed. And suddenly, thunder crashed, and the house blinked its eyes again, the lights turning off and on in a split second. Eve and I huddled close as we followed Butch from the foyer further on through the cavernous house. First, we passed through a dining room. A long table spanned the entire length of the room, and I counted about twenty place settings as we passed. And all along the walls of that great hall were several stuffed heads, everything from bears to boars, all groomed and mounted there like a shrine to death, equal parts museum and morgue. Thunder rolled, the lights dimmed, and the whole house trembled. I, too, was shaken deep down within. Between the dead people in those paintings back in the foyer and the dead animals along the walls of the dining room, I wondered if anybody ever made it out of that house alive.

As we continued on to the next adjoining room, I couldn't help but question how somebody could love animals enough to raise and care for them in the barns outside and hate them enough to slaughter them and hang their lifeless heads on the walls inside. And I struggled to imagine what sort of sadistic soul could sit down to enjoy a meal there at that long table while staring directly into the cold, dark eyes of the very animal whose flesh they were devouring. As I contemplated all those duplicities, I considered a life as a vegetarian.

Just beyond the dining room was a grand sitting room with several couches, tables, and chairs. A tall grandfather clock stood in one corner of the room, and its pendulum squeaked softly as it swung laggardly from side to side. The second hand on that old clock moved with such a latency that every tick seemed like it might be the last, and I suspected that time was on the verge of standing still. And seeing all the vintage fixtures, old-fashioned furniture, and dusty antiques scattered all around the room only served to bolster my suspicions.

One entire wall of the room had bookshelves built right into it, and those dusty volumes rose from the oriental rugs all the way to the vaulted ceiling. The clusters of cobwebs on some books were so thick you would've thought the spiders spent all their days reading. A rolling ladder leaned against the bookcase, allowing for easy access to the upper stacks. The focal point of the room, however, was an enormous fireplace right in the center, where I imagined guests once gathered close around its warmth to imbibe cocoa and hot toddies during the winter's harshest months. Now, that hearth was cold and dark and bereft of life, save for the spiders who spun their webs amidst the dust and soot. A large tapestry was displayed directly above, and embroidered on it in big cursive letters were the words "Leave Your Worries at the Door." Try as though I might, I found that commandment impossible to obey.

"Howdy!" he called, and suddenly the room went dark. Thunder crashed down outside with such percussive clatter I might've believed it was raining grenades. When the home's slow blink was over and the lights were restored, I saw him sitting there for the first time. "Come on in!" the old man beckoned from his big chair. He smiled wide, and I swear there were more eyes on his face than there were teeth in his mouth. The chair he sat in was just about as dingy as he was, and had he not spoken, he could have remained camouflaged there in filth. He wore a set of stained long underwear: two pieces, a top and bottom. And the cotton knickers were held up by a garish pair of rainbow suspenders. His gut hung over his waistband and rested on his thighs like a sleeping babe.

But aside from his swollen belly, amazingly, the rest of him was thin, withered, and emaciated.

His hands rested comfortably on his thin thighs, and I did a double take at the sight of his fingernails. They were long, curved, and pointed at the ends, like the talons of a bird of prey. As I stared at those frightful fingers, I cringed at the thought of what shape the old man's *toes* must've been in. Toenails so long, the poor thing could probably climb a tree with no hands!

"Welcome, welcome!" he greeted us again gleefully as we inched near. A long wispy beard extended from his chin all the way down to his stomach, and the gray hair on his head was longer than Eve's and mine combined. It draped over his shoulders like an old shawl. "Get a load'a you!" He looked Eve up and down like she was a used car up for auction. "What's your name, sweet thang?" he gummed.

"Her name is Angie," I interjected before foolish Eve had the chance to give the old man her real name.

"Angie? Dat dare shole is a perdy name. I used to call my third wife Angie," the old man reminisced. "Too bad her name was Louise." He wheezed out a hearty laugh that culminated in a nasty, wet cough. "Angie," he added between hacks, "was her sister!" He laughed again. And when his laughter waned, he squinted at me like I was a fresh cut of meat in the butcher's window, a collection of breasts, legs, and thighs. "Mmm..." He licked his lips. "And what about you, suga'? What they call you?"

"I'm Maria," I tendered with a curtsy and a smile.

"That name fits you like a glove, darlin'." He nodded his head greedily, as if someone had just offered him a second helping of his favorite meal. "You make a

196

fella' wanna whisk you away and Maria! Get it? Marry ya'?" he clarified before exploding into another fit of wild laughter. Then he erupted into a fit of wild coughing that made me wonder if I would be witnessing *two* deaths that week.

"Angie and Maria," he said with a sigh as his coughs subsided, "you gals got to be the finest negresses I've ever seen."

"Negresses?!" Eve and I repeated together.

Then the old man leaned in and whispered. "I always had me a thang for car'mel." He stuck out his tongue and flicked it like a snake, wagging it up and down and back and forth, like the tail of a dog at dinnertime, simulating the intimate act of cunnilingus. With his mouth there all agape, a putrid odor passed over his gums and filled the space between us with such a pungency, I believed a skunk nearby would have abdicated from the animal kingdom and relinquished its stripe willingly to that smelly old man.

Just then, I noticed the nearly empty bottle of bourbon on the console table beside his chair. He had downed just about an entire fifth all by himself. And honey, Jim Beam saved his life that night. The only thing that kept me from wringing his scrawny neck like a wet rag—other than the fact that I preferred not to touch him— was my realization that the old man had consumed more fluids than a drowning victim, and now he was higher than a giraffe's ass!

"Is this what becomes of Santa during the off-peak seasons?" Eve whispered in my ear, pointing at the bearded, big-bellied, belligerent old drunk, and she and I

197

laughed out loud, trying to contain our giggles with our hands like two schoolgirls.

"You gals find somethin' funny?" the old man asked, his voice dropping an octave.

"Sorry for laughing, sir." Eve placed a hand over her heart to demonstrate her sincerity. "You just have such a wonderful sense of humor." She smiled.

"Where you say you keep the keys?" Butch interrupted, stealing the old man's attention.

"Over yonder...on the hook in the kitchen." The old man pointed.

"This nice gentleman just sold us a new ride, since our car broke down on the side of the road." Butch winked. "Y'all stay here and keep him company while I check out the truck."

"I promise to take real good care of these lil' fillies while you're gone, Jerome," the old man vowed. "Scout's honor!" he added, saluting Butch like a soldier. The veins in his hand looked like a cluster of roadways on a topographical map, and again, I winced at the sight of his fingernails. They made his hand look grotesquely long and misshapen, like the roots of a dead tree dug up by storm. "Sit, sit!" the old man insisted as Butch left the room. Eve and I each staked out a place to sit that wasn't covered in dust. The old man must have seen our hesitancy. "Plenty room on my lap," he invited with a lecherous laugh.

"You're so funny." Eve waved at the old man, dismissing his remarks playfully. "I appreciate a gentleman who can make me laugh." She smiled.

"You know what? Why don't I leave you two lovebirds alone, and you can get to know Angie a lil' bit while I help...uh...Jerome with the truck," I suggested.

And before either one of them could object, I excused myself to find Butch.

"Looks like ya' got me all to ya'self, kiddo," I heard the old man say to Eve as I left the sitting room and passed into the kitchen. "I bet that was your plan all along." He hacked out another violent laugh that sounded painful to my ears, wheezing, hissing, whistling, and screeching like a freight train coming to a grinding halt.

The kitchen was enormous, and I imagined that in its heyday, it had been home to at least a half-dozen cooks and wait staff all hustling and bustling to get affairs in order and dinner on the table. One wall contained a dumbwaiter's shaft. And as if that wasn't luxury enough, I spied a spiraling butler's staircase in the back of the kitchen, where I imagined trays filled with treats were served to the residents at their bedsides—room service at its finest. Along the walls of the kitchen were several hutches filled with china, glasses, candelabras, votives, teapots and pitchers, platters and plates. The dust on them was visible from clear across the room and made me want to sneeze just looking. And dangling above the island in the center of the kitchen was a hanging pot rack that showcased a plethora of stainless steel cookware and utensils. As I passed underneath, I could see the cocoon of cobwebs that swallowed those pots whole like a slow-moving fungus.

Walking through that kitchen, I felt like an archeologist beholding the remarkably preserved ruins of an ancient civilization, like a paleontologist standing inside the giant footprint of a woolly mammoth. I was amazed at the history in the room, and a little bit of sadness descended upon me as I beheld the soulless space. Once bourgeoning with life and activity, once teeming with voices and commotion, it was now extinct, defunct, and silent, rendered useless by Father Time.

But then, as I passed my own reflection in the glass of one of those china cabinets, I began to imagine myself standing in that kitchen just fifty short years ago, and I knew that I would have never been on the receiving end of all those services being performed on that plantation. I wouldn't have been one of the ones sitting at that long dinner table in the dining room sampling those elegant entrees. I wouldn't have been the one descending those fancy front stairs to present myself at parties, the one dancing around the foyer hobnobbing with the guests. No, honey. I wouldn't have been the one being woken up to breakfast in bed. I would've been the one doing the waking! I would've been the one polishing those pots and pans to a high shine and rubbing down the saddles out back with oil and wax. Reality slapped me like a scorned lover, and I realized that my station in that home would not have been as one of the hosts, but as one of the help! My black skin would have relegated me to being just another "negress", and the more I thought about it, the more I wanted to light a match to that godforsaken place and dance around the flames like a cavewoman.

I looked out the kitchen window, and aside from the wind and rain that raged all across the farm, I saw Butch's silhouette heading into one of the barns. I took a deep breath and braced myself before opening the back door and following him into the storm. The rain pounded riotously, pummeling me on all sides like a vengeful mob. By the time I made it to the barn, I looked like a corpse that had just washed ashore, my hair soaking wet, my dress heavy and clinging to my skin. The wind had stolen my breath, and I found myself doubled over in the doorway like I'd just run a mile.

I stepped cautiously inside the dank, dark barn. Several gooseneck lanterns fitted with low-wattage bulbs were affixed along the walls, but their dull output was nearly powerless against the darkness of the night. Through the shadows, I was able to make out two aisles on either side of the barn, and both were lined with rows of stalls and pens. About a dozen loose chickens squawked and squabbled as they chased one another through the barn. Those were the only animals I could see, but I heard clearly the snorting and nickering of horses in the near distance, obviously nervous and agitated by the raging storm.

Lightning flashed and illuminated the big barn for an instant. It was then that I noticed there were several large troughs all around, overflowing with water and filled to the brim with animal feed. And I saw endless bales of hay stacked high against the walls. The barn had a second level that circled overhead like an interior balcony, accessible only by tall ladders leaning all throughout the space. That upper loft served as a mow and was stocked with additional hay bales and large bags of grain and feed.

As my gaze panned over the barn's mezzanine and up into the rafters, I noticed a pair of eyes staring back at me. They were pensive and untrusting, like a gumshoe detective, cold and interrogative. I froze. As I squinted to see who those eyes belonged to, the stranger in the rafters returned my question, asking, "Who?" It was then that I realized those were the big gray eyes of a big gray barn owl. "Who?" it asked again, and I exhaled a sigh of relief. As I stepped further inside the old barn, hay crunching beneath the soles of my feet, the feathered detective zeroed in on me with his private eyes and watched my every move from above, blinking its big eyeballs like shutters and recording my every action like an aerial surveillance camera.

I heard noises and shuffling and followed my ears down the leftmost aisle. And after traveling a few yards, I made out an indistinct mass among the shadows along one of the walls of the barn. Butch stood in front of it, and he made a swift yanking motion that caused specks of dirt and hay to kick up into the air. I covered my eyes momentarily until the particles settled, and once they did, I fixed my eyes on the old brown pick-up truck that Butch had unveiled. The truck looked so rusty and worn beneath the dull lanterns, it made my Milsey seem like a Formula One racecar in comparison.

"I thought I told you to stay inside and keep the old man company," Butch chastised as he noticed me panting there. I was breathing deeply, still trying to catch my breath. But as I inhaled the sickening stench of manure, amplified so close to the source, I considered holding my breath and asphyxiating myself to death as a far more favorable alternative.

"Eve can handle the old man by herself. Shit, she deal wit' drunks for a living, don't she?" I rebutted. "Besides," I added as I stepped closer, "you said you would tell me what you knew about Samson when we got where we goin'. Well…we here. Lay it on me. Who was he?"

Butch sighed as he circled the ancient automobile, "Well, first I started by showin' ya boyfriend's picture around, but I had to stop that quick. You woulda' thought I pulled a rattlesnake outta' my pocket the way folks was gaspin'." Butch laughed as he recalled. "Just the mention of that dude's name made people jump up from the tables."

"Oh no, I knew it! He was some kind of gangster, wasn't he?" I cringed.

"Nah. Nothin' like that. He was a nice enough guy."

"Then what are you talkin' about? People jumpin' up from the tables and gaspin' why?"

"Well, I'll put it to ya' like this...I found out there's at least one chick that ain't at all attracted to this pretty boy," Butch said with a chuckle as he pulled Samson's photo from the breast pocket of his blazer.

"Who's that?" I asked, taking the photo back.

"Lady Luck."

"Huh?"

"Ya' boyfriend is bad luck, Mantha. If you tripped over a black cat and broke a mirror while walkin' backwards under a ladder on Friday the thirteenth, you'd still have a better chance of hittin' the Powerball than ole boy here." Butch laughed, pointing to the photo I held in my hands. "He had a reputation for being toxic at the table, man. Everything he touched turned to shit. If that fool bet on black, the wheel would pump out red all night...like a doggone blood bank. The only way he could win at blackjack is if they changed the rules to twenty-five." He laughed again. "And at the craps table? Shit. He got more snake eyes than the reptile exhibit over at Zoo Atlanta! I'm tellin' you, Mantha, just the mention of the name Samson make people jump 'cause they think his bad luck is contagious. He should'a changed his name to something more acceptable...like Beelzebub." The boy beast howled with laughter as he opened the driver's side door of the truck.

"Dammit!" he exclaimed as a chicken jumped down out of the driver's seat, shedding feathers into the air. "Stupid chickens!"

I mulled over Butch's words, and I had to admit that Samson's luck did appear to be on the fritz, considering the fact that he was dead. That's about as unlucky as one can be. And it was true that ever since I'd met him, my own life had been spiraling out of control—even more than usual. Perhaps he *was* contagious. I thought back on our moments of intimacy there in that hotel room. I'd had a purse full of prophylactics, but no condom could have protected me from this kind of disease. There was no vaccine or inoculation that could make me immune to bad luck, no scientist's serum or witchdoctor's brew to protect me from misfortune of this caliber and kind. The hours that followed my encounter with Samson had been filled with nothing but mayhem, and Butch's prognosis was the only thing that seemed to explain all this. I was now the carrier of the hard luck gene. The curse had been transmitted to me, and I was the new host for the virus. And as long as all that bad luck continued to flow through my veins and consume my being, I knew that Francine wasn't the only dark cloud looming over my head.

"That's all? So what if Samson *is* bad luck. You and me ain't exactly no raffle winners ourselves. I need to figure out what killed Samson before the cops figure that it was *me*!"

"Relax. There's more," Butch said as he stuck the key in the ignition and turned it slowly. The engine sputtered but stubbornly refused to turn over. Butch reached down, mashed on a lever, and with a loud pop, the hood of the old truck crept open sluggishly, like the slow yawn of a lazy dog. "Turns out," Butch continued, emerging from the cab and walking around to the front of the truck, "ya' boyfriend closet got more skeletons in it than a public cemetery." Butch chuckled as he secured the hood. Then he bent over and stuck his head deep inside, as if he were trying to sniff the motor. "Not only was he a walkin' chain letter wit' all that damn bad luck," Butch continued, his voice echoing from under the hood, "he also had a cocaine habit."

"A cocaine habit?" I repeated in disbelief.

"Yep! A bad one. He seen more white powder than a ski instructor in the Swiss Alps. Every chance he got, he snuck off to snort up." Then Butch stood upright and looked me straight in the eye. "You shole know how to pick 'em!" He laughed again before diving back under the rusty hood.

Samson a cocaine addict? I thought about all the many minutes Samson had spent in the bathroom before our tryst back at the Bell Sheraton, and things began to make sense. He'd excused himself to the restroom saying he'd had a long night and just wanted to wash away the troubles of the day. Instead of freshening up, more likely he'd been in that bathroom snortin' up! That would have explained the crazed look in his eyes when he emerged from the bathroom and approached me so salaciously, when he peeled my dress off my shoulders like the skin of a banana and grabbed me by the nape of my neck. I remember feeling like he had the strength of ten men when he lifted me into his arms and carried me to the bedroom. No wonder. He was probably hopped up on drugs. The intensity in his eyes had likely been more than simple desire. He was flying high, and I was just a passenger along for the ride.

I surmised that it must have been that last bump of cocaine that killed him. Maybe he'd scored a bad batch from somewhere. Maybe, in all the excitement of the evening, he'd cut too much and inhaled a fatal dose. Maybe his poor heart just couldn't withstand all that strain: the booze, the drugs, the steamy foreplay, all the sensual strokes and carnal kisses, and dirty talk whispered between us. We were insatiable that night, probing one another with ravenous desire. The passion we'd felt, the decadent debauchery, so voracious and wild, had been a full ten on the Richter scale. I suppose that as we trembled there together, shifting and shaking and rubbing up against one another like tectonic plates, the shockwaves and vibrations that thundered through our bodies had caused his poor heart to become weak and susceptible. And it had only been a cosmic coincidence that my innocent lips administered the kiss of death.

But how could I prove that? How could I mount an ironclad defense and exonerate myself on a mere hunch? A rumor really? I needed more information, more evidence, more insight into the mysterious man who'd stumbled into my life only to die so suddenly on top of me. I prayed that as I continued upon my journey and collected more pieces to this peculiar puzzle, the picture, now so broken and distorted, would soon be made plain and clear.

Just then, the hood slammed shut. Butch made his way back around to the driver's side, where he climbed up into the cab, sat down, and closed the door. He turned the key again, and the truck growled to a start like a dragon waking after centuries of slumber. The engine roared as Butch stepped on the gas, and a dark cloud of smoke poured out of the old truck's tailpipe. Even amidst the darkness, the smoke was visible, and the odor of gasoline and motor oil sent the chickens scattering. Thunder rumbled wildly, shaking the barn's old bones, and I, too, wanted to run for cover like a chicken.

"See?" Butch called out as he rolled down the window. Of course, nothing about that old truck was automatic, so Butch had to turn the stiff crank manually in order for the window to descend. "A little creativity, ingenuity, and elbow grease...and a man can build his own luck!" He laughed, and suddenly a stiff wind began to whip through the barn, launching bits of hay up into the air. I covered my face to protect my eyes.

Through the barn walls, I heard the rain as it intensified, pounding the ground outside. The wind chimes that hung from the gutters of the old house began to rattle violently under the brutality of those punishing winds. Francine scratched on the roof and beat upon the walls of the barn, hissing threats and curses through the warm night, and I knew undoubtedly that those sudden and merciless rains were just the beginning, a mere preview of the frightening dangers still yet to come.

I doubted if that old jalopy would make it around the corner on a *sunny* day, let alone a stormy night like this. And as Butch revved the old truck's engine amidst that rumbling thunder, I wondered who would win the fight between cruel Francine and the madman Butch, armed with all his homemade luck. Both of them were wild, tempestuous, and unpredictable. Both of them were cold, heartless, and cruel. And neither of them had a conscience or a care. Again, I wondered who would come out on top. Who would win this battle of wills? And my old friend the owl echoed my inquiries, asking "Who?" over and over into the abysmal night.

CHAPTER 18: SANTA'S CLAUSE...

I gazed through the barn doors out into the storm, and was astonished as I bore witness to the old plantation's rapid transformation. The grassy fields and towering cornstalks that had once neatly enclosed the estate began to look more like untamed jungles, soupy swamps, wild wastelands, savage and unkempt. Water rose all around us as if the farm were a sinking ship, and tree branches swung sorrowfully from side to side like hands waving goodbye.

Butch and I draped ourselves in the tarp that had once covered the old truck and ran back out into the night, the tarp flapping behind us like a cape. The rain that crashed down all around us sounded like applause, like thousands of hands clapping at the end of a sold-out show. But there was nothing at all entertaining about that thunderous ovation, the raindrops pulverizing us both even despite our makeshift umbrella, and the winds tossing us about like a skiff out on the sea. We bowed our heads to keep the water out of our eyes and huddled close as Francine battered us brutally, snatching at the vinyl tarp like a kleptomaniac. With our feet sloshing through puddles and our ankles wading through mud, the trek back to the house seemed unending. Just as lightning flashed and lit up the night for a moment, I peeked out from under the tarp and stole a glimpse ahead. I was relieved to see the old home still standing there, although it looked as though it might succumb to the tempest any minute and be blown away like a pile of leaves.

Butch and I busted through the back door like two runners breaking through the finishing tape and tying for first. Lightning captured the photo finish like a flash bulb from above. And as we slipped and skated on the slick kitchen tiles, tracking mud across the limestone, it took the both of us and all our strength combined to close the door on Francine, her gale-force gusts pounding the other side like a battering ram.

After we regained our composure and wiped our feet thoroughly on the back-door mat, we headed back toward the sitting room to rejoin Eve and our haggard host.

"No!" Eve cried out as we entered. The lights flickered overhead as thunder crashed down outside. I flinched at the sound of her objection, and Butch reached for the dagger in his breast pocket. "You're wrong!" Eve shouted at the little old man.

"I am *not* wrong!" he protested.

"Are too! There's no such word as squoze!" She giggled. Upon hearing Eve's laughter, Butch took his hand off of the knife and began to stand down from red alert like a soldier newly at ease. I began to breathe again too, and I wondered how many more scares my poor heart could withstand.

"Is too!" the old man insisted.

"Use it in a sentence then."

The old man cleared his throat. "Last night, it snew, and I was so cold I squoze my blanket tight," he stated indignantly.

"The past tense of squeeze is squeezed," Eve replied, placing extra emphasis on the "-ed," "not squoze. There's no such word as squoze!" She laughed again. "And..." she added, "there's no such word as snew either. You can't say it *snew* last night. You have to say it *snowed*!"

"Freeze, froze. Squeeze, squoze!" the old man declared, as if his statement had settled the argument. "Blow, blew. Snow, snew!" He paused to allow his logic to permeate Eve's understanding.

"Oh my God!" An exasperated Eve threw her arms in the air before erupting in laughter. The snaggletooth stranger smiled wide too, delighted to have made Eve laugh so heartily. "No way you read all those books up there and don't know how to say it snowed." Eve pointed at the immense bookcase mounted all along the wall. "They must be just for show."

"Naw," the old man said, shaking his head, "I read 'em. Every last one, cover to cover. Some nights, I prefer a good book over a good woman." He winked. "I love books. And I love words. Even the made-up ones!" He chuckled. "I got all kinds of books up there, darlin'. Dickens, Melville, and Hemingway. Steinbeck, Faulkner, and Twain. Fitzgerald, Salinger, and Tolstoy. All kinds of literary giants hidden on those little shelves." He aimed his claws at the burgeoning bookcase. "I got fables and allegories, famous speeches full of rhetoric and pomp. I got tell-all biographies uncovering truths, and I even got a few tawdry ones filled with nothin' but lies. Some books based on fiction, some books based on fact. All kinds of stories up there. You name it! Cowboys and Indians… murder and the macabre…ogres and gnomes…giant men and magic beans and aliens from outer space. And that's all just one book!" he said with a snicker, flashing a toothless smile. Butch and I were all smiles too as we emerged from the shadows and approached the fast friends.

"Whew!" I exclaimed as I rubbed my arms. My skin was still wet to the touch, and the slight breeze that

211

blew perpetually through the old house made me feel as though I were standing beneath an air conditioner. "I'm chilly!" I remarked, my shoulders bouncing up and down.

"Chilly?!" the old man repeated. "I thought you said your name was Maria!" Then he and Eve exploded again in laughter.

"You two seem to be getting along famously," I said as I took a seat.

"Yes, we are. Willie here is my new best friend," Eve decreed, winking at the old man.

"Sorry, Maria," the old man said to me. "You've been replaced!" Then he and Eve laughed again, the old man's cackles strangled sporadically by coughs.

"Well, sorry to put an end to all the fun, but we gotta be goin' now," Butch interjected.

"Noooo!" Willie whined. "Stay a while longer. I don't get many visitors these days 'cept for the hands that come and look after the farm during the week. And they ain't much for conversation unless it's about a sow or a cow, a hog or a horse. Stay a spell!" he pleaded. "Besides, it's rainin' enough cats and dogs out there to turn the worl' into a kennel! I bet we can get us a fire goin' right here." He pointed at the barren fireplace. "And I got plenty booze to go around." He pulled a metal flask from the crevice of his chair as if it were a pocket intended for storage.

"Aww…you're so sweet," Eve said with a sigh.

"Yeah, we appreciate your hospitality, mister, but we really gotta be on our way," Butch maintained, reaching into his pants pocket. "So, let me pay you for the truck, and we'll move on." Butch pulled out a roll of freshly pilfered hundred-dollar bills and began counting out payment for the tattered truck. "Me and the girls here gotta get to work in the morning…rain or shine," Butch added. As he extended his hand to the old man, the crisp bills spread open in his palm like a Japanese fan.

"You think I believe that?" The old man chuckled.

"Huh?" Butch asked, the money still there in his outstretched hand.

"I got swollen ankles and poor circulation. I got arthritis and tendonitis. High blood pressure. High cholesterol. Diabetes. I go through mo' diapers than a set of newborn quintuplets, and these days, my spine is shaped like the letter 'S.' My memory ain't what it used to be. And my taste buds stopped tastin' over ten years ago! It don't make me no difference 'cause, hell, I ain't got but one tooth left in my mouth, and can't eat nothin' no how, unless it's mashed up like a soup. After ninety-one years on this green earth, I got mo' thangs *wrong* wit' me than right. And I got more days behind me than I got ahead. But I tell ya' one thang. My vision is 20/20. I can see a sheep shittin' in Sri Lanka! And I can for damn sure see, even from all the way over here, that lil' Angie's nametag says 'Eve'." The old man pointed his decrepit fingernail at the pretty waitress. Butch and I both turned our heads to study Eve's dress, and I gasped when I noticed her Wild Goose nametag still affixed.

"And I tell you what else I know!" the old man continued. "These 20/20 eyes of mine also saw you three pull up into my driveway tonight, and I know good and damn well y'all ain't break down on the side of the road. Lyin' and givin' fake names. Flouncin' around here in ya' fancy clothes, flashin' wads of cash, counting out hundreds like the Sultan of Brunei! I know a bunch of crooks when I see 'em. Hell, I used to be one myself," the old man added,

213

laughing again, "before I put my head on straight and got my life together!"

"What chu' gettin' at old man?" Butch said, posturing, and I saw the violence churning in his mind. "Lemme guess…you want more money."

"I'm sayin'," Willie continued, "that I'm sure we can come to an agreement, an understanding, a meeting of the minds." The old man smiled, but there was something sinister about that twisted grin. It wasn't a happy, lighthearted smile brought on by joy. It was creepy and eerie and menacing, like the smile on a jack-o'-lantern, prankish and mischievous, like the face of a joker lurking deep within a deck of playing cards. "If you three can't stay here and keep an old man company, fine. Don't. You can take me with you!"

"Take you with us?!" Butch, Eve, and I repeated all together.

"You must be hittin' that bottle harder than I thought!" Butch scoffed.

"You'll take me with you…or I'll be forced to contact the authorities and report three suspicious characters who drove up to my home late on a stormy night with pockets full of cash lookin' to ditch their automobile. I'm sure there's a crime out there somewhere whose suspects match that description." He chortled.

"I'd like to see you try. The phone all the way on the other side of the room." Butch pointed. "And you gotta make it past me first, old man!"

"That's where you're wrong, sonny." The old man reached inside the neckline of his thermal underwear and pulled out an odd-looking chain. "Behold!" Willie announced. "One of the few benefits of getting old. This here is my Emergency Alert necklace. Like I said, son. I'm ninety-one years old. One push of this button, and I'll have every police car, fire truck, and ambulance in the county right at my doorstep in a matter of minutes. When you get to be over eighty, sometimes they send the coroner too, just in case!" The old man laughed again. "Now, unless you want the authorities to descend upon this place like a SWAT team, I suggest you reconsider my ultimatum."

Butch's chest tightened, his fists clenched, and his face turned red as a sunburned albino. The old man's crooked fingers had pushed Butch's buttons, and now Butch's temper was powering up like a nuclear reactor, charging rapidly like an alkaline battery. I felt the heat rising off of him all the way from my chair, and suddenly I was no longer cold. His nostrils flared, his jawline hardened, and he snarled at the old man like a werewolf hungry for a midnight snack. Eve and I braced ourselves for impact.

"Come on now, sonny. Don't be angry. Where's your heart?" Willie's sad eyes widened, and for a moment, the gray-haired geezer looked more like a toddler on the verge of tears. "Have some compassion for an old man and, if you're lucky, one day you might make it to be my age too! Although..." he paused in thought, "after while, being old stops bein' lucky...and starts feelin' more like a curse. If you keep livin' long enough, there'll come a day when your mama and daddy will pass away...and then your wife... your sisters...your brothers...one by one... everybody you love. You live long enough, son, and you even start outlivin' your chi'ren..." He bowed his head and sighed. "Next thang ya' know, your only friends are your

215

memories…the stories your mama once told you when she tucked you in at night…the smell of fried chicken and biscuits when your family sat down for supper…the songs that played while you held your honey close and slow-danced at your wedding…and a lifetime of Christmas mornings. One day, you'll look around and see that all you got…is all those memories. That's why so many old folks tend to get lost inside they minds. Dementia? Alzheimer's? Pssh! That ain't nothin' but us old folks busy lookin' for what we lost…wandering the labyrinths of our thoughts…meandering through the mazes of our minds…searchin' the depths of our subconscious to catch one last subliminal glimpse of a mother's face or to feel the warmth of daddy's arms around you just one more time. All us old folks wanna do is get back to that place in time when we used to live and love…so we can live and love again. I tell you, if I stay here one mo' night by myself all alone in this old house, I'm liable to get lost inside my mind and be stuck for good. I might not ever find my way back out!" He clutched the armrests tightly with his birdlike talons as though he were trying to anchor himself here in reality.

"That's the saddest thing I ever heard," Eve said with a frown.

"I'll tell ya' what's sad," poor Willie continued. "Some nights, I lay awake, and I can hear death knockin', scratchin' on the walls with his razor-sharp scythe, draggin' his ole rusty chains all through the house, lookin' for me…and whisperin' my name. Willie! Willie!" The old man demonstrated. "That's why I took to sleepin' upright in this here chair at night. That way, I can see the reaper comin' and enjoy one last swallow of bourbon before I join everybody else on the other side. Take me with you," Willie beseeched, staring up into Butch's cold and calculating eyes. "Help an old man live out his last few days with some excitement. Otherwise, I'll die right here where y'all found me...if I don't go crazy first." The old man punctuated his plea with a chorus of coughs.

"Aww...can he come?" Eve pleaded, yanking at Butch's sleeve like a child. "What harm can he do? I'll take care of him and make sure he doesn't get in the way. Please don't hurt him. Let him come with us."

Time seemed to stand still as all three of us looked to Butch for his ruling on the matter, and I was shocked to see that the madman was no longer mad. I expected Butch to issue a thinly veiled threat and to carry that threat out expeditiously if willful Willie refused to comply. But Butch remained composed and collected. I may have even witnessed a glimmer of empathy in his eyes as he beheld the feeble old man wasting away there in his tall chair, tucked away in the empty house like an abandoned puppy, unfed and forgotten.

"Here." Butch stuffed the money back in his pocket, pulled out a handful of keys, and handed them to me. "If the old guy is comin' with us, ain't no way he'll make it out to the barn in this rain. Bring the truck around front, and I'll carry him out." I rose to follow Butch's orders. "Eve," Butch continued, "help me get him ready. See if you can find him some clothes or something to wear and—" Before Butch could finish his mandate, Eve jumped up and hugged him.

"Thank you!" she cried, overcome with joy for our newfound travel companion.

"Yeah, well, pretend the old guy is your pet. You feed him, you take care of him, you clean up after him, and you betta' do all that outta' *your* cut, not mine!" Butch barked. Eve nodded with a smile and raced over to hug the old man, sealing the contract with a kiss on the cheek.

I excused myself from the room, keys in hand, and found the vinyl tarp still on the kitchen floor by the back door, where Butch and I had left it to dry. I donned the tarp again, wrapping it around me like a poncho, and ran back out into the rain. Thankfully, the winds had died a bit, but I could tell that Francine was alive and well. The ground was like a marsh beneath my feet, and with each step, the mud threatened to yank off my rhinestone heels and bury them in the earth like quicksand. But I continued, unfazed. I'd been walking in heels since I was fourteen years old, and if struttin' one's stuff was a professional sport, I would be in the Hall of Fame. I could do a backflip on a tightrope while blindfolded and drinking a glass of water and never lose my balance in six-inch pumps! And as I traipsed on through all that muck and mire, I proved myself to be expert in all terrains.

The driver's side door was unlocked. I stepped in and sat down. I fumbled with the keys for a minute under the dark of night, and by the time I found the right one, my hands were trembling. As I inserted the key in the ignition, a million and one thoughts swarmed around my head like honeybees in a hive: chaotic, frenzied, frantic, yet all working together somehow. Among them were the dead man Samson, vengeful Francine, the poor widow Jackie, and sweet little Samson Junior. I thought of Mrs. Barrister back at the Golden Egg, the entire Madison City police department, who wanted Butch's head on a platter, and now the newest player in this continuing saga: the frail, languid old man named Willie, who'd begged to join us on our journey.

The events of the last few days were turning into a twisted version of The Wizard of Oz. Just like Dorothy's tornado, Francine had started it all as Samson and I trudged through the rain to meet one another at Black Jack's Tavern. And Samson was my wicked witch. His mysterious death had started me on this never-ending quest through strange and unfamiliar lands. And all along the way, the cast of characters kept growing. First Butch, then Eve, and now Willie.

In *my* story though, there was no wonderful wizard. No good witch to tell me what to do. There was no magic in my shoes, and clicking my heels was futile. Unlike Dorothy, none of my companions cared about getting me back home safely, about returning my life to a sense of normalcy, about my welfare and wellbeing, my security, or my best interests. Each of them were out for their own, serving their own agendas, pushing their own purposes, in pursuit of their own grand adventures. They'd be perfectly happy to remain in Oz forever—even if that meant stranding me here with them.

The vehicle started on the very first try, and the engine's deep growl startled me for a second. I slipped it into gear and pulled out slowly. I had set out that morning to dig myself out of a hole, but Butch had only buried me deeper, six feet under and counting. I'd been detoured and derailed, and precious time had been lost. Suddenly, thunder broke so loudly it sounded as though it were only inches above my head. And as lightning pierced the sky, a jolt ran through me too, perhaps Francine warning me to reconsider my decision. Butch had entrusted me with all the keys, including those belonging to the Ferrari. And so, when the tires rolled to a stop, I shifted gears, took a deep breath, and sped off into the night, abandoning our foursome to continue my journey alone, burning rubber all over the yellow brick road.

CHAPTER 19: ALL SCREWED UP...

As I crossed over the county line, leaving Madison City behind, I exhaled a sigh of relief. The wind and rain had let up a bit, but driving through the storm proved to be no less challenging. Fallen tree limbs obscured the blacktop as my tires treaded more water than a swim teacher at the YWCA. The moon was still being held captive behind an army of clouds, and absent its bright glow, the night was exceptionally dark. I knew I could be easily spotted by police behind the wheel of such an exotic car, so I took full advantage of that extra gloom, driving the midnight-blue Ferrari FF most of the way with its headlights off, a phantom moving swiftly in the night.

I turned the radio on as low as I could get it and heard the forecast being whispered over the Ferrari's mighty motor. The newscaster reported that the death toll in Cuba had risen to a whopping sixty-one as bodies were still being pulled from the rubble and devastation. The hurricane was now lingering over the Bahamas and feasting on all those without adequate shelter. For hours, Francine had been trampling through the Atlantic like a giant in steel boots, foraging the earth for life, but according to the news, it seemed as though she were winding down now, tiring out like a breathless boxer late in the twelfth. She still packed quite a punch, the announcer explained, but her winds were slowly dissipating, and her rains were beginning to subside. The weatherman insisted that Francine would soon piddle out and make her way east, but as far as I could see, the rain showed no signs of stopping. I hydroplaned on through the streets, and despite my skepticism, the stranger

221

on the radio gave the world his word that the worst was finally over.

As I crossed back over into southeast Atlanta—the section of the city suffering from an unofficial police lockdown in the wake of last month's bank robbery—I was thankful for the high winds that made helicopter surveillance impossible. And as I turned into the lot adjacent to Butch's development, I almost wept when I saw my Milsey still there. My heart rejoiced at the sight of her, like a mother reunited with her child after an eternity apart. Without hubcaps, minus a proper paintjob, and now— thanks to Butch—stripped naked of her license plates, my poor baby looked abandoned. I pulled up alongside her and turned off the Ferrari. Then I reached into the Ferrari's center console to retrieve Butch's Swiss army knife so that I could reaffix Milsey's plates. But as I dug for the knife, my fingertips brushed the cold, hard metal of the two guns Butch had stolen from the Wild Goose's suborned security. A shiver went through my body as I realized just how deep I was in this mess. Stolen money, stolen property, a stolen car, and now stolen guns?! Immediately I heard Ms. Jane's words of warning broadcasting across my mind like a public service announcement: *If you'll lie, you'll steal. And if you'll steal, you'll kill!* I'd already lied. I'd already stolen. And now I held there in my hands the very tools I would need to fulfill the rest of that fateful prophecy: the soon-to-be murder weapons, according to Ms. Jane's predictions.

The sudden tap on my window stopped my heart and made me gasp. He had moved so stealthily through the parking lot I hadn't even seen or heard him approaching. I looked up and saw his face peering through the driver's

222

side window, and the evil grimace that glared back at me made me wonder if those angry eyes would be the last thing I saw before succumbing to my own homicide right there on the street.

"Out!" he demanded. I'd been running from him with all my might, but like a skilled hunter, he had tracked me down with ease and plucked me out of obscurity. "Out of the car!" He rapped on the window as he spoke, punctuating each syllable with a knock on the tempered glass. I rolled the window down a half-inch.

"Can I help you?"

"Can you help me?!" The rage colored his face red and made him look like a ripened tomato growing there. "Where's my rent?!"

"I'm workin' on it! Give me a few more days, Mr. Tennison!" He clutched his wooden clipboard beneath his arm like an angry football coach pacing the sidelines of a losing game. Aside from the redness of his rage, his face was blanched a stark white, no doubt the result of being confined to a desk for most of the daylight hours and missing out on the kisses being offered by Georgia's gentle sun. Runnels of sweat poured down over his temples despite the breeze that blew across the lot. And the incessant stress of managing the development and all its many tenants had dug permanent trenches into his sallow skin, wrinkles so deep they looked more like fine lacerations.

"A few more days?!" he repeated with a bewildered look in his eyes. "You've already had two weeks! Now I've been very patient with you, Miss Moore, and I even turned a blind eye to the way you've been traipsing in and out of here all hours of the day and night dressed like a

223

showgirl! As you know, this is a family development. But one thing I will *not* ignore is a freeloader who plays me for a fool!" As he yelled, his cheeks hung low and swung around like the sad jowls of an old mastiff, and the loose skin in his crimson neck made him look like a wild turkey squabbling orders at me and pecking at my door.

"I'm tryin' my best, Mr. Tennison. You know I been goin' through a rough patch lately, and I just need a little grace from you."

"What do you think this is?" His hot breaths momentarily fogged the glass between us. "You think I'm runnin' a goddamned charity here? Your rent is not a philanthropic endeavor, young lady! It's not some charitable donation you give out of the benevolence of your heart, whatever you can spare. You have a lease! Which means you have an obligation to pay your rent every month…on time…in full…just like everybody else around here. No excuses!"

"But Mr. Tennison…"

"What are you, deaf? I just told you no excuses. That means no buts! You've been late on the rent every month since you've been back, and you weren't exactly a model tenant before you went away in the first place. I don't know what that sweet old lady sees in you, but if it wasn't for Ms. Jane, you'd have been out on the streets eons ago! Now listen. You've got seventy-two hours to come up with the full rent plus late fees, or I'm throwing your crap out on the curb and renting that unit to somebody with a job!"

"I *have* a job, Mr. Tennison, but things are slow for me right now!"

"Do you even know what a job is? A job is when you drag your ass outta' bed each and every day whether you like it or not, put on some decent clothes, get in your car, and go somewhere to do some work and earn some money! Now, this part may be a little tricky for the likes of you, but your clothes remain *on* the whole time, and your feet have to stay on the *ground*! That's what real people do, Miss Moore. That's how everybody else in this development makes the rent each month. Try an honest day's work! Get a *real* job!"

"I hear you, Mr. Tennison, but it ain't that easy. You said it yourself how much of a mess I am, so you know I need more than seventy-two hours. Please, Mr. Tennison!" I guess there was something extra pathetic about my pitiful plea that made him pause to evaluate my sincerity. After a few moments, he let out a long sigh.

"You've got one week!" He pointed his index finger at me like it was a loaded weapon, cocked and ready. "But that's it!"

"One week, sir. I understand. Thank you, Mr. Tennison! Thank you!"

"Arrrgh," he growled. Then he turned and stomped away like he was Godzilla tearing through Tokyo.

Mr. Tennison had ripped me a new one, chile. Chewed me up and spit me out! A shark attack would've left less carnage! But despite his tough tones and cold candor, I couldn't deny his truth. I just wished he—or anybody else for that matter—could have seen things from my perspective. I wasn't jobless for a lack of trying, and there was nobody alive who wanted to see me on the up and up more than me. But in order to get on the up and up, first, I needed somebody to *help* me up! I needed

225

somebody to give me a chance, to cut me a break. Mr. Tennison and Ms. Jane were constantly preaching to me the obvious gospel of what kind of life I needed to lead, but neither of them could tell me specifically how to attain it. Just because I can clearly see the mountains in the distance, doesn't mean that I can just hop in my car and drive to 'em. There's a whole lot of road between here and there, and without a map, compass, or guide—without direction—I felt defeated, like I might as well just stay home altogether and close my curtains on that beautiful view.

And so their words served no purpose in my life other than to berate me and cause me pain, to make me sick over circumstances I couldn't change, to make me hate my reflection and pray for a swift end. But like most poor folks, I couldn't afford to wallow in self-pity and despair. I had to make ends meet, no matter how far apart they seemed to be. Mr. Tennison had given me a strict deadline and one last chance. I needed to amass some big money fast, and I knew my usual blue-collar quickies and street corner hustles would never suffice. I needed someone of means to lay a couple of Gs on me, and with Samson, that's exactly what I'd gotten. Except, in his case, the G must have stood for "grief," because ever since I'd made his acquaintance, that's all I seemed to encounter.

That acrimonious ambush by Mr. Tennison in the parking lot that night was the event that both precipitated and necessitated me waiting there at Black Jack's Tavern in spite of Samson's tardiness. The mere thought of me living out on the streets—again—compelled me to keep that barstool warm while I drowned my sorrows in cheap wine. And truthfully, honey, that was just a waste of booze. My sorrows were professional swimmers, and like fish, they refused to drown.

I stepped out into the rain, crossed in front of the racecar, and knelt before its bumper. I unfolded the flat-edged knife and went to work. But between the pouring rain, the darkness of the night, and Butch's superior strength in tightening the plates in the first place, the damned screw wouldn't budge. After almost ten minutes on my knees in the rain, I gave up. I desperately wanted to get my plates off that stolen car, but I had survived too much in my lifetime to risk dying of pneumonia now. So I got up and ran over to Milsey's trunk where I found my duffel bag tucked away inside. I grabbed the bag, slammed the trunk, and ran back over to the FF. I hurried to open the passenger door and climbed inside the Ferrari's backseat, where I began to peel off my wet dress.

The rain had given me a thorough shower, and I dried my skin with a towel from my bag. I slipped on a fresh pair of panties and a dry bra, and squeezed my hips into a pair of stretch denim jeans. I found a light off-the-shoulder sweater amongst my garments and slipped a pair of closed-toe heels over my feet. Then I dumped the contents of my cute little clutch back into my larger everyday purse.

I reached forward to adjust the rearview mirror so I could style my hair from the backseat, and my pale reflection startled me for a moment. The rain had washed away my pigment and turned my lips blue, cold, and cadaverous. I remedied this with a little bit of liquid foundation and a quick application of honey plum blush. I slicked my curls back with a hard brush and a dollop of mousse and wrapped my ponytail into a neat bun. A pair of oversized hoop earrings and a fresh coat of cherry red lipstick completed the look. Then I climbed between the front seats and plopped back down behind the wheel.

I wanted to ditch the stolen car, the guns, and all the money and just go back home to clean up my ransacked apartment. I wanted to pay Mr. Tennison what I owed him and go on about the business of living my life. But none of those actions were possible at the moment. Just like that stubborn license plate of mine that clung so tightly to the stolen Ferrari's bumper, I knew that I, too, had been screwed. And my journey had only one direction: forward.

So, I dug into my purse, pulled out the widow's list, and circled my next stop, Samson's last place of employment according to his wife: a twenty-four-hour eatery over in Dunwoody. I started the engine and placed the car in gear. Then I headed for the highway. But I wasn't alone.

Thunder rumbled from above, Francine clearing her throat and announcing her presence. Great big trees bowed like peasants before the mighty wind. And that brutal breeze tossed the Ferrari around as though it were a tin can in an alley and not a two-ton automobile. The FF and I were alone on the road, and as we struggled to stay on the pavement, I remember feeling like Francine was taking her aggressions out on me—like she'd somehow singled me out amongst millions and made me the target of her hostility. I felt like this pounding was getting personal! But I had a personal mission of my own that could not wait, a precarious duty that had driven me out into this downpour. I was on a quest for answers, and only those answers could offer me vindication and exonerate me once and for all. So, I bit down hard and kept on going, speeding ever deeper into the path of the storm.

The widow's directions were easy enough to follow, and as I pulled up to Pete's Put Yo' Foot In It Soul Food Diner and spied the unsavory clientele loitering out front beneath its awning, instantly I knew I should've put *my* foot on the *gas* and kept on driving! But instead, I flicked on my blinker and turned into the busy lot, determined to face my destiny head on—like most fatal collisions.

CHAPTER 20: SOUL PROPRIETORSHIP...

I had barely opened the car door, and already I had the full attention of all the undesirables lurking in front of the restaurant. For a moment, I thought I was a stray kitten with all the catcalls I received. Their libidinous whistles sounded like a bunch of tea kettles as they called out to me like sailors on weekend pass. My umbrella totally obscured me from the neck up, so I knew they hadn't even seen my face yet. All I was to them was female anatomy headed their way, stacked in the back and blessed in the chest. I was used to being objectified, eroticized, and exotified, and so I rolled my eyes and kept on moving, undaunted. After all, if it weren't for ignorant men who lacked self-control, I'd be out of business! Over the years, obnoxious jerks had been my most consistent clientele and my most faithful financiers. I didn't care if their IQs were in the single digits so long as their payments were in the triple.

The diner was a small one-story building built from brick that sat on a lot about five times its size. And on top of the eatery, a tall marquee rose high into the night. That neon sign was fully animated and depicted a goofy-looking man in a chef's hat dipping his big toe repeatedly into what looked like a cauldron filled with soup. And beneath the animation, the restaurant's full name was colorfully displayed: Pete's Put Yo' Foot In It Soul Food Diner. There was an old colloquialism spoken in kitchens all across the south, and naturally, that neon sign brought it readily to mind. When someone says you put your foot in something in a culinary context, that means you've successfully placed your own personal stamp on whatever

230

it is you were making. And as I inhaled the smoky aroma of barbecue pumping from the rooftop vents, I suspected that the owner of that little dive had placed his foot and every other appendage into each of those dishes. He was obviously not just a cook, but an artist expertly blending herbs and spices and skillfully handcrafting decadent delights. And evidently, his customers agreed. His culinary creations were held in such high esteem that patrons were willing to fight Francine for just a taste of his flavorsome flair.

"Why you lookin' so sad, lil' mama?" one man shouted as I collapsed my umbrella at the diner's entrance and shook it dry.

"No reason to be happy," I replied in truth as I disappeared inside.

A cluster of small bells jingled above the doorway and announced my entrance into the restaurant. I could almost feel the eyeballs zooming in and probing me head to toe. I felt vulnerable standing there, an obvious outlier to the rest of the working-class customers.

"I'll take ya' ovah here, suga!" a voice called out from the back of the restaurant. I looked up and saw the smile of a short brown waitress beckoning me with two fingers in the air. I was relieved to have been acknowledged so quickly, and moreover, I was glad to make my way toward the rear of the restaurant, where I would no longer be a spectacle.

There was a long countertop that stretched across the entire length of the establishment, and just beyond that counter was a bustling kitchen. Enormous pots and giant pans simmered over high heats, and their metal lids rattled and trembled as if they might blow any minute and be catapulted into the air. That busy galley looked more like the boiler-room of an ocean liner. Clouds of steam escaped from the steel stovetops, spewing wet heat up into the atmosphere, and thick smoke billowed from the cast-iron grills. A crew of chocolate workers scurried back and forth, scampering from station to station, full speed ahead. And the unsightly sweat stains that marred their beat-up aprons, coupled with the perspiration that poured from their brows, made me wonder if those poor folks weren't slowly melting, chocolate people turning into fudge.

On the other side of the diner, opposite the lively kitchen, there were a bunch of booths, each one packed tight. Folks sat hunched in front of racks of ribs and bowed their heads before big baskets of french fries and slaw. Tall pitchers of sweet tea sweated onto tabletops. And even despite the classic slow jams that played softly through the overhead speakers, the spirited sounds of lip smacking, finger licking, and the occasional gleeful grunt created a steady drone all throughout the space, a white noise that threatened to mask the music.

"It's sad to think…we're not gonna make it," Gladys Knight lamented over the loudspeaker. "And it's gotten to the point…where we just can't fake it." She crooned that famous breakup ballad, and The Pips echoed her sweetly in hushed tones. "For some ungodly reason…we just won't let it die." Voices from all over the restaurant joined in and turned the quartet into a choir. "I guess neither one of us…wants to be the first to say goodbye."

"You meetin' somebody, honey?" the waitress asked as I approached. She looked to be in her mid to late forties, but could have possibly been younger. Her face was pretty and welcoming, but the cheap synthetic wig that straddled her scalp added at least ten years to her appearance. I believe it was supposed to be styled as a bob, but it looked more like the war-torn helmet of a *soldier* named Bob. She wore a shabby pair of comfortable flats, and as I stood there in my five-inch heels I towered over her like a Florida palm.

"No, just me. Party of one," I replied with a smile.

"Alrighty then." She turned momentarily to grab something from a nearby table, and it was then that I noticed her oddly-shaped figure. She was slender on the top, with a flat belly, small waist, and tiny breasts. But just below her waistline, where her apron belt was tied, a rotund behind poked out and protruded. She looked like she was nine months pregnant and carrying the baby on her back! It was almost obscene to me, and honey, I've seen it all. She turned sideways to grab me a napkin and silverware, and I swear she had the profile of a centaur! "Go on and have a seat at the counter then, baby, and I'll be right with you." The mythical creature flashed me a bright smile and handed me a laminated menu.

"Just be thankful," Curtis Mayfield advised, "for what you've got." Suddenly, a spell was cast over the room, and heads began to nod in a synchronized dance. The crowd became entranced as necks swayed back and forth, smooth and easy like tree branches caught up in the summer breeze. And before I knew it, my own neck was swinging freely to that gentle groove, and I tapped my feet like a bona fide percussionist. "Though you may not drive a great big Cadillac…diamond in the back, sunroof top, diggin' the scene with a gangsta' lean…"

"Whoo-hoo!" the crowd cried out.

I sat down on a stool at the counter and perused the entrees. The first page looked fairly standard: wings and ribs, biscuits and gravy, and so on. But page two and beyond? Chile, I almost had a heart attack just readin' it! Neck bones and cow tails, hog maws and gizzards, chit'lins and tripe, fatback and souse. I saw pig snouts and pig ears and pig tails and pig skin. Only thing missin' was the oink! I took my eyes off the menu for a minute to contemplate what I'd just read, and I observed a big jar on the countertop next to me with a label that said "Pickled Pigs Feet". It's a wonder pigs weren't on the endangered species list with chefs like Pete running things. Seemed like anything that ended up on the slaughterhouse floor ended up on that menu afterwards, offered as a delicacy, twelve dollars a plate.

Now, don't get me wrong. I was born and raised in Mississippi, so there was nothing at that diner I hadn't seen before, but the sound of searing flesh coming from the kitchen and the smell of bacon in the air put me in mind of the heads hanging in the dining room of old man Willie's mansion. In the reflection of that glossy menu, I saw the resin-coated eyes of moose, elk, deer, and wild boar staring back at me. Immediately I lost what little appetite I had and found myself struggling to keep down the food I'd already eaten.

"Turn off the lights..." Teddy Pendergrass instructed over the intercom. "And light a candle," he whispered. "Tonight, I'm in a romantic mood...yeah." Fingers snapped as the crowd sang softly together in corporate karaoke.

"Okay, hon, what'll ya' have?" The waitress now stood on the other side of the counter, with the kitchen at

234

her back. She pulled a tiny notepad from her apron pocket and retrieved the pen that was tucked behind her ear.

"Just a cup of coffee, please."

"Coffee? Das it?" A befuddled look froze on her face.

"Yep. That's it for now." I slid the menu across the countertop in her direction.

"You must be on a diet. Girl, me too. According to my pedometer"—she pointed to a plastic bracelet on her wrist— "today, I walked twelve thousand steps!" Then she leaned over and whispered, "Unfortunately, most of 'em was to and from the refrigerator!" She and I laughed together, and I took an immediate liking to her down-to-earth, homespun charm.

Just then, a short, stocky fellow ran up and placed a tray of food on the countertop beside her and disappeared back into the busy kitchen. "Thanks, JoJo," the waitress called after his shadow. A gratuitous portion of barbecued brisket was stacked between two thick slices of Texas toast, and on the side, there was a big square hunk of mac and cheese and a mountain of fresh collards greens. The aroma of vinegar and hot sauce stung my nose and made my eyes water. The waitress stole a piece of fried okra from the basket and deposited it on her tongue like a royal taste tester. "Earl!" she shouted over her shoulder. Almost instantly, a long and lean young man manifested out of the haze and smoke and stood by her side, ready and reporting for duty. "Run this out to table seven," she ordered. And her lanky lackey grabbed the tray and took off like he was running anchor in a relay race and the brisket was his baton.

"Loooooooooooove them…and…leave them. That's what I used to do," Rick James confessed. "Use and abuse them…then I laid eyes on you!" The crowd came to life like they'd been carved by Geppetto, and a few couples even stood up to slow dance to the balladeer's sweet exhortation. "You…turned… on…my…fiiiiiiiiiiire… baby!" The room was so electric I swear those folks could've powered the city through a blackout. I struggled to keep my attention with the waitress.

"Right now," she continued, "I'm on the new turnip diet."

"Turnip diet?" I repeated.

"Un-huh. I eat everythang that turnip on my plate!" We laughed like two old friends, slapping the counter as our eyes watered. And each time the laughter subsided, we took one look at each other, and it ignited all over again like a stubborn blaze.

"Well, I'm not on a diet," I explained between convulsions. "Just needed a lil' pick-me-up and thought I'd stop in for a cup of joe."

"Well, at least lemme cut chu' a slice of pie," she insisted.

"Don't do it, sista!" came a voice from behind. A tall, snuff-colored man in a cowboy hat and pointy boots sidled up to the counter alongside me. He held a tray of food in his hands and set it down on the countertop.

"Come again?" I asked.

"The pie nasty. The food nasty. I don't even like they tea. You betta' hope they get yo' coffee right!" the cowboy confided in me.

"Wus wrong wit' the pie?" the short waitress asked, placing her hands on her widespread hips.

236

"Just 'cause they call 'em sweet potatoes, don't mean you ain't got to add no sugar," he replied. "Damn pie taste like tar!" Then he turned to me and flashed his veneers. "Are my teeth brown?"

"Naw, don't worry," the waitress reassured him. "They still yella'." The other patrons at the counter all laughed, and I covered my mouth to hide my own snigger.

"See dis here?" He pointed at the giggling waitress. "Eveythang lousy here...including the service!"

"Aww, now I'm just foolin' wit' chu', honey." She offered a warm smile. "Ain't nothing wrong wit' dat pie. Quiet as it's kept," she added in a whisper, "I had two slices earlier today myself."

"Well, you musta' ate up all the *sweet* and left behind the potato!" The customers at the counter laughed again, and this time, they were joined by a few of those in the booths behind me.

"If you got a complaint, mister, take it up wit' da chef!"

"Fine. Go git him!"

"Fine. I will," she retorted. "Pete!" she called into the boisterous kitchen. "Peeeeete!" she repeated.

"Yeah, yeah...I'm comin'," a voice responded from somewhere in the back. And moments later, a short, plump gentleman emerged from the chaos of the kitchen. He looked oddly familiar to me, but I couldn't quite place where I knew him from. A bushy mustache straddled his upper lip. It was course, wild, and thick, like a painter's dried up brush. He wiped his perspiring face with the bottom of his apron, but his dour, brooding expression could not be removed. He pulled a white hat from his back pocket and placed it on his head, and suddenly I

237

remembered where I'd seen his face before: the goofy marquee outside! In real life, though, his big, round face was missing that inviting smile, that hospitable grin that made passersby turn in off the interstate and park their cars.

Just then, one of the kitchen workers slipped and dropped a small bowl of sticky sauce on the floor behind the counter. "Watch what chu doin' now, Terrence!" Pete, the proprietor, scolded. "Go get something to clean this mess up and make sure you get it up good...fo' we have every roach in kingdom come up in here! Roaches be done moved in and took over...next thang you know, they buildin' schools and roads, settin' up housin' and runnin' for office."

"Shit, they gotta move outta' *my* house first!" the waitress interjected, launching the surrounding patrons into another hearty laugh.

"What chu' call me up here for, Birdie?" the chef reprimanded. "You see I'm busy wit' da' late night rush."

"This man say he got a bone to pick wit' chu'," the waitress replied, pointing at the cowboy standing beside me. "Look like a turkey bone." She pointed at his plate.

"You again, man? Wus wrong now?!" Pete said with a sigh.

"I'll tell ya' wus wrong," the man in the hat began. "Look at dis! Cold potatoes, half-mashed, half-raw. Peas and carrots all mushed up together. Look like somebody done already ate 'em! And look at this raggedy-ass piece of turkey...sliced so thin you can read the newspaper thu' it. Man, I got birds in my yard make a better sandwich!"

"Now hol' on! Wait just a minute!" Pete postured. "You must not know who I am, sucka'! I am the String Bean King!"

238

"Shole is!" called out someone in the crowd.

"I am the Chicken Champion!" the chef declared.

"Right on!" shouted another.

"I am the Gizzaaaard Wizaaaard!" he proclaimed in a singsong voice, like a boxing ring announcer at the start of a bout. His antics sent the restaurant into a boisterous cheer. "And you betta' believe I know all there is to know about that turkey!" He pointed at the cowboy's plate. "I can tell you if he had a wife and how many feathers she had!" The crowd exploded in raucous laughter.

"Bullshit! Man, you full of it!" The tall man waved his hand in dismissal.

"I'm serious!" Pete swore. "I put a lotta' work into that bird! Lemme tell you, I marinated that turkey in ten different spices and herbs, smoked it outside for a whole day, then slow-roasted it in the oven wit' fresh garlic before stuffin' it wit' homemade southern-style cornbread dressin'. Then I fried it!! If he could, that turkey would get up and take a bite out of his *own* ass!" The crowd laughed again.

"Well, hell...you done baked it, fried it, smoked it, toasted it, and roasted it. No wonder iss so damn dry!" the cowboy concluded. The chef gasped, clutched his chest, and stumbled backwards as if he'd just been shot at close range. "That turkey spent mo' time back there in yo' *kitchen* than it did in the *egg*!" The crowd erupted.

"You cuttin' in high cotton now, jack!" Pete warned. "Say something else 'bout my cookin', and I'll leap across this counter and make you eat every word!"

"If they taste better than this slop *you* servin', I'll gladly eat 'em!" the cowboy heckled, and the crowd chuckled.

"Hold me back! Somebody hold me back!" Pete yelled as he slung one of his short legs high up on the counter and tried to climb over. Laughter swept through the restaurant with such a thunderous roar, Francine would've been jealous.

"Get on down from there, fool!" the waitress commanded. "Get down before you tear yo' pants and somethin' else gets hurt besides yo' pride!" Pete did as he was told and dismounted the countertop.

"And you! Fool number two!" Birdie addressed the cowboy complainant. "You got all this criticism, but yet you come in here more often than *I* do…and shit, I work here! At least they payin' *me* to show up. Wus yo' excuse?"

"I live across the street."

"Boy, git' on way from here. Git!" She shooed the man, and he moseyed away with a smile. The crowd laughed again, and some even clapped. As the cowboy made his exit stage left, I got the sneaking suspicion that this type of comic fodder was all an act, all part of the novelty of Pete's Diner, part of the reason why people came there in droves and made Pete and his staff the highlight of their evenings and their feature destination. Folks all across the room sat up tall in their seats to listen to the playful banter and funny insults being traded back and forth, studying the actions and interactions of the diner's vivid cast of characters. And as they dined on the soulful cuisine, they feasted on the soulful music that pumped through the overhead system. Just like when brothers hang out at the barbershop and sisters make a day of the salon, there was a cultural exchange taking place there in that country diner. Food, music, and laughter attending to the souls of the weary. People finding spiritual ablution in a tall cup of coffee. And there was just enough comfort there in a sweet slice of pecan pie to mitigate the bitterness of the outside world.

"Crime is…increasing," Marvin Gaye reported. "Trigger happy…policing. Panic…is spreading. God knows where…we're heading. Oh, make me wanna holler and throw up both my hands…" Folks slipped their hands in the air, and without having to utter a word, they testified. "Yeah, it makes me wanna holler and throw up both my hands…"

"What brings you here, sugar?" the waitress inquired, pouring a dark-roasted brew from a tall carafe. "We ain't exactly known for our coffee, and you dressed up like you got a hot date and can't be late!" She slid the mug to me along with a bowl of sweeteners and cream.

"Well, maybe you can help me, actually. I need to ask a couple questions 'bout one of the employees here." I pulled Samson's photo from my purse and flashed it at the waitress.

"What chu say yo' name was?" she asked me curiously.

"Tina. Tina Henderson," I lied. "Nice to meet you." I extended my hand.

"Pleasure's mine, Tina. I'm Birdie Jenkins. Hostess extraordinaire. And I hate to tell you this, honey, 'cause you seem like a nice lady, but yo' boyfriend in the picture is a married man. And he got a baby too!"

"Oh no, he's not my boyfriend. It's nothin' like that. I know he has a wife and son."

"Really? Well ya' could've fooled me, 'cause you exactly his type."

"Oh? And what type is that?" I asked reluctantly.

"Breathin'!" She grabbed my hand as she laughed and immediately melted my defenses. "You talkin' 'bout a flirt? Chile, that boy seen mo' ass than a toilet seat!" She laughed again.

"That's his wife's problem, not mine," I promised. "He and I aren't dating."

"Well, if he ain't cattin' around wit' chu', then why you got his picture in yo' purse?" She leaned in and whispered. "You some kinda' cop? I ain't too keen on cops," she warned.

"Me? A cop?" I laughed at the notion. "No, no. He and I crossed paths recently, and I just need to know a few things about him. That's all."

"Well, he mostly just bus tables out on the floor, but sometimes, he help out in the kitchen. He ain't been to work in a few weeks, so if you lookin' for him, I can't help you. I don't know him very well to tell you the truth, but I'm sure Pete be glad to help you." And before I could inquire with her any further, she called out, "Peeeeete!"

"Dammit, Birdie! What now?" the chef shouted back from behind a veil of smoke and over the din of the sizzling grills.

"Lady up here wanna ask you a couple questions!" Birdie called back.

Pete reemerged from the depths of the sweltering kitchen and made a bee line right over to me. "You got a complaint for me too?!" the owner asked angrily, like he was a cross-examining attorney and I was a liar up on the witness stand.

"No, sir. Everything smells and looks delicious, actually." I smiled wide.

"Dis here Tina Henderson," Birdie introduced. "She wanna ask you a couple questions 'bout Samson."

"Who?" the chef asked.

"You know, Samson! The baldheaded boy wit' da big muscles. He work weeknights out front bussin' tables."

"Oh, you mean Baldy?"

"Yeah, Baldy!" the waitress confirmed.

"What about him?" Pete turned back to me.

"I just wanted to ask you a couple questions, sir. That's all."

"Well, come on back behind the counter, and we can talk in my office. I got a hundred pounds of chicken to finish cleanin', or else we gon' have ourselves a riot up in here!"

The waitress pointed the way, and I rose from my stool to traverse the perimeter of the counter back toward the restaurant's entrance. I lifted the counter door, passed underneath, and crossed over into the kitchen area to join Pete. The many minions working in the kitchen spied me with wonderment, and I knew that I was probably the first patron they'd ever seen step foot into that restricted zone.

"Right this way." Pete motioned, and I crossed in front of him. "Walk straight to the back," Pete directed, and I led the way down one of the kitchen's slim aisles. The heat was almost insufferable as I traveled deeper into the belly of the building. I looked over my shoulder and saw Pete's smiling face still behind me. "Straight on through the doors, honey," the chef directed. "Straight on through the doors." I turned back around to face front and stepped through a pair of white swinging doors and into the chef's makeshift office there in the rear of the kitchen. I was surprised to see several gentlemen in dark suits sitting around a large conference-style table.

"Hello." I waved. They all smiled and responded in a chorus of hi's and hellos. But before I could utter another word, I felt a cold, hard poke in my back.

"Arms in the air," the chef whispered. And suddenly, all the men rose from the table, pulled the guns from their holsters, and aimed them at my face. The chef twisted the nozzle of his gun deeper into my lower back, and just like Marvin Gaye had foreshadowed only moments before, the pain made me wanna holler and throw up both my hands!

CHAPTER 21: WET DREAMS!

I remember our first time, me and you on Mama's
couch. Uh-huh. You remember. I was wearing my best
dress, the red one you liked so much. Red was my favorite
color too. First, you told me that I was pretty and smart.
Then we kissed. And kissed. And kissed again. That
alone would've been enough, but then you placed a hand
on my thigh and slid the other one down my spine, sent
tranquility running through my body like my blood had
turned to wine. Your tongue licked me in private places
and reached deep down my throat. Your kisses were wet as
waterfalls; I could barely stay afloat. My eyes rolled back
into my head, where visions of you loving me ran wild. I
got lost inside your passion as your fingertips defiled. And
when you rested your heavy chest on my virgin breasts and
pulled my hips to yours? Mmm…it was just as I had
pictured… It was all that and more.

Your hands were dangerous, the way that they
attacked me, tugging and pulling at me, in sensual brutality.
At first, it hurt a little, but you soothed me with your kiss.
You nibbled on my earlobe and sent me into bliss. Every
single inch of me lay there longing for the pain. My eyes
rolled back up inside my head again, like they were looking
for my brain. Our bodies intertwined, all of yours and all
of mine, folding into one another, glued in sweat. Between
us. Beneath us. Sweat slick like oil and salty on your lips
as you squeezed my breasts and grabbed my hips. You
strummed on me like an old guitar, sang me like a sax.
Your fingertips skipped along me like a piano, to the top of
the scale and back. I was your music. You were my muse.
I was your rhythm. You were my blues. I squeezed you

tighter and dug my nails into your skin. You felt like black satin in my hands, and I squeezed you hard again.

I was only twelve; you were almost forty. I was too young to choose you; you decided for me. You sent me headed for insanity the first time you put your hands on me. You placed me on the verge of ecstasy with no hope for return. From then on, I yearned for it. I burned within. I should have been focused on school, but I was too busy being your fool: scribbling your name in notebooks and pining for your kiss, doodling your image on napkins, and writing poems like this. I wanted to shout our love from the rooftops, to climb the nearest mountain and yell. But I promised you my silence. I swore I'd never tell..................................

I gasped and rose into a fit of coughing. For some reason, I was breathless and cold. As I paused to allow the air to refill my deflated lungs, I took a moment to try and make some sense of that strange hallucination. Was this buried memory now being exhumed by my brain to remind me of something long forgotten? Or was it an allegory, some kind of metaphor conjured by my subconscious to warn me of events still to come? My emotions were spilling all over the place, and trying to contain them was like trying to scoop up a runny egg with a metal spoon: impossible. Before I could wake myself fully, I was already asleep again, cast back into the land of dreams and hopes and fears, doomed to endure yet another round of restless repose.

|•|•|•|•|•|•|•|•|•|•|•|•|•|•|•|•|•|•|•|•|•|•|•|

We'd been ducking and dodging Mama for weeks, and it was starting to gnaw at my conscience. I told you how I felt about it, but you dismissed my fears as nonsense. And then, later that night, I remember you crept into my room. You surprised me with chocolates and a bottle of perfume. I felt terrible opening that box for reasons I could scarcely describe. Somehow, your gift felt insincere to me, like it was some sort of bribe. I tried to break things off again right there, and I wanted to tell Mama. I couldn't stand the pressure of the lying and the sneaking; I hated all the drama. You looked at me with those sad eyes, so big and brown, and you asked me to hear you out; you begged me to sit back down.

I knew I shouldn't have sat on that chair. Shouldn't have let you play with my hair. And even if it was only just a peck, I shouldn't have let you kiss me on the neck. I heard the marching band in my head, but louder still were the words you said. "I love you," you whispered all over me, spreading lies like KY Jelly, before mounting my belly. You told me to kiss you, and like a fool, I obeyed. This time, not love, but a baby was made.

I lay there in a bed of my own blood and tears, serenaded by screams. Screams soaring like ghosts up and down the tunneling corridors, the cries of women and little girls just like me, scared and scarred, lonely and alone, strapped down and spread open, then poked and prodded like meat on the grill, forceps used as tongs. My angel was born, and I held her for a little while. Instantly, I fell in love; I couldn't contain my smile. They took her so they could weigh her and count her fingers and toes. Then a social worker whisked her from the room and gave her to God only knows.

Who ushered me into that cold, cold Hell? That's something only a devil can do. You sent me to that cold, cold Hell. The devil, my darling, is you. And so now, I'm afraid I'll have to kill you. The family you destroyed must be avenged. Three generations of women ruined by you. And for that, you cannot make amends. No, I won't accept your apology. Yes, it's too late to surrender. You're only sorry it caught up with you, and that makes you the worst kind of offender. BOOM.............................

I woke up, lurching violently to what sounded like a gunshot in my ear. My whole body was drenched in a cold sweat, and breathing seemed impossible, as if I were sitting on the surface of the moon. I heard another loud boom and realized it was nothing more than Francine lurking somewhere close. And more than ever, I was thankful for her torrential tantrums sending so much thunder and rain. It seemed like my mind had gone haywire: synapses disconnected, neurons misfiring. Something was wrong with my brain! With all the weird dreams and distant memories running rampant through my malfunctioning mind and straddling my subconscious, I was like a climber clinging to a cliff, trying desperately not to slip and fall down into a ravine of hazy fog. Francine became a friend to me, extending her hand and helping me to climb back up aboard reality. Her thunder reminded me which world was real, which sounds were actual, which visions were mere illusion and which ones were factual. And of all the many emotions my screwball senses perceived, Francine told me which, if any, could truly be believed.

There was nothing but darkness everywhere, and I couldn't see a thing. I heard voices nearby, but all the sounds around me collided with one another in a deafening cacophony, loud and indistinct, like a dozen radios being played simultaneously, each one on a different station with frequencies scrambled. I felt so scared there in the dark that I started to panic again and buck wildly like a bronco. It was then that I realized that I was tied up at the wrists and ankles. I bore down with all my might to try and break free of the ropes that bound me there, but my strength was insufficient, and my resistance futile. I felt like every muscle in my body had somehow atrophied, and I was rendered immobile, completely lame and powerless.

I began to cry. And as I sat there, teary-eyed, staring into the black abyss, I realized then that the darkness I sensed all around me was nothing more than the simple result of my eyes having been closed this whole time. I tried to open them, but it felt like my eyelids were made of steel, each lash weighing a ton. I tried again to open them and failed. I tried again and again and maybe a dozen times more until finally I managed to lift those stubborn gates and cast my gaze on the world around me.

It was breathtaking, the way the lights danced and the pretty shapes hovered over my head and twirled around the room. And the room itself was revolving gently, gracefully counterclockwise. As I sat there, I saw teeny little bubbles drifting leisurely on a soft wind, and periodically they'd all explode together like fireworks, a million brilliant stars bursting forth and raining down on my face. I smiled and laughed, grateful to be free of Earth's monotony and happy to take residence in this beautiful new world hidden deep inside the viewfinder of a kaleidoscope.

Without warning, I felt a hard slap against my face, but it wasn't administered by someone's hand. The hard

slap I felt was the cold sting of a lengthy spray of water.
And suddenly, I was drowning. My hallucination popped
open like a zit, and my fantasy world ruptured and oozed to
an end right before my eyes. Immediately I was fully
aware again. I was fully awake: lucid, coherent, and
terrified!

"Who are you?!" Pete stood before me, asking. A
man in a dark suit stood beside him, holding a dripping,
high-velocity hose. As I sat there gasping, my hair and
face soaking wet, I spied five lightbulbs hanging from the
ceiling in a straight line right down the middle of the room.
One such bulb swung just above my chair. And with the
help of its light, I saw that the floor was made of concrete
and there was dampness all around, water collecting in
puddles all over. I heard the constant gurgling of a drain
nearby and gathered that I must have been in the diner's
basement.

Several metal racks were assembled all throughout
the space. Big bags of sugar, flour, cornmeal, rice, and
dried beans were stacked high all along the rickety racks
and made the room look like one great big pantry. Wooden
slats lined the brick walls as well, and those makeshift
shelves were packed tight with big economy-sized cans,
jars, and bottles. There was enough mayonnaise, ketchup,
mustard, and relish there for a million meals. Every item
on every shelf, every can on every rack, each bag and
bottle, was labeled with a giant number, evidence of an
airtight inventory system hard at work, someone governing
the massive storeroom, and crunching numbers with a fine-
point pencil. The man with the hose aimed his weapon at
me again and fired, attacking me like a dedicated fireman

up against a blazing inferno. "Who are you?!" Pete
shouted again.

The water stung my face and went way up into my
nostrils and mouth. I was breathless, just as I had been
when I'd risen from that first dream. And the cold water all
over my face and running down my back reminded me of
the cold sweat I'd felt when I'd risen from the second
dream. Had I been under interrogation this whole time?
Could the breathlessness and cold sweats I'd felt before
have been the hose at work then too?

"You askin' me who I am. Who the hell are
you?!!" I fired back. One of the other suits lunged forward
with his fist cocked, but Pete lifted a hand, and the goon
halted in his tracks. "First, you stick a gun in my back.
Then you tie me up and drug me. Then you got the nerve
to get mad when I can't answer questions?!" And
suddenly, I surprised myself by leaning over the arm of my
chair and vomiting.

"Man, I told you that was too much nitrous oxide!"
Pete scolded one of the men. "I told you to *sedate* her. Not
put her in a coma!" The goon bowed his head in shame.
Then Pete turned his attention back to me. "Amateurs," he
mumbled under his breath. The powerful hose had
knocked my bun loose, and my wet curls hung down low
over my face. Pete pushed them to the side, and I flinched
beneath his unfamiliar touch. I felt woozy, presumably
from the drugs, and my stomach was knotted up tighter
than a hangman's noose. "Listen, honey," Pete began.
"I'm a nice man. I am." He clutched his heart as if he
were pledging allegiance to the flag. "But I need you to
understand that I got a good thing goin' on here and I don't
like folks meddlin' and askin' too many questions." Pete

251

paced the floor. "Especially when they come up in here askin' questions about a motherfucka' who double-crossed me. So, from here on out, if it's all the same to you"—he paused and tipped his chef's hat in my direction— "I'll ask the questions. Let's start again with question one. Who are you?" The hoodlum with the hose sprayed me again, and I found myself gurgling louder than the drain in the corner.

"My name," I whispered between gasps, "is Tina...Tina Henderson."

"How I know dat?! Huh?! You walkin' 'round here wit' no wallet...no ID. How I know you are who you say you are? And where is Samson?!" The hose assaulted me again, stinging my eyes and adding to the tears that were already there.

"I can explain!" I shouted. "Lemme explain, please!" I wheezed.

"Go on," Pete permitted. "Continue. But I'm warning you." He shook his index finger at me. "Whatever it is that's about to come outta' yo' mouth betta' sound like the truth to me, or I'll have my man here drown you right there in that chair." He motioned to the man with the hose, and the aquatic assassin readied his fingers on the trigger. "Now who are you, and where is Samson?"

"I promise I don't know where Samson is. I'm lookin' for him too!" I pleaded.

"Why?! Who are you to him? We know you ain't his wife, 'cause we done already paid her a visit!"

"I'm nobody, sir! I barely even know him!" The fireman lifted his hose once more, and I hurried up and blurted out the rest of my story before I could be doused again. "I met him a few days ago. He picked me up in a bar, and we went back to my place and...you know..." I

252

lowered my head, pretending to be ashamed. "One thing led to another, and when I woke up the next morning, he was gone. And he took my wallet with him, my credit cards, my license, my cash. Everything!" I admit I felt a little guilty projecting my wrongdoings onto Samson. I was the one who had stolen *his* wallet, and here I was blaming a corpse for my crimes. "He mentioned to me that he worked at the best soul food joint in Georgia and told me he would bring me here for dinner one day. That was before he robbed me, of course. I'm just tryna' find him so I can get my stuff back... That's all!" The chef probed my face for a sign of sincerity, a trace of truth.

"Think about it, sir. Why would I come up in here askin' about Samson if I knew he double-crossed you? Why would I step knowingly into harm's way? Why would I venture into the lion's den and risk gettin' myself mauled to death? I don't know what Samson did that's got you all so mad, but I swear it ain't got nothin' to do wit' me!" The chef paused to ponder my remarks. Then he sprang to life like a jack-in-the-box.

"I won't tell you what he did. I'll *show* you!" Pete walked swiftly over to one of the metal racks and began yanking down one of the big bags of rice from a shelf high above his head. It had to be at least fifty pounds, and secretly I wished it would fall down and crush him like the roach he resembled. But instead, a few of his henchman joined him there and helped the short chef retrieve the heavy sack from that upper ledge. They each grabbed a corner, brought the sack over to me, and set it down gently. Then Pete pulled a long blade from his hip and poked a tiny hole in the top of the bag. Instead of grains of rice, a mysterious white powder spilled from the hole in the sack.

253

"Not even Birdie and the others know about my lil' side business. But somehow that junkie Samson found out what we were doin' down here and stole two bags just like this one. Bag number forty-eight and bag number fifty-one." Pete pointed to the empty spaces on the metal racks where the bags had been. "That's almost fifty kilos! You know how much that is out on the streets? I need to find him before he sells my shit! Or worse yet, before it disappears up his big nose. And guess what? You gon' help me look for him!"

"What?!" I cried. "I don't even know where he is myself! That's why I came here in the first place!"

"Well, we done searched the city high and low for that boy, and no luck. But you! You done tracked down his employer. And Birdie said you knew he had a son before she told you 'bout him. You even somehow managed to obtain a photo of him to aid you in yo' search." Pete pulled my picture of Samson from his huge apron pocket. "How in the hell you do that?" Pete studied the photo in his hands, then held it up to my face like it was the smoking gun, exhibit A in an ironclad case.

"I don't know how you did it," he said with a laugh, "but somehow, you managed to make more headway with Samson in the last few days than my men have in weeks. Granted, they ain't the sharpest bunch..." He glared again at the dimwit who drugged me to excess. "But you"—he bestowed upon me a look of wonder and amazement— "you must be pretty resourceful, Miss Henderson. And you got moxie! A man stole something from you, and you made it yo' mission to track his ass down. I like that! You and me both want the same thing. We wanna find that bastard and get back what's ours! I need someone bold and clever like you on my team. So now...you work for me," the don decreed.

"Work for you?!" I repeated, confusion choking my understanding.

"You know way too much about my operation"—he pointed around the room— "for me to just let you walk outta' here alive, young lady. And you seem to be having more success at sniffing Samson out than the rest of us. So, you're hired!" Pete proclaimed.

"I'm not looking for a job, sir."

"I'm not offering you one." He laughed. "An offer," he explained, "can be declined. You ain't got no choice in this matter, Miss Henderson. The job is yours...effective immediately." He laughed again. "The pay is nominal, but the benefits package can't be beat. You see, Miss Henderson, if you work for me, you get to keep on breathing. And if you don't, you die."

"Come on now! If I was so smart, I wouldn't have gotten my wallet stolen in the first place! If I had half a brain, you think I woulda' walked up in yo' restaurant and sat down at yo' counter? I've already gotten myself in enough danger over this fool Samson, and I won't do it! I ain't no private investigator! And I'm not getting' myself mixed up in a drug ring over no missin' wallet. It ain't worth it!"

All the goons inched toward me, like I'd just insulted their pappy and smeared their family name. The violence showed on each of their faces, and I knew I'd said too much. The chef held up a hand, and again, all the men froze, as if someone had yanked on their leashes. Then Pete turned into a hyena, laughing wildly, as if *he* had been the one plied with nitrous oxide, the laughing gas that had made me so loopy before.

"Listen, Miss Henderson." He leaned in and whispered. His calm tones sounded menacing to me and sent more shivers through my body than that high-powered hose. "I can fillet a five-hundred-pound steer in just under ten minutes. One big fat slab of beef"—he stretched his arms wide to demonstrate the proportions— "reduced to the juiciest, most succulent portions of meat you ever laid eyes on. First, I take that foreshank and carve out the brisket, slice up that flank real good, and make grillin' steaks. I dissect the rib cage like a trained surgeon and make up a rib roast, ribeye steaks, baby back ribs, all that!" The chef licked his lips as if the raw meat itself had whet his appetite. Perhaps I *had* stumbled into a lion's den after all. "My favorite part is that loin. Mmm…" He salivated.

"Ya' see, that's where you get your porterhouse from, and your tenderloin and your filet mignon, the most delectable cuts. Then I dice up that chuck for stew meat and ground that round into burgers. We known for our quarter pounders," he boasted. "And baby, you should see me. I'm like a duck in water. When I get my knives goin', I'm like Michelangelo carving out David from a block of fine marble, like a sculptor chiseling out swans from a hunk of ice. Girl, I'm David Copperfield pullin' an elephant out of an envelope, doing the impossible, making something outta' nothing. And all it takes me is ten short minutes. Six hundred seconds. You must be 'bout what? A buck fifty? Maybe 'bout a hundred and sixty pounds?" He pulled the long blade from his side again and thrust it swiftly in my direction like Zorro on the attack. "How long you think it'll take me to fillet *you*, Miss Henderson?"

I don't know if it was the pain I felt from the blade poking my abdomen or the lingering pangs stemming from my association with Samson, but my eyes began to well up again. Tears threatened to spill from my eyelids like water over an embankment. It seemed like I was making enemies everywhere I turned, and just like the cans and bottles on the shelves all around me, my days felt like they, too, were numbered. And speaking of numbers.

"A hundred and sixty pounds? Really?!! You lucky my hands are tied, or I'd slap your mustache off!" I cursed the chef, and he laughed. It was guttural and grand. His booming voice echoed back and forth between the brick walls, bounced off the concrete floors, and filled the soggy cellar. And that haunting cackle served to substantiate him in my mind as a truly evil villain.

"I like you, Miss Henderson. I do. And I'll tell ya' somethin'. It shole would hurt me deep if you disappointed me. I'm givin' you a grand opportunity here. I'm giving you the chance to grow old and gray…to see your children walk down the aisle someday…to rock your grandbabies to sleep in your favorite chair. Don't blow it." I gulped. "I want Samson alive. You can hurt him, but don't kill him. You leave that to me. You got forty-eight hours."

He made a slight motion to one of his goons with a simple tilt of his head. And next thing I knew? Darkness. Silence. I was weightless. Like a leaf drifting up on the breeze, I was suspended in midair. Then I was floating in outer space. Then I was a spirit without a body…a glimmer of light dancing in the distance.

|•|•|•|•|•|•|•|•|•|•|•|•|•|•|•|•|•|•|•|•|•|•|•

I gasped and sprang up in my chair with a jolt. I was panting like a dog in chase. It took a moment for me to slow my breaths and quiet my mind. I guess I'd fallen back to sleep. I couldn't recall any strange dreams or haunting nightmares this time around. Perhaps I hadn't been dreaming at all? I wasn't sure. But despite that little bit of uncertainty, I felt much more alert this time. I wasn't seeing stars and colors, and my mind was stationary, no more spinning. I lay back and settled into my seat, staring out at the road ahead. Daylight peeked over the horizon before me, but there was no sun, just clouds lumped together like cotton bolls, soft as cotton balls, crawling slowly across the crepuscular skies. A soft rain fell down all around, and for a moment, I was lulled. I found myself hypnotized by the windshield wipers that moved rhythmically from side to side.

Suddenly, I became aware of the fact that my neck was quite stiff, and I sat up tall in my seat to stretch my weary limbs. I looked to my right and saw the scenery moving past my window: grassy meadows, amber colored fields, and dew-kissed paddocks. The cows and horses all paused together and lifted their necks to study the Ferrari as it drove past their pastures. *Wait*, my brain whispered to me softly. *If the Ferrari is on the move and you aren't driving it...then who is?* I turned to my left and locked eyes with a stranger.

"I'm Asani," the unfamiliar man announced. The handle of his gun peeked out from behind the waistband of his dark gray suit, and instantly I forgot how to breathe. "You can call me Ace." The look on my face must have expressed all my apprehensions and exposed all my fears. "Don't panic. Don't trip. Relax." He held out a reassuring hand. "I'm not here to hurt you, I promise. We're just on our way to get some coffee. That's all."

"Who the hell are you? And what the hell are you doin' driving my car?" I asked. By this time, my back was pressed squarely against the passenger door even despite the FF's taut seatbelts.

"Relax," the stranger said again, one hand on the wheel and the other extended between us. His palm lay flat, and he lowered it slowly as if he were trying to push down my anxieties. "Pete sent you on assignment, remember? You're supposed to find Samson and, with any luck, retrieve what he stole. That ring a bell?" I nodded. "Well, think of me as Pete's insurance policy. I'm here to make sure you keep your word and do what Pete asked you to do. I'm here to make sure you don't get hurt and to make sure you don't do nothin' stupid either...like blab to the cops about our private affairs. We understand each other?" I nodded again. "I guess I'm kinda' like...your chaperone." He smiled. "Don't play no games with me, and you and me won't have no trouble. Got it?" I swallowed hard.

What had I gotten myself into now? Forty-eight hours ago, my biggest fear had been that Mr. Tennison might put me out on the streets. Now, I found myself mixed up in the nefarious activities of an organized crime syndicate. One false move, and they might put me *under* the streets, six feet deep in a pine box. Now here I was, cruising the countryside in a stolen car, being chauffeured by an armed and dangerous stranger, a career criminal, probably a hitman or assassin—all the while being chased by the police, my landlord, Mrs. Barrister, Butch, Eve, Willie, and Francine! They chased me like townspeople going after a suspected witch. Armed with their pitchforks and their prejudices, they were ready to burn me alive at the stake. And as they chased me, I found myself in a chase too. I was in hot pursuit of a cold body, a dead man, an unidentified corpse lying in the county morgue. And my assignment was to bring him back alive. Talk about a mission impossible! How could I bring back a dead man? I'd been blessed with a lot of skills, endowed with many talents, but honey, resurrection power wasn't one of 'em!

The stranger continued to drive on down the road, and he placed his fingers consolingly in mine. Meanwhile, I marveled over my lousy luck. Even while sitting there holding an Ace, somehow, I still wound up with the losing hand.

CHAPTER 22: SMOKING GUNS...

"Please tell me you got a cigarette?" I asked the mysterious miscreant. It had been two days since my last one, and I felt like a fiend going through withdrawal. My nerves were bouncing all over the place like a jar full of crickets, and I needed something to ease my mind, to calm my spirit. More than anything, I needed to come up with a plan of escape for this present predicament, but I just couldn't think straight. While the FF moved freely through the countryside, every road my mind ventured down seemed to end in a cul-de-sac, and I kept getting turned around. I needed a Newport!

It's so amazing what a cigarette can do. There's a certain clarity that comes from sipping on one of those slender sticks. Instantly the slate of your mind is cleared of clutter, and you find yourself free to ponder more important matters. And if you're anything like me, chile, just hearing that wrapper squeak when you tear into that pack for the first time and hearing the foil crunch when you're digging for that smoke? Mmm...it's like opening presents on Christmas morning. And when you finally break that seal and the aroma escapes the carton and wafts up to kiss you on the nose, there's this soothing, hopeful feeling that descends upon you just knowing that soon you'll be savoring that smooth taste. The effects of Pete's drugs had just worn off, and I was already looking to replace one poison with another, nicotine for nitrous.

"Nope, sorry. I don't smoke. And neither should you. Those things'll kill ya'," said the man with the gun.

"Is that so?" I asked facetiously.

"Yes, that *is* so," he said, mocking my glib tone. "You wouldn't sit in your garage with the motor running, would you?"

"Umm…no," I reluctantly replied.

"Of course you wouldn't. Not unless you were tryna' kill yourself from carbon monoxide poisoning. Would you sniff a bottle of ammonia? Would you breathe from a tank labeled 'Cyanide'? No. But every time you light a cigarette, that's exactly what you doin'. Over seven thousand chemicals in tobacco smoke. Seven thousand!" he reiterated. "Carbon monoxide, ammonia, and cyanide only account for three!"

"And who are you? The surgeon general?" I snapped. Even though I had plenty of issues in my life to be worried over and anxious about, I believe it was my plummeting nicotine levels that placed me on such razor-sharp edge that morning and made me so crabby and cantankerous. At that very moment, all I wanted was a cigarette. The mere thought of it consumed my mind, body, and spirit like a deity demanding to be worshipped. And Ace's disrespect and irreverence toward my sudden spiritual fervor made me all the more ardent in my defense.

"Whatever," he muttered. "Obviously, you don't like to be wrong." He adjusted the rearview mirror.

"Just spare me the sanctimonious speeches, okay. Lotta' nerve you got admonishing me for smokin'." I turned away to observe the cows.

"Cigarettes kill. That's a fact." He slapped the steering wheel.

"Oh, and bullets don't? What's your gun loaded with? Ice cream and sprinkles? Every single day, almost three hundred people across this country are maimed or killed by gun violence. That, too, is a fact."

"Yeah, and *quadruple* that amount die daily from cigarettes! You can throw out all the stats and numbers you want, but no matter how you look at it, smoking kills far more people than guns. It's simple math." He laughed smugly.

"How's this for simple math? All it takes is *one* bullet," I said, holding up a finger, "but one *cigarette* ain't never killed nobody!"

"Well," he began. "The fact is—"

"And even if cigarettes claim more lives than guns in the long run," I interrupted, "how can you compare a violent, painful, bloody shooting death to a mild chemical exposure over the course a lifetime?" Just *talking* about smoking seemed to have sharpened my mind like a cat's claws, and I was feeling like my old self.

"But," he began again, "studies have shown—"

"I'm done with this argument." I held up my palm between us as if I were holding his words at bay, blocking his opinions from entering my ears. "Let's just agree to disagree. You don't tell me to stop smokin', and I won't tell you to stop shootin'. Deal?"

"Argument?" He laughed. "I would have to get a word in edgewise for this to be an argument." He laughed again. "And for the record, I'm not the one making comparisons. *You're* the one who went and brought up gun violence. And since you mentioned it, I spoke on it. Bottom line? Cigarettes do far more harm than guns and pose a far greater threat to people's overall health and well-being. If you can't see that, you need to get cha' eyes checked."

"Say what you will, tough guy," I sneered, "but if you had to choose whether to be shot to death right now or to smoke a pack a day over the next forty years, chile, please. You'd go through more Camels than a taxi stand in Saudi Arabia!" A brooding expression washed over his face as he contemplated my remarks. It seemed my logic had silenced him, and I'd won the debate.

"So I was right then," he concluded.

"What?!" I turned my full body toward him. "How are you right?" I contested.

"I said you don't like to be wrong. And that makes me right." He smiled, still staring at the road ahead.

"Of course I don't like to be wrong. Duh! Name me one person who *likes* to be wrong. I'll wait." I held up my wrist and stared at my watch. "Aaaant! Time's up!"

"Fine," he conceded. "You do to suit yourself. Smoke a million cigarettes if you want. See if I care." We rode the rest of the way in silence, and while the gangster glowered, I gloated.

The roads were completely clear, as if the Earth had been evacuated during the night. There was an eerie stillness in the air, and I felt sorry for the sky. Battered and bruised all night by the sadistic storm, now it was black and blue all over. I wanted to turn on the radio and see what the news had to say, but I didn't want to make any sudden or unauthorized moves with the sullen gunman sitting by my side. After a few miles more, we crossed over into Roswell and pulled into the parking lot of Debbie's Donuts. The Ferrari came to a stop.

"Now, listen up," Ace said, pulling the keys from the ignition. "When we get inside, I don't want you talkin' to nobody. I don't even want you *lookin'* at nobody. Just smile and stay near me. No funny business. And if you thinkin' 'bout tryna' make a run for it, just remember. I've been authorized to make good on every one of my boss's threats." He pointed to the gun on his hip. "And I definitely don't wanna hurt you. That's not my style."

"What am I, five? I know how to behave in a store. Save the briefing for your next hostage." I'd been threatened so many times lately, I found myself almost completely desensitized. "Besides. I couldn't run even if I wanted to. I'm a smoker, remember?" I coughed and stuck out my tongue.

Ace shook his head stoically, as if he were exercising great restraint. Then he pulled a gray fedora from under his seat and stepped out into the rain. As soon as his back was turned to me, I rushed to lift the center console to grab one of the guns that lay there hidden. They were gone. I lowered the console in a hurry as Ace walked around the front of the car and met me on the passenger side. I stepped outside to join him in the rain as he held an umbrella over my head.

"Your pocketbook's beneath the seat if you need it." He pointed.

"Thank you," I said as I bent back down to retrieve my purse. While I was down there, I felt around underneath the seat. What had become of the guns and the Swiss army knife? Had the sacks in the trunk been discovered too? I was shaken up, but I tried my best not to let the disconcertion show on my face. I'd been acting all big and bad with Ace only because I was counting on those secret weapons. But somehow, my secret had been let out. And like a sucker strolling around with a "Kick Me" sign on my back, I was the last to know.

I swung my pocketbook casually over my shoulder and centered myself under Ace's umbrella. Then I did some of the best acting of my life, pretending not to be terrified as I walked the parking lot like a pirate's plank. Now that we were out of the car, I noticed for the first time that Ace was quite tall, maybe six three or six four. I almost had to run to match his long strides. Even in the absence of the sun, his copper skin glowed under the morning light like an orb of glass plucked from a fiery furnace. His eyes were honey-colored, and his lips were full and red as if they'd been painted on. His haircut was neat and close, and the short, fine hairs that lay beneath his hat were remarkably lustrous and colored in a sandy brown. As we approached the store's entrance, he pulled the door open, and his blazer became tight in the arms as his biceps constricted. He held the door and gestured for me to enter first. I crossed in front of the chivalrous chauffeur, but I knew that, like any other man, he was only pretending to be polite so he could ogle my ass as I sauntered by.

Debbie's wasn't much more than a kitchen, a counter, and a few tables—six to be exact. But in a glass encasement behind the granite counter, a colorful exhibition of pastries, Danishes, and donuts was displayed on nearly a dozen long shelves. Chocolate muffins and blueberry scones. Bear claws full of jelly and eclairs filled with cream. Those sweet treats impregnated the air with all kinds of syrupy scents, and with each breath, I could already feel my thighs spreading.

It was 7am on a Saturday morning, and the patronage was understandably scant. A few old men sat at the counter entertaining a gray-haired waitress, and a couple more elderly gentleman occupied two of the square tables. They didn't seem to know one another, yet they traded sections of the same newspaper between sips of black coffee. Ace and I approached the counter, and the waitress excused herself from her senior citizen suitors to take our orders near the vintage cash register.

"Mornin'!" she exclaimed as she made her way over. "What can I do ya' for?" Her cheeks and lips were a bright rouge, and her eyeshadow was the color of the ocean, a bright blue-green. Dark eyeliner traced her eyelids and made her look a bit sad even despite her wide smile. Her gray hair looked as hard as a helmet and was styled like Washington's wig on the one-dollar bill. You could almost *see* the hairspray on it, and I worried for her safety working back there in that hot kitchen with such combustible curls. Her large breasts sat up high, just beneath her chin, and threatened to leap right out of her uniform like a couple of kangaroos. Her nametag was placed, quite provocatively, alongside her copious cleavage. And the letters on it spelled the name "Debbie".

"A coffee please. And a scrambled egg on toast," Ace ordered.

"That for here or to go, sweetie?" Debbie asked, typing numbers into the antiquated keyboard.

"Here," he answered. Then he turned to me. "What chu' want?"

"Not hungry," I replied.

"Make that two coffees, please," he said to the waitress. "And...add an order of pancakes with blueberry syrup," he continued. How dare he order for me! Didn't I just say I wasn't hungry? I was so annoyed, I rolled my eyes one at a time. "Trust me," he leaned in and

267

whispered. "You gotta eat something. And after you taste Debbie's pancakes, you'll be glad you did." He smiled.

Trust him? Was he serious? Through his suit jacket, I could still see the faint imprint of the gun on his hip. And I sneered again derisively. *Trust me*. Those two words must be on page one of The Asshole Handbook— required reading for all men. Ace was pretending to care, pretending to be an advocate for my interests. Meanwhile, the gun on his hip told a different story. That gun spoke the truth! Like every man I'd encountered before him, Ace smiled at me outwardly, all the while plotting inwardly to destroy me the minute I became obsolete or unnecessary. I refused to be conned again, and I ignored those soft words and that bright smile—even despite its dimples.

"Okay, loves. Pick a seat and take a load off. Coffee comin' right up!" Debbie directed, and Ace and I staked out a table near the window.

"So, what's the plan?" We'd barely sat down, and already Ace was ready to talk business.

"I don't have a plan. This lil' adventure wasn't my idea, remember?"

"True. But from what I understand, you were already lookin' for Samson though, right?"

"Yeah, so?"

"Well…let's pretend you never had that little run-in with Pete last night and you never got tangled up with me. Suppose you just came to the diner lookin' for Samson and he wasn't there. What would your next move be?"

I paused to ponder the question. "Well…" Just as I was beginning to answer, Debbie arrived with our coffees and interrupted my summation.

"Henry, put down that paper and finish those flapjacks before they get cold!" Debbie scolded one of the men a few tables over.

"I'm full!" the old man shouted back over the sports section. "My eyes were bigger than my stomach."

"Not from where I'm standin', they ain't!" she let out a loud hoot, and all the other men joined her in a round of laughter. "Now eat up!" Debbie demanded. Then she set our coffees before us, along with a tin cup filled with fresh cream. "Food'll be out in a jiffy, loves. Y'all sit tight!" she promised as she left the table.

"Thank you," Ace called after her. Then he turned back to me. "You were saying?" he asked as he grabbed several packets of sugar from a dish on the table.

"Um..." I poured a little cream into my coffee and watched it blush, turning from black to beige in a magical moment, like the forming of a thought, so swift and resolute. "If the diner had been a dead end, I would've just gone on to the next place."

"The next place?"

"Yeah." I reached for my purse. "I scribbled a few notes here." I unzipped my bag and dug for the widow's list. I didn't want to offer up too many details about the list. If Pete and his gangsters knew what those words were and what they all meant, they might just circumvent me all together and renege on our agreement. Then, next thing you know, I've mysteriously disappeared, and there's a new lunch special on the butcher's menu: a *Tina* melt, served up with a pickle on rye.

As I found the list, I also found it quite telling that Ace seemed totally comfortable with me reaching inside my purse. His nonchalance confirmed for me that he'd already gone through it for weapons and found it to be benign. And if he'd been the one to search my purse, I deduced that he had probably been the one to search the car as well. He was most likely the one who'd recovered the weapons concealed there inside. But where were they now?

"I have a few more leads to follow," I said, examining the crumpled list. "Hopefully, one of 'em will take us to Samson." Of course, I knew finding Samson alive would be harder than finding clean undies on laundry day, but I figured maybe I could uncover some information that would steer Pete toward his stolen property. And if Pete found his lost drugs or at least found out what happened to them, maybe he'd release me from this debt and spare my life. Maybe.

"Sounds good. So where we headed next?" Ace asked between slurps of coffee. Piping hot steam rose from his mug like smoke over an active volcano.

"Not sure. I placed a call in to a friend of mine yesterday, and she's supposed to help me turn up some information on one of the leads. I need to call her back this morning to see what she found out. I think that'll probably determine where we go next."

"And who is this friend?" An eyebrow rose high on his forehead.

"None of your business," I replied. He glared across the table at me. "If you want me to trust you, you gotta trust me too," I insisted. "Now, my friend was kind enough to help me out with this favor, and I'm not about to repay her kindness by gettin' her mixed up in a drug cartel." We peered into each other's eyes like we were having a staring match, a blinking contest, our strong wills at war.

"Fair enough," he acquiesced. "I'll trust you on this, but don't make me regret it." He sighed.

"Egg sandwich," Debbie announced as she approached the table again. "And a stack of buttermilk pancakes with homemade blueberry syrup. My granny's recipe!" she added with a wink, setting both plates down on the table. "Eat up, now!"

"So..." Ace scooped up the hot sandwich and blew on it softly with his thick lips. For it to be just a simple egg on toast, that heaping sandwich looked huge there, even despite Ace's big hands, like it had been made from the egg of an albatross. "Where ya' from?" Ace asked, taking a big bite of the steaming sandwich. An excess of butter and grease dripped down onto his plate.

"Where am I from?" I sneered. "If you think I'm about to tell you all my personal business, yo' brain must be scrambled harder than that egg you eatin'," I replied, staring at the mountain of carbs before me.

"You're really rude. You know that?"

"Oh? Well, if I'm rude, what does that make you?!" I retorted.

"Believe it or not, I'm actually a really nice guy." The look in his eyes told me that he actually believed what he was saying.

"If you're a nice guy, then let me go." I pointed toward the door.

"You know I can't do that. I'd like to. But my hands are tied."

"Yeah? So were mine. All night. My hands were tied and so were my ankles. I was drugged and tortured for

271

hours while all you suits just stood around and watched. A *real* nice guy wouldn't have let that happen. A *real* nice guy would have stepped forward out of the shadows and done something. So pardon me if my feelings for you aren't exactly warm and fuzzy." I reached for my fork.

"I get that," he said, and he almost looked sincere. "What happened to you last night was terrible. And it was unforgiveable. But today is a new day. You're safe now. And I intend to keep you that way…so long as we can work together, and you continue to cooperate." He picked his sandwich back up. "I won't ask you anymore questions. And if you prefer, we can sit here and eat in silence. How's that?" He took another bite.

"Thank you," I replied. I stared down at my plate, unsure where to begin. I counted six pancakes in that towering stack, and I was trying my hardest not to count the calories. Rich and gooey syrup dripped down over the sides of the buttermilk heap and gathered at the bottom of the platter in a pool of blue. Fresh blueberries were sprinkled all over, and a huge dollop of butter melted slowly in the center and drizzled down over the edges. I couldn't deny. It truly was a beautiful breakfast.

"Toast?"

"Yes, please." Each slice was black as tar and burnt to a Cajun crisp, but I was hungry. And so were the others. All around me, I heard the sounds of knives scraping, everyone chipping away at the rock-hard bread to break through to the edible parts. A chainsaw and jackhammer could have served as acceptable silverware for a meal like this, right alongside our forks and knives. I smiled and proceeded on down the line.

"Ham?" offered a little old lady in a hairnet.

"Yes, please," I replied, and she dropped a thick wedge of pink meat onto my styrofoam plate. Thick chunks of fat protruded from the meat's surface. I held the plate to my nose and sniffed. Then I dissected the meat with my plastic fork and examined its texture like a coroner conducting an autopsy. My analysis determined conclusively that the mystery meat wasn't ham at all, but ham's evil imposter: spam. "Keep the line moving, please," the old lady directed, and I lumbered on over to the next station.

"Eggs?" offered a portly woman with a round face. Her hair was covered by a tall, black and white habit that draped over her shoulders and ran down her back. I did a double take as I watched her stir the big foil pan of scrambled eggs that rested on the Sternos between us. The eggs weren't pure yellow, but variegated oddly with tinges of blue and green. At the time, that bizarre sight ranked high amongst the strangest things I'd ever seen. I now know that sometimes a large batch of scrambled eggs may turn green when the eggs are left in an aluminum pan for too long over direct heat. It's a common occurrence in the food service industry, but as an inexperienced sixteen-year-old, I was nonetheless repulsed.

I'd been waiting for over an hour in the cold to be admitted into the Blessed Sacrament Soup Kitchen. It was the holiday season, and as Christmas carols were blazoned all over the airwaves, nearly all the homes and stores in town were decorated inside and out with lights and shimmering tinsel. From the loquacious old ladies loitering at bus stops right down to the stickup kids and street-corner thugs, everyone in town seemed a tad more cheerful with Christmas fast approaching. And even the poorest among us had giving on the mind. Not me, though. I hadn't eaten in days and was far too filled with pride to ask for help. But when my stomach began to tighten up like an angry fist that morning and I'd found myself battling debilitating cramps, I learned firsthand that one cannot subsist on pride alone. So, I made myself join the long line of vagrants and vagabonds that wrapped all around the gates of the Blessed Sacrament Cathedral. Nuns and volunteers directed us through the old church as they disseminated tracts about salvation and preached repentance. I smiled and obliged them, but it wasn't my soul that hungered. It was my stomach. All I truly wanted was a meal.

I was living in East Nashville's Bordeaux section and working under the table at a neighborhood laundromat. My chief duties were sweeping, mopping, vacuuming out the lint traps, and polishing down the machines. And once a week, I had to don a tall pair of rubber hip boots and climb down into the drainage vat out back to scrub the grates clean of sludge and scum. Needless to say, it was a dirty job. Dirtier still were my other avocations. By night, I was soliciting my services outside a gas station convenience store down the block from the room I was renting: convincing snaggletooth old men on Social Security into buying me dinner, and selling kisses to pimply-faced frat boys for a chunk of their allowance.

Despite the many prestigious colleges and universities bordering Bordeaux, all of which hosted a myriad of budding intellectuals each year from all across the country, high schools in the area had a dropout rate of nearly fifty percent back then. And as a result, the streets were overrun with local kids just like Butch and me: underemployed, lacking education, and from unstable homes. We were like stray dogs and cats fighting each other for scraps and scratching at the butcher's back door hoping for handouts.

Butch was living right around the corner from me and had joined a street gang called the Dragons. As the newest member of that savage crew, Butch quickly broadened his criminal horizons and graduated from petty theft into the lucrative land of drugs. His days and nights were spent peddling poison to an endless cavalcade of troubled souls: stricken and impoverished men and women looking for the quickest way to escape reality and aimless boys and girls with nothing certain in their futures but the promise of death. Hypnotized by addiction, they roamed the streets endlessly, haunting the night like ghosts, apparitions in baggy jeans. Those days in Bourdeaux were among some of the lowest in my life, and as I stood there before that basement buffet staring at a plate full of green eggs and spam, I resisted the urge to overturn the tables like the Grinch who stole Christmas.

"Psst!" I heard someone signal. I turned around and saw a girl who looked to be about my same age. She smiled at me and pointed toward a table set up against one of the basement walls. The table was filled with little boxes of cereal and packets of instant oatmeal. And at the far end, there were platters filled with bananas, grapes, oranges, and apples. I made my way to the wall, filled a couple of bowls with apple cinnamon oatmeal and granola cereal, and loaded my tray with fruit. Then I sat down across from my newfound friend at one of the tables in the giant hall.

I tore into my cereal, and as the milk dribbled over my lips and down my chin, I gained the attention of just about everyone nearby. I ravaged my oatmeal and gorged on grapes, and even the homeless looked at me with sympathy in their eyes while the nuns added me to their prayers. I came up for air when I'd heard her laughing. Sitting there stuffing my face like hamster cheeks, I probably should've been embarrassed at the spectacle I'd made of myself. But something about her smile made me feel welcomed and accepted, just as I was, flaws and all.

Her name was Elizabeth Lawrence. She was a living mural, tattoos descending her neck and covering her entire body right down to her fingers and toes. Her hair was jet black except for the tips, which were dyed a bright blue. Her lip, tongue, eyebrow, and nose were pierced with metal spikes, and all her makeup was black. Her lipstick, her eyeshadow, her nail polish? Black as coal. And so was her clothing, a skintight cat suit handstitched from scraps of denim and leather. The nuns had draped her in a brown blanket to conceal that outfit, that hair, those tattoos, and all the other characteristics they found indecent. And while I sat there devouring my breakfast like a pig in a pen, my toes made contact with something hard under the table. I looked down and saw her big, black guitar case.

From the moment we met that cold morning at Blessed Sacrament, Liz and I were joined at the hip like Siamese twins. I'd spend the night at her place. She'd spend the night at mine. Born and raised in Denver, the daughter of two doctors, she'd found herself trapped in a world of advanced placement classes and SAT prep, slowly rotting away in quiet suburbia. That is, until one day, with her sights set on stardom, she hopped on a Greyhound bound for Nashville and never looked back. But after just a few short weeks, Liz soon discovered that the road to fame isn't always paved. Sometimes, it's rocky, twisting and turning through a wilderness of regret. Back home, she'd had everything she wanted and had never gone without. But on the road, Liz found herself at the mercy of others, surviving off the charity of strangers as she sang songs on sidewalks for spare change and half-eaten sandwiches.

I used to love to hear her sing those familiar folk songs and play on that beat-up guitar. Her appearance may have seemed cold or even threatening to some at first: a gruff girl with wild blue hair caressing her guitar with tattooed hands. But her voice was warm and inviting, a sweet surprise, never loud, never booming, always meek, always mild, easy and light like whispers on the breeze. And when she plucked out chords on that acoustic guitar and serenaded spectators with that golden throat, a reverent hush filled any space she inhabited, mouths agog and ears in awe of her glorious gift.

It was Valentine's Day. I'd slept over at her place the night before in my usual pile of blankets on the floor, and we'd stayed up half the night talking loud and eating discount chocolates. When I rose that morning, I saw that she was already awake, still in bed, lying on her back and staring up at the ceiling, lost in thought. I wished her good morning, and when she didn't respond, I sat beside her on the bed. It was then that I noticed her eyes. They were bloodshot. Her lips were chafed and blue. I called for an ambulance. I did CPR. I rubbed on her skin to warm it back up, but there was no change. The paramedics arrived and found no pulse. They took her away on a stretcher with a sheet over her head, leaving me alone to contemplate the timing of my dear friend's death. Valentine's Day. Twenty-four hours set aside to celebrate matters of the

277

heart, and yet this was the day that her poor heart stopped. I stalked the medical examiner's office for days until, finally, a clerk there took pity on me and revealed the official cause of death: an air embolism.

Liz was the sister I never had, but no matter how close she and I became, all along, her true best friend had been heroin. That heroin spoke to her in a secret language that only they two could comprehend. It woke her in the middle of the night and led her from her bed and out into the streets to chase dealers down alleyways for a ten-dollar fix. It whispered to her in the morning, and while most folks rose to cook themselves a breakfast of bacon and eggs, Liz stood before her stove, melting crystals with a heated spoon, cooking up a sweet serum to be injected into her veins. Hidden deep within the elaborate artwork on her colorful body were endless track marks, tiny puncture wounds scabbed over and over again. I know all this because I brought Butch with me to her funeral and he recognized her corpse as one of his customers.

An air embolism—a rare diagnosis. Administered by that last needle, the tiny air bubble had traveled slowly through her veins and arrested her heart. I was young and inexperienced with the signs of drug use, totally oblivious to the demons that haunted Liz. I spent the next few days in the local library photocopying pages from reference books and studying medical journals full of medical jargon I could scarcely understand, gleaning all I could about needles and drug addiction. I blamed myself for not being smarter and wiser, for not being more perceptive of her suffering. If only I'd recognized the warning signs. Probably the most glaring indication was the way that her mood would change drastically from day to day. Some

278

days, she was lighthearted and exuberant, full of laughter and jokes. And some days, she was disengaged, numb to the world, despondent, and dejected. I thought she was just being your typical artist type: brooding, moody, and eccentric. But all the while, it had been the addiction eating away at Liz like an infectious disease right before my blinded eyes, devouring her soul, slow and meticulously, piece by piece by piece. She was gone long before she left us. She was dead way before she died.

Following that harrowing experience, I begged Butch to quit the gang, and we left Nashville behind. I made a solemn vow to myself that I would never ever get mixed up in drugs. And as I sat there in Debbie's donut shop staring into the face of a gangster, my stomach churned inside and made eating impossible. The choices I'd made recently had caused me to break my promise from years ago. I had vowed to steer clear of drugs, and here I was on a quest to *find* them. Suddenly, Ace's handsome face seemed horrid and ugly to me, covered in a caul of hideous hypocrisy. Ace had the audacity to lecture me about the dangers of smoking, and meanwhile, he was a purveyor of poison, guarding the interests and investments of a drug consortium, supporting an industry that trafficked toxins all over the state. *He* was an air embolism, a silent killer injecting himself into the veins of poor communities, moving slow and undetected, stopping hearts along the way.

Illicit street drugs may not kill as many folks each day as cigarettes or guns statistically speaking, but that's only because it's nearly impossible to quantify the magnitude of their impact. The truth is they ruin a hundred percent of the lives they affect. I've seen firsthand how they lead folks spiraling down dark paths, eroding morality along the way, turning noblemen into scoundrels. No matter which side of the game you're on, whether you're a dealer or an addict, you'll do whatever it takes for drugs, even kill and connive. And you'll perpetrate these hateful acts even against the folks you love the most. That's the irony of addiction. Liz's flame had been extinguished far too soon. And I blamed men like Pete and Ace for—once again—holding the hose. They were the root cause of my dear friend's demise. And now, as I sat there acting as their agent, so was I.

CHAPTER 23: 10 MINUTES & 60 SECONDS...

"I'll make that phone call now. It's just after eight,"
I said, looking at my watch. I'd taken a few bites of my
pancakes and a couple sips of coffee, but I couldn't seem to
activate my appetite. Ace had eaten his colossal sandwich
and was now digging his fork into my plate. If he'd had a
heart, I'm certain all the butter and grease he consumed that
morning would have surely arrested it. I hate to waste
food, and so, on one hand, I was grateful for his greed. On
the other, I wished I had a little arsenic. I would've
sprinkled it over those hot cakes like confectioner's sugar
and laughed as he went into convulsions, foam spilling
from his big, opinionated mouth.

"Here." Ace reached into his breast pocket and
pulled out a phone. "You can use my cell," he offered.

"I'd rather not," I carefully declined. "I'd prefer to
use the phone over there." I pointed to the payphone just
outside the window mounted on a post in front of Debbie's
restaurant.

"What's the difference?" Ace asked.

"The difference is A: I'd like some privacy and B:
I'd rather not leave the phone number of my confidential
informant on your cell phone call log. That okay with
you?" I pursed my lips.

"Fine," he granted with a grunt.

"I need change, though." I held out my open hand.
The gunman sighed and dug into his pants. He placed six
quarters in my palm, and I rose from the table reaching for
my bag. With the swift precision of a viper striking at its
prey, he grabbed my wrist, and I froze in my tracks.

"Make your call"—he nodded toward the payphone on the other side of the window— "and come right back. You don't need your purse. Put it down, please." I set my pocketbook back down on the chair beside me. "In ten minutes, I'm trusting you to be back here in that seat. Got that?"

"Yeah, I got it," I snarled, breaking free of his grasp and leaving the table.

"Wait," he called after me. "Here." He handed me the umbrella, and for a split second, I contemplated beating the crap out of him with it! But as his biceps bulged beneath his blazer and threatened to tear his suit open like the Hulk, I thought better of it and rolled my eyes instead. Ace offered me the umbrella so I wouldn't get soaked in rain, and simultaneously, the gun on his hip was offering me bullets and threatening to soak me in blood. As I turned to leave the restaurant, I rolled my eyes a second time, once for each of his two faces.

I opened the door and made my way toward the payphone. And as I walked, I could feel Ace's eyes on my back like the infrared light on a marksman's rifle. Perhaps I was playing this all wrong and I should've been kinder to my captor. Perhaps I should've been meaner? After being bamboozled so many times recently, I didn't know what the hell to think. The part of my brain that managed wisdom was less developed than an embryo, and lately my instincts were as unreliable as tabloids and public transportation.

In a moment, I was standing before the payphone just outside the shop. I held the umbrella's long rod awkwardly in the crook of my neck so I could free my hands to hold the receiver and deposit my change. Then I dialed my favorite number.

282

"Good morning," she answered on the first ring, her voice sounding like honey in my ear.

"Ugh...Ms. Jane. Am I glad to hear your voice."

"Hey, baby! I been thinkin' 'bout chu' all night. How thangs go wit' you and Butch? Y'all learn anything else about the dead man?"

"Well...yes and no," I said with a sigh. Then I took another deep breath and rattled off the story of Butch's heist, the subsequent police chase that led us to old man Willie's house, and then my desperate attempt to elude Butch by stealing back the stolen car and leaving him stranded there with Eve.

"What?! I tole you that fool was crazy!" she exclaimed. "He got a screw loose!"

"I know, Ms. Jane."

"Boy ain't got no candy in his piñata!"

"I know, Ms. Jane."

"Don't know whether to tie his behind or scratch his shoe!"

"I know, Ms. Jane. I know. But," I said, sighing again, "there's more."

"Please deposit twenty-five cents..." warned the automated voice. I dropped another quarter in the slot before the operator could finish her threat, and then I recounted the story of my visit to Pete's place and my brief stint as a POW in the diner's dungeon. I concluded with the story of Ace, the man who held me captive like a Labrador on a leash, the man who sat there eyeing me through the window even as I spoke, issuing intimidations with his gaze. "Can you believe this mess?" I cried out, the threat of tears choking my throat. "Why me?!" I dropped another quarter in the slot.

"You know what, honey? The good book says do unto others as you would have done unto you."

"I know what the Bible says, Ms. Jane…"

"It also says you reap what you sow," she continued.

"I know that too, Ms. Jane."

"The Hindus and Buddhists call it karma. That's where whatever you did in your past affects your present, and your actions right now impact the future. The Chinese have something sorta similar… They say yin and yang. I like dat one." She chuckled. "That's where opposing forces interconnect and interact and counteract and give rise to one another…like night and day, like winter and spring…light and darkness. According to ancient Chinese philosophers, the universe is governed by equilibrium, balance, harmony…cause and effect…things acting on one another."

"Umm…okay…" I replied. I knew there was no stopping Ms. Jane once she got started on one of her tangents. And even if I tried to interrupt, she probably couldn't hear me anyway from way up there on her soapbox.

"Some folks simply say what goes around comes around," she continued. "And I know you heard that what goes up must come down. Even Sir Isaac Newton, a man of science, the famous physicist and mathematician, said for every *action* there is an equal and opposite *reaction*."

"What the hell does this have to do with anything, Ms. Jane?!" My patience was worn down to the nubs and thinner than a sheet of paper.

"Well, honey, what I'm tryna' say is…no matter where we come from, whatever walk of life…regardless of religion, culture, creed…irrespective of spirituality, cosmology, ontology, or our own personal philosophical beliefs…different folks may say it different ways and call it different things, but honey…there is a fundamental principle, an inviolable law, a golden rule that acts upon the air, the land, the sea, and every living thing in between: Don't be a jackass! Simple as that! You got to treat people well and do the right thing! Until you wrap your mind around that fact, your days will be filled with nothin' but pain and calamity, chile! You ask why me? You wanna know why trouble seems to follow you everywhere you go? Iss 'cause you doin' such a good job of leadin' the way! Sleepin' wit' men for money, breakin' up homes, stealin', and conning folks. I know you don't think much of yourself, but honey, your actions have the power to set events into motion! And if you think about it, that's actually *good* news! That means that if you really want thangs to stop goin' wrong…all you gotta do is take responsibility and start doin' *right*!"

I had no time for Ms. Jane that morning. Actin' all high and mighty like Jesus among us! And I had zero patience for her mystical cogitations, esoteric ramblings, and didactic sermonettes. Zero! And honey, that was me roundin' up! I contemplated pretending to have a bad connection and hanging up in Ms. Jane's ear, but I had called her that morning for a reason, and the clock was ticking fast. I deposited another quarter.

"Ms. Jane, I hear you…and I promise I'll work on changing all my wicked ways tomorrow. But for right now, I gotta focus on the issues before me that can't be deferred. Now, did you have a chance to find out anything

285

about the name I gave you yesterday? Nathan Dobbs? They call him Doughboy."

"I shole did. I don't know how much help iss gon' be, but I turned up a few things. For starters, he ain't just Nathan Dobbs. He's *Reverend* Nathan Dobbs. He pastor a church up there in Buckhead on Paces Ferry Road called The Church of the Open Door. A trusted source told me he runs a community outreach program with farmers in the state, where they make food donations to feed families in need in exchange for a tax write-off. His church even has a partnership with the Board of Education and offers afterschool tutoring to high school students and night classes for adults studying for the GED. They have Bible Study on Wednesday nights and again on Thursday at noon. That way, folks can swing by the church on they lunch break to pick up on what they missed the night before. They choir just won the state championship in January. I remember reading about it in the paper. When all this is over, I think me and the girls might just pay his church a little visit. Sound like the good Lord is movin' in a mighty way over there in Buckhead."

"His congregation call him Doughboy?"

"No, chile, they don't call him no Doughboy," Ms. Jane scoffed. "He got that name way back when he was still out there in the worl' chasin' after sin. When the good Lord whispered in his ear and called him out of darkness and into the marvelous light, he shed his former self and left that name behind. He's Reverend Dobbs now by all accounts."

"Crap!" I exclaimed. "Today is Saturday!"

"So?"

"I gotta wait till tomorrow to talk to him, don't I?"

"Did you forget already, chile?" Ms. Jane laughed. "It's called The Church of the Open Door. You can go there anytime. The gates to the kingdom are always open, honey. And to tell you the truth, I can't think of no better place for you to be at a time like this than in the house of the Lord."

"Please deposit twenty-five cents for the next three minutes," warned the automated voice. "If twenty-five cents is not deposited within fifteen seconds, your call will be disconnected." I had thirty seconds to spare before Ace made Swiss cheese out of me, so I said my goodbyes, hung up the phone, and hurried back inside to take my seat at the gunman's table.

"Welp! We're goin' to church!" I announced as I sat down.

"Church?" Ace repeated.

"You heard me. Church! Big building. Pews. Steeple on top? Surely you've heard of it," I said sarcastically. "It seems our friend Samson was in pretty tight with a pastor over in North Atlanta."

"A pastor?" Ace echoed again.

"What am I, speakin' in tongues? Yes, a pastor. At a church. His name is Reverend Dobbs." I probably should've kept my cool, but I just couldn't help it. Everything about Ace annoyed me that morning. He was like a six foot four gnat, all up in my face and too big to swat. "You got somethin' against church?"

"Nah...I'm just surprised. I mean, I've only seen Samson once or twice myself, but he didn't strike me as the religious type."

"Me neither. But I suppose there's no real type. They say God watches over babies and fools. And we both know Samson ain't no baby." Ace laughed as he took another sip of his coffee. "I guess even fools like Samson need a little inspiration from time to time. Maybe this Pastor Dobbs knows him well and can help shed some light or offer some insight that might help us. Maybe he counseled him in some way and knows something we don't. Either way, this is just about the only lead we got right now, so let's see where it takes us."

"Okay. You're the boss." Ace raised his hand and signaled for Debbie's attention. "Check, please," he called across the room, and the waitress headed over to the old cash register to print out our receipt.

"I'll need to change my clothes first," I mentioned as I looked down at my outfit. Thanks to Pete's hose, my clothes were incredibly clean but nonetheless inappropriate.

"Why? What's wrong with what you got on?"

"I can't go into a church lookin' like this. Low-cut top and six-inch heels? This push-up bra got my boobs standin' up like they ready to sing in the choir! And look at these jeans." I stood up to illustrate my point. "They tight as a tourniquet." I sat back down. "No, I definitely need to change my clothes. In this getup, I'm liable to be struck by lightning soon as my heels hit the parking lot—that's if the ushers don't tackle me to the ground first."

"I like those jeans, actually." Ace winked before lifting his mug to down the last of his coffee.

"And from the looks of this storm out there," I said, ignoring Ace's advances and pointing out the window, "getting struck by lightning is a real possibility." The rain was soft but steady, and the sky was still dark despite the onset of morning. I might've believed there was a fire

288

somewhere nearby causing all those dark clouds if I weren't already familiar with Francine's handiwork.

"My duffel bag is in the trunk, and I got something in there I can slip into that'll be more appropriate." I searched Ace's face for a sign of reluctance. I figured if he had tampered with the trunk and removed the sacks of money, then certainly he wouldn't want me anywhere near there.

"Cool," he replied, his face showing about as much emotion as a card shark poker player with Botox injections. Like white words on a white page, he was impossible to read.

"Here ya' go, loves." Debbie laid the bill on the table between us, along with a couple of toothpicks and two peppermint candies. "Y'all come back now, ya' hear?" she sang as she waved and walked away.

"We sure will," Ace promised with a smile, literally lying through his teeth. The only way I imagined ever coming back to Debbie's dump was if I was reincarnated and came back as a donut! Ace pulled a twenty from his wallet, threw it on the table, and we both rose to leave. He held the door for me on the way out and held the umbrella over my head as we crossed the lot. In his gray suit, he looked like he was on Secret Service detail and I was the world's worst president, a collection of failures wrapped in flesh—indecisive, with poor judgement, and a past more checkered than a racing flag.

"Pop the trunk, please," I requested as we approached the FF. Ace squeezed the electronic remote on the Ferrari's keyring, and the trunk rose slowly as we approached the front of the car. Ace handed me the umbrella, unlocked the car doors, and got in on the driver's side while I proceeded on to the trunk. I held my breath the whole way, hoping that the bags were still there. And when I finally made it to the rear of the car and looked down into the trunk, I almost fainted. My duffel bag was just where I had left it. Only my duffel bag. The sacks were gone, and so was the pigment in my skin and the air in my lungs.

I grabbed my duffel and slammed the trunk. Then I got in on the passenger side and climbed into the backseat to change my clothes. I slammed the passenger door behind me too.

"Everything okay?" Ace turned the key, and the FF growled to a start.

"No, everything is not okay. Everything is really screwed up, actually, if you hadn't noticed."

"What's wrong?" Ace spied me through the rearview mirror and cocked his head with concern.

"What's right?" I answered his question with a question as I tore into my duffel. I was borderline hysterical, plucking garments from my bag one by one like a magician pulling scarves from an endless sleeve. And after a second, I just flipped the bag upside down and poured everything out into a pile on the backseat: make-up, deodorant, clothes, and all.

"What the hell is wrong with you all of a sudden?" Ace asked.

"Listen. I know you and I aren't on the same side. I know I'm just some dumb broad that you got stuck babysitting today. I know you're allegiance is to Pete and you're all about the business of selling drugs or beatin' people up or whatever it is you do. Fine. I get that. But can I just have sixty seconds of real talk with you? Sixty seconds where you actually tell me the truth? Can I have that? Sixty seconds." Ace eyed me again through the rearview mirror, and just as his gaze met mine, a tear spilled from my eye. I wiped it away quickly as I struggled to compose myself in the backseat.

"Alright," Ace said with a sigh before turning off the engine. "Sixty seconds."

"What did you do with the stuff that was in this car?"

"What stuff?"

"The truth, Ace! You know damn well what *stuff* I'm talkin' about. And don't blame it on Pete. I'm not a fool. If Pete had found the *stuff* that was in this car, he would've dragged me back down to that cellar for another round of interrogation—if he didn't kill me first. Now, I'm askin' you again. What did *you* do with the *stuff* that was in this car?" Ace was silent as he stared directly ahead.

"Ace!" I implored.

"Look. Pete asked me to tag along with you, and naturally, I checked your purse. I found your car keys, and of course, yours was the only Ferrari in the lot. So, while you were still in la-la land, I did a sweep of the car, and I admit I found some pretty interesting *stuff* inside."

"And what did you do with it?" Another tear escaped my eye. Ace turned around in his seat to face me.

"I removed it for your protection. And for mine. No way I was gonna let you ride shotgun with two *real* guns in the console between us. I'm no fool either. And I saw with my own eyes how close Pete came to killing you last night when he thought you were a threat. I knew if I told him about those sacks in the trunk and the weapons you had in here, he would've assumed you were in cahoots

291

with Samson and he would've slit your throat…just like he promised. Then, he would've taken the money and called it even."

"And what do you care if I live or die? Or if Pete confiscated all my money? You don't even know me. What's your angle? You ain't exactly no boy scout."

"I could tell by the look in your eyes that you didn't know what the hell Pete was talkin' about last night. You didn't steal that cocaine. So I figured…why let you suffer for Samson's crimes? And you're right. I'm not a good guy. But I'm not a bad guy either. I know this may be hard for you to believe given our present circumstances, but actually, we *are* on the same side. I'm not your enemy. And I'm not a drug dealer either for the record. I'm not a fighter, nor am I a killer. First and foremost, I'm a guardian. I protect people. And that's what I'm here to do today for you. That's the capacity I stand in right now; that's the hat I'm wearing." He lifted his fedora. "Now, don't be mistaken. I'll put up my fists if necessary, and yes, I won't hesitate to draw my gun if it comes down to it, but *only* if it comes down to it, when I absolutely have to, when the situation leaves me no other choice. I was saddled with the responsibility of accompanying you on this assignment, finding what Samson stole, and bringing us all back safely. And so, I emptied the center console to protect myself from you. And I emptied the trunk to protect you from Pete."

"And where'd you put it all?"

"I put everything in *my* car for safekeeping," Ace explained.

"*Your* car?"

"Yeah," he confirmed. "*My* car."

"Look, Ace. Samson already stole my wallet, my license, my credit cards. Promise you won't steal my life savings too. I just closed out the last of my accounts and bought this damn car...every last dime to my name is in those sacks. Every cent of my mother's inheritance!" Now, I'll admit that was a whopper, the biggest lie I'd told yet. The only thing I'd inherited from my mama was my poor taste in men, but I needed to try and offer a suitable and somewhat plausible explanation for the fancy ride and cash deposit bags in my possession. "Samson already took advantage of me while I was grieving. Please, don't you do the same."

"Here." Ace pulled another set of keys from his pocket and handed them to me.

"What are these?"

"Those are the keys to my Audi. You want real talk? Fine. I'm gonna level with you, Tina. The reason Pete picked me to guard you today is 'cause I was the one guarding the pantry the night Samson robbed it. I need this win. Okay? I need to earn back Pete's trust. So please. Consider these keys as collateral. You help me get back what belongs to Pete, and I'll help you get back what belongs to you. How's that?"

I nodded as I clutched the keys. For all I knew, those could've been the keys to anything. Or nothing at all. Ace could've been telling me a boldface lie, but for the time being, our little agreement offered me at the very least an inkling of peace. His words gave me a glimmer of hope, which was a hell of a lot more than I'd had a few moments before.

"Promise me that you'll keep your word, Ace. Please?"

"Aaaant! Time's up!" Ace pointed at his watch and laughed. Then he turned back around to face front. "Don't feel too good when somebody does it to *you*, does it?" He flashed a smile at me through the rearview mirror as he started the FF back up again. "Now tell me where we headed. Longest sixty seconds of my life."

I sighed and went back to the task of sorting through my clothes. "Next stop...The Church of the Open Door in Buckhead...North Atlanta," I directed from the backseat.

"Wrong."

"Say what?" I looked up.

"Our next stop is the nearest convenience store," Ace replied, shifting the car into gear.

"What you need from there?"

"I need to get *you* a pack of cigarettes. No offense, but you aren't exactly pleasant company. Locked up in this car with you while you go through nicotine withdrawal? Mad one minute and sad the next? No thanks. I'd rather be stuck on an elevator with Hannibal Lecter...and him holdin' a bottle of hot sauce."

CHAPTER 24: A CHURCH SEARCH!

I was never very big on spirituality. And as for organized religion? I just couldn't relate. I guess I probably needed *my* religion to be chaotic—just like the rest of my life. When I was a kid, Mama went through a brief period where she was particularly devout. This was back in the day before she remarried, and my stepdaddy became her deity. Mama and I were a team of two then, and we went to church nearly every night of the week—work permitting. Tuesday night for Prayer Service, Wednesday night for Bible Study. Thursday night was Choir Rehearsal and again on Saturday morning. I think Wednesday night Bible Study was my least favorite. You talkin' 'bout boring? Chile, I used to stare at my watch like it was the TV!

And of course, all of our Sundays were donated to the church like old clothes and canned goods, and there were multiple services and meetings spanning the entire day, from sunup to sundown and beyond. Hours on end, I spent in church, but no matter what kind of services I attended, I never quite connected. Rarely was I a participant; usually I was just an observer. I never had any transcendent encounters with a higher power. I'd never tarried, never spoken in tongues until the spirit descended upon me and made me want to dance or run around in circles like so many others. I'd never fasted or prayed with supplication until mountains had been moved. I just didn't seem to have the knack for all that. Heck, every time I tried to meditate I fell asleep!

Mama used to get me up out of my bed and drag me to service every Sunday, and even though I liked Sunday services more than all the other church events combined, and usually enjoyed myself, I just didn't really see the point. Soon as the congregation hummed its last hymn and the preacher closed in prayer, Mama and I usually left just as we had come—only a few cents poorer with the way the deacons demanded our tithes and offerings like bookies collecting on a debt. We left church feeling good, but by the time we boarded the 107 Local headed back home, our cloud nine had dissipated faster than the fumes from the bus's exhaust. We went right back to wrestling the same demons, fighting the same endless fight, trying to keep food on our table and the landlord off our back. Church never seemed to have much lasting effect on Mama and me, but nevertheless, I admit those Sunday mornings I spent in church as a kid were usually a welcome distraction, a pinch of sunshine in an otherwise dreary life.

I remember sitting beside Mama on our regular pew, and as the sun shone brightly through the tall, stained-glass windows, I would stare up at the colorful images that surrounded the sanctuary on all sides. Those giant windows were like biblical billboards, artful advertisements for salvation and hope. A favorite of mine was the nativity, so beautifully detailed. The sweet little baby Jesus, wrapped in swaddling clothes, was lying in a manger filled with hay. And kneeling there right beside him was mother Mary and gentle Joseph. The three wise men stood off to the side, all draped in colorful cloths and offering gifts to the infant king. And my favorite part was all the animals, the donkeys and goats and sheep that bowed at Jesus's makeshift bedside. Even they seemed to be humbled by the halo hovering just above the savior's curls.

And then, in another scene, there he was all grown up. The bearded Jesus, hair blowing in the breeze, walking on water with outstretched arms. I liked that one too. But even despite the sunlight that passed through those windows and illuminated each image so brightly, some of the depictions were dark and dismal, such as the one of Christ being marched through the streets of Jerusalem, shouldering the cross upon his back as it dragged on the ground behind him. You could almost see the splinters that shredded his skin, and you could just about feel the painful chafing as his back rubbed up against the raw, untreated wood.

And never shall I forget the sad scene of Christ's emaciated body nailed up on that cross. No built-in bench or ledge to stand on, his body was nailed directly to those posts like a flesh-colored tapestry for the world to see. His own body weight pulled against those nails, and as I sat there studying the vivid imagery, I imagined that every breath he took must have been excruciating as he hoisted himself there, battling gravity and fatigue.

One scene offered a gratuitous close-up, and you could see in great detail the rusty spikes that were hammered right into the metacarpals of his open hands and the metatarsals of his weary feet. And if that weren't gruesome and gory enough, his enemies mocked his claim to the throne by adorning his head with a crown of prickly thorns, the blood trickling down his brow and stinging his eyes like salt. Watching that window was like looking at an R-rated movie for a little kid like me. All that was missing was the popcorn! That window depicted an unparalleled cruelty, a sadistic and torturous vendetta carried out against Christ. And yet, even as he balanced

297

himself there, hanging high off the ground by his flesh, way up on the hill of Golgotha—the gallows of ancient Jerusalem—he was compassionate until the end. Two convicted thieves hung alongside him, and Jesus offered paradise to the one who believed him in faith to be the son of God. And as for the men who were responsible for his torment and death? Rather than curse them like they so rightly deserved, he said a prayer instead. "Father, forgive them, for they know not what they do."

I think that's where I developed my love for art. That vivid glass, so colorful and clear, spoke to my immature mind in a language it understood. I would stare up at those vibrant murals and admire the images, all the stories frozen in the glass. Each window spoke of something new, and even though it was Sunday morning, I sat there watching them like they were Saturday cartoons.

Meanwhile, the stern-faced ushers in their white gloves and hats directed folks into the church with all the focus and intensity of air traffic controllers guiding in jumbo jets. And after the choirs processed down the aisles, sang their songs, and took their seats, the real show would begin.

I can still hear Reverend Woodson hooting and hollering from the pulpit, his silk oversized robe trailing behind him like a shadow as he paced the stage. And folks all over the building would be standing up and shouting, even the ones who had rolled in on wheelchairs. I'm serious, honey! You wouldn't catch any sad, somnolent sermons coming out of his mouth. Reverend Woodson could preach a *funeral*, and they'd have to bolt down the caskets! His energy was electric, his charisma was magnetic, and his delivery was dynamite! He'd read a few

passages from somewhere in the text, and then he'd dissect
each sentence like a surgeon, breaking down words and
building them back up like he was working construction.
Every sermon was delicately woven. There was an
eloquent introduction, a powerful presentation of the main
idea, with supporting details and real-world examples, and
finally a climatic closing that nearly set the roof ablaze.

But just when you thought he was done and had
brought the sermon on home, he went and flipped the
lesson around in such a way that our hats nearly flew off
our heads due to our minds being so thoroughly blown.
Suddenly, you saw things from a brand-new angle, a
completely different perspective, and in an alternate light.
And there in the glow of that enlightenment, all the
complexities, paradoxes, and vicissitudes of life were laid
plain before you like a map of the universe. I wish I could
go back in time to hear some of those sermons again.
Maybe this time, I'd pay attention.

|•|•|•|•|•|•|•|•|•|•|•|•|•|•|•|•|•|•|•|•|•|•|

It was half past nine when Ace and I pulled into the
lot, and just as its name suggested, the doors of the church
were wide open, and the lot was nearly full. I'd
successfully changed clothes in the narrow backseat like a
contortionist fit for the big top, and now I donned a yellow
sundress with colorful flowers embroidered all over it.
Then I changed purses again, transferring a few items from
my big, cumbersome pocketbook into my dainty evening
clutch. On my feet, I wore a pair of cork bottom wedges.
And at a mere three inches off the ground—three inches

less than usual—Ace dwarfed me as I took my place beside him under the umbrella. Unlike everything else in my life that morning, my curls were uncharacteristically cooperative, so I elected to wear my hair down for a change. I'd reapplied my makeup and even chain-smoked three cigarettes outside of the 7-Eleven while Ace waited in the car, safe from the secondhand smoke. All things considered, I felt surprisingly good.

"Wow! God shole been kind to y'all!" an old lady shouted with a smile as she drove past and noticed Ace and I emerging from the fancy Ferrari all dressed up. I smiled politely, and Ace tipped his hat. Then we crossed the lot together and walked toward the front entrance.

The church was actually an old bank that had gone under years ago in the wake of the last recession. At some point, it had been purchased and converted into a sacred space by Reverend Dobbs and the church's trustees. There weren't any stained-glass windows surrounding it, and I admit I was a little disappointed. From the outside, the edifice looked more like an old courthouse, with at least thirty steps leading up to its tall wooden doors. And as Ace and I approached the stairs, I knew that whether it was a courthouse or a house of prayer, either way, judgement awaited us within.

Out of nowhere, I felt a bit uneasy. Suddenly, my stomach was queasy, like I'd eaten worms for breakfast and they were still alive and squirming in my gut. And the pensive look exhibited all over Ace's usually inscrutable face told me that he was nervous too for reasons of his own. Aside from the occasional soup kitchen here and there during bouts of hardship, I hadn't stepped foot in a church since I was a little girl. I had no idea what to expect or what kinds of memories would come flooding back to me once I got inside. Maybe warm memories of Mama and the nice quiet life she and I'd shared together before it all went to Hell—pardon the pun. Maybe I'd run into a mean usher who reminded me of my old Sunday school teacher Ms. Knight, who used to smack my hand down when I asked too many questions. As we began climbing the stairs, I wondered if I would don a smile on the other side of those doors? Or a frown? And I debated with myself if I should continue on or turn around. So many questions were circling my mind. But in the midst of all my fear and reluctance, Pete's assignment made the choice quite clear. I had to keep walking or die. Naturally, I chose the former.

"Listen, Tina," Ace said as we ascended. "I don't think you should use your real name in here. I know you probably ain't too keen on lyin' in church, but let's play it safe and leave a clean trail, okay?"

"Makes sense," I agreed. As it was, I could barely keep track of all my aliases, but thankfully Ace didn't know that.

"And I think we should be married."

"Come again?" My eyebrow rose so high on my forehead it almost crossed over my hairline and bum-rushed my bangs!

"No, not like that." Ace laughed. "Don't flatter yourself. I'm not proposing...yet." He smiled, and his deep dimples winked in my direction. "I'm sayin' we should *pretend* to be married because it seems to me like mostly couples go to church together, right?"

"Hell if I know," I answered earnestly. "But yeah, I think we should be married too. Otherwise, they might think we shackin' up together, and we don't need folks whispering about us already." I laughed. "Actually, wait a minute. I got a better idea!" I stopped walking right then, partly because I wanted Ace's undivided attention, but mostly because the three cigarettes I'd smoked earlier had caught up with me and I was already out of breath. "Let's pretend to be engaged! That way, we can talk to the pastor about marrying us, and that'll give us a reason to get in there to see him."

"Good thinking." Ace nodded. "Okay, so why don't you be Carmen Wilson, and I'll be…uh…Christopher Smith. That work?"

"Nice to meet you, Chris," I declared with a curtsy.

"Likewise, Carmen." Ace smiled and bowed. The climb up the rest of the way seemed unending, like we were two tiny black ants ascending the Pyramids at Giza. And as we hiked, a stiff wind began to rise, chasing leaves and litter across the lot. That wind turned our umbrella inside out and exposed us to the elements. The cold rain on my face reminded me of Pete's hose, and for a moment, I was breathless again. I looked up and saw the evidence of Francine rousing from another nap. A herd of black clouds rushed over the horizon like bison stampeding across the sky. Thunder popped and snapped above our heads, Francine cracking her knuckles before a fight. Ace and I ran the rest of the way, and when we finally reached the summit of those stairs, we burst through the doorway to escape the rain. Aside from the wind that followed us inside, I was surprised to see that the lobby of the church was empty.

"Where is everybody?" I wondered aloud, still catching my breath. All those cars parked outside in the lot and the eerie silence and desolation inside the church made me feel like I was sneaking into a private party thrown in my honor, like, at any moment, all my closest friends were due to jump out and yell, "Surprise!"

"Beats me," Ace replied. Then he pulled open one of the inside doors that led into the sanctuary, and instantly, we were blown away.

"Ride on, King Jesus! No man can a-hinder me! Ride on, King Jesus ride on...no man can a-hinder me. No man can a-hinder me!" The doors of the sanctuary must've been soundproofed, because as soon as Ace pulled on that handle, it seemed like a concert began right on cue, as if Ace and I were the guests of honor and the choir had been anticipating our arrival.

"In that great gettin' up mornin', fare ye well, fare ye well! In that great gettin' up mornin', fare ye well, fare ye well!" There had to be at least a hundred voices in that chorus, and each one was pouring out passion like there were souls up on the moon that needed saving. The choir sang a cappella, accompanied only by the stamping of feet and the clapping of hands. And their voices soared high up into the nave of the cathedral as if they were the next battalion of Joshua's army trying to tear down the walls of Jericho for a second time.

"When I get to Heaven, gonna wear a robe! No man can a-hinder me. Gonna see King Jesus sittin' on the throne! No man can a-hinder me." A Hammond B3 organ joined in on the action and sang a stirring solo through the Leslie speaker. That organ screeched, scratched, and got downright ugly. And I thought the organist might've been part octopus with the way he pushed and pulled on the drawbars and walked the bassline with his feet—never once missing the beat! A piano flirted with that powerful organ, offering accents here and there and sprinkling arpeggios over the tune like raindrops, soft and sweet. And then, as the choir repeated that last refrain over and over, they quieted down into almost a hush, punching the lyrics breathily and light. "No man can a-hinder me. No man can a-hinder me," they declared again and again. The pianist zipped his fingers up and down the scale so skillfully I thought he might beat the black off that piano. And the organist played chords so sugary sweet my tooth began to ache. Honey, I closed my eyes and saw colors. Until I felt Ace's finger tapping me on my shoulder.

"This is just choir rehearsal," Ace assessed. "Let's go. The pastor ain't in here." We backed out of the sanctuary and headed down a long hall that wrapped around the perimeter of the edifice. And as we walked, we passed several rooms along the way. I suppose those rooms used to be offices when the building was a bank. Now they'd been repurposed by the parishioners to serve the needs of the church. One large room we passed contained rows of rocking chairs. Several large women held small babies on their laps and sang to them softly as they fed them bottles of milk. Some stood and bounced the babies on their hips as they paced the floors of that rainbow room, pointing out shapes and colors to the awestricken babes. I estimated at least twenty-five kids being cared for there in that nursery, presumably so that moms and dads could worship without worry elsewhere within the cavernous cathedral.

One room looked like a drycleaner's storefront. Inside were racks filled with red and purple choir robes, and a half dozen men and women were busy steaming the sleeves and ironing the collars and lapels. Another room must have been the bank's conference room. It was now a boardroom for the church trustees and other benevolent benefactors. A bunch of men in suits and a few women in big hats stood around the room in clusters. They smiled and laughed and nodded at one another, and their informality told me that either their meeting had already ended or hadn't yet begun. As I stood there watching in the window, I was deeply astonished by the conference table that divided that big room in half. That table was so unbelievably long it could've made the Last Supper look like a midnight snack.

Ace and I proceeded on down the winding corridor, and occasionally an old man or woman, maybe a young boy or girl would pass us, walking in the opposite direction back toward the sanctuary. Each of those strangers smiled and sang a howdy or hello, and immediately I was rapt with fascination. Ms. Jane had already informed me of all the church's outreach efforts, and they'd been impressive. I'd heard the choir for myself, and wow, they were phenomenal! My eyes had already beheld the beautiful building with its high ceilings, pristine pillars, and marble floors polished to an immaculate shine. All those factors stunned me independently, and collectively I was amazed. But what really took the cake was the warmth. And I don't mean the temperature. I'm talking about the warmth I saw reflected in the eyes of those we passed in the hall. I'm talking about the good-natured volunteers I spied through the windows of those rooms: men and women offering their time and talents in service, exhibiting care and kindness to one another so freely, so generously. And they did so on their own volition, not even knowing that they were being surveilled and scrutinized by cynics like Ace and me.

Riding mama's coattails to and from church as a kid, I'd witnessed so many saccharin smiles and hesitant hugs exchanged in my presence that part of me was convinced that the last bit of *real* love to inhabit most churches was Christ's celebrated sacrifice thousands of years before. But in a matter of minutes, The Church of the Open Door had managed to open the door of my heart and challenge my childhood notions. And as our heels clicked beneath us and echoed across the tunneling corridors, something interesting happened. I found myself exhaling all my burdens and encumbrances. In their place, I began to inhale the love that infused the air around us like the sweet scent of an expensive perfume.

Up until that moment, my life had been nothing more than a series of sad stories strung together by a withering thread. And even as I walked through the church, I could still feel that thin thread unraveling. My existence was a long, drawn-out tale of unrequited love: me giving all of myself to one undeserving person after the next and receiving nothing in return but dollars and disappointments. With the exception of Ms. Jane, I'd never known real affection, just a lifetime of candy-coated contempt and disdain disguised as devotion. But despite my inexperience with real and true love, somehow it was obvious to me there that morning, like when you meet a distant relative for the first time: you may have never seen their face before, yet it's somehow still familiar. As I continued to breathe it in, letting it fill my lungs and flow to all my empty spaces, I knew that love was not dead and gone. It was still alive and here for the taking. And I thought that if all those folks in that building could manage to obtain inner joy and a sense of purpose and pride, maybe—just maybe—I could have all that too. Maybe there was hope yet for a sinner like me.

"Here we go." Ace pointed. "Pastor's office," he said, reading the sign that donned the door. Ace and I gave each other one last look and took a deep breath before I rang the buzzer. And as I pushed on that little button, my body still filled with new breath, still nurturing a new awakening, I found myself praying—something I hadn't done in decades.

I'd brought a gunman with me into the house of the Lord, along with a fake name and a hidden agenda. And we were only seconds away from waltzing into the pastor's office and lying right to his face, searching for clues to lead us to a dead man's stash. I'm usually able to lower the volume on my conscience after a lifetime of practice, but standing there before the pastor's chambers, the guilt was almost unbearable. And so, I prayed for forgiveness. Just like the thief I'd seen as a child, hanging on the hill alongside Christ, I prayed to be pardoned. I asked to be absolved. I petitioned for a miracle. Instead of opening the pastor's door, I wanted to open my eyes and wake up from this nightmare, to be unfettered once and for all from *this* reality and to ascend into another, to graduate from this woeful realm into the next. God was a perfect stranger to me—in the truest sense—yet I prayed to Him with all my might. But just like most letters addressed to an unknown recipient, it seemed my prayers were returned to sender, unopened and unanswered. Nothing happened. I felt snubbed and shunned. I felt refused, rejected, and denied. And ironically, I was somehow comforted by those familiar feelings. After all, I'd known them all my life.

CHAPTER 25: WHOLLY MATRIMONY!

"Come in," called a voice through the intercom, and the door unlocked with a click and a buzz. Ace and I looked at each other curiously, because the voice—albeit heavy and slightly low—did not belong to a man. I opened the door slowly and stepped inside wearing a grin as my guise. Behind a large oak desk was a heavyset woman with big, round glasses. She sat hunched over her keyboard, typing quite vigorously into a desktop computer. A few gray hairs were mixed into her curls, so at first, I pegged her for about fifty. But her furrowed eyebrows and fast fingers told me that perhaps those grays were premature, and she was just overworked and under stress like so many others in this world. Maybe she was in her late thirties or early forties? Aside from those few gray hairs, her age was incalculable to me, because two large flat-panel monitors stood high on her desk, blocking part of my view of her face. Those monitors had to be at least twenty-four inches each in diameter, and they made her look like an audio engineer at the helm of a giant mixing board mastering tracks in a professional recording studio. The monitors, a hard drive, and a massive inkjet printer covered the bulk of her workstation, and a multiline phone and rolodex inhabited the rest. And teetering on the edge of her desk, threatening to fall any minute, was a gold nameplate that read "Sister Sheila Anne Sumpter – Executive Steward."

It was immediately obvious to me that Sister Sumpter was the hub of the entire operation, the business center for all the church's interests and activities. One wall of that office housed a full row of filing cabinets, where I imagined all kinds of permits and plans were archived fastidiously and payrolls and personnel files were organized with care. And behind Sister Sumpter's big, brown desk rose a tall bookcase embedded right into the wall, not unlike the one back at Willie's place, only this one was neat and clean with not a spider in sight. Those shelves were packed tight with encyclopedias, biblical concordances, dictionaries, and big Bibles in a multitude of translations. And interspersed all throughout were hundreds of books on the subject of theology, dating back centuries and written by scholars from all over the globe. Beholding all those volumes up there, I couldn't help but wonder: What questions were so profound and pervasive that they warranted the procurement of so many books? And if life's questions couldn't be answered by all those great thinkers, what hope did a nitwit like me have for finding peace in this world?

"Good morning," Sister Sumpter sang, never once lifting her eyes from her work.

Hi!" I exclaimed in reply as I approached. Ace closed the door gently behind us and took his place by my side. "I'm Carmen, and this is my fiancé Chris." I motioned toward Ace, and he removed his hat. As he held that fedora in his fingers, I noticed that his big hands were trembling a bit, like he was approaching a highway checkpoint with a dead body in his trunk. I was sure Ace's closet had more *skeletons* in it than hangers, him being a career criminal and all, so I thought he'd be better at hiding his discomfort. His reaction to being in church that morning reminded me of my own reaction to being at the Wild Goose the night before.

309

Sitting there among Atlanta's elite, I'd felt like I was trapped in a confined space and had forgotten to put on my deodorant. I was convinced that everyone could smell me and it was only a matter of time before I'd be sniffed out and publicly shamed. Ace's vulnerability standing there that morning made him seem almost human to me and not just a goon with a gun. And without even knowing why, I'll admit I began to feel a little bit sorry for the man. But I had to cut my empathy short and get back to the business before us. I turned my attention again to the pair of eyes behind the desk. "We're here to see Pastor Dobbs. Is he in?"

"I'm afraid Pastor is indisposed. Is there something I can help you with?" She stole a quick sip from a mug beside her computer. There were so many things on her desk that I hadn't seen the mug before.

"Indisposed? What does that mean?" Ace asked.

"It *means*," Sister Sumpter expounded, "he's currently wrapped up in a meeting in his chambers." She pointed over her shoulder toward a door beside the bookcase. Her eyes never left the monitors.

"Can we just talk to him for a moment?" I implored.

"Nope! Absolutely not! As it is, he's already behind schedule today. And truth be told, he shouldn't even be having no Saturday meetings. He needs to be preparing for tomorrow's sermon!" she insisted. "You folks can say hello and shake his hand after service tomorrow, just like everybody else," she added quite matter-of-factly.

"All we need is a moment," I pleaded. "You see…my fiancé and I"—I smiled up at Ace and grabbed his hand— "would like to speak with Pastor Dobbs about the possibility of him marrying us."

"Well, why didn't you say so?!" Sister Sumpter smiled, finally looking up from her computer as if she'd been waiting all morning for that little bit of good news. "There are few things as wonderful as the announcement of a young couple deciding to walk down the aisle and enter into the covenant of marriage before God and the world. Pastor will be glad to have his schedule interrupted for news like that!" Sister Sumpter said, her face beaming. And now that her whole face was fully visible to me, no longer obscured by those monstrous monitors, I saw that she was actually quite beautiful. She was the color of caramel and had round, rosy cheeks. Tiny freckles were sprinkled all over her nose, and her big red lips accommodated a full set of big white teeth. Her smile was the kind of smile that sells toothpaste on TV: trusting and inviting and sincere. She wore a flowered dress beneath her navy-blue blazer, and the gold brooch pinned upon her left breast depicted a beautiful butterfly in flight. "When?" she asked, squinting back at her screen.

"When what?" I replied.

"When is the wedding, sugar?" she asked again.

"Oh, yes...the wedding...uh...we're hoping for some time in September, but we're flexible on the date."

"Well, that makes it easy then." She consulted the calendar on her computer. "Pastor Dobbs only has one weekend free in September, so it'll have to be Saturday the twenty-first. How's that?"

"Perfect!" I exclaimed as I locked arms with Ace. His muscles were so tense beneath his clothes, you would've thought his gray suit was made of armor, fashioned from steel instead of satin. I looked up to examine the serious look in his stern eyes, and I swear if his jaws tightened up any harder, his face would've been ready to grace Mount Rushmore.

"You okay, sweetie?" Sister Sumpter must've seen Ace's anxiety too. With her gold glasses perched on the edge of her speckled nose, she looked up and eyed Ace with concern.

"Yes, ma'am," Ace answered. "Don't mind me…just gettin' over a cold." He coughed.

"Honey, please." Sister Sumpter rose from her desk—or *almost* rose that is. At a mere four foot ten or so, she was scarcely taller standing than she was sitting down. "The only cold I see is those cold *feet* you standin' on, young man!" She laughed as she turned her back to us. "Y'all have a seat, and I'll be right wit' cha'," she directed over her shoulder, trying to pull down a big, black binder from the bookcase behind her desk. Though the binder was only eye level to me, Sister Sumpter had to stand up on the tips of her toes and reach her arm up high to get it, like she was imitating the Statue of Liberty. Ace and I sat down on the two leather club chairs that faced the desk. The leather seats were quite plush, yet Ace and I were still uncomfortable.

"Okey-dokey!" Sister Sumpter exclaimed as she sat back down at her desk, the black binder opened before her. Then she angled the monitors and slid them to the side so she could address Ace and I properly head on. "What you say your name was again, honey?" She looked up over her glasses.

"I'm Carmen Wilson, and this is Christopher Smith," I reintroduced. Sister Sumpter pulled a pencil from a caddy on her desk and began writing our names in the giant book.

"Car…men…Wil…son," she spoke as she wrote, "and Chris…topher…Smith. Got it!" She put down her pencil and picked up her mug. "Okay, lady and gentleman"—she took a swig of coffee— "Pastor likes to get some preliminary information from all couples seeking to be wed. And to that end, I'm gonna administer a short questionnaire. Please note, your responses to these questions will be graded today by me. A passing grade will result in Pastor Dobbs officiating the ceremony as requested, and I'll even bring you in to meet with him today. Any score less than passing, and I'm afraid you two will need to sign up for couples' classes and reapply in three months."

"Three months?!" Ace and I repeated.

"Wow! Those are some pretty stiff terms," I said with a smile.

"Not as stiff as those marriage vows you 'bout to take, honey!" Sister Sumpter said with a smirk. "Pastor likes to make sure couples really know what it means to promise fidelity and loyalty and commitment to one another for richer or poorer, in sickness and in health. If more couples stopped to contemplate the terms of their *marriage* contract, there'd be less folks in court hashing out the terms of their divorce! I mean, think about it! There's a whole branch of the court system dedicated exclusively to divorce, but we don't put half as much time and effort and energy into planning the marriage! And don't be deceived, honey. Planning the wedding and planning the *marriage* are two totally different things! God wants you to have a happy and healthy union." She smiled at Ace and me.

"And I've designed these questions to assess your long-term compatibility." She took another sip.

"And what makes you qualified to make such a determination? Why can't we speak with the pastor?" Ace persisted.

"Well…" Sister Sumpter put her mug down slowly and removed her eyeglasses, and I knew Ace was in for a thorough tongue lashing. "In *third* place is my Master of Divinity from Emory. Running a close *second* is my PhD from Princeton Theological. And first and foremost, you wanna know what makes me an authority on this subject? My four marriages!" She held up four manicured fingers. "I have nearly three decades' worth of credentials, and honey, it took me a whole lot of heartache and heartbreak to get to where I am today. I've borrowed from all of my studies, all the good book's teachings, and all my life's experiences to develop this here test."

She held the binder in her hands. "This questionnaire will help the two of you to determine whether or not your legs are strong enough for a journey through life together and if your foundation is solid enough to build upon. It took me four trips down the aisle to get it right, and I've dedicated the majority of my ministry to making sure young couples such as yourselves get the information they need the *first* time. Question one!" The cleric cleared her throat and placed her glasses back on her face. "How'd you two meet?"

Ace and I looked at each other with hesitance, neither of us wanting to say the wrong thing and contradict the other. In our arrogance, we'd hastily slapped together this cover and hadn't thought through any of the details. Who knew we'd be interrogated by this marital magistrate?

314

"Well…" I began. I wanted to keep my answers as honest as possible while I sat there on holy ground, so I chose my words carefully and edited the particulars as I described the circumstances of my first encounters with Ace. I thought back to when I was Pete's hostage. "When Chris first saw me, I was in a dark place and at a very low point in my life." That was my way of telling Sister Sumpter about that basement. The dark place and low point I referred to were not only metaphorical but geographical. "And I was kind of in a bind." I remembered the ropes that had bound me there for so long. "I was in a place where…I felt like I was drowning… hopeless and all washed up." I pictured Pete's hose spraying in my direction. "There were people all around me, but none of them would help," I said, referring to Pete's goons who'd surrounded me there, cheering Pete on like spectators at a sporting event. "And when it was all over, when the worst had come and gone, there was Chris. Right by my side." I recalled waking up earlier that morning in the Ferrari's passenger seat with Ace next to me behind the wheel.

"Mmm…" Sister Sumpter nodded her head solemnly as she scribbled notes into her book. "Very nice…very nice…" She nodded again. "And when did you first know she was the one?" she asked of Ace.

"Uh…I don't know what to say." He shrugged and laughed nervously.

"It's okay, sugar." Sister Sumpter smiled. "Most men who sit in that seat are uncomfortable sharing their feelings, but don't worry. I already had my breakfast this morning, so I promise I won't bite!" She chuckled. "Just take your time, think about the question, and answer

honestly. When did you first know Carmen was the one?"
Ace looked down at his knees and stared a while as if he
were afraid his legs might run off without him. Then he
turned and locked eyes with me.

"I knew she was the one the moment I saw her. She
was in trouble. She was vulnerable. She was scared. And
there was nothing I could do about it. And the fact that I
couldn't swoop in and save her from her situation…the fact
that I couldn't be there for her and make everything
alright…it made me sick to my stomach…physically sick.
But…as time went on…I saw how strong she was. How
brave she was. The way she stood up to her circumstances
and wouldn't back down. The way she confronted her
situation and wouldn't quit? I saw a fortitude deep down
within her so powerful and tough that I realized…she'd
never needed saving to begin with. She was no damsel in
distress. She didn't need me to ride in to the rescue on a
white horse. She was her own knight in shining armor.
She didn't need me or anybody else. She was complete in
and of herself…she was whole…lacking nothing. And I've
been in awe of her ever since, looking up to her like a
redwood tree, humbled in the shadow of her resilience."

Ace was most likely acting, but where on earth did
he get the script?! Where did those words come from?
Yes, he was probably just playing a role for Sister Sumpter,
but I was deeply impressed. I was almost moved. He told
that story like there were cameras in the corner and he was
trying to secure an Emmy nomination or win the Tony for
Best Supporting Actor. And I wasn't the only one who'd
been touched by his performance.

"Mmm," Sister Sumpter sighed. "Good answer
honey…good answer!" She smiled and winked at Ace like

she wanted to steal him for herself and make him husband number five. Then she scribbled again wildly into her big, black book.

While she wrote, for some reason, Ace and I could barely look at one another. My eyes darted around the room, desperate not to look in his direction, and he studied his knees again like he was preparing to paint their likeness on canvas. I was ninety-nine percent sure that Ace's admission was just a farce intended to fool the evaluation, but honey, that remaining one percent left a tension in the air so thick we almost needed gas masks just to breathe. I'd only known Ace a matter of hours, yes, but I had to admit we'd done a whole lot of living in that small stretch of time. But still, he was a stranger to me. I didn't know him well enough to like him or loathe him, to love him or hate him. And there was no plausible explanation or reasonable foundation for the feelings budding between us. But if there was one lesson my life had taught me time and time again, it was that the human heart is rarely rational. With no rhyme or reason, without cause or cure, sometimes we just like who we like, and simply love who we love. And no matter how fast or far we run away, somehow what's destined to be will always be.

"Alrighty...and Carmen"—Sister Sumpter looked up from her big book and turned her attention over to me— "what do you hope to achieve in the future? And how do you believe Chris can help you to attain that goal?"

"What do I hope to achieve in the future?"

"Yes, and how do you believe Chris here"—she pointed at Ace— "can help you to attain that goal?" This question proved quite difficult for me to answer truthfully, mainly because I didn't have the slightest clue of how it *should* be answered. Future? Goals?! I was stumped. This was uncharted territory for a girl like me, and I found myself at a loss for words. "It's okay, sugar," Sister Sumpter soothed. "Take your time," she added in a whisper. And for once, I gave no forethought to what I would say. I just shot from the hip and spoke from the heart.

"Honestly, Sister Sumpter, I don't know." I shrugged and threw my hands up flippantly. "Maybe this makes me a bad candidate for marriage, but so be it. I can't lie. To be honest with you, I've never been the type of person to give much thought toward the future. My whole life, I've always lived for the moment, for the right here and the right now. I never had the luxury to sit back and dream. Never had the time nor the opportunity to think ahead, make plans, and prepare."

"And why is that?" she asked, her voice bearing a note of concern as she tapped on her mechanical pencil with her French tips.

"Why? Because I was always too busy surviving from day to day, that's why. Sometimes, hour by hour. I been fighting my whole life to carve out a space for myself in this world. Begging and borrowing, struggling just to score a meal and make the rent. The fact that I'm still here is nothing short of a miracle." I forced my lips into a smile, and I can only imagine how strange and out of place it must have looked sitting there on my sad face. "As a matter of fact, when Chris and I first met, I wasn't sure if I'd see another tomorrow; I didn't even know if I'd make it through the night. You wanna know what's in my future and how Chris can help? Well, he's just about the only person in my life who doesn't wanna hurt me in some way.

318

So right now, he *is* my future. He's my *only* help," I
concluded. And suddenly, I was saddened to realize that
my remarks were more *true* than false.

Sister Sumpter continued writing in her book, and
when she looked up at me finally, there was warmth and
compassion in her eyes. She reached over and pulled her
desk drawer open. Then she reached inside it and dug for a
minute until finally she produced a box of Kleenex. I
almost rolled my eyes. *What a sap!* I thought to myself.
Nothing I'd said was so heartfelt and profound as to
warrant tissues and tears. Obviously, Sister Sumpter had
been doing couples therapy far too long, and her career in
counseling had made her excessively empathetic and overly
emotional.

She snatched a tissue from the box and instead of
using it herself, she leaned forward over her desk and
handed it to me. Was *I* crying? The look of consolation in
Sister Sumpter's eyes and the wonder all over Ace's face
answered my question. I grabbed the tissue and hurried to
soak up those stray tears, totally embarrassed by the
betrayal of my emotions. I mean, really! Emotions are
supposed to let *you* know how you feel about something.
But my emotions were broadcasting my innermost thoughts
to the world. They'd gone behind my back and told
everybody my business like a gossiping hairdresser. And I
was left in the dark like I'd forgotten to pay my electric
bill! I continued to wipe away those slanderous tears, and
Ace reached over to hold my hand.

"Ugh!" Sister Sumpter exclaimed, slamming the
big, black book shut. "I've heard enough, and I've seen
plenty!" She held her mug to her lips and guzzled the rest
of her coffee like a barfly at last call.

"Is everything okay?" Ace rose in his chair.

"Is everything okay?!" Sister Sumpter repeated, almost spitting out her sweet drink. "Is everything okay?!!" she echoed again. "Everything is *wonderful*!" she proclaimed. "In all my years, I've never seen two people more in love!"

"Really?" Ace and I asked together, astonishment in our voices and disbelief in our eyes. *In love?!* I repeated to myself. Hearing that ridiculous diagnosis, I was convinced that Sister Sumpter was sippin' on Kahlua, not coffee!

"Aww...don't be modest, children. What you two have is beautiful! You should be declaring it from the mountaintops with confidence, not whispering it with diffidence! You should be boastful about it, not bashful! You don't know how many folks have passed through this office with not even an ounce of what you two have. Some people forge a relationship out of mere convenience—it's strictly symbiotic. He ain't got no way to get to work, and she got a brand-new car. Boom! Instant couple! That's all it takes!" Sister Sumpter scoffed. "And some folks don't have no reason at *all* to be together. They go out a few times and think just 'cause they had a few dates and haven't killed each other yet, they should become a couple. Then they stay together for a while...no passion, no excitement...each one settling for the other. And after a few years, they figure, hey, the next natural step must be a wedding 'cause that's what everybody else is doin', right? Next thing you know, they find themselves locked in a miserable marriage, a painful prison serving twenty-five to life. But not you two! Anybody with eyes can see there's something special brewing here. And so, in my professional, spiritual, and personal opinion, on September twenty-first, I think you two should *run* down the aisle!"

"Thank you!" I exclaimed.

"So you'll let us in to see Pastor Dobbs then?" Ace asked.

"Certainly!" Sister Sumpter smiled. "Right this way!" She rose to her feet—or more accurately, she *stood* to her feet; her short stature forbade her from rising.

Ace and I trailed behind her eagerly, just one step behind her shadow. We'd done it! We had passed round one of the gauntlet. Sister Sumpter reached up to press the buzzer to the pastor's chambers, and Ace and I beamed at each other with pride. Without delay, the door unlocked with a click and a buzz, and the three of us entered in a rush.

The pastor's chambers were dark and quaint but beautifully designed. That fine room had most likely been the executive suite of the former bank's president, the place where six-figure deals were hashed out in private, executed with a handshake, a cigar, and a smile. Just about identical to Sister Sumpter's space, the pastor's chambers included a big, brown desk with two leather club chairs in front of it. But the pastor's walls were covered in a dark cherrywood paneling that was polished to a high shine. Another big bookcase was embedded in the wall behind the pastor's desk, and crammed on those shelves were even more volumes, all of them thick as phonebooks.

"Sorry to interrupt, Pastor, but this is your favorite kind of news!" Sister Sumpter announced. The pastor's chair was facing the bookcase, and its tall leather back completely concealed the clergyman. As the pastor's tall chair began to spin around slowly, Ace and I straightened our clothes and practiced our smiles so as to make the best possible presentation for the renowned reverend. And once the spinning stopped, the three of us were greeted warmly with a big, boyish smile.

"Well, if it isn't my long-lost cousin Clara! So we meet again!" Butch waved. If the shock and surprise of seeing Butch there didn't kill me first, I was sure Butch would do the honors himself any minute. And so, for the first time all morning, I was actually grateful to be in church. With the choir crooning just around the corner and the sanctuary already filled, my corpse was in the prime location for its funeral and final farewell!

CHAPTER 26: SHALL WE PREY?

"Cousin Clara?!" Sister Sumpter repeated. "You two related?" She pointed at Butch and me. "And I thought you said your name was Carmen?!" She placed a hand on her hip and squinted at me over her glasses like her eyes had laser powers.

"You told *me* your name was Tina!" Ace added in my ear.

"Tina?!" shouted Sister Sumpter, her voice jumping an octave in an instant like a coloratura soprano. "What in the world is goin' on here?" she asked of no one in particular. Then she turned her attention back to Butch, the pastor's imposter. "What you doin' in Pastor's chair, Mr. Jones?! Pastor don't like nobody sittin' at his desk!" she warned.

"Don't worry." Butch smiled as he leaned back. "I asked him nicely." He laughed.

"Butch, how'd you know to come here?" I asked the man-child.

"Butch?!" Sister Sumpter repeated, and for a second, I thought there was a parrot in the room.

"I made a copy of that lil' list of yours." Butch grinned as he rocked back and forth in the leather recliner.

"You made a copy?!"

"Yep! Right here." He tapped at his temple. "I got a pretty good memory, ya' know. And Ms. Jane ain't the only somebody who can find stuff out. I knew we'd catch up to you sooner or later."

"We?" I asked, and suddenly I heard a click coming from a door beside the pastor's bookcase. The plaque on the door read "Pastoral Washroom" in big fancy lettering.

All those rooms inside of rooms inside of rooms? I felt like I was traveling through the Twilight Zone and trapped inside a Russian nesting doll!

"Pastor, is that you?!" Sister Sumpter cried out. And when the door finally creaked open all the way, a man emerged. A very old man. Snaggletooth Willie limped slowly through the doorway as pretty Eve helped him along like a human cane.

"Hi, Maria!" Willie shouted through that toothless grin, flapping his arthritic fingers in an enthusiastic wave. Excitement danced in his eyes as if I were his prodigal daughter returning home at last.

"Maria?!" Sister Sumpter's confusion strangled her like a python as her eyes nearly bulged out of their sockets.

"Her name's not Maria, silly," Eve corrected Willie with a nudge. "It's Mantha, remember?" she added, her sparkling smile flashing in my direction. "Hi, Mantha!" She waved.

"How many names you got, girl?!" Sister Sumpter shouted, her eyes widening like panoramic lenses. "Lawd hammercy, y'all gon' make me catch a heart attack!" She clutched her chest. "Where is Pastor? Pastor Dobbs?!" she called into the washroom. "Pastor Dobbs?!" she called again. Hearing no reply, she marched past Willie and Eve to inspect the lavatory herself. Finding no one there, she turned back around and stepped back into the chambers with the rest of us. "Who are you people?!" Sister Sumpter screamed. "And where is Pastor Dobbs?" She stomped her foot.

Just then, I heard a strange sound coming from behind me. I turned around, but there was nothing there. Ace must have heard it too. He closed the door to the pastor's chambers, and hidden behind its slow swing, a long-legged man sat on the floor there with his knees against his chest and his back propped up against the wall. He was dressed in a seersucker suit that had faint blue vertical stripes running down its length. His face was covered with a burlap sack, probably a feedbag from Willie's farm. And the sack was held in place over his head by a thick rope tied tightly around his neck and shoulders. His hands, too, were tied behind his back, and a bit of blood seeped through the top of that sack from where he'd been hit over the head. Sister Sumpter had said earlier that Pastor Dobbs was tied up in a meeting, but the poor thing had no idea just how right she was!

"Mmmm…" There the sound was again, the wounded pastor moaning, disoriented and lost in the darkness of that opaque sack.

"Pastor Dobbs!" Sister Sumpter cried as she pushed past Willie, Eve, Ace, and me to kneel beside the poor pastor and minister to his wounds. She pulled at the ropes, and the reverend moaned louder as the square knots tightened around his neck.

"I wouldn't touch him if I were you," Butch said with a smirk. "You pull at those knots the wrong way, and you'll snap his windpipe and suffocate him. This church'll be lookin' for a new pastor." Butch was no boy scout, but after a lifetime of stickups, holdups, burglaries, and petty thefts, he sure could tie knots like one! Sister Sumpter pulled her hands away quickly and sat there silently with tears in her eyes.

"Will somebody tell me what the hell is goin' on here?" Ace shouted as he backed away from Sister Sumpter, the pastor, and me. I could see the wheels turning

325

in his mind, his tactical training as a gangster kicking in. He backed up slowly until he was standing in the corner, the best vantage point for assessing the room and the safest spot for guarding against any potential surprises from behind. His square jaw, coupled with the focused look in his eyes, told me that he was ready to reach for his gun any minute. And the fact that he hadn't done so already proved to me that Ace had been telling me the honest truth earlier when he'd promised he only pulled his weapon as a last resort. He'd been telling me the truth ever since he'd met me, and I'd been busy spreading lies like birdseed, handfuls at a time. And while I spun tales like a black widow spider, Ace had been falling steadily like Francine's rains—but not for me. He'd been falling for Tina Henderson, the fake me, the temporary woman, the spoof, the sham, the illusion in the glass. If Ace knew my true identity, the real me, plain old Mantha Moore, he would probably be sick to his stomach to know that all this time he'd been escorting an escort and falling for a felon!

"I'll tell you what's goin' on!" Butch rose. And before he was all the way to his feet, Ace pulled his gun finally and aimed it at the man-child. Eve and Sister Sumpter screamed. Meanwhile, Willie smiled wide like he'd been flipping through the channels and just stumbled across his favorite program. "Take it easy, friend." Butch slid his hands up in the air slowly and smiled. "I'm not the enemy. The enemy is standin' right there." Butch pointed at me.

"Quiet!" Ace shouted at Butch. Then Ace turned to me. "Here." He pulled something from his pocket and tossed it to me. And when I caught it and opened my hands, I was surprised to see that it was the Swiss army

326

knife that had been taken from the Ferrari's center console. "Cut him loose," Ace directed, and I knelt down beside Pastor Dobbs and Sister Sumpter and began cutting at the ropes.

"Is that my knife?" Butch asked, and an eyebrow rose on Ace's forehead. "Yep! That's my knife alright. I recognize the handle," Butch added. "I musta' left it in the car."

"Who is this clown?" Ace asked me, never taking an eye off Butch. "He your boyfriend or something? He damn sure ain't no cousin."

"He's not my boyfriend! And he's not my cousin either. I don't know who he is anymore," I answered, still sawing at the ropes. I didn't know how best to explain Butch without contradicting and further incriminating myself. I'd already lied to Ace about the sacks in the trunk. How could I take that back? And I certainly didn't know how to explain Willie and Eve. That would've been a long story, and the one thing we were short on that morning was time. So I focused instead on the task before me, sawing nervously against the ropes in my hand. The pastor moaned and squirmed beneath my touch, and Sister Sumpter whispered prayers up into the air. I hoped she'd have better luck getting through than I did.

"Nah, man...I ain't her boyfriend," Butch said. "I would never wanna get mixed up wit' a chick like dat." He pointed at me with disdain. "She dangerous. Ain't that right?" Butch asked me.

"I told you to shut-up," Ace warned.

"Hey, man, I'm just tryna' tell you the truth. She like to kill her boyfriends, don't you?" Butch said, addressing me again.

"Don't you say another word to her!" Ace widened his stance like he was readying himself for the shot.

"Fine man, ask her yourself!" Butch yelled back. "Ask her what she did to her last boyfriend. What was his name? Err...uh...Samson! That's it. Ask her about how she made love to him and then killed him and left him to rot in a motel room!" Eve, Willie, and Sister Sumpter all gasped together. And Ace looked at me like he was seeing me for the first time, like he was a blind man testing out new eyes.

"Is that true?" Ace asked me, still aiming the gun at Butch. "You killed Samson?" As I continued to cut at the thick ropes amidst accusations of being a murderer, Sister Sumpter scooted away from me slowly, like she feared for her safety with me holding that knife. "Did you kill Samson?!" Ace asked again. The tension in the room was thick as molasses, and sitting there, I was more uncomfortable than a hen laying a square egg!

"No! I didn't kill nobody. I swear! He just...he just died." My eyes watered as I recalled Samson's lifeless face looking down at me as we lay together on that hotel mattress.

"So you mean to tell me this whole time you got me lookin' for a dead man?!" Ace asked in disgust.

"Ace, I couldn't tell Pete that Samson was dead 'cause the only way he'd let me out of that basement alive was if I promised to find Samson and bring him back. And I didn't tell you the truth because I didn't know if I could trust you before. I know it looks bad, but I didn't kill Samson, I promise... He must've overdosed or something. The only reason why I dropped by the diner last night was because I was lookin' for clues. I was just tryna' figure out what killed him!" I pleaded, a tear escaping my eye.

"Don't you dare cry," Ace whispered solemnly. "You been foolin' me with those tears ever since I met you. Playin' me for a sucker!"

"No, that's not true. You gotta believe me!" I begged, and just as another tear fell from my eyes, the knife in my hand finally cut through the stubborn ropes that wrapped around and squeezed the pastor's neck like a hungry anaconda. Sister Sumpter leapt forward to help me untangle the ropes and free the pastor's face from the burlap sack. And when we finally snatched that bag off, the man underneath gasped and coughed as his lungs filled with fresh air.

His jawline was covered by a thick goatee, and his salt and pepper hair was trimmed into a neat fade. His complexion was like maple syrup: thick, rich, and brown. And his almond-shaped eyes were deep, dark, and discerning. I could imagine the ladies of the congregation fighting for a seat in the front row, so they could wink and bat their eyes at the handsome minister. There were bruises all over his face, and blood trickled down the side of his head. Sister Sumpter pulled the handkerchief from the pastor's jacket pocket and began wiping the crimson drops from his face. And we both smiled at him sweetly in guarantee that everything would be okay.

"*You're* Pastor Dobbs?!" Ace cried out all of a sudden, and immediately the sympathetic smiles that Sister Sumpter and I displayed collapsed faster than a house of cards. The handsome pastor, still coming out of his disoriented stupor, looked up and locked eyes with Ace. And suddenly, a frightful realization took hold of his face like he'd just seen a monster. The two men exchanged gazes in silence, and without warning, Ace took his gun off of Butch and pointed it at the pastor. Sister Sumpter screamed, and she and I jumped back up and out of the path of Ace's revolver.

"Ace, what are you doin'?!" I cried.

"Dis fool ain't no pastor. Seem like everybody in here playin' a role today!" Ace accused.

"Yo'self included...*Ace*!" Sister Sumpter shouted as she stepped forward. "Talkin' 'bout I'm Chris wit' cold feet," she mocked. "I gave you fools a quiz on marriage and I should'a been administering a lie detector test!" Sister Sumpter scolded the two of us. "Now you leave my pastor alone, you hoodlum!" She stared Ace down—or more accurately, she stared him *up*, as he towered over her even from across the room. "You too late to rob the *bank*, fool, 'cause that closed down years ago. This is a place of worship now, young man! You're standing in the house of the Lord! Only thing we rich on around here is grace and mercy! And there ain't nothin' in here for you to take...unless you lookin' for salvation and a little hope! So go on! Git! Find someplace else to steal from!" She pointed toward the door.

"You really don't know, do you?" Ace asked Sister Sumpter, and the confusion in her eyes returned. "You think *I'm* a thief?! Your '*pastor*,'" Ace mocked, "is one of the biggest thieves in all of the southern United States!"

"What?!" Sister Sumpter gasped.

"Ace, what are you talkin' about?" I asked.

"That ain't no pastor!" Ace sneered. "That's Doughboy!" For a moment, I was just as confused as Sister Sumpter. I'd never mentioned Pastor Dobbs' old nickname

330

to Ace, mainly because it didn't seem relevant. "He changed his hair and lost the beard, but I'd know those eyes anywhere. Tell everybody who you really are!" Ace insisted. Then he pulled down on the hammer of his revolver, and we all heard the click as a bullet climbed into the chamber. Willie and Eve gasped as they sat back and watched the show. Butch, of course, was all smiles, excited at the prospect of blood being spilled. The pastor took a deep breath and cleared his throat.

"I'm Reverend Nathan Michael Dobbs," he replied, his gaze going cross-eyed every few seconds as he stared down the barrel of Ace's gun. "I'm the pastor of this church. I haven't used the name Doughboy in years."

"Doughboy?" Sister Sumpter repeated, bewilderment devouring her face like flesh-eating bacteria. "Lord hammercy! Does everybody in here have two and three names?!"

"That ain't my name anymore, Sheila," the reverend said. "We all have a past. Every one of us has a personal testimony of where God has brought us from. When the Lord found me, I was Doughboy. But he changed me into the man you know today, the man that's been leading this flock diligently ever since. Don't lose faith in me now."

"But Ace, how do *you* know him?" I asked, pointing at the pastor.

"Doughboy here," Ace said, eying the reverend, "is Pete's old business partner, one of the founders of our little organization. Pete and Doughboy ran the diner together back in the day. Pete made the meals, and Doughboy here made the desserts. That's where he got his nickname from. Used to make all kinds of cobblers and cakes, pies and pastries." I thought back to the sweet potato pie that the cowboy had complained about back at Pete's place, and Ace's explanation made sense. Without benefit of a pastry chef onsite, the diner's desserts seemed to be suffering. "Pete and Doughboy ran the restaurant together, and on the side, they hustled together, laying the groundwork for an empire."

"So they used the diner as a cover to keep down suspicions and launder the revenue discreetly," I concluded.

"Exactly," Ace confirmed. "Until Doughboy here got greedy. Ain't that right, Doughboy?" Ace took a step closer.

"Now you hold on a minute, son!" the pastor refuted from the floor. "That was years ago! I'm tellin' you. I'm a changed man now. Second Corinthians five and seventeen says 'Therefore if any man be in Christ, he is a new creature: old things are passed away; behold, all things are become new.' I'm tellin' you, son...I'm a different man now, washed in the cleansing blood of the Lamb!"

"So what?!" Ace shouted. "Maybe *God* forgave you, but I promise you Pete didn't! And if you really are a new man, if you so righteous like you claim to be, how come in all these years you never went back and repaid the money you stole? Huh?! Here I was nervous to be in church again after all these years, and you ain't even a real pastor. I know you, man. I've seen your kind before. You just like my daddy. Huffin' and puffin' and parading around the pulpit on Sunday morning...as if you weren't just drinking and fightin' all up in the bar on Saturday night. Raising Hell while you preach about Heaven. I know you, man. You probably got a girlfriend on every pew, don't chu'?" The pastor bowed his head. "Yeah, I know you real good, man." Ace shifted from side to side, and the gun began to tremble in his hands. "You just like my pop! Castin' judgement left and right…everywhere but in the mirror. Throwin' stones by day and comin' home each night to a glass house. I know who you are, man, and I'd be doin' the world a favor by blowin' yo' brains out right now!"

"Ace," I said calmly, trying to quell the rage inside him. "Don't do it," I pleaded. "Look at me." Ace took his eyes off of the pious pastor for a moment and looked into my eyes. "He's not your father." I knew Ace had been nervous to come to church that morning, and now I knew why. Walking up those stairs meant confronting the past he'd been running from for years. And when he'd opened the door to that sanctuary and heard the choir sing, he'd opened up a locked box buried deep inside his mind, spilling secrets and memories everywhere and short-circuiting his senses. And of course, I knew all about that. I'd been running my whole life too. So, as I stared up into Ace's face, those eyes were like mirrors. They reflected back the same exact struggles I'd been wrestling with. I recognized the same hurt and longing hidden there inside Ace that I'd been fighting within myself. And suddenly, it was clear. An ace is only worth one point at the blackjack table and should never stand alone. And yet, right there, in that brief second, as I examined his eyes with my own, an ace was all I wanted. My Ace was somehow enough.

"She's right. Don't hurt him!" Eve offered. Suddenly, the gaze that entangled Ace and I was broken, and he turned his attention back to the pastor.

"Yeah," added Willie. "What if you're wrong, son, and he really is a reverend?" Willie reasoned. "Shootin' a preacher...that's got to be 'bout what? Seven years bad luck?" he asked Sister Sumpter. "I can't remember." Willie waved his crooked fingers in dismissal. "I'm not big on all this religious mumbo-jumbo. It's all just hocus-pocus to me!" Willie sniggered, his laughs culminating in a series of coughs.

"You sound like you 'bout ready to kick the bucket and go ask God in person!" Sister Sumpter rolled her eyes. Then she turned to Ace. "Don't do it, honey," she said softly. "Listen to us. Be a better man than your father was! Prove that *you* have some integrity."

"It's too late," Ace replied. "It's already done."

"Ace, you said you weren't a killer!" I reminded him.

"Yeah...and you said your name was Tina," he offered in reply. "But don't worry," he said to Sister Sumpter. "I won't kill him." Then he turned to the pastor. "I'm gonna bring you back to face Pete, and I'll let *him* kill you. I couldn't find Samson, but I think finding Doughboy will do." Ace leaned in closer and centered himself in the pastor's gaze.

"God may have shown you mercy, but Pete's gonna give you justice! That's right. He's gonna give you exactly what you deserve. And you know how he's gonna do it?" Ace asked. "He's gonna tie you down on his cutting table and butcher you alive...piece by piece. He's gonna make you watch him while he saws off your arms and legs. And every time you pass out, you know what he's gonna do? He's gonna turn his hose on you and wake you right back up!"

"Jesus!" Sister Sumpter summoned. She shouted that name with such a fervency that I half expected the good Lord to manifest out of thin air to stand right before her like a genie in a bottle!

"I'll admit it." The pastor lowered his head again. "There was a time when the only thing that mattered to me was money. I robbed and cheated to get what I wanted, and I didn't care who I hurt. I wish I could say that Pete was the only somebody I ever double-crossed. But to be honest, he wasn't the first nor the last. Pete was just one of many men that I lied to and stole from while I was living in sin chasing after the treasures of this world. But I'm tellin' you, son, I'm not the same man I once was. Now I'm a servant of the Lord! And that's the absolute, unequivocal, God's honest truth."

For a moment, we were all spellbound by his impromptu sermon. Every one of us in that room had done things in our lives that we weren't proud of; we all had secrets that brought us shame. We all had regrets—at least *almost* all of us. Butch's sociopathy may have precluded him from feeling real regret, so I wasn't sure about him. But certainly, the pastor's admission tugged at the heartstrings of the rest of us. I looked up at Ace, and I could tell he wasn't quite convinced, though.

"Fine," Ace said. "Answer me this then." He stepped in closer. "How you know Samson? Huh? What's the connection? I'm supposed to believe it's all just a big ole coincidence that Samson steals a hundred kilos of coke with a street value of six and a half million dollars and his trail leads to you, a man who just so happens to be a former kingpin in a drug cartel? A man who did the same exact thing *himself* once before? Admit it! You sent Samson

335

over there to get a job at Pete's place so he could infiltrate
the staff on your behalf and execute an inside job, right?
Right?! You stealin' from Pete again, ain't chu?!" Ace
accused. "Ain't chu?!"

We all studied the pastor's eyes for an explanation.
And after a few moments, the pastor lifted his head and
looked toward the ceiling, as if he were hoping to see God
up there. Then he sighed and opened his mouth to respond
to Ace's allegations, to bare his soul and set the record
straight once and for all. We prepared our ears for his
answer.

But suddenly, out of nowhere, a thick brown book
sailed across the room and hit Ace on the side of the head,
and the gunman stumbled and fell into the wall. As he
faltered, Butch leapt across the desk like a jungle cat
pouncing at its prey and landed on Ace's back. He plucked
the revolver from Ace's fingers and hit Ace over the head
with the gun's grip. The whole thing happened so fast and
the moment seemed so surreal that it was like somebody
had started fast-forwarding a movie I was watching. By the
time Sister Sumpter and I let out our screams, the whole
thing was nearly over.

"Ace!" I cried out as I lunged forward to help. But
in the two seconds it took for me to make it across the
room, Butch was already standing over Ace and pointing
the pistol in my face. And as my gentle giant lay on the
floor motionless, knocked out cold, his blood splattered
across the pages of the hymnal Butch had thrown, I took
Sister Sumpter's advice. For the first time in my life, I
thought about the future. Standing there nose to nose with
that revolver while the man I was falling for lay there,
fallen, unconscious at the man-child's feet, I made plans to

fulfill the prophecy. I'd lied. I'd stolen. And now there was only one thing left to do...

I had to kill Butch.

Dara Dionne Welms

CHAPTER 27: HELL BREAKING LOOSE!

"Thank you, young man!" Pastor Dobbs exclaimed as he rose to his feet. Sister Sumpter helped him up, offering her body as a crutch.

"Don't thank me yet, brother." Butch smiled. "I didn't slay this giant to help you out." Butch kicked Ace's leg, and my muscleman didn't even flinch. "I did it to help me! Now, what's this I hear about a six-million-dollar stash of coke?!"

"Didn't you hear what I said, son?" the pastor asked in exasperation. "I'm a man of the cloth now!" the pastor persisted.

"You must not know who you talkin' to, brother!" Butch laughed, his gun still aimed at me. "You got this place guarded like Fort Knox…soundproof rooms all up and throughout… You got electronic doors with built-in bolts…and the sister over here said the building used to be a bank. Is that right? So that means you got a vault on the premises, don't it? This is the perfect place for a covert operation. All the security benefits of a bank, and the church as the perfect decoy."

"Covert operation? Decoy?" Pastor Dobbs echoed.

"That's insane," chimed in Sister Sumpter. "We can't help if we inherited the security features of the former establishment. And I know for a fact that the vault is broken! Ain't that right, Pastor? It's stuck and can't be opened."

"That's right! That vault is useless, son, no way in and no way out. Now, how many times I gotta tell you folks?" Pastor Dobbs shouted indignantly. "This is a

338

church! And I'm a pastor! Just like Sheila said before…the only business we're in around here is the business of spreading love and helping people to live happier, healthier lives! Now please leave. You done already tied me up and beat me senseless for no good reason. Go on now and leave us be!"

"Man, please. You ain't foolin' nobody! I got a nose for nonsense, my friend, and I know you runnin' drugs through here just like ole boy said!" Butch accused.

"Butch! So what if he is!" I interjected, the gun still pointed at my face. "What difference does it make to you? You got plenty money of your own right outside in the parking lot," I lied. "Just take the car and go! And you can keep my cut… I don't want it!"

"Thanks." Butch smiled. "I appreciate the kind offer…but I think I want *his* money too!" Butch turned his smile to Pastor Dobbs.

"What money?!" The pastor shouted back. Then he reached into his pockets and turned them inside out. "If there's money here, I swear it's news to us! And look at me, son"—the pastor pointed at his clothes— "I bought this suit on clearance over at Zoot Yourself, buy one get one free! If I had six million dollars at my disposal, wouldn't I be wearin' Armani or somethin'?"

"He's right!" Sister Sumpter agreed. "Our tithes, offerings, and endowments don't hardly cover the mortgage, payroll, lights, and utilities. Trust me! I'm the one who balances the books and manages our fiscal ledger!"

"Lemme get the keys to the ride, Mantha." Butch held out his hand.

"They're in his pocket." I pointed at Ace. Butch backed up slowly and knelt down to retrieve the keys from Ace's pants, all the while aiming the gun at me.

"Don't you know we broke down twice comin' up here in Willie's old truck?" Butch laughed as he frisked Ace. "After you pulled that lil' stunt of yours and stole the keys, I had to hotwire it. You know how hard it is to manipulate frayed wires in the pouring rain?" Butch shook his head as he pulled the keys from Ace's front pocket. Then he stood up and tossed them over to Eve. "Catch!" he called out, and Eve reached up and caught the keys in midair. "You take Willie to the car. I'll be right out," he instructed.

"Come on, Willie," Eve coached as she and the old man began to head for the exit.

"If you folks got a suggestion box around here," Willie said to Sister Sumpter, "I suggest y'all get this building a ramp! All them steps out front, I think we passed through Saturn's rings on the way up here!" he scoffed. Once the door closed behind them, Butch turned his attention back to Pastor Dobbs.

"Good. They're gone," Butch said with a sigh of relief. "I didn't want them to see what I'm about to do." And suddenly, Butch turned the gun on Ace and fired. The bullet went into Ace's back as he lay there still. Sister Sumpter and I both screamed and ran over to Ace. The pastor's almond-shaped eyes spread so wide they looked painful on his face. "See?" Butch said to Pastor Dobbs while Sister Sumpter and I scrambled like EMTs tending to Ace. "Look what you made me do! This senseless bloodshed could have been avoided. Now kindly tell me where the money is." Butch aimed the gun now at Pastor

Dobbs. "Or I'll spray that cheap suit so full of holes people'll think polka dots came back in style!"

"Okay, okay!" Pastor Dobbs shouted. "Thirty-seven, forty-eight, fifty-two, five! That's the passcode to the vault. Take it all...it's yours! There's cash and a couple dozen kilos left if you wanna take it and sell it yourself!"

"Pastor!" Sister Sumpter looked up over her shoulder, still applying pressure to Ace's wound with both of her tiny hands. "You mean to tell me it's all true?!"

"Shut up, Sheila!" the pastor replied. Then he turned back to Butch. "You can have it all, man...just let me go! In an hour's time, I'll be out of the state. You'll never see my face again, brother! I promise!"

"What was that again? Thirty-seven, forty-eight..." Butch asked.

"Thirty-seven, forty-eight, fifty-two, five," the pastor repeated.

"Got it!" Butch exclaimed with a smile. "Nice doin' business wit' cha'! Now, how do I get to the vault?" Butch asked, stepping over Ace's legs.

"I'll take you," the pastor volunteered. "It's right downstairs, but you gonna need the key in order to enter the strongroom." Pastor Dobbs crossed around to the other side of his desk, pulled open the center drawer, and reached way back inside. Meanwhile, Sister Sumpter and I removed Ace's jacket and tied it over his wound like a makeshift tourniquet. I checked his pulse and felt a faint vibration, the life leaving his body, seeping out slowly with every weakened breath.

"Hold on, Ace," I whispered through my tears. "Don't die." Those weren't exactly the first words I'd hoped to whisper in my true love's ear, but for the time being, they'd have to do. Sister Sumpter was crying too in the wake of the pastor's betrayal. We looked into one another's eyes, and as we examined each other's tears, we vowed together in silence to avenge our broken hearts.

"Aah...here it is!" Pastor Dobbs declared as he pulled his arm from the desk drawer. It was only after I'd heard the gunshot that I saw the small silver pistol in the pastor's hand. Sister Sumpter and I screamed in horror as the bullet hit Butch square in the shoulder and propelled him backwards into the wall. And even as he fell back, the man-child managed to retaliate, squeezing the trigger and firing a few shots of his own. Butch's bullets pierced the pastor in the chest, and the blood oozed through his seersucker suit and spattered across the room. And when the skirmish was over, Pastor Dobbs stood still for a moment and looked around the room. "S-s-s-sorry," he stuttered as he locked eyes with Sister Sumpter. Then he leaned forward and collapsed over his desk, blood pouring from his body like it was a punctured plastic bag.

"Pastor!" Sister Sumpter screamed as she raced over to cry over the corpse. And while she tended to her love and I tended to mine, Butch used the wall as leverage to stand himself upright. Blood spilled from his shoulder and soaked through his clothes, yet the madman seemed unaffected and numb to the pain. He stepped forward and examined his assailant closely to make sure that he was dead. And when he was satisfied with the prognosis, he lifted the gun again and aimed it at Sister Sumpter.

"Butch, no! What are you doing?" I asked the madman as I jumped to my feet. "She ain't done nothin' to you! It's me you want! Kill *me* if you gonna kill somebody!"

"Oh, I'll deal with you in a minute," Butch promised. "But first, I'mma take care of the old lady here." Sister Sumpter slipped her hands into the air, but I suspected her surrender wasn't to Butch. The three of us stood there alone, yet the sweet sister seemed to be entertaining angels in her view.

"Why, Butch?!" I appealed. "She ain't got nothin' to do with this!"

"You know I can't leave no witnesses, Mantha," Butch explained. "This lady know our names… Shit, she even know our aliases! She know 'bout the money outside in the car, *and* she know all about the money I'm finna' steal from the vault downstairs. Ain't no other way." Sister Sumpter closed her eyes and began whispering prayers as she prepared herself to face her fate.

"Butch, please don't!" I pleaded as I stepped forward. "There's gotta be another way!" I begged again. And as Butch's eyes narrowed in on Sister Sumpter's sweet face and his finger tickled the trigger, I leapt forward and plunged the Swiss army knife deep into his side. The gun went off accidently, and the bullet pierced an encyclopedia only inches above Sister Sumpter's head. It seemed her colossal faith and meager stature had partnered together to oil death's grasp and save her life. Sister Sumpter opened her eyes slowly, surprised to find herself still here on this side of glory. And when she saw me wrestling with her would-be assassin, she ran around the desk and jumped on the madman's back. She and I tussled with Butch, trying to knock him from his feet. But even in his injured state, the man-child was much too strong and refused to be subdued.

343

In the melee, as I pulled on Butch's fingers with all my might, trying to pry the gun from his iron fist, an idea went off in my head as if my brain were a gun in its own right. I jumped up and ran over to the desk to snatch the *other* pistol from the stiff fingers of the sinister minister. Then I aimed and fired. Butch yelped as the bullet grazed his leg. I tried to shoot again, but I couldn't tell where Butch ended and Sister Sumpter began as the two of them wrestled there on the floor.

The embattled Sister Sumpter fought with all her being as Butch and I tried to capture one another in our sights and shoot each other dead. She scratched and clawed at Butch with her French tips, and I ran over to rejoin her in the fight. And just as I came close, Sister Sumpter managed to lift her stubby leg and knee Butch in the groin. Butch howled like the wolf that he was and curled up like an armadillo. And with our attacker momentarily overcome, I aimed my gun again. But Sister Sumpter grabbed me by the forearm, and I lost the shot. She pulled the door open, and we ran from the pastor's chambers while Butch climbed back up on his feet to give chase.

"Come back here!" Butch yelled as Sister Sumpter and I sprinted across her office and headed for the door. With the madman hot on our heels, we pulled the handle open and spilled into the hall outside. Butch fired again, and the wayward bullet put a deep dent in the steel door.

"This way!" Sister Sumpter pulled me. "The emergency exit!" She pointed the way. And as another shot rang out from behind us and the bullet flew over our heads, Sister Sumpter and I took off racing down the winding corridor like we were poised on the blocks of the hundred-meter dash and had just heard the starting gun. And as we approached the neon exit sign, I turned and shot back over my shoulder. For a moment, I wondered *Where is everyone?* Where was all the commotion, all the screaming and panic that should've surely accompanied the occurrence of shots being fired in a church? And then I remembered Butch's observations: the soundproofed doors of the sanctuary and all those rooms accessible only by buzz entry. I swallowed hard when I realized that no one could hear us and that the sweet sister and I were on our own.

Sister Sumpter reached the exit doors first and pushed them open—or tried to, that is. Just beyond those doors was the ugliest face I'd ever seen. Snarling and howling like a rabid dog and trapping us there inside, descending upon the church like Armageddon, Francine had finally arrived!

CHAPTER 28: SUDDEN DEATH!

The door was only open a few seconds. But in the
presence of so much power, bearing witness to such
grandeur and force, I was overwhelmed with awe, and the
seconds seemed like centuries. Francine had been issuing
threats for days, and even the brainy meteorologists had
mistaken her dormancy for departure and confused her
remission with retreat. Everyone had assumed the worst
was over and the coast was finally clear. All the while, it
seemed Francine had been toying with us, sending soft
rains intermittently to lull us all into a false sense of
security so she could creep up from behind and make her
move at last. And now, as I stood in the doorway and
beheld her full magnificence, as my eyes gazed upon her
glory with my mouth there all agape, I was spellbound by
her splendor and nearly blown away—quite literally—by
her wrath.

Those winds sounded like freight trains barreling
by, and my ears popped under the pressure. Signs were
snatched down off their posts, and hundred-year-old trees
were torn right out of the ground like they were nothing
more than shrubs and weeds. Lampposts leaned in the
wind like they were trying to light up the asphalt, and trash
and debris tumbled across the parking lot like they were
alive and desperate to get away. The storm ripped the
bumpers off of cars, yanked antennas and satellite dishes
down from rooftops, and stole the mailboxes from nearby
lawns. Hubcaps glided by like Frisbees, and garbage cans
soared through the sky like they'd grown wings of their
own and learned how to fly. Water poured into the parking

lot while the storm pounded the pavement. And as the wind blew those waters all around, I saw them transforming right on into waves as if the sea had come ashore.

Sister Sumpter and I struggled to close the door again, and as we pulled on the handle with all our might, I looked up and saw the sheer size of the storm. It was like seeing a blue whale come up for air right alongside my skiff, like standing at the base of a New York City skyscraper and looking straight up. Francine towered over me, a hundred feet high, yet it felt like we were nose to nose. With her eye glaring at me, so vile and mean, and thunder grumbling deep in her belly, with her mouth wide open, spewing hot winds with each sultry, steamy breath, Francine hovered overhead like she was a swarm of bees and I'd just thrown a stone at her hive. As she salivated, hungering for flesh and thirsting for blood, rain dripping from her chin like spit, dribble, and drool, I knew that death was upon us and a reckoning was near.

Queen Francine had swooped down from her throne and declared war upon the world, and the only thing that was clear on that dark and dismal day, was the fact that she had no intention of leaving until she'd been heard. She'd come with a message for mankind, with a warning for all of humanity, a bulletin from above, hot off the heavenly press. She'd come to remind us of the pecking order, the ancient hierarchy of the universe, time, and space: man's perennial place beneath nature and our eternal appointment to the bottom rung. She was here to teach us a lesson, to steer us back to our rightful place, to show us, once and for all, who's in charge. And as thunder crashed down again just above our heads, anyone with an ear heard Her Majesty loud and clear.

347

Sister Sumpter and I quickly closed the door and ran on down the hall as Butch's footsteps advanced from behind. I could hear the irregularity in the rhythm of his stride, like he was dragging one of his feet. And that unevenness in his gait told me that the bullet to his leg had been more effective than I'd thought.

"Give it up, ladies!" Butch's voice circled over our heads like a vulture over two desert carcasses. "You're trapped!" His wounds may have slowed him a bit, but the indomitable Butch proved that he would not be stopped. "Nowhere to go from here!" he shouted. And as the sister and I rounded the curve of the hall, we approached a room up on our right. I ran to the window to get someone's attention.

"No!" Sister Sumpter shouted in a whisper. "We can't endanger anybody else! You heard him! He'll kill any witnesses. Only way to keep the members safe is to get to an empty room and find a phone!"

"A phone?" I repeated. "You seen outside. No way the cops are gonna be able to get to us in time! We gotta find somewhere to hide and get there quick! And I know just the place." I grabbed Sister Sumpter's hand and raced for the stairwell. We burst through the door and scuttled down the steps like crabs down an embankment. And when we reached the bottom, we burst through the basement doors like two swimmers coming up for air.

The basement of the church was strikingly grand. The floors were tiled in alternating beige and brown and polished to a sparkling shine. Two rows of tall pillars held up a beautiful domed ceiling, and planters filled with big, green trees were placed before each pillar, transforming the former bank into a banquet hall fit for fellowship, fraternity, and the breaking of bread. There were endless rows of long rectangular tables spanning the length of the cavernous room, each one covered with burgundy cloths and surrounded by matching chairs. Bamboo runners stretched from one end of each table to the other and were anchored on both sides by big floral bouquets. Multicolored candles served as centerpieces on every row, and their fragrances infused the atmosphere with a subtle mix of sweet and sugary scents.

All around the perimeter of the room were endless safe deposit boxes built right into the walls. Their stainless-steel faces were lustrous even despite the absence of windows and the softness of the lights. Hanging from the ceilings along the edges of the room were heavy gold drapes tied back by thick, decorative ropes. They were wide open now, but I imagined that those drapes would be drawn to a close during church events so as to keep the safe deposit boxes out of plain sight.

On one side of the room, there were about twenty or so service carts neatly arranged. Inherited from the former bank as a means of transporting cash and coins, I guessed that those carts had been repurposed by the church to deliver food and serve beverages to the gentle masses. Assembled in stacks behind the carts were at least a hundred extra chairs, and leaning up against the wall behind the chairs were dozens more rectangular tables, all props used to convert the cold, stark strongroom into the perfect venue for a multitude of elegant affairs.

On the other end of the resplendent room, framed right in the center of the wall, was an enormous vault, the prime focus of the entire space. The vault consisted of a huge circular door about seven or eight feet in diameter and made of thick, shiny steel. Right in the center of the circle was a small dial with numbers on it and a huge metal wheel such as might be seen aboard a ship or submarine. A massive locking mechanism held the vault secure, big bolts anchoring the door into the floor and embedding it into the wall like a colossal piece of sculpture. A tall podium was erected right before the huge vault, where, I supposed, the pastor stood and addressed his flock and gave benediction before meals. The steel circle offered itself as the perfect backdrop, a built-in showpiece for the charlatan shepherd.

Standing there in the middle of that hallowed hall and gazing around the room, I heard our breaths bouncing back and forth across the vacuous ceilings as we panted and gasped like two old ladies on life support. Aside from our breaths, the room was completely silent and still, and I knew that hiding from Butch wouldn't be easy. One peep from either one of us, and Butch would catch us effortlessly, like he was fly fishing in the kitchen sink. And without doubt, I knew that once he caught us, he'd skin and gut us each like the catch of the day and bring an untimely end to our earthly visit.

"Close the drapes!" I whispered. "Hurry!"

Sister Sumpter and I raced around the room, unlatching the drapes. And one by one, the curtains came cascading down to shield the safe deposit boxes. Just then, I heard sounds coming from the stairwell, and I knew Butch was on his way. I hurried to assess the room one last time, looking for shadows and places where Sister Sumpter and I could camouflage ourselves out of the madman's view. Truthfully, I didn't care where we hid. I just needed to stay unseen long enough to set my sights on Butch. Then I'd unload my weapon into him, just like he'd done to

Ace. The storage area where the tables and chairs were stacked looked fairly promising as a suitable place to hide. And I thought perhaps we could entangle ourselves in the drapes or dive beneath one of the tables. Maybe we'd take refuge behind the tall podium that stood at the head of the room. Whatever we decided, we had to act fast, so I grabbed Sister Sumpter's hand, and she and I hid in the best place I could think.

Hampered by the stiffening of his leg, Butch hobbled through the entrance after a few minutes, and I heard his footsteps in the distance. Sister Sumpter and I sat silently, petrified with fear as the madman paced the marble floors.

"Come out, come out, wherever you are…" Butch taunted us in song. Then he laughed, his gleeful guffaws echoing around the room. "I know you down here. No other place y'all could'a went. You can run…but you can't hide," he warned as Sister Sumpter and I held our breath as best we could. "Ahaaa!" Butch exclaimed, tearing back a section of curtain along one of the walls. "I like this game! Reminds me of when we used to play hide-and-seek when we was kids. Remember dat?" Butch laughed, and the bass in his voice reverberated across the room like a subwoofer amp. "Ready or not…here I come…" he goaded with a chuckle. "Those were the good ole days, weren't they? We used to play all day…swimmin' in the quarry…divin' for turtles and toads. Then we'd sit and skip rocks across the water while our clothes dried. Remember dat, Mantha? We used to ride our bikes back and forth, pretending we were racecar drivers, puttin' cards in the spokes to make it sound like we had motors. And when it rained, we used to take shelter under the train tracks and play jacks, shoot marbles, trade baseball cards, make mud pies…man! I miss that shit…don't you? Ahaaa!!!" he shouted again as I heard him snatch at one of the tablecloths. Votives and vases shattered against the ground, and I bit my lip to keep from screaming. Sister Sumpter shuddered at the sound of the breaking glass, but the two of us managed to keep our composure, breathing as softly as we could.

Butch laughed again. "Hey…remember that first job we pulled back in Tuscaloosa? That was epic, wasn't it?" As he spoke, I heard him pulling the service carts out of their alignment one by one. "We were in and out before they even knew what happened." I could hear the wheels of the carts rolling slowly across the marble as he made his way to the tables and chairs that stood behind them. "That was fun," he added. "Remember when I broke into that house, tied up those people, and killed that dog?" Butch sighed. "We ate good that night, didn't we? Ahaaa!!!" Butch called out as a stack of chairs came crashing down. The sound was amplified in the hollow room and echoed over and over again, like an explosion in an empty cave.

Next thing I knew, I was trembling like someone had turned down the heat, and Sister Sumpter and I clasped each other's hands tightly, each of us clinging to the other like a lifeline in frigid waters. "You know me, Mantha. You known me longer than anybody! Only friend I ever had," Butch confessed as he lumbered along, dragging that leg behind him.

"You know that everything I ever did, whether it was wrong or right, I did it for us!" he yelled. "When we were two dirty-faced, snot-nosed, barefoot kids catchin' fireflies and climbin' trees…the world was already against us…my mama beatin' my ass everyday…and your stepdaddy grabbin' at yours. We ran away and been runnin' ever since. And you know how we survived all these years? *Me*…me…me…me!" his voice echoed. "Who masterminded all those heists and orchestrated all those schemes to put food in our bellies? *Me*…me…me… me!" The man-child asked and answered. "Who robbed and fought and cheated and stole to keep money in our pockets? *Me*…me…me…me! And why did I do all that? Why have I been stickin' my neck out and riskin' my life year after year, job after job? You wanna know why?"

He paused for a moment, and the silence was deafening. "*You*…you…you…you!" His voice sent a shudder through my soul like there was an earthquake going on inside my body. "But now, all of a sudden, you high and mighty. Now, after all these years, suddenly you know right from wrong. And you wanna look down your nose at me like *I'm* the bad guy?" Butch asked the air. "You just like me! We ain't nothin' but liars, cheaters, and crooks. Always have been since we was kids. And that's all we ever *will* be until the day we die. Which, in your case…will be *today* if you don't come out here and face me!" he threatened. "Unfortunately, ya' friend there has to die. Ain't nothin' I can do about that 'cause, A: she know too much…and B: ain't no more room in the car!" Butch laughed. "But me and you can bounce back from this, Mantha. We can get beyond this, you and me. It's not too late for us."

How did we get here? I asked myself, retracing my steps. Twenty-four hours ago, Butch had been my best friend. And now he was my worst enemy. In my hour of need, I'd gone to Butch for help. I'd begged him to

353

accompany me on this journey, to aid me in this investigation. I'd asked him to put my needs first and to be there for me. And he'd agreed to stand in my corner, to come out swinging when I called his name, ready and willing to go to the mat for me if need be. He was supposed to be my hidden advantage, my secret weapon. But all along, the real secret was that the weapon was aimed at me! Instead of helping me to clear my name, Butch was busy scandalizing it. And though I needed him to be my unsung hero, he turned out to be nothing but a dud, an unsung zero! It hurt me to have to kill him. But I had to protect Sister Sumpter, so the madman left me no other choice.

Suddenly, as we huddled in our hiding place, cloaked in darkness, clinging to one another like static electricity, the two of us silent as stone, Sister Sumpter and I heard Butch as he approached the vault. And after a few seconds, I heard the dial clicking as he twisted the knob slowly and began entering the combination. Thirty-seven. Then he spun the dial in the opposite direction until he came to the second coordinate. Forty-eight. Then he changed directions again and rotated the dial once more. The room was so silent you could hear the pins in the tumbler shifting in their grooves. Fifty-two. Then he went back the other way, caressing the knob with his fingertips until he reached the final digit. Five. Then I heard Butch grab the big steel wheel. It squeaked and squealed as it started to turn. One by one, I heard the notches as they began to unlatch, and echoing all around us were the sounds of the plates aligning and the bolts retracting. Butch pulled hard on that spinning circle, and with one final thunderous click that resonated over our heads, the mighty vault door became unlocked at last. Butch pulled at the handle, and I stirred in darkness, bringing the gun up slowly to set my sights on the man-child. And right then, right there, as Butch pulled on that vault door, I shot him!

I'll never forget the look of surprise that froze upon his face when I locked my eyes on him and he looked up and saw my gaze. He fell to his knees, and in what seemed like slow motion, he hit the ground, his pistol falling from his fingers and sliding across the floor like a hockey puck. Sister Sumpter and I stepped out of the shadows, panting and gasping for air. And as our breaths returned to us slowly but surely, she and I climbed out of the vault, where we'd been hiding all along.

I had a pretty good memory too, and I'd memorized the combination that Pastor Dobbs had rattled off to Butch. In the minutes it took for the battered Butch to descend those basement stairs, Sister Sumpter and I had opened the vault ourselves. But it wasn't until we'd climbed inside and shut the door that we'd realized our mistake. The vault had a built-in intercom system that allowed us to hear, but there was no ventilation system; the two of us could barely breathe. We were trapped. It seemed all that running had led us to a dead end—in every possible sense. To keep from suffocating, we'd begun holding our breath and rationing our oxygen. Butch didn't realize it, but in trying to take our lives, he'd actually saved them. If he hadn't chased us downstairs and opened that vault, who knows how long Sister Sumpter and I would have had before we asphyxiated.

It felt like an eternity as we waited there in fear, not knowing if the next breath would be our last. But Butch was right. He'd said that he and I were just alike, and I knew his words were true. Just like me, Butch could never resist the lure of easy money. He could never ignore the temptation of fast cash. And so, I was certain that he'd set us free; it was only a matter of time. Sister Sumpter straddled one of Pete's sacks while I'd made myself a cushion out of hundred-dollar bills. And as we sat there cowering quietly in that cold dark vault, I was banking on my old friend's greed.

"Come on." Sister Sumpter pulled at my arm. "We need to call the cops!"

|•|•|•|•|•|•|•|•|•|•|•|•|•|•|•|•|•|•|•|•|•|•|•

Sister Sumpter and I waited together in the lobby for hours before the police and ambulances arrived. Apparently, there were so many living victims suffering at the hands of Francine that the police were in no rush to retrieve our three corpses, since they were already a lost cause. She and I sat there in silence, numb, despondent, devoid of all emotion. Perhaps we were still in shock. I cared deeply for Ace, Butch had been my best friend, and Sister Sumpter had been the pastor's right hand. Neither of us could bring ourselves to look in on the bodies again and to face the finality of death. Once had been enough.

Eventually, after the storm had subsided, the police came and took our statements, and the coroner was dispatched to the scene. People paraded out of the church and descended down the front steps like they were disembarking from Noah's ark at the end of the long flood. Those churchgoers exiting the sanctuary to the sight of

356

sirens and lights were oblivious to the events that had taken place right under their roof—and their noses. Francine had picked the city apart, leaving only bones on her plate. And when folks saw the aftermath of the storm, the fallen trees, the severed signs, and the destruction all across the lot, they simply assumed that Francine's tirade had summoned the police and ambulances to their aid. I frowned at the thought of how sad they all would be when they soon discovered their pastor's true identity and heard the news of his sudden death.

The rains had stopped. Glimmers of azure began to poke through the clouds as daylight fought to reclaim the horizon. Even a few brave birds dared to venture out of hiding to dance between broken branches and bathe in parking lot puddles. Queen Francine made her ascension back up to her throne on high. And as the birds stretched their wings again to grace the afternoon skies, their lively chirps announced victory to the world down below. Just like that, the long nightmare was finally over, and my odyssey had come to an end. But another storm, it seemed, was just about to begin.

CHAPTER 29: MAKING A KILLING!

"Well, look who it is… The menace returns!" he
announced as he entered. My back was to the door, but I
didn't even have to turn around to see who it was. I'd
know that voice anywhere. Some nights, I heard it in my
sleep. The fat detective made his way around the long
table, and as he sauntered by, his big buttocks shifting from
side to side in his tan slacks like two watermelons loose
aboard a boat, I could tell by that smug swagger that I was
in for a fight. "Still causing trouble, eh?" The detective
stared me up and down as he pulled out his chair on the
other side of the table. "I see you haven't changed a bit,
Miss Moore," he said as he sat down.

"Yes, and evidently neither have your eating
habits," I offered in reply.

"I'll have you know, I've lost twenty pounds!" he
grunted.

"Honey, a twenty-pound weight loss on you is
about as undetectable as carbon monoxide gas! What are
you doing here? I said all I had to say to the other
officers."

"Those officers were simply here to take your
statement. And now I'm here, lil' lady, to ask you a couple
of questions *about* that statement. Let me begin by
informing you that you have the right to remain silent.
Anything you say can and will be used against you in a
court of law. You have the right to an attorney. If you
cannot afford an attorney, one will be provided for you. Do
you understand the rights I have just read to you? Hell, you

been in the system so long, you could probably read me *my* rights by now!" He laughed.

"Yes, I understand my rights. I understand that I have the right not be treated as a suspect when anyone can clearly see I'm a victim! I have the right not to be interrogated after going through an ordeal like the one I just survived."

"I have a sneaking suspicion you're the one who *caused* the ordeal!" the big man accused.

"Oh, is that how we do our police work these days? We operate on sneaking suspicions? That's all it takes? No wonder so many innocent folks are incarcerated all over the place—young men and women being gunned down in the streets at the hands of unqualified, uneducated, simpleminded, redneck detectives like you acting out of pure speculation!" I folded my arms over my chest. I'd been bullied enough in the last forty-eight hours to last me a lifetime and I was in no mood for the detective's denigration. "Thanks to cops like you, police corruption is at an all-time high!"

"Unqualified? Corruption?!" the detective repeated. "Who's your pimp these days? The ACLU?" He laughed. "I been doin' this job since before you climbed outta' your mother's twat! And you better believe that after eight years on the beat, ten years workin' vice, and another nineteen years as detective, I've grown to be an expert on tramps like you!"

"You've only grown in size, fat ass!" I stuck out my tongue. "And you got some nerve callin' me a tramp. You're just jealous!"

"Me?! Jealous of you?! What the hell for?"

"Cause you're about as sexy as a dead hippopotamus. I mean, look at you! I bet if you had to draw me a map to your asshole, you'd need two sheets of paper! You sit there and look down your pointy little nose at me and call me a tramp, but we both know the only reason you're so chaste and restrained is 'cause nobody wants to touch you!"

"Is that all your tiny, little degenerate brain thinks about?" The detective laughed. "You're so goddamned oversexed, you probably moan every time you wipe your ass!" He laughed again. "And for the record," he added, "I'll have you know I'm a married man!"

"Please give my condolences to your wife!"

"Condolences?" he repeated. "We've been happily married since '86!"

"Well obviously she went blind in '85!" I retorted. "No woman in her right mind with a working set of eyes would get involved with a hateful slob like you!"

"Oh, is that right?"

"That's *quite* right!" I replied.

"Hmm…well maybe I oughta' invite her here to meet you. That way, you could see what a *real* woman looks like!"

"Aww…sweetie." I tilted my head in pity. "Just 'cause she's durable and lifelike doesn't mean your girlfriend is real. It says so right there on the box!" And suddenly, the detective froze for a moment as if the feed to his brain had been interrupted. Then he exploded in laughter, his booming voice filling the cinderblock room.

"Right there on the box?" he repeated, his gelatinous belly wobbling to and fro as he laughed with all his might. "Right there on the box!" he repeated again, slapping the table as a tear escaped his eye. And when his hearty laugh subsided, he said, "You know…believe it or not, Miss Moore…I didn't come in here to argue with you."

"Could'a fooled me." I rolled my eyes.

"The reason I came in here," he continued, "is to put your ass away…this time for good!" And just as he'd done the first time we met, the detective pulled a fat folder up from somewhere down below and slammed it on the table between us. "I'll remind you, Miss Moore, I always get the last laugh. You mind if I call you Miss Moore? Or do you prefer Alice Johnston…from uh…" He opened the manila folder and read from his notes, "from Dugan Financial? Shall I call you Alice? Or would you rather I refer to you as Clara Wells from West Texas? Or maybe I should call you Tina Henderson, is that better?" I cringed in my chair. "No? Don't like any of those? Well, how 'bout I call you Carmen Wilson? Try that one on for size. What do you think? Is that one a keeper? Oh, I know! How about somethin' a lil' more sleek and sexy. How about…Maria," he added in a whisper. "Now that's a nice lil' one-word moniker…floats right off the tongue. Ma-ri-a," he said again, stretching the syllables in his mouth. "Well? Take your pick. Which one will it be?"

"I don't know what you're talkin' about." I folded my arms over my chest again. "And evidently, neither do you. Frankly, I don't care what you call me. Just please don't call me Sam."

The detective chuckled as he removed his glasses to expose his beady bug eyes. "You ever been to the Bell Sheraton Hotel, Miss Moore?"

"I can't recall," I replied.

"Can't recall, eh? Tell me…are you suffering from an early onset of Alzheimer's disease, Miss Moore? Are you taking any medication right now…be it prescribed or over-the-counter…that might include amnesia as a side effect? Are you currently under the influence of methamphetamine or any other psychotropic drugs that might be affecting your memory today, Miss Moore?"

"I can't recall," I replied, smiling wide like I was posing for my obituary. The big little man sighed to himself, placed his glasses back on, and leaned back in his seat. I heard the squeaking as his chair's hind legs were tested to their limits beneath his gargantuan girth.

"You know, Miss Moore…I was pissed when I got that call. Five in the morning, I get the news that a dead body has been left to rot in a hotel room downtown. I got that call, and it was like somebody went and took a shit right on my doorstep. And I tell ya'…I've been cleanin' up crap ever since!" the detective growled. "I mean, talk about a mystery. Half naked man…no wallet on his person…no ID whatsoever. Guy could be King Tut for all I know! Had to send him to the morgue as a John Doe. And of course, it's a hotel room in the heart of downtown, so fingerprints everywhere, and we can't use not a one. A real clusterfuck this was!" The detective shook his head slowly. "But oddly enough, we did find this." The detective leaned forward and pulled a clear, plastic polybag from the manila folder and placed it on the table. "A lady's bra. I don't suppose this looks familiar to you, does it Miss Moore?"

Sitting there, seeing my long-lost bra in the stubby fingers of that fat detective, I fought the urge to panic as the heat rose within. "I can't recall," I replied.

"Can't recall, eh?" the detective repeated. "I guess you pull your titties out so much it's hard to keep track, huh?" He laughed. "You hear a belt unbuckle and you come runnin'…just like my cat when he hears me open up a can of Friskies!"

I knew this was just a tactic intended to provoke me, so I simply ignored the big man's rude remarks. "Are we done here?" I asked, looking at my watch.

"Oh, we're just gettin' started." He smiled. "Thanks to this sexy little bit of evidence"—he tossed the bra in my direction and it landed in the center of the table— "we know there was a woman in that hotel room with him. And then I saw the tan line on the index finger of his right hand, and I realized that one of his rings was missing. You like to steal items from your victims, don't you, Miss Moore?" He winked. "So anyway…we get this John Doe down to the M.E.'s office and run his prints, and boom! The good Lord cuts us a coupon; his prints are in the system! I get a name and address…Samson Brodice…lives over in Lithonia…just a stone's throw from the station. So I make my way to the address on file…Aldine Road… That sound familiar to you, Miss Moore? You ever find yourself on Aldine Road in Lithonia, Georgia?"

"I can't recall," I replied.

"Can't recall," he repeated. "I see. So anyway, I head over to Lithonia so I can break the news to the dead guy's next of kin, and his old lady answers the door. She's got a kid on her hip…looks just like the poor son-of-a-bitch that's layin' on a slab in the morgue. She invites me in…and I get the high honor of being the asshole who has to tell this poor lady that she's a widow now…and from here on out her son's a bastard." The detective shook his head as he recounted the events. "So the poor lady collapses in my arms…totally inconsolable…I mean she's spewin' tears like she's waterin' her roses! So I'm busy apologizing for her loss, and she says somethin' that catches my ear and piques my interest. She says…at least now she'll be able to put all the money to good use. So naturally, I say, 'What money?' And the widow proceeds to tell me about a visit she received from a one Miss Alice Johnston from Dugan Financial, during which this Alice Johnston informs her of an inheritance owed to the dead guy. Can you believe this guy's luck?" The detective laughed. "Somebody leaves him all this money, and the poor schmuck dies before he can see a dime!" He shook his head again. "So I jot this name down…uh…Dugan Financial…you ever heard of Dugan Financial, Miss Moore?" the detective asked me with a smile.

"I can't recall," I replied.

"How did I know you'd say that?" He snickered, and his big belly bounced. "Anyway…so I go to check out this Dugan Financial…and wouldn't ya' know…the damn thing doesn't exist! Can you believe this shit?!" He threw his hands up in the air in a show of exasperation. "So of course…I go back to see the widow so I can get a description of this phantasm, this Alice Johnston, and I say to the widow, I says, 'Tell me everything you told this lady.' So the widow tells me that she gave this ghost from Dugan Financial a list of names and some places where her husband—who, mind you, has been dead this whole time—might be. So I jot down the same list, and I'm back in business!" The detective flashed a sly smile. "One of the places on the list is this jumpin' lil' jazz club over in Madison County…uh…" The detective consulted his notes

364

again. "The Wild Goose. That sound familiar to you, Miss Moore? You ever been a guest at The Wild Goose nightclub?"

"I can't recall," I replied.

"Of course you can't." He smirked. "You really should drop in sometime, though. I'm tellin' you they've got a ribeye there?" He kissed his fingertips. "Whew! Out of sight!" He smiled. "But anyway…that notwithstanding…you won't believe it. This little nightclub gets robbed the *exact* same night that our widow is paid a visit by the mysterious Alice Johnston. And what's even weirder. The owner of the club calls in to report not only a robbery, but a *kidnapping*! Some crazy lunatic takes a hostage with him as he flees the scene, some lady in a tan dress by the name of Clara Wells…from West Texas. That name Clara Wells ring a bell to you, Miss Moore? You know anything about West Texas?"

"I can't recall," I replied.

The detective chuckled. "Interesting," he said after a moment. "So anyway," he continued, "this guy robs the place and takes a hostage, and he's got the whole entire Madison City P.D. dispatched… I mean, every available cop is goin' after this nutjob, right? And eventually they locate his car on the road and catch up to him. I'm talkin' ten…maybe twenty police cars…they're ridin' his ass like a two-dollar whore!" Then he leaned in close. "Surely that's an analogy you can appreciate," he whispered with a smile before leaning back again. "So they're hot on his bumper…and guess what happens? All of a sudden, this guy takes off like he's friggin' Jeff Gordon! Like he stole a motor from NASA and he's got rocket fuel in his tank! He outruns all the cruisers and disappears without a trace like he's goddamn Amelia Earhart!" The detective shook his head again. "So the next morning, wouldn't you know it…a luxury car dealership down over on Main reports a missing car stolen off the lot the night before. A midnight-blue Ferrari FF…a sweet ride!" He whistled. "Handles like a dream and capable of exceeding two hundred ten miles an hour. Now, keep in mind our maximum cruiser speed is a modest one-fifty, so this car outperforms the police by 'bout what? Thirty percent? Give or take? Tell me, Miss Moore. You ever ridden in a midnight-blue Ferrari FF?"

"I can't recall," I replied.

"You're really startin' to worry me, Miss Moore. You know you might wanna get that checked out!" He leaned forward in concern. "You never struck me as being too bright to begin with, but this is pretty bad even for you." The detective threw his head back in laughter. "So anyway…where was I? Oh!" The detective remembered his place. "So the owner of the club calls in a robbery and kidnapping. Madison City Police Department sends a dozen officers to the scene to take witness statements…and would you believe? Other than the lady…uh Mrs. Barnes…or Barrett…Barrister…somethin' like that…other than the owner of the club who called in the alert…nothin'! Two hundred people in the room, and no one's seen a thing!"

As the detective spoke, I recalled the wallets and cellphones that Butch had confiscated from the crowd as he threatened their lives. It seemed his intimidations had been quite effective. Even after Butch was long gone, his victims were still terrified at the mere thought of his return.

"So where does that leave me?" the detective carried on. "Another dead end! No arrests made…and as far as anybody knows, this lady in the tan dress…this Clara Wells…the poor thing"—the detective lowered his head in reverence— "she's still out there…still a hostage somewhere maybe…who the hell knows. But let's move on, shall we?" The detective fumbled through his file, pulling pages out one by one. "Another item on the widow's list is a lil' restaurant over in Dunwoody called…uh…lemme get this right." He fidgeted with his papers again. "Pete's Put Yo' Foot In It Soul Food Diner. Now, if that ain't a crazy name for a restaurant, I don't know what is!" He laughed. "But I'll tell ya' one thing. They got a barbecue sauce over there that'll make ya' wanna yank out one of your *own* ribs and toss it on the grill!" The detective smiled, his eyes glancing up longingly as if he were picturing his plate. "You ever dined at Pete's Put Yo' Foot In It Soul Food Diner, Miss Moore?"

"I can't recall," I replied, and the detective rolled his beady eyes.

"You know, I think you might actually be brain-damaged, Miss Moore. That sure would explain a lot!" He smiled.

"You're the one with the big, dumb grin on your face. Tellin' all these stupid stories. Maybe *your* brain is damaged," I retorted.

"I'm so glad to hear you say something other than 'I can't recall', I'm gonna do you a favor and ignore that remark." The detective placed his hands on top of his bald head and leaned back again in his chair. I could smell his pits from clear across the table, and I wondered if that was part of the interrogation. For a moment, as he fired off fumes in my direction, I thought I might prefer being waterboarded at Guantanamo Bay.

"I learned from his wife," the detective continued, "that Samson Brodice was an employee at this lil' diner, and so I head over there to question the staff. I get to talkin' to the hostess there, and on a hunch, I ask if anybody's come in recently askin' after Samson. Who knows? Maybe she's heard of this Alice Johnston character too. The hostess tells me she's never heard of Alice Johnston but somebody *else* did come in recently askin' questions...a tall, pretty young thing by the name of Tina Henderson. So I ask if this Tina Henderson said anything that might be of assistance in my investigation. The hostess tells me no. This Henderson girl just came in for a cup of coffee, asked if anybody'd seen Samson, and left. That's it. Another dead end!" Birdie had warned me that she didn't like cops. I suppose that while under the scrutiny of that pushy detective with all his invasive questions, she'd decided to protect our sisterhood with silence.

"This investigation is back in the shitter," the detective went on, "and circling the drain like last night's burrito! Until...I get a call early this afternoon about shots fired at TCOD."

"TCOD?"

"The Church of the Open Door," the detective clarified. "Ya' know, it's not every day you hear about a shooting in a church, and not many churches open on a Saturday to begin with. So while this damn hurricane has us all stuck inside the precinct, I log on and do a lil' research on this church, and I see that the pastor's name is Nathan Dobbs. Name sounds familiar to me, and I'm wonderin' why…guy's got no police record…then low and behold…I realize he's one of the names on the widow's list! So once again…I'm back in business!" He smiled, his teeth flashing yellow and orange in his mouth. "You ever meet a man by the name of Nathan Dobbs, Miss Moore? And if you say you can't recall, I'll be happy to slam your head against the table and reset your switch for you!"

"Yes, of course I know who he is. The man was killed right in front of me. I told you guys that!"

"Yes, and who'd you say killed him again?"

"His name is Butch. I told y'all that too. He killed Pastor Dobbs and…the other guy." I didn't want to offer too much insight into my affection for Ace. "He would've killed Sister Sumpter and me too if I hadn't shot him in self-defense."

"Self-defense?" The detective laughed. "Why not plead insanity? At least *that* would be true!" He laughed again. "Seriously, Miss Moore. Why don't you just come clean and stop wasting everybody's time? Go on and admit it. You killed Pastor Dobbs, didn't you? Just like you robbed and killed Samson Brodice!"

"I didn't kill any Samson Brodice!" I yelled back.

"Ahaaa!! So you admit you *did* kill Pastor Dobbs, though!"

"I ain't kill nobody! Don't twist my words! I didn't kill Pastor Dobbs," I told the truth, "and I don't even know anybody named Samson Brodice," I lied.

"What was it? Poison? Is that how you killed Samson Brodice?" the sleuth insisted. "You better start talkin' while you still can lil' lady. Believe it or not, I'm the best friend you've got right now," the detective declared.

369

"Listen." I took a deep breath. "For the umpteenth time…I don't know anything about any Samson Brodice. All I know is that Butch killed Pastor Dobbs because Pastor Dobbs was dirty. He was selling drugs through the church and Butch, who was even dirtier, tried to steal the pastor's money. Just check the vault. It's all there. Money and drugs too! If you don't believe me, just ask Sister Sumpter. She'll tell you!"

"I've already talked to Sheila Sumpter, and she told me plenty…*Carmen Wilson*! Isn't that the name you gave her when you came into her office under false pretenses? Huh? Isn't that the alias you used when you went over there to rob that church? Just like you snuck into the Wild Goose calling yourself Clara Wells and pulled off that heist! Hostage my ass! You were the *mastermind*! Just like you masterminded the death of Samson Brodice… lured him into that hotel…flashed your tits"—he held up the bra in the bag— "ripped off his ring and his wallet and left him for dead! That *is* your M.O, isn't it? Wasn't that how you got your last conviction, as a matter of fact? A stolen wallet? Except, last time, your big mistake was that you left witnesses! After all those men came forward to stand against you and that eyewitness testimony put you away, you stepped your game up, huh, Miss Moore? You decided to kill the john this time around, huh? No more witnesses, huh? Everybody dies!"

"I didn't kill anybody!" I shouted. "Butch shot Pastor Dobbs right in front of Sister Sumpter and me. You can check Butch's gun!"

"Butch's gun?" The detective chuckled. "And where the hell do you suggest I look to find this gun?"

"How the hell should I know? Ask the officers who removed Butch's body what they did with it."

"You may think I'm an idiot, Miss Moore, but I'll tell you a few things I know. I know damn well there was neither gun nor body found in that basement! And you know it too!"

"What?!"

"You heard me! My men checked every inch of that basement and found nothing! Unless you wanna count the six inches of water that seeped in from the storm. If somethin' went on down there, God knows there's no sign of it now...no body, no gun, and the vault is empty! So what am I supposed to believe, Miss Moore?"

"Th-that can't be," I stuttered. "Ask Sister Sumpter!" I implored. "She'll tell you what happened! She was there. She saw it all! Her word has gotta count for something."

"Anybody can see what's goin' on here! It's obvious that Sheila Sumpter is covering for you. That woman's a nervous wreck, probably scared shitless, just like all those other idiots over at The Wild Goose who refused to come forward. I'll bet my next ten paychecks she's only cosigning on this fairytale out of fear and duress. Poor thing probably thinks she's next on your hit list if she admits what she really saw."

"You're twisting the facts!" I shouted. Tears threatened to well up in my eyes, but I refused to give the fat detective the satisfaction of seeing me cry. "This is a trick! Butch is dead. He killed Pastor Dobbs and the other man in the suit, and then he tried to kill Sister Sumpter and me. We got away from him, and he chased us to the basement, where I shot him in self-defense. That's what happened!"

"You're gonna stick to that ridiculous story, eh? That this mysterious Butch guy was killed, then miraculously woke up, continued his crime spree, and absconded with a vault full of money and drugs in the middle of a Category Four storm? Impossible!"

"Evidently, you don't know Butch!"

"And what about Pastor Dobbs? I'm supposed to believe that this pillar of the community, this upstanding citizen and public servant who never even so much as jaywalked his entire life is actually a gun-slinging, drug-trafficking thief? That what you want me to believe, Miss Moore? I just can't see it."

"Did you see yourself bein' born? Of course not! But it happened, didn't it?! You here, ain't chu?! I'm telling you the truth, detective!"

"Yeah, you've been tellin' the *truth* ever since I came in here and sat down, haven't' you? Miss 'I Can't Recall'," he scoffed. "I don't think you know the meaning of the word! Not only are you a compulsive liar, Miss Moore, you're a spoiled, entitled prima donna who thinks that having had a hard life affords you the right to trample over others and treat folks like crap 'cause the world owes you something. Well, I'm here to tell you that it doesn't, Miss Moore. The world doesn't owe you shit!" He pounded his fists on the table, and his papers went flying. "Almost everybody has a sad story to tell. That doesn't mean we all get the right to go around with wanton disregard visiting our misery on others…robbing, cheating, and killing 'cause we're so sad and mad. I've sworn an oath to bring arrogant assholes like you to justice. And

what I'm about to tell you gives me great pleasure." He
closed his rant with a baleful smile, flashing his teeth like
fangs. "Your other victim is out of surgery."

"Other victim? What are you talkin' about?"

"The man you left for dead on the floor of the
pastor's chambers? He's over at University Hospital.
Don't ever go into nursing, Miss Moore. You couldn't tell
a corpse from a canary! You pegged him for dead, but the
paramedics found a pulse and were able to revive him. He
just came out of the O.R. which means we now have
another witness to what went down over there. And soon
as he's awake and lucid, I'm gonna pay him a lil' visit.
That's right, Miss Moore! I'm gonna confirm once and for
all that you've escalated from prostitution and petty theft to
being a full-fledged femme fatale!"

Was Ace alive? Was *Butch* alive?! This had to be a
trick. Ace and Butch were dead! Weren't they? Last I saw
Butch, he was sprawled out in front of the vault. And last I
saw Ace, he was lying on the floor of the pastor's
chambers, his pulse fleeting and his breaths mere whispers.
Sister Sumpter and I had done all we could to plug Ace's
wound and mitigate the loss of blood, but seeing that tall,
musclebound man reduced to a motionless mass, his face
buried deep in the mohair carpet, I was convinced he was a
goner. I'd already said farewell to both of them and made
my eternal peace. I'd chalked their deaths up to being just
another pair of disappointments in the continuing saga of
my life, a story overflowing with so much tragedy and
regret it could make the works of William Shakespeare
look like those of Dr. Seuss. What if Ace *was* alive? For a
moment, I basked in the glow of the bright future I knew he
and I could have together. But if Butch was alive? Heaven

help me! I knew he'd make sure that my future became a thing of the past.

"In the meantime," the detective said, breaking through my thoughts and stealing my attention. "Why don't you take a look outside? I've got a present for you." He smiled, pointing toward the big, glass window to my right that ran the entire length of the wall. The blinds were drawn. "Go on...don't be shy," he coached. I scooted my chair out, and the chair's feet screeched against the linoleum tile. I stood up slowly, wondering what other tricks the detective might've had up his sleeves for me. I crept over to the window, testing each step as if there might've been a trap door in the floor along the way. And when I arrived at the window, I turned the rod slowly and opened up the blinds. And what I saw there on the other side of the glass stole the moisture right out of my mouth and snatched the color from my complexion.

"You remember Jackie Brodice, don't you, Miss Moore?" the detective said from across the room, still reclining in his chair. "She positively identified you today as insurance agent Alice Johnston from Dugan Financial. And I know you remember Theresa Barrister, right?" I shuddered as I saw her face. "She positively identified you today as Clara Wells from West Texas." I could hear the smile in the detective's voice. "And surely you remember Birdie Jenkins?" the big man continued. "She positively identified you today as Tina Henderson, the pretty face that came into the diner asking after Samson—the *same* Samson you claim you don't know." He chuckled. "And of course you know Sheila Sumpter. She positively identified you today as Carmen Wilson and was kind enough to inform me of your other alias too…Maria. That's my favorite of the bunch," he added nonchalantly.

Through the glass, I watched as all four women sat around a table, talking to two officers in uniform, the officers scribbling vigorously in their pads. They didn't see me standing there, and how could they? None of them knew *me*! I'd played a role with each of them, and I could only imagine what they thought of me as they powwowed there together. Four women from four very different walks of life, all united there by their disdain for me. To them, I was a con artist, nothing more than a common criminal. I was a collection of lies wrapped up in a friendly smile, a steaming turd hidden in a fancy purse. I couldn't hear their conversation, but somehow, I knew my name—all of my names—were resting on everyone's lips like a fresh coat of ChapStick.

"Since you can't seem to recall very much, Miss Moore, these ladies were kind enough to come down to the station today to help you recollect." The detective came up from behind and stood alongside me as I peered through the glass. "Don't worry. They can't see in. It's a one-way mirror. I wouldn't want you intimidating any of my witnesses now, would I?" He smiled. "Miss Moore, I want you to think of each of these ladies as a nail in your coffin." He pointed around the room. "Imagine them as soldiers in your firing squad…needles in your lethal injection. These four women contradict every lie you've told here today and place you at the center of it all. Is that just a coincidence? Personally, I don't believe in serendipity. But hey…I'm just an unqualified, uneducated, simpleminded, redneck detective. What do I know?" he said with a snigger.

"Soon as I get in to speak with your other victim over at University Hospital, I'll have a clearer picture of what all is goin' on here, but in the interim, I've got more than enough to bring charges and take you into custody today. Samantha Anna Marie Moore?" He snatched my hand, and I felt something pinch my wrist. I looked down and saw the steel handcuffs clasped over my skin. "You are hereby charged with one count of violation of probation, one count of unlawful possession of a firearm as detailed under the terms of your probation, nine counts of obstruction of justice...that's one count for every time you couldn't recall and deliberately impeded this investigation! And—last but not least—you're under arrest for the murders of Samson Brodice and Nathan Dobbs!"

CHAPTER 30: SUNDAY MOURNING

Drip......drip......drip......drip. No leaky roof this time around. Those were the raw, unadulterated sounds of my tears. Surrounded on all sides by cinderblock and bars, serenaded by the snores of my cellmate, I lay there still all night like I was practicing for my casket. I'd been assigned the top bunk, my nose so close to the stucco ceiling I could almost smell the asbestos in the plaster overhead. Between my claustrophobia, my fear of heights, and the sounds of the mice running along the walls, I don't know what petrified me more. The cotton in my mattress had lost its bounce, and the springs felt like involuntary acupuncture, a million needles digging in my back. Lying there on that cold, hard bunk, feeling vulnerable so high up off the ground, I felt like my bed had been built upon the Rock of Gibraltar, and I was terrified to look down.

The night seemed endless; I thought morning would never come. And when the sun finally did decide to visit my tiny cell, peeking through the small square window like a shy stranger, I spent the bulk of the morning defecating like a nervous dog, my guts tied up in knots. The room was thick with the sour stink of my bowels, and my roommate threatened to reroute my intestines if I took one more dump. And honestly, I wished she would. Maybe she could beat me senseless and rid my mind of all the memories and regrets that plagued me like an incurable disease. Maybe she could drag me back and forth across the concrete floor until I'd forgotten my name and all the struggles and setbacks that haunted me like vengeful ghosts. Maybe she could bash my head into the wall. Then

I'd be telling the honest truth the next time I answered, "I can't recall."

The only thing more upset than my stomach that morning was my spirit. I'd been stripped of my watch, my clothes, and my dignity as I paced my cell in borrowed clothes, a baggy jumpsuit the color of molten lava, bright orange and fiery red. I knew the day was Sunday, but I had no idea the time. And what difference did it make, anyway? That fat detective promised to put me away forever. And counting the minutes of my confinement was about as pointless as counting the drops in the wide-open sea.

"Samantha Moore," the officer called through the bars. "You're free to go."

"Who? Me?" I asked in disbelief. "Free to go?"

"Yes, you! You're free to go," he repeated, "unless you'd prefer to stay here and keep Higgins company." The officer pointed at my surly cellmate, and she snarled at the suggestion. "You comin' or not?!" the officer shouted, his words bouncing off the walls like ping pong balls. I stepped cautiously toward the bars. Was this another one of the detective's tricks? A joke at my expense? A cruel taunt? Would the bars slam shut as soon as I stepped near so everyone could have a laugh? Or would the guard let me pass only to pull the alarm immediately thereafter and claim that I'd escaped? Surely, this was too good to be true. No way they'd just let me out for no reason.

"Officer, can you tell me why I'm being let go?"

"Your bail's been posted," he explained. And instantly I knew. I'd been freed by my dearest friend, Ms. Jane! The relief fell upon me like a warm blanket. Ms. Jane must've heard what had happened at the church and come down here to get me. As I followed the officer down the dimly lit hall, I couldn't wait to see my gentle giant, to wrap my arms around her and to be consoled by her embrace. Once I saw that smiling face and heard her sweet voice, I knew everything would somehow be alright.

The release process was just as lengthy as intake. I signed a stack full of papers and was given back my clothes. And about an hour later, I was sent on my way, escorted to the exit by a gray-haired guard. He pushed a button on the wall, a buzzer sounded over my head, and with that, the bars began to part before me. I began to pass through that final gate and out into the reception area, when suddenly I froze.

"Go on now, Miss," the officer said as he held the gate for me. "We got other things to do today."

I stepped forward, right into the custody of two tall men in gray suits. The iron gate slammed behind me. Where was Ms. Jane? I'd been praying to be reunited with my giant, but as I walked between the shoulders of the two towering men, I realized I should've been more specific. They didn't say a word, and they didn't have to. I knew it was over.

We exited the county lockup, and the fresh air filled my belly like a sweet ambrosia. The sun kissed my nose as I looked up at the sky, and as the three of us approached the dark limousine that awaited us at the curb, I accepted my fate like a dead woman walking. I'd been saddled with the responsibility of locating Samson, and I'd been charged with the task of bringing him back alive and returning the loot that had been pirated from the diner's basement shelves. I'd failed. Samson was dead, and the loot was gone. And in a moment, I knew I'd be dead and gone too.

I couldn't hold up my end of the bargain, but I knew Pete would gladly hold up his—especially when he found out what happened to his main man, Ace. Pete would take great joy in carving me to bits like a Thanksgiving turkey. Or maybe he'd throw me in his pit outside and smoke me like a ham. The giant on my right opened the limo door, and the one on my left pushed me forward. I inhaled deeply, one last breath for the road, and then I climbed into the dark coach to meet my murderer—and then my maker.

"You have a debt to pay."

"Oh…I…uh…you…" I stuttered. Suddenly, I'd forgotten my native language.

"If you're trying to remember your vowels, my dear, I believe it's A…E…I…O…U…and sometimes Y," she corrected. Hidden there in the shadows of that dark limousine was a face I couldn't believe.

"Mrs. Barrister! W-what's goin' on? *You* bailed me out?" It seemed I'd mistaken the men in dark suits for Pete's goons when, in actuality, they were Mrs. Barrister's guards!

"Yes, I posted your bond," Mrs. Barrister confirmed. "That detective really had a hard-on for you, didn't he, my dear? To charge you with a double homicide before *either* of the autopsy results were in? No fingerprint analyses…no ballistics reports? How could he possibly know that the gun you surrendered was even the murder weapon? And with all that criteria left unmet, on what grounds could you be charged with violation of your probation?"

She shook her head. "I was an attorney for thirty years and even did a brief stint as councilwoman over in the third ward… That was mainly so I could overturn local ordinances and expedite the permits I needed to open up the club. That being said, even after a lifetime in law and politics, I've never heard of such foolishness in all my days! I mean, even if we put aside the legalese and talk common sense, why on earth would someone perform all those heinous crimes and then just stick around and *wait* to be arrested? Far be it from me to tell these cops how to do their jobs, but I was appalled at the shoddy police work and at the terrible treatment you received while in their custody. Now, don't get me wrong," she postured. "I'm about ready to slap you silly myself, but that foulmouthed detective was ready to prep you for the gas chamber! And I didn't think that was fair."

Mrs. Barrister picked her purse up from off the floor and reached deep down inside. After a second, her manicured hand emerged clutching a pack of Marlboro Lights. "Care for a smoke?" she offered, extending the pack in my direction. I pulled out a cigarette as Mrs. Barrister cracked the windows with her console controls. And as we held the cigarettes between our lips, Mrs. Barrister pulled out a slender lighter and lit us both. "So…" she continued. "I kindly asked that detective if he'd like to spend his pension in retirement on an island far away just him and his wife? Or would he prefer to spend his nest egg on years of litigation after I filed charges on your behalf against him and his whole godforsaken department…starting with unlawful detainment, false arrest, and coercion for the way he antagonized that poor Sheila Sumpter, trying to convince her to change her story. I expect the charges against you to be dropped by the end of the week." Mrs. Barrister turned and peered out the window as smoke exited her nostrils and escaped through the crack in the glass. Two squirrels were chasing each other up a pole in the parking lot, and immediately I thought of Butch and me.

"But why?" I asked Mrs. Barrister. "Why did you come to my defense? And why did you bail me out? I mean…after everything you heard about me, I know you must think the absolute worst."

"Indeed I do." She turned back to me. "But as I said before, you have a debt to pay. Now tell the driver where you live."

I told the man behind the wheel where to go, and he raised the partition and drove. "Clara Wells," she said, shaking her head slowly. "You really fooled me well with that one, dear. And I'm usually a pretty good judge of character. It's my specialty actually. You see, to me…reading people is like…like pointing out a counterfeit purse." Mrs. Barrister set her pocketbook on the seat between us, and even despite the cigarette smoke that clouded the car, I could smell the genuine leather of her big black Birkin. "First, I take a look at the quality of the stitching, check for loose or crooked threads, irregularities in the spacing, single-stitching versus double-stitching, and so on, etcetera. I inspect the feel of the material and check for inconsistencies in the patterns. Then I test the zippers and closures." She demonstrated. "I check for glue around the grommets. And of course, I read the tags carefully to establish authenticity. But the most significant factor, the most telling sign, is that a *real* bag stands up straight…even on its own." She removed her hands from the purse. "See that? It stands up tall and regal, dignified like a queen. But a fake bag, my dear, will always collapse in on itself the minute you walk away. Reading people is just like reading purses. All you have to do is look closely. The truth is in the details." She smiled.

"From the minute you glided over to that poker table," she continued, staring ahead as if she were reliving the moment in her mind, "and those boys pulled out your chair, I knew you were different. There was something distinctive and unique about you, and I knew you were special somehow. Yes, you seemed a little unsure of yourself, but it was clear that you were smart and quick-witted. And there was an air of sophistication about you, but also a humility that I liked very much. Maybe it was the modest dress and your selection of jewelry. I mean, I knew right away that the diamonds weren't real, but I thought certainly the *woman* was! And that's why you intrigue me. You snuck right under my radar, Miss... I don't even know what to call you."

"Please. Call me Mantha."

"Well, Mantha, when you and I had our lil' chat in the ladies' room and I made those remarks about the other women, was that the moment when you decided to rob me? I realize that was quite the faux pas on my part, and I apologize."

"No, no, no, Mrs. Barrister. I promise you. When I walked into your club, I had absolutely no intention of committing any crimes. I had no idea what that fool was up to."

"You mean Butch?"

"Yes...Butch. You know his name?"

"I do. Sheila Sumpter filled me in on the details. Apparently, she had an encounter with that lunatic too. And according to her, while he was trying to murder the two of you, she overheard some remarks that seem to corroborate your story. Evidently, this Butch fellow admitted in her presence that he was the brains behind the operation. Is that true?"

"Yes!" I exclaimed, probably louder than I should have. I was just so relieved to have someone believe me for a change. "I've known Butch for many years, and honestly, he's been bullying me since we were kids… Only, I didn't realize it until it was too late. Call me naïve…call me stupid…but I thought he was a friend, and I thought he cared about me. When he held that knife to my throat that night in front of the entire room, I swear that wasn't an act, Mrs. Barrister. I was scared for my life. Still am!"

"Yes, well…that may be the case, but I can't let you off the hook that easily, dear. If you don't take responsibility for your role in these events, I'm afraid you'll never learn your lesson. You brought a lion through my front door and unleashed it in my house. You may not have been the one who stalked, pounced, and devoured, but you did release the beast! So stop pretending as though your life is an out-of-body experience beyond your control. You *chose* to befriend that animal, and despite his willful disobedience of the laws of this land, you called him your pal. You turned a blind eye to his criminal acts, and in doing so, you enabled his perversions. Instead of standing up for what was right, you decided to go with the flow, and that makes you complicit in his crimes. And so, I say again, you have a debt to pay."

"Yes, Mrs. Barrister. I plan on paying back every bit that was stolen from you. I promise!"

"Oh, honey, I'm fully insured." She laughed. "You have a debt to pay, but it's not me you owe. It's you! You owe it to *yourself* to try harder…to be better…to transcend the challenges of your past."

"I-I'm sorry. I don't follow."

"Shelia told me about your stepfather and the abuse that you endured." Hearing my poor story being spoken over the millionaire's lips, I was overcome with shame. "And she told me that you ran away at an early age and that you've been running your whole life long. Maybe that explains your unhealthy connection to this Butch fellow… Maybe you're still searching subconsciously for a father figure…someone to boss you around and tell you what to do… Who knows what spawned this sick relationship between you two. Whatever the case…I've gone very far out of my way this morning to tell you this: It's not too late to turn things around. Maybe your parents failed you. So what if your friends let you down. It doesn't even matter that that detective tried to lock you away forever, to clip your wings like a caged bird. The best revenge you can exact upon those who sought to destroy you is to live a life that has purpose…that has meaning…to live loudly and proudly…to leave a permanent mark upon the very world from which they tried so hard to erase you. You've been given a second chance to rise from the ashes of your past. Not everyone gets another chance. That jail we just left is full of men and women who won't have another chance."

And there it was again. Everybody thinks they're so profound and prolific. Mrs. Barrister was reading to me from the same speech as Ms. Jane, Mr. Tennison, and a dozen others. They wanted me to simply pull myself up by my bootstraps. But who am I, Harry Houdini? I mean, who else but a magician can pull themselves up off the ground by the straps of their boots? Mrs. Barrister, like everybody else, was asking me to do the impossible.

"With all due respect, Mrs. Barrister," I interjected. "It's hard to just straighten up and fly right…especially if your spine is crooked and you ain't got no wings! Things aren't that simple. Maybe they are for a rich lady like you, but for somebody like me…it's easier said than done."

"What do you think…I was born rich?" she scoffed. "You think I came out of a box like this? All set up and ready to go?" She threw her head back in laughter. "I weep for your generation!" She shook her head. "You children live in the age of the computer. Everybody has a cellphone on their hip and a tablet in their lap. You're so used to having everything at your fingertips, you think your lives are supposed to change with the push of a button, like the song selection on your iPod. You kids don't know how to struggle, how to sacrifice! You don't know what it means to keep your hand on the plow until the work is done…to labor and toil from sunup to sundown until the harvest is complete. You never had to build a house brick by brick or chop firewood to keep warm for winter. You don't know what it's like to cook from scratch, to chop and cut, to slice and dice. You never had to shuck a tub full of corn or snap and shell a basket of peas till the grit and dirt got stuck under your fingernails…all to get dinner on the table each night. Never had to pluck a million feathers off of a chicken and then cut it up and clean it by yanking out all the guts and innards, bile and fat. All you youngsters know how to do is turn on the microwave and walk away. Or yell orders into a clown's mouth while somebody else brings you fast food. In my day," she said with a chuckle, "fast food was any meal that was ready to eat the same day you started cookin' it!" She threw her head back as she laughed and reminisced.

"And girl, back then, we didn't have any Google," she continued. "If you wanted information you had to carry your behind to the library! You had to check the card catalog and use the Dewey Decimal System. We didn't have any Amazon or eBay. If you wanted something, you had to get off your duff and go get it! It didn't come to *you*! Do you understand what I'm saying?" she asked, and I nodded. "Just by virtue of the limitations on our lives, a work ethic was instilled in all of us. We learned how to roll up our sleeves and get the job done! We learned how to get out there and make things happen, how to manifest the desires of our hearts! And as a result, we know how it feels when your garden finally grows. We know how it feels when you see the roses you planted blowing in the breeze. We know how it feels to sit down in front of a dinner *you* made in a house that *you* built being warmed by a fire *you* started! We know how rewarding it is when hard work finally pays off, and that feeling is addictive, honey. I'd trade in all these modern conveniences any day for the lessons I've learned through hard work and determination…adversity and perseverance…through sweat and through struggle. Nothing wrong with technology, but your generation lost out on those fundamental life lessons. You kids don't know how to fight for what you want, so you settle for less than you deserve. And so, I say to you again. You owe it to yourself to take full advantage of this second chance, my dear, and *I'm* going to show you *how*. How to set your sights on the life you want to lead and make a plan of action…taking it step by step…one leap after the next…never ever stopping until finally you can emerge from the shadows of your history…to walk into the beauty of your destiny! That's my commitment to you, dear. If you're willing, of course."

"Yes! Oh yes, I'm willing and ready! Thank you, Mrs. Barrister!" I exclaimed. And just as my mind took flight and began to imagine all my life might amount to, the long limousine rolled to a stop.

"You live here?" Mrs. Barrister asked, looking out of the window.

"No, ma'am. Give me a second, please." And with that, I climbed out of the limo and looked around. I shuddered as I looked up and saw a familiar face staring back at me from a distance, Pete's effigy greeting me on the diner's neon marquee. It was only 11am, and the restaurant's lot was already packed for the lunchtime rush. I reached into my clutch and pulled out the keys Ace had given me. Now was the moment of truth. Were these his real car keys? Or was I holding a handful of useless metal. I squeezed the keyring remote and heard a horn beep near the back of the lot.

"Have the driver pull around over there, please." I pointed before closing the door. And I followed my ears until finally I stood before Ace's Audi. I pressed the button to release the trunk and walked around to the rear. And at long last, I was reunited with the six sacks that had been plucked from the belly of The Wild Goose.

The limo pulled up shortly, trailed by a tan sedan containing Mrs. Barrister's security detail: the two suits who'd met me at the jail. The gentlemen emerged to assist me in loading the loot into the limousine. And as they swapped the sacks from car to car, I bummed another smoke from Mrs. Barrister and pulled out my red pen. And with it, I wrote a tiny note in tiny letters on the side of the slim cigarette and stuck it beneath Ace's wiper blade. It read:

> *Still think cigarettes*
> *cause more harm than guns?*
> *Please forgive me. Keys behind tire.*
> *Tina xoxo*

I left Ace's keys under the car, hidden out of sight, and Mrs. Barrister dropped me off back at Milsey. Her guards saw to it that I got in my car safely with us so close to Butch's lair. Then we all drove off in our separate directions.

Mrs. Barrister made me promise to show up at the club first thing Monday morning for training. And she promised to teach me how to work an ordinary job like an ordinary person and still turn my life into something *extra*ordinary.

|•|•|•|•|•|•|•|•|•|•|•|•|•|•|•|•|•|•|•|•|•|•|•

Milsey and I somehow managed to navigate the highways without being stopped for her missing plates. And in no time, we pulled into Connelly Homes, and I parked in my regular space at the back of the lot. Staring ahead at my apartment building, I realized that after all I'd been through the last few days, I had nothing to show for it. The money I'd taken from Samson was tucked inside my big purse, and my big purse was tucked inside of the Ferrari with all my other things. Who knows where Eve and Willie were. Was Butch with them? He'd stolen a fortune from Pete and Pastor Dobbs. Would he take the money and run? Or would Butch come back to find me with revenge on his mind?

Every question begat another question, and a whirlwind of thoughts swirled around my head as if there was another hurricane brewing on my brain. With all the money I'd seen and touched with my own two hands? With all the affluence I'd encountered along this journey? I was sick with shame to realize I was no closer to making the rent than I'd been before I'd started. Mrs. Barrister had given me a second chance, but I'd run out of grace with Mr. Tennison. It would be at least a few weeks before I received my first paycheck from The Wild Goose, and in the meantime, how would I eat? And where would I sleep when Mr. Tennison put me out in just a few days' time. The only thing emptier than my pockets that morning was the fuel gauge on Milsey's dash. I couldn't borrow any more money from Ms. Jane. She'd already done enough and had four mouths of her own to feed.

What option did I have other than to take to the streets again, to put on my tightest dress and my tallest heels and scope out a corner where I could join the others: countless girls, all nameless, each one of us harboring her own sad story that no one cares to hear. I was familiar with the routine. We'd put on our war paint, dark eye shadow and bright blush, and march the streets like an aberrant army, Jane Does in the making, each of us destined to die young. We barter our bodies and sell our souls, roaming the sidewalks, pacing a concrete cage, drifting through the night like journeying spirits, stuck between here and there.

Lurking in the shadows and whispering in the dark, we are long legs in high heels, lipstick, leather, and lace. We peddle our flesh from dusk till dawn, from midnight to morning, and sometimes beyond. And every dime we make is already spent on food, gas money, and—if we're lucky—rent.

Maybe I'd be fortunate enough to die before nightfall. Surely dying would release me from all my earthly debts and hide me where not even Butch, Mr. Tennison, or that fat detective could find me. With all the questions and concerns floating around my mind, I longed for the absolution of death, the certainty, the finality, the freedom, the *peace* that would accompany my demise. But as I sat there depressed and drowning in my blues, I remembered something. A little bit of good news.

I popped Milsey's trunk and climbed out of the car. My big purse and duffel bag were long gone, held captive in the Ferrari FF, but I had one treasure left to my name. I'd begged Butch to let me borrow a few of his records, and the man-child had told me no. But when he wasn't looking I smuggled Billie Holiday from one of those stacks and trafficked her out of his apartment like a drug mule. Then I hid her in Milsey's trunk where he'd never think to look. Of course, I'd planned on returning her just as soon as I was done, but I guess the rare record was mine to keep now with Butch out on the run.

And suddenly, I had Billie on the brain. As I walked across the parking lot, feeling lower than a snake, I couldn't wait to hear that lady sing the blues. I couldn't wait to drop that needle on the record, to take off my clothes and shoes, and lose myself in the cushions of my couch. There was nothing but uncertainty in my future, but for a moment, I had no worries, no fears. I was sure that—just as it always had—a little bit of music would be the anecdote to my every ailment, like sugar for my soul.

I rushed into the apartment and headed straight for my overturned stereo. I set it back upright and turned it on. Then I reached for the record hidden deep inside the sleeve, but instead of a black vinyl disc, all I saw was green. Lying flat, packed tightly inside the cardboard sleeve, were dozens of crisp hundred-dollar bills. Ten thousand dollars when I counted them out.

Finding that cash where Billie should have been, I was overwhelmed, and more than anything, I was confused. I mean, I knew Butch's collection was probably worth a lot of money, but this wasn't what I'd had in mind. No wonder Butch had been so protective over those records. But why would someone who didn't even care about music have all those albums stacked high in his apartment? And why would he pull out the vinyl records and stuff the sleeves with cash? And then I remembered. The helicopters. The random police checkpoints. The city under surveillance. Could Butch have been involved in that bank robbery last month? Three officers had been killed at the hands of an unknown assailant. That crime had Butch's name written all over it. But why would he successfully rob a bank and then turn around and rob the Wild Goose? And then the church?!

It was then that I realized just how sick my dear friend was. Like the lure of the roulette wheel to a hopeless gambler, like a gin and tonic to a seasoned alcoholic, like cocaine to a cokehead, wreaking havoc was Butch's drug of choice. Villainy was his vice! He wasn't addicted to money like I'd long thought. He was addicted to the thrill of the hunt, the excitement of the chase, the chaos of the kill, the bloodier the better. Butch was no different than a Hollywood daredevil, attracted to the danger, the action, the adventure of life on the edge. He craved the adrenaline rush that accompanied each death-defying act, reveling in risk, thriving under the threat of his own demise.

There was no hotline for an addiction like his, no weekly meetings to attend, no pills to take or healing elixirs. There was no help and no hope for someone like Butch, and I knew he'd never change. It simply felt way too good…to be bad.

I counted out my rent money and calculated the late fees. I set a few hundred aside to tide me over, and the rest I planned to send to the widow Jackie. It wasn't much, but I knew she'd be grateful to get it. I went to the kitchen to fetch an empty envelope, so I could drop my payment off at the rental office. And as I fumbled through my junk drawer, a bottomless pit of papers, I looked over and saw the footprint that had been left by the creep who'd ransacked my place. That was the one thing that didn't make sense to me. I'd been gallivanting all over Georgia trying to unlock the clues to clear my name and solve this crazy case—and for the most part, I'd done it—but this one last mystery remained. Who'd entered my apartment? And why?

Standing there, I felt like I'd just gotten my car up and running, but there was one more greasy part in my hand, and I didn't know where it went. I felt like I'd just completed a thousand-piece puzzle and found one more jigsaw hiding on the floor. My picture was complete, yet there was this one detail that didn't fit anywhere. I found my envelope and left the kitchen. And as I walked through

393

the ruins of my cozy abode, the mystery nagged at me like a housefly buzzing around my face. It just didn't make any sense!

That is, until suddenly…it did.

CHAPTER 31: TOUGH CALL!

"I just wanna know why."

"Why what?"

"Why'd you do it?"

"Why'd I do what?"

"You broke into my apartment! Admit it!" The four girls ran up to stand beside Ms. Jane as she stood in the doorway. I could tell they didn't like my tone of voice. And as they growled at me like a pack of pit bulls, I knew they were ready to defend their grandmother's honor with violence.

"Y'all go on back in the kitchen and finish eatin'!" Ms. Jane instructed. "Go on! Git! This here is grown folks' bid'ness!" And the girls slinked back over to the table, issuing threats with their ghoulish gazes.

"Come on in," she invited, and I stepped in and took a seat on the sofa. The gentle giant hobbled over to her big chair and sat down slowly. "Well, go on," she insisted, mashing down on the lever and bringing her legs up to recline. "Say your piece."

"You know where I been all night, Ms. Jane?"

"Shole do. A lil' birdy tole me you was in county lockup."

"That's right. And while I lay awake all night, I had a chance to think. The night that Samson died, I came home and found my place torn apart. No sign of forced entry...no broken windows...my locks were all intact. Looking back, I realize somebody must've had a key. And you're the only somebody I entrusted with my spare key, Ms. Jane."

She was silent.

"And I know you knocked my ficus off the ledge and spilled soil on my kitchen floor, because there's nobody in all of Georgia but you, Ms. Jane, who could make a footprint that damn big." I pointed at Ms. Jane's big slippers as her toes pointed up in the chair.

Still she was silent.

"Of course, I got scared, and I came to you, Ms. Jane. You were my sounding board, and I told you all about my troubles. I told you all about Samson and how he died on top of me in that hotel room. And after I got it off my chest, I fell asleep right here on this couch. And next thing I knew, you were waking me up the next morning. The day had barely started, and there was Samson's story on the news. Now, looking back, I ask myself, how could that be? Checkout was at noon, so how could Samson's body have been discovered before dawn? His death was my little secret…that is…until I told you, Ms. Jane."

She didn't utter a word.

"The detective who interrogated me yesterday told me he received a phone call about the body at 5am. Only *you* could have tipped off the authorities. I've been checkin' in with you at every turn…keeping you updated…and all the while…*you* were the one who set all this mess into motion. You were the one who dispatched me on this quest to *find* the truth…and all along, you were *withholding* it. And I wanna know why!" A tear fell from my eye.

"Well…" Ms. Jane sighed, and I knew I was in for a story. "I ain't never been able to fit into a size six, honey. Not even when I *was* six!" She chuckled. "I was already five foot nine by the time I made it to fourth grade, and you should'a seen me." She smiled as she recalled. "I towered over everybody in my class like I was one of them NBA players. And chile, the custodian loved me 'cause I could change a lightbulb without a ladder!" She laughed again. "Folks used to call me Giant Jane. My whole life, I ain't never been able to go into a store and try on clothes. Never once seen the inside of a fittin' room...or been able to find my size right there on the rack. And Lord knows I ain't never been able to wear a whole bunch of fancy shoes like all you young gals do. Ain't a stiletto in the worl' made in a men's size sixteen wide!" Her shoulders bounced up and down as she chuckled to herself.

"So, over the years...I guess by default...I took a real liking to things like jewelry...perfumes...stuff like dat. You can't go wrong wit' a pair of earrings. They come one-size-only." She laughed again. "So, on Thursday, I noticed I was missin' a pair of diamond studs. Gone right outta' my jewelry box. Half-carat diamonds set in fourteen karat gold. Cost four hundred dollars at Pat's Pawnshop! Of course, Pat owed me a favor, so I got 'em for free. But anyway...my pretty earrings were gone without a trace! First thought I had, I'm sorry to say, was that maybe you took 'em. I mean, we both know you have a tendency to take thangs that don't exactly belong to you from time to time." I conceded with a nod. "And just about all yo' jewelry is fake." I agreed again.

"And so, I admit, I got angry. I grabbed your spare keys from the drawer, and I let myself into your apartment, and I searched every nook and cranny. I knew you took my earrings. I just knew it! And when I thought about how many times I'd bailed you outta' trouble and invited you into my home and served you a hot meal right there at my table, I was livid! I tore that place apart, and when I didn't

397

find what I was lookin' for, I just came on back home and waited to confront you. Then, when you came knockin' on my door later that night lookin' like what the cat dragged in and tole me 'bout the man who died, I decided to use this experience as a teachable moment. And so, I did it. While you were asleep that night out here on the couch, I phoned in the anonymous tip that led the police to that hotel."

"Teachable moment?! What lesson did you expect me to learn by goin' behind my back and reportin' me to the police?"

"I didn't report *you* to the police. I reported a body in a hotel room. I never told the police one thing about you, honey!"

"I don't get it, Ms. Jane! I mean, first of all, I never stole any earrings. I would never take from you, Ms. Jane! Never! But you didn't call the cops to report stolen earrings. You called them to report a dead body. If you hadn't done that, I would've never left your apartment that morning! I wouldn't have gotten myself arrested and almost killed!"

"Now wait just a minute!" She pressed on the lever and rose in her chair. "I didn't tell you to call on that fool Butch and steal a car and rob a casino! That was all *you*! I told the cops about the body because, at the time, I thought you'd stolen from me…and involving the authorities was the only way I could get through to you. I figured maybe that would light a fire under you and scare you straight!"

"Do you understand that I almost *died*, Ms. Jane? More than once! Not to mention the night I spent in jail. You were wrong, Ms. Jane!"

"I admit I was wrong about the earrings!" she acknowledged. "I learned later that Kyla went and wore 'em out the house. And you betta' believe I wore out her behind! But at the end of the day, it didn't matter who took the earrings, baby. I still needed to get your attention. You needed a wake-up call! I mean, here I've gone and leveraged every bit of credit and good faith I had to get Mr. Tennison to let you keep your apartment while you were away in jail. And you hadn't been out three months and were already back to yo' old ways! I thought that maybe if you had another brush with the law, you would stop taking your freedom for granted and make some changes. I didn't wish no harm against you, baby, but I hope that now that you had a few encounters with death, you'll value your *life* a little more and stop throwin' it away…and riskin' it out there in them streets!"

"You were wrong, Ms. Jane!"

"Maybe I was." She rose from her seat. "But I did it because I love you, girl! Can't you see? I love you just like one of my own babies!" She pointed to the kitchen. "It tears me apart to see you living this way. Every time you walk out yo' door, I wonder if you'll ever come back. Or if I'll be reading about you in the newspaper the next day or seein' yo' face on the news. I hate to see you livin' so far beneath your potential. You so smart…and yet so doggone stupid! So insightful…and at the same time blind as a bat! I sat right there the other night"—she pointed at the recliner— "and I tried to talk some sense into you…just like I've done a thousand times. And you sat there and ignored me. You needed help, Mantha, and I was at my wit's end. I didn't know what else to do wit' you! So I made the call! I made that call to help you, and if I had to do it all over, I'd do it again. Hate me if you must, but I stick by my decision. And honey, at six foot eight, you betta' believe I shade every bit of ground I stand!"

I'd never seen Ms. Jane cry before, but suddenly there it was. She always seemed so strong and impenetrable, a fortress made of flesh. I stood up and walked around the coffee table to stand before the giant. Her four guard dogs put down their bologna sandwiches and rose up in their chairs.

"If I didn't think you'd kick my behind, I'd slap you into next week," I said. Then I buried my head in her belly and hugged her tightly. "I know you meant well and that you love me, Ms. Jane. I love you too," I vowed. "And I promise to stop making you worry. From here on out…I'm gonna make you proud."

THE END

Please Don't Call Me Sam!

Dara Dionne Welms

CHAPTER 31½: WANT MOORE?

Psst! It's me, Mantha! If you're reading this message, then I suppose that means you stumbled across my memoir and made it to the end! I thank you. Yes, *you,* honey! But the end is only the beginning.

If you liked this book and didn't find it to be an insufferable waste of time, then please—from my heart to yours—I beg you! I *implore* you! Please tell someone about me! Share this book with a friend. Hell, share it with a foe! Tell your coworkers. Tell your family! Tell anybody! Tell *every*body! Your boyfriends, your girlfriends, your husbands, your wives. There's even a thing or two within these pages for your mistresses! Send a tweet, post a little something on Facebook, shout me out on the Gram. Even if you have to send up a smoke signal, honey, do it!

For years, I sat locked away deep inside the inner recesses of Dara Dionne Welms's brain, scratching and clawing and trying my hardest to climb out of obscurity. And for far too long, I was nothing more than handwritten notes scribbled on Post-its while Dara rode the train to and from work. I was random thoughts and crude drawings doodled on the crumpled edges of chewing gum wrappers and the backs of paper napkins. Before I was Pete's prisoner, I was Dara's. And now that I'm out, now that I'm finally free from Dara's dungeon, free from the cluttered cages of Dara's mind, no longer entangled in the snares of procrastination and doubt, honey, I need to make up for lost time! I'm tired of being somebody's secret! I want everybody to know my name!

And that's where *you* come in, my friend. In order to help me, in order to keep new Mantha Moore Mysteries coming your way, I need you to do your part. Please light a flame in your community and pass the torch. Visit my website and join my mailing list so you and I can stay connected. Feel free to comment and share your favorite moments and your favorite characters. I don't care how you decide to make your mark on this movement. I'll leave that up to you. But however you choose to tell others about me, all I ask is that when you do? Please don't call me Sam!

www.ManthaMooreMysteries.com

Credits

"'Tis So Sweet to Trust in Jesus" – Music by William J. Kirkpatrick, Lyrics by Louisa M. R. Stead, 1882

"How High the Moon" – Music by Morgan Lewis, Lyrics by Nancy Hamilton, 1940

"Neither One of Us (Wants to be the First to Say Goodbye)" – Written by Jim Weatherly, Performed by Gladys Knight & the Pips, 1972

"Be Thankful for What You Got" – Written by William DeVaughn, 1972, Performed by Curtis Mayfield, 1974

"Turn Off the Lights" – Written by Kenny Gamble & Leon Huff, Performed by Teddy Pendergrass, 1979

"Fire and Desire" – Written by Rick James, Performed by Rick James & Teena Marie, 1981

"Inner City Blues (Make Me Wanna Holler)" – Written by Marvin Gaye & James Nyx, Jr., Performed by Marvin Gaye, 1971

Text Dividers Created by Freepik

Acknowledgements

Thank you to Sonya Dublin-Galli for being my muse. If it weren't for you, this book would still be a collection of thoughts and dreams, a bunch of maybes and what ifs. Thank you for accountability!

Thank you to Nancy Ortiz for being my cheerleader and coach. Your honesty and candor gave me the gentle, nurturing guidance I needed to make this project happen.

Thank you to Anelle Narcisse for your listening ear and sound business advice. Let's continue to chase these dreams together!

Thank you to Wanda J. Austin, an impeccable teacher, friend, and mentor. Thank you for believing in me from the start and for all of your kind words of encouragement throughout my life. I am forever indebted.

Thank you to Julia "Kito" Kirtley, Sekou Williams, Alfonso Williams III, Vivian Ray, Shirley Hicks, Shinnerrie Jackson, Jenean Roberts, Nikkea Foster, Adrena Cunningham, Constance "Connie" Moore, Dayna Holliman, Deshaun Sneed, Safia Brooks, Audrey & Steven Baldwin, Tanga & Doug Wilson, Mark Eubanks, and Dale MacDougal for all the late night and early morning conversations that motivated me to stay on this path.

Thank you to the Ghetto Crew (Le'Kisha Mingo, Dora Payne, Tawanda Barber, Barbara Cole, Chonda

Orders, Brad Sarboukh, Toshona Wright-Sutton, Brenda Gladding, and Jerome Roberts) for all the calls, texts, emails, visits, outings, prayers, laughs, and endless encouragement over the years! Each of you is a gift to my life!

Last, but never least, a very special thank you to my amazing extended family for the ways in which you enrich my life each and every day! I love you all!

About the Author

Inspired by the likes of J. California Cooper, James Baldwin, Alice Walker, and Walter Mosley, Dara Dionne Welms is a lifelong lover of the written word and an admirer of folklore and storytelling. Majoring in Creative Writing and African-American Studies at Oberlin College, for the last decade, Welms has served as an account executive with a design firm in SoHo NYC and is a first-time novelist. Welms is a native of Trenton, New Jersey, and currently resides in Newark.

www.ingramcontent.com/pod-product-compliance
Lightning Source LLC
Chambersburg PA
CBHW020929020726
47495CB00002B/411